Family is Forever

Family is Forever

Rita Potter

SAPPHIRE BOOKS

SALINAS, CALIFORNIA

Editor - Tara Young
Book Design - LJ Reynolds
Cover Design - Fineline Cover Design

Sapphire Books Publishing, LLC
P.O. Box 8142
Salinas, CA 93912
www.sapphirebooks.com

Printed in the United States of America
First Edition – November 2023

Rita's other books

As We Know it Series
Upheaval
Survival
Betrayal

Stand Alone
Broken Not Shattered
Thundering Pines
Whitewater Awakening
Out of The Ashes
Love or Hate

Dedication

For Terra and Chumley: My little family

Acknowledgment

I'd like to thank Sapphire Books and Chris for letting me tell my eclectic tales.

Thanks to my editor, Tara. With each book, I'm sure it will be the one I get right, and you'll have little editing to do. With each book, I'm wrong.

Thanks to my friends in the Sapphic writing community. I've been blessed to find a group that feels like home, like family.

Thanks to my work family. We've been traveling this road together for nearly thirty years, and I love you guys.

Thanks to my mentor Jae. Words can't express how much I respect and admire you.

Thanks to my Save the Cat beta readers Shalon and Camille. You two have been a wonderful addition to my writing life, and I look forward to seeing my name in your acknowledgments.

I've run out of ways to thank Cade, Nan, and Michele. You truly are my dream team. You always challenge me to make my work better. I thank you from the bottom of my heart.

Thanks to Terra. You've been by my side for over twenty years. Some days, it feels like we've been together forever, in a good way, while other times, it seems like only yesterday. I can't wait to see what the next twenty years brings.

Oh, and to Chumley, whew, I'd have hell to pay if I missed him. Our family wasn't complete until you wandered in. That should appease him, for now.

And thank you to my readers, who continue to follow me on this amazing journey.

Chapter One

"Perfect," Jaycee Ward said as she raised her fingers to her mouth. She smacked her lips together and threw her hand into the air in an exaggerated chef's kiss. Her face heated, and her gaze darted around her kitchen.

Dumbass. Nobody was there to see, but still she felt foolish. It wasn't as if she'd cured cancer or anything. Successfully baking macarons wasn't worthy of such a flamboyant celebration.

She pulled in her shoulders, and the smile left her face. It was probably a stupid idea to bake them in the first place. What kind of idiot thought that French macarons had a place beside turkey, stuffing, and sweet potatoes? Maybe she should have baked pumpkin pies instead. This was her sixteenth year making macarons, so it was too late to be self-conscious.

She recounted the square tins piled on the counter. The tally was the same as the last six times she'd counted. There was a small container for each of the nine kids, and a large platter for the dessert table. A slight smile parted her lips as she remembered the year she'd not packaged individual tins for the kids. *Big mistake.* She'd almost been disowned.

A sharp pain stabbed at her chest, and she struggled to breathe. *No.* She wouldn't do this to herself. Not today. She snatched the containers off the counter and shoved them into the box, making sure to count them one more time as she placed them inside.

Jaycee took a deep breath and looked down at her blue jeans. Maybe she should change into something a little nicer. Possibly her work clothes. She was one of those rare people who felt more comfortable in dress clothes than casual. Put her in a pair of nice slacks, a button-down shirt with a bow tie, and suspenders, and she was ready to take on the world. In blue jeans, she felt inadequate.

Tessa always accused her of hiding behind her signature *costume*. Jaycee snorted. "Hmph." What did Tessa know anyway? Just because Jaycee wanted to look nice didn't mean she was hiding from anything.

She ran her hand down the front of her thermal shirt, smoothing out imperceptible wrinkles. With one more deep breath, she picked up the box and headed for the garage. As she reached for the doorknob, she froze. She stared down at her sock-covered feet. *Damn it.* She needed to relax and get it together.

It had been fifteen years ago that she'd attended her first Thanksgiving at the Wilsons' house. It wasn't as if this was her first rodeo, yet this year was different.

She hurried through the vast house to the primary bedroom and pulled open the door to the walk-in closet. Her enormous shoe rack took up only a small portion of the expansive back wall in the half-empty closet.

Jaycee glared at the rows of shoes. Why the hell did she have so many? Most she hadn't worn in years. She picked up a pair of alligator skin cowboy boots and turned them around in her hands. Maybe she should wear them. Throw caution to the wind. She slid the boot back into its slot and reached for her favorite pair of Air Jordans.

She put two fingers in her mouth to wet them, then wiped off a tiny spot of dirt on the toe. Now she was ready to go. In her favorite shoes, she strode across the house with a little more bounce in her step.

ﾟ。ﾟ。ﾟ。ﾟ

Jaycee sped north on Interstate 43 toward Cedarsburg. She'd taken this route so many times over the past fifteen years that her Range Rover could practically get there on its own. Give technology a few more years, and it probably would.

Her heart rate accelerated as she took the exit ramp toward Cedarsburg. She glanced at the clock. Plenty of time. It was just past eleven, and the feast didn't begin until noon. *Shit.* What if they'd changed the time this year?

Maybe this was a bad idea, but she continued toward the familiar subdivision, anyway. The kids would be disappointed if they didn't get their Thanksgiving macarons. She patted the box she'd seat belted into the seat next to her. Possibly excessive, but she didn't want all her hard work to go to waste if she had to stop suddenly.

She smiled as she turned onto the tree-lined street. The trees were nearly bare and had been since the heavy winds that whipped through Wisconsin last week. Unfortunately, she'd been too busy at work to take the time to enjoy the changing colors, and now it was too late, at least for this season.

The neighborhood lost some of its charm once the leaves fell, but once Christmas decorations were hung, it would regain its appeal. Judging by the number of cars lining the street, most families were celebrating here rather than traveling for the holiday. And why not? The homes were large enough to accommodate most family gatherings. Jaycee flipped her blinker and turned onto the Wilsons' street. The cul-de-sac was nearly full. That was what happened when the kids got older. It wasn't long ago that there was only one car per family. Four cars—that was it. Now several of the kids drove themselves, likely having other places to go after the meal.

She pulled to a stop several houses down but didn't turn off the engine. Jaycee shivered. It wouldn't be long before snow would fly. Why did it seem that every year she was shocked when it happened? She shook her head at her ridiculousness. After all, she'd lived in Wisconsin since she was three, so snow shouldn't be a surprise.

No doubt, she was stalling. She rested her hand on the box and didn't make a move to open her door; instead, she lifted the lid and pulled out the small tins, leaving the big one in the bottom. The ride had been smooth with light traffic, so likely none of the cookies had been jostled, but she'd better check just to be on the safe side.

Carefully, she set the small tins on the floor before prying the lid off the large container. Nothing seemed to be amiss. A rainbow of colors greeted her, each signifying a distinct flavor. She grinned, remembering the year she'd played a trick on the kids and colored each macaron a different color than their flavor. The lime ones were purple, the strawberry yellow, the lemon pink, and so on. The kids had found it to be great fun—the adults not so much.

Lost in her thoughts, she hadn't been paying

attention to her surroundings, so when a loud rap sounded against her window, she squealed and threw the lid into the air.

As she turned, she met the gaze of what appeared to be a very annoyed Tessa Wilson. Jaycee swallowed hard before she lowered the window. "Oh, god, you scared me." She put on her best smile.

Tessa didn't return the smile. "What the hell are you doing here?"

So this was how it was going to go. *Okay.* She just needed to breathe and stay calm. "Hi, Tessa."

"I'll ask you again. What the fuck are you doing here?"

Jaycee decided against pointing out that Tessa wasn't actually saying it again since she'd replaced *hell* with *fuck.* Somehow, Jaycee thought Tessa wouldn't find that distinction helpful.

"Are you just going to sit there and stare at me?" Tessa asked, her face getting redder as she spoke.

"Um, sorry. I was just startled." Jaycee needed to get control of the conversation, so she reached down and picked up a tin off the floorboard. "I brought macarons."

Tessa's mouth dropped open, and she didn't speak for several beats. "Seriously?" She turned her head and looked away before she spun back around. Anger burned in her eyes. "We do not want your goddamned cookies."

Jaycee's hand shook, so she set the tin on the seat and slid her hand under her leg. "But, uh, I thought, um…well, maybe the kids would."

"No!" Tessa pointed her finger toward Jaycee's face. "They don't want any, either."

Even though Jaycee didn't think it was right

for Tessa to speak for them, it was another thing she decided not to voice. "I don't have to come in. I could give you the box, and, um, you could hand them out."

"When are you going to get it into your head that you're no longer a part of this family?" Tessa clenched her jaw after she delivered the line and fixed Jaycee with one of her patented glares. A look that Jaycee had come to know well over the years.

The words cut into Jaycee like a knife. Leave it to Tessa to go right for the jugular. There was no soft pedaling when it came to her. Still, Jaycee couldn't go without a fight. "It's not official yet, so technically, I still am."

"Only because you're sitting on the paperwork." Tessa's face fell, and she sighed. It was as if all the anger flooded from her body, leaving her exhausted. "Why do you have to make this so difficult?"

Jaycee blinked back tears. She wouldn't cry in front of Tessa, again. Especially knowing how much Tessa hated it. "Maybe if you were losing your entire family, you'd understand."

Tessa threw her hands into the air and slapped her palm against her own forehead. "Ugh, I am not having this conversation with you again. It's not my fault you don't have a family of your own." She leveled her gaze and locked eyes with Jaycee. "And I won't feel guilty for it."

"I'm not asking you to." Jaycee felt the anger bubbling inside her, but she knew it would only end badly if she didn't keep it at bay. "I just don't understand why our divorce means I have to divorce your family, too."

"That's just how it works." Tessa's eyes flashed in anger again. "They. Are. My. Family."

Jaycee's hand clenched into a fist. "Who went to all of our nieces' and nephews' ball games, their band concerts, their plays—?"

"That's not the goddamned point."

"Who took your mom to doctor's appointments when she had cancer? Helped your dad fix his boat—?"

Tessa thrust her finger into the window, coming close to poking Jaycee's face. She likely would have had Jaycee not leaned back. "It's not my fault that your job allowed you more flexibility. I couldn't exactly reschedule appointments with my patients every time the Wilson clan had a problem."

"But you didn't mind that I did," Jaycee said under her breath, but she knew it was loud enough for Tessa to hear.

"Fuck that," Tessa practically yelled. "I don't think you showing your clients houses qualifies with the same urgency as me performing lifesaving surgery."

And there it was, the same argument Tessa always used. "It still doesn't make my contribution any less valuable."

Tessa sighed, and her shoulders dropped. "I can't do this anymore."

Jaycee stared into Tessa's tired eyes. "We could still try counseling." Jaycee tried to keep her voice even.

Tessa clamped her teeth together, which made it appear as if she were growling. "I've told you it's too late for that. People grow apart all the time. Just accept it—and move on."

"Easy for you to say." Jaycee let out a snort. "You only lost me, which apparently isn't much of a loss since you don't even seem to like me."

Tessa rolled her eyes toward the sky but didn't respond.

"But I lose not just you, but an entire family." Jaycee blinked several times, willing her tears back.

"And I'll say it again." Tessa spoke slowly as if she were speaking to a small child. "You need to go create your own family, not just keep chasing after mine."

"But they've been mine for the past fifteen years." Jaycee didn't try to hide the pleading tone in her voice.

"And there lies the crux of the problem." Tessa shook her head. "I'm not sure when you fell out of love with me or if you ever did love me. All these years, it's been my family that you were truly in love with and couldn't leave."

Tessa's words stung, mostly because they were true. How should she respond? A flash of red whizzed past and temporarily distracted her from their conversation. "What the hell was that?"

Tessa's eyes widened. "You need to go."

Jaycee watched the red car pull up to the curb on the other side of the cul-de-sac. The car must be electric since it drove past with only a whisper. Expensive, no doubt. She smiled, hoping to lighten the tension. "What? Do you have a hot date?" Jaycee laughed, but Tessa didn't.

"Just go, please," Tessa said.

The Tesla's door flew open, and a shapely leg, clad in three-inch heels, slid out. A tallish woman with long flowing blond hair stepped from the car. She pulled the trench coat around herself, but not before Jaycee could make out the tight black dress she wore.

"I'm done with this conversation," Tessa said.

"What the fuck? She *is* your date."

"We've been separated for nearly a year. I think I'm allowed to date." Tessa crossed her arms over her chest.

The woman called Tessa's name from across the way.

Tessa turned and held up her hand. "I'll be right there." She turned back to Jaycee. "I'm going inside, and you need to leave."

"You had to bring her to Thanksgiving?" Jaycee put her hand against her chest. "And flaunt her in front of me?"

"Oh, for fuck's sake, I'm not flaunting anything." Tessa's face reddened. "How the hell did I know you'd behave like a crazy stalker and show up to see it?"

Tessa had a point, but Jaycee wasn't ready to admit it. Especially while the pain in her chest practically cut off her breath. She wanted to say something more, something angry, but the other part of her wanted to go climb under a blanket fort and never come out.

Jaycee started the Range Rover, and without another word to Tessa, she rolled up the window. She shoved the car into gear and peeled around the cul-de-sac, hoping her tires might toss up a few pieces of loose gravel along the way.

All the better if one bounced up and caught Ms. Black Dress by surprise. Jaycee didn't even look in the woman's direction as she flew past her.

She found herself speeding through town but didn't remember driving out of the subdivision. With the back of her hand, Jaycee swiped away the tears streaming down her cheeks. "Shit. Shit. Fucking shit,"

Jaycee screamed, hoping it would make her feel better. It didn't work.

She weaved around the sparse holiday traffic and accelerated through a yellow stoplight that might have been closer to red, but she didn't care. Irrationally, she believed if she could just get out of Cedarsburg everything would be better.

With the ramp toward I-43 in sight, she plowed through another nearly red light and swerved around a jackass going way too slow before she powered onto the southbound ramp. Instead of slowing as it curved, she stomped on the gas, frantic to leave Cedarsburg and the Wilsons behind.

Her tears didn't stop; instead, they seemed to flow harder. Angrily, she ran the sleeve of her coat over her eyes, and the rough material scraped across her eyelids. *Good.* Maybe she'd rip them off. Could someone die from torn-off eyelids?

She knew she was being ridiculous and overly dramatic, but it was only to keep the pain at bay. Anger was much easier to handle than hurt. At the speed she was going, she would be at the exit toward home soon.

Her stomach clenched. The thought of wandering the cavernous house alone threatened to overwhelm her. *No.* She couldn't go there now. Maybe she should go throw the fucking macarons into Lake Michigan.

She glanced at the tins that had tumbled over on the floor. Better yet, she could chuck the cookies out the window one by one and give herself a point for every passing car she hit.

Wow. She needed to get a grip. Since when was she someone who threw cookies at other drivers? Would that qualify as road rage?

After she flew past her exit, her heart rate slowed. She'd drive into Milwaukee, her city, the brew capital of the world. Since Tessa moved out, she'd driven around the city countless times when she couldn't bear to return home to an empty house. It usually brought her peace.

Normally, she'd drive the neighborhoods, checking out her current listings or homes she'd recently sold. She enjoyed getting a glimpse of how the new homeowners changed the property. It reminded her of the impermanence of everything. A home, just like a family, was supposed to be forever, wasn't it?

Chapter Two

"Shit," Piper Marsden said to no one as she glared at the piles of uncooked food on the stainless steel countertop.

Mrs. Akers, who sat at a table in the corner of the large kitchen, looked up from the pie she was painstakingly cutting. The same one she'd been working on for the past five minutes. "Did you say something, dear?"

"Um, sorry. I didn't mean to disturb you." Piper smiled at her, hoping to avoid a lengthy conversation. She loved Mrs. Akers, but right now, she didn't have time for one of her winding stories.

"It's okay, honey." Mrs. Akers motioned to the pumpkin pies that surrounded her. "But I do need to focus if I'm going to get all these cut up properly."

"Of course, I need to leave you to your work," Piper said in a rush, seeing the opportunity for her escape.

Mrs. Akers glanced around the room and frowned. "I hope the others get here soon."

Piper faked another smile. She wasn't about to tell her that the volunteers wouldn't be coming. "I better go check."

As she made a beeline for the door, she was forced to pass the counter, where the uncooked food mocked her. In the past hour, she'd shuffled the food items around but had accomplished little else.

Stupid COVID. And stupid her. It had been shortsighted to have only one church group assigned to meal prep, but they'd been so enthusiastic about working together that she'd not considered the consequences, until the entire choir had come down with COVID.

Shit. What if the other group scheduled to serve got sick, too? She couldn't think that way or she'd end up rocking in the corner with her thumb shoved in her mouth.

Maybe Pastor Bob had found replacements, although he hadn't sounded optimistic, saying it was Thanksgiving after all. *No kidding*. As if she didn't know that. The boxes and boxes of food were a dead giveaway.

Piper took a deep breath before she pushed against the swinging door. She needed to stop having snarky thoughts, or karma was going to bite her harder in the ass. *Positive thinking*. That was what she needed.

Something wonderful would be waiting for her on the other side of the door. Possibly an entire replacement crew of volunteers. Maybe the pastor pulled off a miracle.

With renewed confidence, she burst through the door.

She quickly scanned the room, and her face fell. *No miracle*. Although, DOTS, the Dreams of Tomorrow Shelter, did look especially festive today. Thank god she'd set up the tables and decorated last night.

As if the people coming for meals didn't have enough troubles, they could add having to eat her cooking to the list. The thought made her stomach lurch. *Shit.* She didn't have a clue what she was doing in the kitchen, and even if she did, there was no way she and Mrs. Akers could cook a meal for over two hundred fifty people.

Ugh. She wanted to scream. Why had she told Sergio and Caleb she could handle this? If they hadn't gone to Sergio's parents' house in Chicago, she'd call them and beg them for help, but she was on her own.

She was going to let everyone down. They'd entrusted her, and she blew it. Her gaze landed on the children's turkey drawings that decorated the walls, and her eyes welled with tears. Worst of all, she'd let down all the people who looked forward to the meal. The people who relied on it.

A lump caught in her throat. *No.* She would not fail them. She couldn't.

Piper stood up straight and steeled her jaw. *Get over yourself.* She'd lived through much worse, so this wouldn't defeat her.

She scanned the room, looking for potential help when she noticed a tall woman in a stocking cap standing just inside the door talking with Ole Freddie. The woman clutched a large box to her chest, and by the way her gaze darted around the shelter's large all-purpose room, she appeared a bit uncomfortable. Piper hadn't seen her around before, but the holidays usually brought extra people in.

Despite the stocking cap, which was many times part of the patrons' standard garb, the rest of the woman's outfit looked too clean for her to be living on the street.

A volunteer? Maybe Pastor Bob had come through after all. Piper hurried across the large room toward Freddie and the woman.

As she approached, she was able to take in more. The woman was definitely not homeless. Although her clothing was casual, it was also expensive. The Air Jordans she wore had to cost over two hundred dollars. Plus, the woman didn't have the telltale grime embedded in her face from life on the streets. Nor did her eyes show the strain that came from not knowing where her next meal would come from or if she'd have a warm place to lay her head at night.

When Piper was only a few yards away, she couldn't help but notice the softness of the woman's features, which was a juxtaposition to her tall sturdy frame. Despite having a masculine vibe, her long eyelashes, dimpled cheek, and nearly flawless skin gave her an unquestionable femininity.

Damn. She was cute. *Seriously?* Piper had more to do than ogle this stranger. A stranger who looked like she needed rescuing from Freddie.

She must be one of Pastor Bob's replacement volunteers. Hopefully, she was one of many who would flood the shelter.

Piper smoothed the front of her sweater and put on her most cheerful smile as she approached. "I'm so glad you could make it." Piper extended her hand to the woman. "I'm Piper. Piper Marsden."

The woman's eyes narrowed, but she held out her hand. "Jaycee."

Piper clamped Jaycee's hand. The grip was warm and firm. "J.C.? What does that stand for?"

"Jesus Christ." Ole Freddie cackled.

Piper shot him a look. She couldn't afford chasing away her only volunteer.

"Um…it doesn't stand for anything." J.C. must have noticed Piper's puzzled look because she added,

"It's spelled J-A-Y-C-E-E."

"Oh, what a pretty name," Piper said, hoping to put her at ease.

By the way Jaycee kept looking over her shoulder at the exit, Piper feared she might bolt at any minute. Sometimes people coming to a homeless shelter for the first time were a bit overwhelmed, and having Ole Freddie be the first to greet her hadn't helped. It wasn't lost on Piper that Jaycee hadn't given a last name. Sometimes people preferred to stay anonymous, so they weren't hounded for donations.

When Jaycee didn't respond, Piper forged on. "Please tell me you know how to cook."

"Yeah." Jaycees brow creased.

"Excellent." Piper put her hand on Jaycee's elbow. "We better get you into the kitchen then." Piper turned. "Sorry, Ole Freddie, you'll have to get to know Jaycee another time. She has work to do."

He winked. "Don't think I'll let a pretty lady like this get away for long." He smiled at Jaycee. "Maybe we can chat over a piece of pumpkin pie."

Jaycee's eyes widened, and she nodded slightly. *Good lord.* This woman was definitely a noob, but she'd be in the kitchen most of the time, so it should be all right. Piper waited for him to wander off before she said, "Are any others coming?"

"I...um...I'm not sure." Jaycee's gaze darted around the room.

Shit. "That's okay. I take it you don't sing in the choir." Piper gently tugged on Jaycee's arm to get her to follow. Maybe a little small talk would loosen her up. Jaycee clung to her box like someone might take it. At least she must be dedicated if she brought her own utensils.

"Sing?" Jaycee finally said after they'd walked several steps.

"Apparently not." Piper laughed at the repulsed look on Jaycee's face. She must not be a fan of the church choir. "That's okay. I sing about as well as I cook, so I understand."

They'd made it halfway across the large room. Piper had intentionally walked fast, so nobody would try to stop her and talk. Everyone at the shelter knew to stand back when she was on a mission. It served her well.

Despite Jaycee's head swiveling from side to side as she took in the surroundings, she easily kept up with Piper. It was one of the advantages of being tall, which was something Piper knew nothing about.

"Where are you taking me?" Jaycee said when they were nearly past all the tables.

Piper stifled a sigh. For someone who came prepared with her own box of utensils, Jaycee seemed a little clueless. *Stop.* Piper wasn't being fair. After all, Jaycee had come out on Thanksgiving, on a moment's notice. By her reactions, she'd never done anything like this before, so Piper needed to put her at ease.

Piper slowed and gazed into Jaycee's expressive brown eyes. "Sorry. I'm just a little frazzled. I'm sure you understand." Piper was careful not to say anything negative about Jaycee's fellow church members. "I mean, COVID's not their fault."

"Maybe I missed it, but did you tell me where we're going?"

They'd arrived at the doors to the kitchen. With a flourish, Piper threw open the door, waved her hand toward the mountain of food, and said, "Your canvas awaits." Maybe a humorous approach would wipe the look of apprehension off Jaycee's face.

Jaycee pointed at the pile of boxes. "Is that the, um, food for the meal?"

Piper's shoulders sagged. "I think so. It's everything they delivered this week."

Jaycee's eyes widened. "How many people are you expecting to serve?"

"We're figuring around two hundred and fifty."

"How much do they plan on eating?"

"As much as they want." Piper glared. Just because they were homeless didn't mean she'd skimp on their holiday meal.

"I didn't mean any offense." Jaycee held up her hand. "That just looks like way more food than you'll need."

Piper put her hand against her forehead. A headache was brewing. "Sergio and Caleb are normally in charge of the meals, so they did all the ordering. I just pulled it out of the storeroom. This isn't my domain." Piper leaned against a pile of boxes, suddenly exhausted. "The volunteers said they could handle it."

"When is the meal supposed to be served?"

"Four o'clock."

Jaycee looked at her watch, and her gaze snapped to Piper. "That's less than four hours."

Piper groaned. "Don't remind me."

Jaycee pointed to Mrs. Akers, who was bent over her pies not paying them any attention. "The two of you planned on cooking the entire meal yourselves?"

Piper shook her head. "Mrs. Akers only cuts the pies."

Jaycee's eyes widened farther if that were possible. "You planned on doing it all yourself?"

"I was on my way to recruit volunteers when

you showed up."

Jaycee looked between the boxes and Piper. "And you think the two of us can do this?"

Piper let out a loud sigh. Something she hadn't intended on doing. "No. I wanted to get you set up, and then I was gonna round you up a few helpers. Unless a few more of your friends are planning on coming."

"Ah, nope." Jaycee's face registered a cross between confusion and annoyance. At least that was how Piper saw it, but right now, she was so stressed she probably wasn't reading anything right.

"I should go recruit then." Piper backed toward the door. "Be back soon." Before Jaycee could respond, she turned and hurried from the room.

Chapter Three

*J*aycee stared at the door for at least a minute after Piper scurried out.

What the hell just happened? Was this the way all shelters worked? She'd simply wanted to drop off her macarons so someone could enjoy them. She certainly hadn't expected to be put to work.

Why had she just stood and gaped while Piper ordered her around? Granted, Piper was adorable, in a chaotic and frenetic sort of way, but still.

Shell shock. That must be it. First, she'd been traumatized by Tessa, and then she'd stepped out of her comfort zone and showed up at the shelter. Only to be accosted at the door by the old guy, what had Piper called him? Ole Freddie?

He'd been in the middle of telling her about his war wound and had just reached for his shirt to hike it up when Piper interrupted. *Thank god.* Jaycee was pretty sure she wasn't prepared to see what he'd been about to show her.

And what was all Piper's talk about COVID and singing? It was just weird. When Piper returned, Jaycee would tell her that she couldn't stay. In the meantime, she might as well check out the menu.

Jaycee scanned the industrial kitchen. It was a mass of stainless steel. Not aesthetically pleasing but practical. She guessed that was the point. Substance over style.

Jaycee made her way around the boxes and found the meal plan Piper said she'd find on the countertop. Standard fare, nothing fancy, turkey slices, stuffing, mashed potatoes and gravy, green bean casserole, yams, rolls, and pumpkin pie. She glanced at the old woman in the corner. At least the pumpkin pies were already cooked. One thing she could check off the list.

Jaycee was pretty sure this was way too much food. The entire kitchen was filled with boxes, crates, and bags. Her gaze landed on the bags of potatoes piled against one wall. *Holy hell.* Four stacks of five bags. Twenty? How many pounds were in each bag?

She walked over and looked at the label. *Fifty pounds.* As she did the math in her head, she looked toward the ceiling. Twenty times fifty was a thousand pounds. *Shit.* Doubtful that they'd need four pounds of potatoes per guest.

Jaycee shook her head and chuckled. Obviously, Piper had no clue what she was doing. A quick scan of the rest of the ingredients told her there was too much of everything. No wonder Piper seemed so overwhelmed.

She glanced at the door and back at the boxes. How long would Piper be gone? Jaycee supposed she could help a little while she waited since it would be rude to just sneak out.

Potatoes? She pulled out her phone and Googled potato servings. *Hmm.* Surprisingly, the answer came back forty-eight pounds for one hundred people. Three bags should be more than enough. She toted one bag at a time and set them at one end of a long counter that looked to be a food prep area.

With the potatoes figured out, she moved on to the stuffing. Google said it would take about one ounce of dry mix to feed one person. *Hmph.* Not the way she ate stuffing, it wouldn't. She found the boxes labeled stuffing. *Holy shit.* There were six cases with two ten-pound bags in each box. Who the hell did the order? She snatched one box and took it to another area of the counter. That would give each person nearly one and a half ounces each. *Much better.*

This was kinda fun. Before she moved on to the yams, she moved the extra boxes of stuffing next to the potatoes to get them out of the way. She located six boxes of yams. Thankfully, they were in cans, unlike the potatoes. Jaycee studied the case. The label said, six #10 cans. What the hell was a number ten can?

She pulled open the top of the case. *Fuck.* The cans were enormous. She chuckled. *Number ten?* She'd have named it a big ass can, or at least a #50. After a trip around Google, she decided that fifteen cans should do it.

Jaycee grinned as she lined up the cans. Fifteen was a perfect number to make a pyramid. The base row started with five cans, the next four, until she put the one crowning can on top. One of the cans wasn't quite centered, so she twisted it slightly.

She stepped back to examine her work but shook her head. No, she wanted to finish getting the supplies in order before Piper returned, so she could slip out of here before the meal prep started.

No doubt, Piper would come back with more than enough help.

࠸࠹࠺࠻

"Now I need everyone to be on their best behavior." Piper wagged her finger at the group standing in front of her. "Jaycee seems a bit…um… let's just say skittish, so we can't be chasing her off if we want everyone to have a good meal."

"What about the church people?" Mitzy whined. "I thought the meal was supposed to be for us."

Piper bit her lip. Even though homeless, Mitzy was still a typical teenager, so it wouldn't do any good for Piper to challenge her. "It is." Piper moved up beside Mitzy and tried to put her arm around Mitzy's shoulder. Being nearly a foot and a half shorter, Piper had to settle on putting it around Mitzy's waist instead. "I really appreciate this. You." Piper turned to Donovan. "Both of you."

Donovan gave her a shy smile and patted Mitzy's arm. "Come on. Piper's been good to us. We can do it. Just this once."

Mitzy grunted and flipped her wrist. Her long fingers were capped by bright red fingernails. "If I break a nail, someone will pay."

When Mitzy wasn't looking, Donovan shook his head and smiled at Piper. The two made quite the pair. Piper hoped Jaycee was ready to deal with them, but Piper had no choice. The volunteer pool was slim pickings.

"Okay. Remember, let's put our best foot forward when we work with Jaycee." Piper forced a smile as she looked at the motley crew she'd soon present to Jaycee. "Let's go."

With more confidence than she felt, Piper strode across the room. She hoped Jaycee wouldn't be annoyed at how long it had taken to assemble a team. Negotiations with the group had been, shall she say, a little heated. She had to hand it to them; they'd been tough negotiators. They'd bought themselves special privileges through Christmas. Piper knew they would have helped for free, but she always tried to show them as much respect as she could. After all, she knew how it felt to be invisible.

Piper paused outside the door. Was she ready for this? Or the bigger question, was Jaycee?

She pushed the door open and marched into the kitchen with her squad trailing behind her. Piper stopped short. "What did you do?" she said without thinking.

Jaycee's face colored. "Um, I just...I sorted out what you needed." She pointed to the large pile of supplies against the wall. "I don't think you need those."

Piper put her hand on her hip. "What do you mean, I don't need it?"

Jaycee held up her phone. "I, uh, I Googled how much food you needed for the meal. I don't know who ordered all that, but it's way too much."

Ole Freddie chuckled and pointed at the pile. "Is that everything that was in the storage room?"

"Yeah," Piper said with a frown.

He laughed again. "Planning on serving all the food for the entire month in one day?"

"What?" Realization began to dawn. Piper groaned. "You mean I almost wiped us out of food?"

Ole Freddie laughed harder, and the others joined in, even Jaycee. "And you hauled it all out here by yourself?" he asked.

"Yes!" Piper stood up taller.

He reached out and squeezed her biceps. "For a little thing, you have some moxie."

She ignored him and pointed toward the counter. "So that's all we need?"

Jaycee nodded. "I think so."

Piper pointed at the pyramid of yam cans. She smiled. "And what's this?"

Jaycee returned her smile. "A yamid?"

Piper laughed. "Well, it's a very nice yamid." She could finally breathe for the first time today. Seeing the ingredients laid out made the task at hand seem a little less formidable. Not that she knew what she was doing, but she suddenly felt hopeful.

Jaycee started to open her mouth to speak, but Piper cut her off. "Oh, I almost forgot. I need to introduce you to your team."

❧❧❧❧

Damn it. Jaycee had just opened her mouth to announce her exit when Piper cut her off.

"What was that?" Jaycee asked, sure she hadn't heard Piper right.

"Your team. Your squad." Piper dramatically waved her arm around to the group standing behind her. "Or should I say sous chefs?"

Jaycee's jaw started to fall open, so she clamped it shut. Surely, Piper was joking, but her expression was serious. Dry sense of humor? No, Piper didn't strike her as the dry humor type.

She should respond with something, but she couldn't stop staring. Two children who didn't look to be older than five, a strange pair of teenagers who held hands and giggled seemingly oblivious to the others in the room, a woman who appeared to be talking to herself, and Ole Freddie.

"We're ready for our assignments," Piper said a little too enthusiastically and clapped her hands together for emphasis. "Put us to work."

"You want me to…to…" Jaycee glanced at the food lining the counters. "To direct this meal?"

"You're the only one that knows how to cook." Piper beamed at her and bounced from one foot to the other. "We're ready."

Seriously? This was not happening. Jaycee had nearly made her escape, but now what? Could she leave them with no hope of producing a meal and let so many people go hungry on Thanksgiving Day? *Fuck.* Her gaze slowly drifted over the team. Not much to work with. It would take a miracle to pull this off, but then again, what else did she have to do? Her empty house flashed through her mind. She'd sit alone, eating popcorn and watching the football game. Jaycee shuddered at the thought—her mind made up.

"Introduce me to the crew," Jaycee said, wondering if she'd regret those words.

Piper's face lit up. Her smile was infectious. She had a wide mouth with thin lips, but it was the deep valleys that separated her cheeks from her mouth that drew Jaycee's attention.

Piper's dark brown eyes danced as she put her hand on Freddie's shoulder. "You've already met Ole Freddie."

Jaycee nodded.

"And this is Loretta." Piper moved close to the mousy woman, who kept her eyes cast to the ground, but Piper didn't touch her. Loretta mumbled something under her breath, but Piper continued as if she hadn't heard. "Loretta works best if you give her a project she can focus on, um, on her own."

Jaycee nodded again, picking up on Piper's subtle instruction.

Piper slid between the two teenagers and put her arm around them. "And these two...these two are gonna be your superstars." Piper beamed up at the tall, wide-shouldered girl who must have been at least six-foot-six in her several-inch heels. "This is Mitzy." She turned to the short baby-faced boy who stood only about an inch taller than Piper. "And this is Donovan."

"Nice to meet you," Jaycee said.

Donovan smiled and nodded, but Mitzy just looked bored and stared at her fingernails.

Great. Surly teenagers, just what she wanted to deal with. Jaycee's thoughts went to Josh and Megan. They'd gone through that stage a few years ago, and she'd found her way through it, so she could surely do the same with Mitzy and Donovan. But the memory of her niece and nephew, if she could call them that anymore, made her heart hurt.

"Hey, are you okay?" Piper asked.

Jaycee blinked. *Shit.* She hadn't meant to let her thoughts show on her face, but apparently, she had. "Yeah, yeah. Just thinking about how I'm going to deploy the troops."

"Wait." Piper held up her hand. "I haven't introduced you to your final volunteers. She motioned for the tiny kids. The bigger of the two, the boy looked to be no older than five. "These are my children, Paxton and Maddie."

Jaycee's eyes widened. "They're going to help?"

Piper frowned. "They're great helpers."

"How old are they?" Jaycee tried not to stare, but she didn't see how these two would do much more than get in the way.

Paxton stepped forward and held out his hand.

"I'm eight and Maddie's six."

Jaycee took his hand and stared.

Ole Freddie laughed. "They're small like their momma. She's been getting them into places for free for years."

"Hush." Piper glared at him. "Don't pay him any attention."

Maddie smiled a toothless smile. "Momma says I can pass for four as long as I don't talk."

Piper shook her head. "Six going on eighteen. But we don't have time for any more stories. We need to get to work."

Jaycee was shell-shocked since she had no clue how they would pull this off. After the introductions, she had even more doubts, but she pounded her fist on the counter with more conviction than she felt. "Let's get cooking."

"It's going to get hot in here." Piper pointed at Jaycee's hat. "Don't you want to take that off?"

"No!" Jaycee said a little more forcefully than she'd intended. "I mean, no, I'm quite comfortable in it."

"Suit yourself," Piper said with a shrug.

Jaycee adjusted her hat, making sure that none of her telltale short but thick, white blond hair peeked out from underneath. She picked up the recipe cards and held them up. "Who wants to do what?"

Loretta shuffled up, mumbling under her breath. She gazed up into Jaycee's eyes and seemed to be looking into her soul. "Gravy," she said clearly.

"Thank you." Jaycee handed her the recipe.

Loretta took the card and moved closer. "I know you," she said before she began muttering again.

Jaycee froze and stared straight ahead.

Piper moved in beside Loretta but didn't touch her. "Come on, sweetie. I'll help you get your ingredients together."

Loretta shot one last look at Jaycee and walked away muttering, "That's the bus woman. Big face. White hair. Park benches. White hair."

Jaycee pulled her stocking cap farther down on her head.

Piper glanced over her shoulder, shook her head, and mouthed, "Sorry."

Chapter Four

Piper ran the back of her hand across her forehead, wiping away beads of sweat. Who knew cooking could be so strenuous? She tore open another bag of tiny marshmallows and started to pour them into the pan.

"Did you forget something?" Jaycee said over her shoulder.

Piper looked up into Jaycee's soft brown eyes and smiled. "Shit. The brown sugar." Piper reached behind her for the bag, but Jaycee had already picked it up and held it out to her.

Jaycee pointed at the other pans. "Did you remember to put it on those?"

Piper bit her lip. Had she? "Ah…I think so."

Jaycee laughed. It was such a soothing sound. Some people had loud, grating laughs, but not Jaycee. Hers was low and melodic. It was easy on Piper's ears and didn't trigger her startle response.

"I'll check them." Jaycee nodded toward the pan in front of Piper. "You keep working on that one."

With a glance inside the bag, Piper made her decision and dumped the remaining sugar on top of the yams.

"Holy shit, are you trying to put someone into a diabetic coma?" Jaycee asked.

Piper jumped and nearly lost her grip on the brown sugar.

"I didn't mean to scare you." Jaycee put her hand on Piper's back.

"I just have an overactive startle response." Piper's heart raced, so she took two deep breaths. "Everyone around here knows not to come up behind me."

"Yep, one night, she just about took me down with a broomstick," Ole Freddie said as he walked past with a tray of turkey slices. "Never snuck up on her again."

"Stop telling tales." Piper waved her hand at him but winked.

He shrugged and continued to the oven.

"What's his story?" Jaycee asked, then quickly added, "if it's okay to ask. He just seems like a really nice guy."

"He is." Piper smiled. "The war was hard on him."

"Vietnam?"

Piper shook her head. Jaycee was obviously making the same mistake many people who met Ole Freddie made. "No. The Gulf War."

"Gulf War?"

"He's only fifty-four."

Jaycee's eyes widened. "Oh. I didn't realize."

"He's been on the street for a long time. It ages people." Piper refrained from saying that all the booze aged him, as well. It wasn't her story to tell. Seeing the discomfort on Jaycee's face, Piper decided a change of subject was in order. She motioned with her head toward Mitzy and Donovan. "You seem to have a way with teenagers."

"Did you miss the broken nail saga?" Jaycee ripped open another bag of brown sugar and sprinkled it over a pan of yams.

"I don't think anyone could have." Piper pulled another can off the yam pyramid and clamped the can opener around it. "I think the ruckus was likely heard in Green Bay."

Jaycee smirked. "It was rather dramatic. I'm just glad I found a task more suited to Mitzy's talents. I'm surprised that a girl so…uh…so hardy is quite so prissy."

Piper bit her lip, so she wouldn't laugh. Another story that wasn't hers to tell. She thought Jaycee had figured out that both teenagers were transgender but apparently not. "She and Donovan are all over the green bean casserole, though," Piper said.

"I think it's the crispy onions. They've eaten as many as they've used."

"Yeah, I noticed." Piper shook her head. "I still admire the way you patiently managed the fingernail incident. I've never known anyone to break a nail peeling potatoes."

"Your kids saved my ass." Jaycee glanced at Paxton and Maddie, who were diligently scraping their peelers across a potato. "I can't believe how hard they've worked."

A lump caught in Piper's throat. What the hell was the matter? The stress of the day must be getting to her. She blinked a few times and looked down at the pan, not wanting Jaycee to see her reaction. "They're good kids." What an understatement, she thought.

"I can tell. It's a sign of good parenting."

Piper's stomach roiled. She needed to extract herself from this conversation, so she threw out the first thing that came to mind. "How long have you been with the church?"

"What church?"

"What do you mean, what church?" Piper stared at Jaycee, who stared back at her. "The one that sent you."

"Sent me?" Jaycee crinkled her nose.

"First Baptist." When Piper saw the look of confusion still on Jaycee's face she said, "Pastor Bob."

Jaycee shook her head. "I don't know a Pastor Bob, and I don't go to any church."

"But…" Piper pointed over her shoulder toward the door. "But you came in to volunteer."

"Actually, I didn't."

"What?" This conversation was getting stranger and stranger. She'd been having a great time working with Jaycee, but now she was beginning to think she'd been under so much stress that she'd dreamed her up. Nope, she was definitely real. *Shit.* What if she was homeless and had just come for the meal? After all, she clung to her stocking cap like it was a security blanket. But being homeless certainly wasn't a sin, just not what Piper had expected.

"I came in to donate…wait." Jaycee hurried across the kitchen and picked up a box. She brought it back and set it on the counter. "I came in to drop these off." She pulled out a tin and opened the lid.

Piper peered down at the colorful cookies. "What are those?"

"Macarons." Jaycee smiled.

"Macaroons? I've heard of those."

"No, no. Macarons. Rhymes with gone." Jaycee held the tin out toward Piper. "See."

Piper peeked at the multicolored cookies. "I always thought they were called macaroons."

"Macaroons are puffy coconut cookies."

Piper frowned. "Why the hell would they name cookies so close to the same thing? That's like having Oreos and Oreas."

Jaycee laughed. "Different countries. Macaroons are Italian, and macarons are French."

"Ah, that explains it." Piper wasn't sure if it did, but she didn't want to appear ignorant. Besides, she wanted to get to the bottom of this mystery. "If you came to drop off cookies, then why did you say you were here to volunteer?"

"I didn't." Jaycee rubbed her hand over her stocking cap but didn't take it off.

Piper started to argue but stopped and replayed the earlier conversation in her head. Then she let out a loud laugh. "Oh, my god, you didn't."

"I know I didn't." Jaycee's voice came out in a higher pitch.

"Then why did you stay?"

Jaycee met Piper's gaze. "Because you asked me to. You needed me."

Piper stared into Jaycee's eyes for several seconds before she responded. "Seriously?"

"You looked like you needed help. I planned on leaving after I got the food sorted out for you."

"So why didn't you?"

A blush spread on Jaycee's cheeks, and her gaze darted around the room.

Piper let out another laugh. "Because you saw the team I had to work with."

Jaycee looked over the top of Piper's head. "They've been great."

"But you weren't so sure in the beginning?"

"I...well...I had my doubts." Jaycee shuffled from foot to foot. "But I was wrong."

On impulse, Piper stepped forward and wrapped her arms around Jaycee. "Thank you so much for staying."

Jaycee stiffened at first but then melted into Piper's embrace and squeezed her tightly.

Piper's first reaction was to pull away, not because it felt wrong, but because it felt so right. It had been a long time since she'd hugged anyone from outside the shelter. Jaycee smelled of shampoo and soap not the street. Piper breathed in Jaycee's scent, hoping she wouldn't notice.

"What's going on over there?" Mitzy called from across the kitchen. "Aren't you supposed to be working?"

Piper stepped out of Jaycee's embrace and hoped her face wasn't as red as it felt. She needed to get control of the situation. She held up her hand. "I almost broke a nail, and Jaycee was comforting me."

Mitzy glared, but then her lips quivered, and she burst out laughing. "Good one."

The rest of the group laughed, except for Loretta, who intently stared into the pot of gravy she was stirring. Counting to ten as she stirred clockwise, before she reversed and stirred ten times counterclockwise. She'd been lost in her rhythm for the past twenty minutes.

Once the laughter died away and the others had returned to their duties, Piper said, "Thank you for staying. I couldn't have done this without you."

Jaycee smiled big enough to bring out her dimple. "Yeah, you would have cooked the food for the entire month."

"I know, right." Piper grinned and waved her hand around the food. "This is much more manageable for the team."

"Speaking of the team." Jaycee nodded in the direction of Mrs. Akers. "What is she doing with the measuring tape?"

"Making sure every piece is the same size."

"Seriously?" Jaycee's eyes widened. "I thought maybe she had some weird method of keeping count."

"Nope. She demands that all the pieces are the same size. That's why she won't let anyone else help. Says we'll do it wrong."

"That's priceless."

"Yeah, right. You should've been here for the row we had a few years ago. She insisted that all the pies be baked in nine-inch pans and was turning away bigger ones." Piper shook her head. "It took a minute to convince her that turning down donated food at a shelter was not a good thing."

"How did you convince her?"

"Sergio took care of it." Piper smirked at the memory. "He grabbed a knife and started hacking at one of the pies, saying he'd have to do it himself if she wasn't going to do it. I thought she was going to pass out."

Jaycee laughed and sneaked a glance at Mrs. Akers, who was intently measuring and scoring the pie. "What happened to the mangled pie?"

"That's the best part. She bought the pie off the shelter for twenty-five dollars just to keep it off the table." Piper leaned over and whispered, "I suspect she threw it in the dumpster."

"Oh, so she's not one of the...um...the clients... or people who are homeless."

"We call them patrons. At least we do here. The language is always evolving. Advocates are pushing for unhoused or unhomed, but it hasn't caught on here yet. I try to at least say people without houses, but even I mess up."

"It's hard to keep up with the right words."

"Exactly. Some terms are so disparaging, demoralizing, and degrading, we call it the three D's."

Piper smiled. "I've had volunteers that have used every incorrect term in the book, but the patrons love them, and others that have all the right words, but the patrons avoid them."

"Why?"

"Our patrons have well-developed bullshit meters." Piper put her hand against her own chest. "Words don't matter as much to them as what's in here." Piper flicked her gaze toward Mrs. Akers. "To answer your question, she's not without housing. She's just one of our staunchest volunteers."

"How nice."

"It's good for her, and it's good for us. A win-win."

Paxton interrupted their conversation. "We have another batch that needs to be cut up."

"Duty calls," Jaycee said. She paused for a moment and appeared to want to say more, but then she stopped. Her soft eyes didn't exactly harden, but they lost some of their warmth. "Don't forget the brown sugar."

"Aye, aye, captain." Piper said, hoping to bring the twinkle back to Jaycee's eyes.

Chapter Five

aycee stood in the far corner of the kitchen and watched as the new batch of volunteers filed in. "So these are the servers?" Jaycee said to Mrs. Akers.

"Yep. Our job is done." She smiled at the pies stacked on racks around her. "I try not to watch the barbarians serve." She shook her head, and her gray curls bobbed around her face. "How hard is it to lift a piece of pie out of the pan? But they rip into them without any regard to my work. Savages."

Jaycee smiled and patted Mrs. Akers's shoulder. "You do wonderful work. Artistry," Jaycee said, feeling magnanimous.

"I like you." Mrs. Akers beamed up at her. "You should volunteer here more often."

Jaycee froze. Despite the fun she'd had, this was surely a one-time thing. She couldn't rely on a homeless shelter to uplift her, even though it had today. Jaycee grunted in response when she sensed Mrs. Akers's gaze on her.

Mrs. Akers groaned as she rose from the table. "I should go mingle. It's always nice to talk with the patrons."

Jaycee turned to her. "Thanks again for all your help."

"The thanks belongs to you." Mrs. Akers patted Jaycee's arm. "You saved Piper's ass."

Without thinking, Jaycee looked across the room at Piper's ass. Jaycee's face heated, and she turned back to Mrs. Akers. "It's been my pleasure."

"She's a dynamo." Mrs. Akers winked. "I think she could use someone like you around here."

Before Jaycee could process the meaning of Mrs. Akers's words, Mrs. Akers shuffled away, chuckling as she went.

What the hell was that about? Jaycee pushed it aside as the ramblings of an old woman. For the first time today, she got the chance to really study Piper.

Piper was holding court with the volunteers. All smiled and nodded as she spoke. A huge smile played on Piper's lips, creating the smile valleys that drew Jaycee's gaze. Jaycee wasn't sure if she'd ever seen anyone with quite that pronounced or deep lines. They suited Piper, though.

Mrs. Akers was right; Piper was a dynamo. It was a stretch if she were five-two, but her presence made her seem much taller. Dressed in a simple brown and orange sweater that screamed Thanksgiving and a pair of black jeans, she looked professional without being stuffy. She wasn't pretty in the traditional sense, but her magnetic energy made it hard for Jaycee to look away.

Her dishwater blond hair was slightly stringy and could use a little TLC from a stylist, although the way it fell on her shoulders gave her a carefree vibe. But it was her intense brown eyes that drew Jaycee in. There was an intelligence behind her eyes, as well as a dash of playfulness, but there was something else Jaycee couldn't identify.

Piper must have sensed Jaycee staring because she met Jaycee's gaze and waved.

Jaycee wiggled her fingers and started to look away when Piper made an exaggerated motion with her arm, beckoning Jaycee. *Shit.* Jaycee didn't want to join the group. She'd noticed a woman she'd sold a house to amongst the volunteers, and she certainly didn't want to be recognized.

Thinking quickly, Jaycee drew her legs together, bent slightly, crossed her arms over her groin, and motioned toward the restroom with her head. Before Piper could respond, she hustled from the room.

In the bathroom, she plopped down on the toilet and rested her back against the bowl. That was a narrow escape. She wasn't ready for anyone here to know who she was. Loretta had been a close enough call. Luckily, nobody listened to her ramblings, but she'd obviously seen Jaycee's picture plastered all over the city buses.

She hated them, and she had to turn away every time one passed. The gigantic billboard that made her look like King Kong standing next to a skyscraper was the most cringeworthy. Nobody looked good blown up twelve feet tall, but her marketers had insisted on it since she was the face of Re-Ward Realty.

She still couldn't believe she'd allowed such a ridiculous play on her last name. If it were today, she'd never agree to it, but when she was young and starting out, she did whatever the marketers told her. Begrudgingly, she had to admit it had worked since she was the number one Realtor in Milwaukee, hopefully, soon to be in the entire state of Wisconsin as her business continued to spread.

Jaycee tended to be a bit more reserved, but Tessa had convinced her that she needed to be the face of the company. Now she was stuck with her short white blond hair with chunky dark streaks, even when she wanted to grow it out or dye it. And everyone expected her to arrive at a showing, wearing her bow tie and suspenders.

The few times she'd tried to wear something else, the customers' disapproving looks and comments on her attire had chased her back to her *uniform*.

She closed her eyes and took a deep breath. What a day she'd had. She'd not had time to process the scene at the Wilsons' house this morning. In some ways, it seemed a million miles away.

The bathroom door creaked open. "Jaycee, are you in here?" Piper's voice was low.

"Uh, yeah." Jaycee's eyes popped open. "Yeah. I'm here."

"Is everything okay?" Piper's voice was tentative.

"Yeah, yeah. It's fine." Jaycee felt ridiculous having this conversation through the bathroom door.

"Did someone do something to upset you? Did I?"

"No, no. Not at all." Jaycee sighed. "I just needed a little break."

Piper laughed. "Don't tell anyone, but this is where I hide out, too, so I totally understand. But you are going to join us for dinner, aren't you?"

No! Jaycee's mind screamed, but the tone in Piper's voice made her pause. Was Jaycee imagining it or was there a hint of hope twinged with apprehension. *Really?* She'd become an expert on Piper's tone in an afternoon and could read her through the bathroom stall. She needed to get over herself.

"If you don't want to, it's okay," Piper said. This time, there was no mistaking the sadness in her voice.

"You've already done so much."

"I'd love to stay" rolled out of Jaycee's mouth. Why the hell did she say that?

"Excellent." It sounded as if Piper had clapped her hands together. "The team will be so excited to have you."

"Uh, I'll be out in a minute." Jaycee hoped that Piper would get the hint that she didn't want the awkwardness of emerging from the stall with Piper looking on.

"Oh, god. Of course. I'll let you finish up in here. Take your time." Piper groaned. "Pretend I didn't just say that. I'm going to slink on out of here."

Jaycee laughed and heard Piper chuckling before the door closed behind her.

Well, she'd agreed to stay. Too late to back out now. She pulled her stocking cap off and tousled her damp hair. It felt good to let her head breathe for a bit. The hat was warm—too warm, but she'd have to put it on before she went back out. Her stupid hair would be a dead giveaway to who she was.

She leaned back against the bowl. She'd just stay here for a few more minutes.

※.※.※.※

"I ate too much." Piper patted her stomach. "You might need a forklift to get me up."

Mitzy groaned and turned in her chair, so her profile faced Piper. "I'm not eating for a week, or I'm gonna lose my girlish figure." She flipped the bottom of her hair with her hand. "The curse of being a woman."

"Then I'll take that." Donovan grabbed Mitzy's half-eaten piece of pie. He rubbed his flat stomach.

"The joy of being a man."

Everyone at the table laughed, even Jaycee now that she was in the know. It had taken everything Piper had not to laugh when the realization hit Jaycee. Her expression was priceless as it went from confusion to shock to acceptance in a span of about fifteen seconds. She'd shot Piper a questioning look, and Piper had simply nodded.

No words were exchanged, but Piper was sure Jaycee understood that Mitzy and Donovan were transgender. She'd not only seemed accepting, but also appeared to embrace them at an even deeper level. They'd had a few volunteers they hadn't asked back because of their prejudice. It pleased Piper that Jaycee passed the test.

Not that Jaycee would ever come back. It was a one-time fluke. Piper's chest tightened. Today had been one of the best days she could remember. It was likely just the heightened adrenaline.

"Piper!" Ole Freddie's voice was loud. "Are you listening?"

"Huh?" Piper said.

"Where were you, girl?" Mitzy said. "It certainly wasn't here."

"Uh, sorry. It's been a long day." Piper gestured to the nearly empty tables. "But we did it."

All the volunteers had left, and only a few stragglers remained scattered around the room. Most of the regulars had likely retired to the sleeping area.

"Thanks to our super volunteer." Ole Freddie grinned.

"Oh, yes. Where are my manners?" Piper sat up taller in her chair. She couldn't let fatigue set in now. "We certainly couldn't have done it without Jaycee."

She met Jaycee's gaze. "You saved Thanksgiving."

"To Jaycee." Mitzy lifted her glass of tea.

The others followed suit and lifted their glasses. "To Jaycee," they said in unison.

Jaycee's cheeks turned a deep crimson. Piper couldn't help but gape. She really was an attractive woman, especially when she flashed that dimple.

"Stop." Jaycee waved her hand at them and then covered her face.

"And to think, she just came in to drop off cookies," Ole Freddie said.

"Mac-a-ruhns," Piper corrected.

Jaycee dropped her hand from her face and greeted Piper with a huge grin. "You got it. Oh, shit, we never served them."

"We're having leftovers tomorrow, so we can put them out then." When Piper saw the disappointment on Jaycee's face, she leapt from the table. "But we can all sample them now."

"But everyone's full," Jaycee said.

"Nonsense," Donovan said. "I've got plenty of room."

"I've even got room for a fancy French dessert," Mitzy said and put her pinky in the air as she took a drink of her tea.

Piper shot Mitzy a glance. "How did you know they were French?"

Mitzy's eyebrows shot up. "I wasn't born on the street, ya know."

Every now and then, Mitzy or Donovan surprised Piper, and this was one of those moments. They'd shown up at the shelter about six months ago, and they'd been tight-lipped about their past.

Each person and each story were different, some

were open books, while others took a long time to let anyone in, if they ever did.

Jaycee stood, too. "I'll help you. I can pick out the best ones."

"Aren't they all the same?" Piper asked.

Jaycee rolled her eyes toward the ceiling. "Apparently, I have a few things to teach you about macarons."

As they walked to the kitchen, Jaycee gave her a lesson on baking macarons.

"You mean you can only bake them in certain weather?" Piper asked.

"Not exactly. I've baked them when I shouldn't have, but then they don't turn out as good."

"Ugh." Piper slapped her hand against her forehead. "Baking mac-a-ruhns seems complicated."

Jaycee rewarded her with a laugh. "It's never good to bake them when there's too much humidity in the air."

"So you can't bake them when it rains?"

"I prefer not to, but sometimes it can't be avoided." They'd reached the box that Jaycee had set in the corner, but she made no move to open it. "They're finicky. The ingredients must be prepared just right, or you won't get a good set."

"You saw my cooking prowess, or lack thereof." Piper grinned. "I don't even know what that means."

Jaycee flipped open the box and pulled out the large tin that she'd brought out earlier. She carefully removed the lid and plucked out a cookie. She tapped the hard outer shell. "It's all in the shell. It should have the perfect crunch but should never be hollow." Jaycee ran her finger over the smooth surface. "It should be smooth with rounded corners. But the true mark of a well-made macaron is the feet."

"Feet?" Piper laughed. "Now your cookies have feet?"

Jaycee moved in closer to Piper and held a cookie out in front of her. "See right here." Jaycee pointed at what looked like a ridge on the inside of the cookie.

"What am I looking at?"

"These." She lightly touched the macaron. "The feet. They should be small and unbroken, or something went wrong."

Piper stepped back, and she studied Jaycee. "Are you messing with me? Just making this shit up?"

"No." Jaycee laughed. "Google it."

Piper pulled one of the smaller tins out of the box. "So you went to all the trouble to make the perfect macaron to bring to the shelter?"

Jaycee shuffled her feet and closed the tin. "No. Not exactly."

Piper narrowed her eyes, suddenly curious. The rule at the center was to let people tell you what they wanted, but Piper's curiosity got the better of her. "Can I ask why you baked them?"

Jaycee sighed, and a pained expression crossed her face before she put on a smile that didn't reach her eyes. "My Thanksgiving plans fell through. I always package up individual tins for my nieces and nephews. And well, um, since I didn't get the chance to visit them, I didn't want them to go to waste."

Piper sensed there was more to the story, but she decided not to press Jaycee. Something told her that Jaycee had revealed more than she'd wanted to by the way she clutched the tin. "I'm sad that your plans fell through, but I'm happy to be the benefactor. I'm sure the others will be, too."

Jaycee's shoulders relaxed, and the tension left her face. "I hope they like them."

"Sounds like Mitzy's had them before." Piper put the small tin back in the box and closed it. "I'm pretty sure you just earned points with her."

"You seem surprised."

"That you earned points?" Piper gave Jaycee a sideways glance as they walked.

"No, that Mitzy had eaten them before."

"The thing you'll learn around here." *Oh, god.* Did she just insinuate that Jaycee would be back? It was too late to backpedal now, so she forged on. "The thing is. Everyone is different about their past. Some will tell you their life stories the moment you meet them, while others won't."

"Why do you suppose that is?"

"Too painful," Piper answered.

※ ※ ※ ※

As Jaycee ran the rag over the table one last time, she glanced at the clock. She still couldn't believe it was almost nine. She'd been at the shelter for almost eight hours.

"Thanks again for helping." Piper pushed a broom around the last table. "I would have been here until midnight without you."

Jaycee lifted her rag from the table and studied Piper. "You look tired."

Piper nodded. "I am. It's been a good day, no, a great one, but I'm ready to fall into bed."

"Hopefully you'll get the rest of the weekend to relax."

"If only." Piper smiled. "I have a paper to write for my Public Policy class."

"You're taking classes, too?"

"Yep, I'm getting my master's degree in Public Administration. Only a year to go."

"Wow." Jaycee nodded toward the far table, where Paxton and Maddie lay with their heads on their folded coats. "School, a job, plus you're raising such good little humans."

Piper's weary eyes filled with love, and she put her hand on her chest. "They're my heart. I couldn't ask for better."

"I still can't believe how hard they worked. Most kids would have been whining the entire time."

Piper's eyes welled, but she blinked twice, and the tears didn't come. "I'm not sure how I got so blessed."

"Do they ever complain?"

A strange look crossed Piper's face before she said, "No, not really." She opened her mouth but then abruptly closed it.

"Everything okay?" Jaycee asked, noticing the change in Piper.

Piper nodded. "Just overly tired."

"Would you like me to give you and the kids a ride home?"

"No."

"Oh, okay."

"We don't live far, and I have a few things to finish before I call it a day."

"Can I help?"

Piper shook her head. "No. It's paperwork. The daily logs."

Jaycee nodded. In her business, she understood paperwork. "Well, I better let you get to it, so you can get the little ones to bed." Jaycee glanced over at the sleeping children, and a twinge of sadness hit her. She'd not get the opportunity to say goodbye to them. Piper leaned her broom against a table and walked toward Jaycee. Despite the dark circles that had formed under her eyes, they still burned with intensity. And her step was a little slower, but it didn't take away from her dynamic energy.

Piper stopped a few feet from Jaycee. "I want to thank you again. For everything."

Jaycee smiled. "I meant it when I said, it's been a pleasure."

"Likewise. Um, if you ever want to volunteer again or just drop in, you know where to find us." Piper smoothed out her sweater. "I'm sure the others would love to see you."

Jaycee raised her eyebrows, and before she gave it any thought she said, "Just the others?"

"Busted." Piper held up her hands. "I'd love to see you, too."

"Okay." *Ugh.* Was that the best she could do? She'd wanted to say something more, something profound, but words escaped her. It was time for her to leave before she made things any more awkward. "Enjoy the rest of your holiday weekend."

"You too."

"And tell the kids thanks for me."

"I will."

Just go, Jaycee thought, but her feet stayed rooted to the floor. "If it's not too much sugar for them, give them one of the tins of macarons."

"I can't believe how much they loved them. Especially Paxton."

Jaycee smiled. "He gobbled up the strawberry ones."

"Since he was little, strawberries have always been his favorite food." Piper shook her head. "Strange, but at least it's healthy."

Jaycee smiled and nodded, unsure what to say next.

Piper bit her lip. "Hey, don't forget your coat."

Ah. That was her cue. Piper wanted her out. "I didn't wear one. I thought I was just going to run in and out."

"Touché." Piper's forehead creased. "Are you going to be warm enough?"

"I'll be fine." Jaycee motioned over her shoulder. "I'm only parked about half a block down the street."

Piper nodded.

Yep. It was getting more awkward by the minute. They'd spent the day chattering like old friends, but this small talk was making Jaycee's skin crawl. She pulled her stocking cap down a bit to signify that she was leaving. "It was great meeting you." She took a step toward the exit but turned and looked over her shoulder. "Take care."

"You too." Exhaustion was back in Piper's eyes.

Jaycee wished she could erase it, but that was silly. Piper just needed a good night's sleep. "Goodbye." Jaycee took another step toward the door but this time didn't look back over her shoulder.

"Goodbye." Piper's voice was low.

Jaycee fought the urge to turn and ask for another hug like they'd shared earlier. Maybe that would erase Piper's weariness.

Sure. How arrogant to think she would be able to have that effect on Piper. She picked up her pace on her way to the exit. She pushed through the door and didn't look back.

Chapter Six

And you wore that smelly stocking cap the entire time?" Georgette made a gagging sound and covered her nose with both hands.

"It isn't smelly." Jaycee leaned back in her desk chair. "You're such a drama queen."

As if to prove Jaycee's point, Georgette leaned forward in her chair, plucked a file folder off Jaycee's desk, and fanned herself with it. "Eight hours of head sweat. It must have smelled worse than Stanley's work boots after a day in the fields."

"Eww, would you stop?" Jaycee wrinkled her nose. "That's just gross."

"You're not the one that has to wash his socks." Georgette pretended to swoon. "I can bring one in so we can do a sniff-off."

"Stop." Jaycee pointed toward the door. "Or you can just take your happy ass out of here."

"Don't you go swearing at me, missy," Georgette said, her Southern accent getting more pronounced with each word.

Jaycee rolled her eyes. "How many times do I have to tell you that you're not in Alabama anymore? Hell, you've lived in Wisconsin for what, forty-five years?"

"And how many times do I have to tell y'all," Georgette shifted in her chair, so she could put her hand on her hip, "you can take the girl out of the

South, but you can't take the South out of the girl?"

"Girl?" Jaycee raised one eyebrow, knowing she'd get a rise out of her assistant.

"Bless your heart," Georgette said.

"Would you stop being a stereotype and listen to me?"

Georgette chuckled. "Oh, give me some sugar and quit being ugly."

Jaycee pursed her lips and frowned, feigning outrage. They both knew Georgette was laying on her schtick for Jaycee's benefit. Georgette had seen her through her darkest times. After Tessa asked for a divorce, Jaycee had spent many an hour crying on Georgette's shoulder.

Georgette had worked for Jaycee for eighteen years. Longer than she'd been with Tessa. Actually, Georgette was her closest friend, if she could count her sixty-five-year-old personal assistant as a friend. She'd been so busy with the Wilson clan and building her business that she'd not taken time for making friendships. She hadn't thought she needed to.

Now look where she was. *Alone.* Her family of fifteen years pulled out from under her.

"Nope." Georgette waved the folder at Jaycee. "No! You're not going to think about her."

Jaycee stared at Georgette slack-jawed. How could Georgette always tell what she was thinking? It was irritating.

"And stop giving me that annoyed look." Georgette dropped the folder back onto Jaycee's desk.

"Fine." Just to rile Georgette, Jaycee gave her a fake smile that she knew looked more like a grimace.

"Don't give me your constipated raccoon look, either."

"And how do you know what a constipated raccoon looks like?"

"I've known my fair share of raccoons."

"Constipated ones?"

Georgette rolled her eyes. "Are you planning on telling me more about that little hottie you met?"

"I didn't say she was a little hottie."

"Right. When I talked to you on Friday, it was Piper this and Piper that."

Georgette had a point, but Jaycee would never admit it. When Georgette called to check on her Friday morning, Jaycee had been able to tell her a little about Piper before Georgette's grandkids had woken up, demanding time with Grandma.

"I didn't talk about her that much." Jaycee knew her protest was hollow.

"Sure, you didn't." Georgette waved Jaycee off before she could respond. "But back to this beanie. Why did you wear it the entire time?"

"Weren't you listening? I didn't want anyone to figure out who I was."

Georgette snorted. "Sometimes I wonder how you built this business. When it comes to real estate, you have more savvy than anyone I know, but when it comes to other things, you're the most naïve person I've ever met. Do you really think a hat is going to disguise all that you've got going on?" She stared at Jaycee across her desk, then circled her hand as if framing Jaycee's face.

"I don't have anything going on." Jaycee scowled.

"Whatever." Georgette snorted. "Can we just finish the conversation about your day at the homeless shelter before your client gets here?"

For the next half hour, Jaycee ran through the

highlights of her Thanksgiving Day while Georgette nodded and interjected an *I see* or *interesting*.

When Jaycee finished, she met Georgette's gaze and said, "So that about sums it up."

Georgette smirked. "So this Piper is a looker, huh?"

"Really? That's what you took out of everything I said?"

"Nope. It's what I took out of how your eyes lit up every time you said her name."

"Did not." Jaycee didn't even try to launch a better protest.

"Sweetie, if that's the best you got, I'm not even gonna argue with you." Georgette rubbed her chin. "So she's got kids. Any father in the picture...a husband?"

Jaycee shook her head. "I don't think so. I didn't ask her directly, but I'm ninety-nine-point-nine percent sure she's on her own."

"I'll go with those odds." Georgette made a gesture in the air as if she were checking a box. "Single. And she's working toward a master's degree in Public Administration?"

"Yeah, she'll be done in a little over a year."

"Educated. Smart." Georgette made two more air checks. "And she wants to continue working with the homeless when she graduates?"

"Yeah. She wants to be able to influence services on a larger scale. Make systemic changes."

"Ambitious and compassionate. Check. Check," Georgette said as she gestured. "Plus, she's easy on the eyes?"

Heat rose up Jaycee's neck, and she couldn't stop the goofy grin that played on her lips.

Georgette held up her hand. "That's answer

enough. What are you going to do about it?"

"Do about it? What's there to do? I volunteered one day at the homeless shelter. That's it."

"You're not going back?"

"She did invite me." Jaycee fidgeted in her seat. "But I doubt I'll go."

"Why the hell not?" Georgette pounded the desk, causing Jaycee to jump.

"Jesus, you scared the shit out of me."

"Jumpy?"

"No." Jaycee scowled, hating that Georgette saw through her. All weekend, she'd been unusually jumpy as if her nerve endings were right below the surface of her skin. "It's just been such a fucked-up year that I don't even know what to think."

"I know, honey." Georgette's eyes softened. "But meeting Piper is a good thing."

"I doubt if this is a thing." Jaycee threw her hands up in exasperation. "Tessa had just ripped me a new one and shoved in my face that the only family I have is gone." Jaycee rubbed her chest. "This is the first holiday without them. Well, the first major one. I was in a bad place. Obviously, I overreacted to a little kindness from strangers. How pathetic is that?"

Georgette's eyes welled with tears.

"No." Jaycee pointed. "You can't do that. I can't do it. Besides, I have no right to feel sorry for myself after I saw what real adversity is. Have you ever been to a homeless shelter?"

"I can't say I have."

Images from Thursday flooded her mind and all the faces and stories they'd shared. "It was strange. Despite the hardships, there was a spirit...an energy I can't even explain."

"I'm not sure I could have done it." Georgette shook her head. "Their stories would have been too depressing."

"That's the thing. I expected it to be a somber place, but I can't remember a time I laughed so hard." Jaycee ran her hand along her jaw. "My cheeks hurt the next morning."

"Did you tell Piper what happened with Tessa that morning before you showed up at the shelter?"

Jaycee shook her head. "No. I just told her my holiday plans got derailed. She didn't need to hear my inconsequential tales of woe."

"You need to stop doing that." Georgette frowned. "You can't keep pushing it down and working a hundred hours a week."

"Eighty." Jaycee grinned. "But it's been good for business."

"Typical Jaycee." Georgette shook her head. "Everything you've felt this last ten months is legit. You suffered a huge loss, so you don't get over it with a snap of your fingers." She snapped her fingers as she said it. "You must grieve, and calling your feelings inconsequential is demeaning."

"Fine." Jaycee clapped her hand against her chest. "I just want to stop hurting, and I want my family back. I'd do anything if I could get Tessa to see what she's done. To change her mind."

"Ugh." Georgette grabbed a handful of her own hair and pretended to pull. "No. No. No! I thought you were getting somewhere. I hoped Thursday was the turning point. That your experience would help you turn the corner."

"Just because I had a good time at the shelter. Wow, I can't even believe those words just came out of my mouth. Who says they had a good time at the homeless shelter?"

"Anyone that's had the privilege of volunteering there, I'd imagine."

"I suppose." Jaycee sighed, and her shoulders dropped. "It helped me survive the day, but that's all there was to it."

"Uh-huh." Jaycee wasn't sure how Georgette made two small words sound sarcastic and condescending, but she did.

"It was a nice distraction, but it wasn't real."

"Eventually, you're going to have to move on. Pick up the pieces and build a new life."

But Jaycee didn't want a new life. She wanted her old one back.

Chapter Seven

Jaycee slammed the door of her Range Rover and put her head against the steering wheel. What had gotten into her lately? If she kept it up, she was going to blow this sale.

She'd returned to her vehicle under the pretense of getting a spec sheet when she'd had one in her folio all along. It had given her time to escape and think things through before she'd tanked the deal. Hopefully, the buyer hadn't seen the look of disgust on her face when he spoke of razing the five million dollar home so he could build a house to his specifications.

Something had changed in her since her day at the shelter. Even though it was nearly three weeks ago, it still played in her mind. She hadn't returned, but the experience wasn't far from her thoughts.

She'd not been able to look at her clients the same way anymore. As she was putting people in million-dollar homes, others remained on the street struggling to survive.

And this clown wanted to tear down a six thousand-square-foot house, which wasn't even twenty-five years old, because he didn't like the primary bedroom. A place this size could have accommodated so many people who didn't have a roof over their heads.

Guilt washed over her. The thought of the disparity between her clients and Ole Freddie made her want to cry. She shook her head hard, hoping to rattle some sense into herself.

She gazed out over Lake Michigan, a sight she'd never get tired of. The wind had picked up over the past hour and was creating tiny whitecaps on the water. She'd always loved watching a storm roll in across the lake, but she'd even started to call into question her love of storms.

Daytime storms meant that people like Mitzy and Donovan would likely be huddled together below an overpass, sheltered under an old tarp, or lingering under the awning of a hotel until someone chased them away or until the shelter opened for the evening.

A nighttime storm would mean most would be out of the rain, except for people like Ole Freddie. He'd told her he only slept in the shelter on rare occasions. When she'd pressed him, he'd said it was too dangerous. After Piper gave him a disapproving glare, he'd admitted he preferred his freedom.

Damn it. She needed to get her ass back inside and do her job. The customers were eager to buy, so it wouldn't take much to get the sale. She shrugged when she realized she didn't care.

Enough. She pulled the spec sheet from her folio and pushed open the door. With a hard set to her jaw, she marched back toward the house where her clients awaited.

She'd close the deal and then donate half of her proceeds to the shelter. She held her head up. She wouldn't tarnish her business out of a sense of guilt; instead, she'd use her resources to make a difference.

With renewed determination, she pushed open the front door. This sale would be for the shelter.

≈∥≈∥≈

Jaycee swirled the wine around in her glass and stared at the fireplace. It wouldn't start itself, but she had no motivation to get up. Besides, it wasn't even dark yet, and fires were best at night. She'd closed the deal. Her buyers had gone too high in her estimation, but they'd wanted the property and weren't willing to risk losing it. They'd told her they wouldn't quibble over two hundred fifty thousand dollars.

When had her life become this—working with someone who thought two hundred fifty thousand dollars was quibbling numbers? *Enough.* She'd worked hard to build her business. Besides, she'd created employment for over a hundred people, so she couldn't let guilt gnaw at her.

Jaycee glanced at the large pile of boxes in the corner of the room. On impulse, she'd gone to the shelter's website. DOTS had an extensive wish list of supplies it needed, so she'd bought everything on the list. The stack had been sitting in the corner of her living room for the last two weeks.

Dumbass. She couldn't exactly walk in with her arms piled high without raising eyebrows. They'd not figured out who she was, and she wanted to keep it that way. Money changed things. The last thing she wanted was for Piper to find out her net worth.

After sloshing the wine around in her glass, she took a large gulp. Not exactly the way wine was meant to be enjoyed. *Coward.* She'd thought of taking a box or two to the shelter ever since the delivery had arrived, but there it all still sat.

With determination, she stood and marched to the kitchen. She started to pour the wine down the drain but stopped. Sure, she was going to the homeless shelter, so she'd toss fifty dollars' worth of wine. *Nope.* She carefully set the glass aside. She'd drink it when she got home. Did this mean she was actually going to do it? She glanced out the kitchen window. Heavy dark clouds filled the sky, and the wind whipped around, announcing the likelihood of snow later this evening. Looks like the forecasters were going to get this one right.

Maybe she should wait until the weather was better. Sure, the homeless people had that luxury, didn't they? The thought was enough to motivate her. She had warm coats in her stash of boxes. With the weather, it made sense to take those to the shelter now. Then she'd have Georgette arrange an anonymous shipment of the rest of the supplies.

It was too late for her to back out now since she'd have to live with the thought of Mitzy and Donovan huddled with threadbare coats if she didn't do her part.

It had been three weeks; would they even remember her? Probably not, but she could do a quick drop and get out. She'd be back home sipping on her wine before she knew it, her conscience clean.

Why did the thought of them not recognizing her make her feel so bad? Because she was being ridiculous. They had bigger things to think about than a privileged woman who helped one day and plied them with macarons. A woman who hadn't returned since.

Guilt pushed her forward. When she arrived at the stairs, she took them two at a time. She'd change out of her bow tie and suspenders, don her stocking cap, and be ready to go.

Chapter Eight

"What did you do?" Piper snapped at Maddie and immediately regretted it when she saw her daughter's sad eyes. "It's okay, sweetie."

"Sorry, Mommy." Maddie's bottom lip trembled. "I'm a clumsy dodo bird."

"No." Piper pulled Maddie against her side. "It's just a little paint. We can clean it up." A little paint might have been an understatement since it was dripping off the table onto the floor. "Let's get some rags."

"But I ruined Santa." Maddie held up her picture. Santa's face was covered in red paint.

"That was your practice Santa." Piper kissed the top of Maddie's head. "You can do another one after we sop up this spill."

Maddie's glistening eyes lit up. "Do we have time before dinner?"

"If we hurry." Piper motioned to the paint that continued to dribble onto the floor. "Let's go."

Maddie started to follow her and then froze.

Piper turned back. "What's the matter?"

"Is Ole Freddie going to be mad at me?"

"Why would he be mad?" Piper's brow creased.

Maddie pointed at the chair that now had paint on it, too. "That's where he always sits for dinner."

Piper stifled her laugh since Maddie had such a horrified look on her face. "Ole Freddie loves you, so he'll understand. Besides, we'll clean it up so good that he'll never even know."

Piper thought it would get Maddie moving forward, but instead, Maddie put her hands on her hips and glowered at Piper.

"What's that look for?" Piper asked.

"We have to tell Ole Freddie. It wouldn't be right not to," Maddie said in a scolding voice.

Out of the mouths of babes. How had her six-year-old become so wise? At least Piper had raised her well. "You're right. It would be wrong to keep it from him, but I know he won't mind."

Maddie studied her for a second and then nodded.

"Ready to help clean up?"

Maddie took her hand. As they walked toward the supply closet, Maddie said, "How come you're angry?"

"Angry? I told you it was okay."

"But you were angry when it happened."

Piper had hoped Maddie had forgotten she'd snapped at her. Piper opened her mouth to apologize, but Maddie continued.

"And you're sad-angry."

Piper took a deep breath. She'd hoped the kids hadn't noticed her mood swings. Since they'd been on their own after Emma left, the holidays were always the hardest. After she'd laughed so much and had so much fun on Thanksgiving Day, the best in years, she thought maybe her holiday blues were in the past. Then Jaycee never came back.

Piper had been sure Jaycee would return, but each day that passed, Piper felt more ridiculous. What did she think, that they'd become BFFs? Piper scoffed at her own idiocy. People like Jaycee didn't hang out in homeless shelters.

Piper squeezed Maddie's hand and considered lying to her. All she'd have to do was deny being sad-angry, but she knew what damage that could do. Maddie would begin to doubt her own ability to assess other people and their feelings. "You're a perceptive little girl. Mommy has been sad-angry sometimes."

Maddie gazed up at her with her big brown eyes. "It's okay to be sad-angry. We all feel bad sometimes."

Piper smiled. How could she be in a bad mood when she was blessed with her two precious children? "Thanks, honey."

"I know you don't like Christmas." Maddie looked down at the floor. "But is it okay that I do?"

"Of course it is." Piper's jaw clenched. *Damn it.* She'd never wanted to be someone who took the joy out of Christmas for her children just because she hated it. "How about you and Paxton teach me how to love Christmas more?"

Maddie's face lit up. "Paxton will be happy. He loves Christmas, too. But he says we can't talk about it."

"Why not?"

"Because it makes you sad."

Piper wanted to cry. What had she done?

Maddie squeezed Piper's hand and said, "Paxton says you're happy all the rest of the time, so we just need to be extra good for now." Her gaze dropped to the floor. "Then I went and spilled paint all over."

Piper stopped walking and bent in front of Maddie. She wrapped her arms around her and held her tightly. "Mommy's sorry. She'll do better."

"You're the best mommy ever." Maddie's small voice came out with conviction.

Piper didn't feel like the *best mommy ever*. Most days, she didn't even feel like an adequate mom. Today was one of those days. "What do you say we get things cleaned up? Then we'll see if we have enough time for you to paint another Santa before dinner. If not, I'll help you afterward."

"All right." Maddie skipped to the supply closet, already moving on from the conversation, while Piper tried to swallow down the lump in her throat.

❄❄❄❄

Jaycee turned her back and pushed her buttocks against the shelter door. It swung open easier than she thought it would, and she nearly toppled in. She chuckled. That would have made quite the sight. Her body sprawled out on the floor with boxes covering her.

Once inside, she scanned the empty room. On Thanksgiving, she hadn't noticed how nondescript the large room was. Full of people, it had seemed homey, but now it reminded her of a school cafeteria. The Thanksgiving decorations had been replaced by Christmas decorations, but they couldn't hide the institutional feeling of the rows of metal tables and unmatched chairs.

A Christmas tree stood in one corner, but it looked small in such a large room. The lights blinked erratically as if accenting the sparse trimmings. Jaycee made a mental note. *Buy more ornaments.*

It was eerily quiet. Must be too early for dinner. Her gaze landed on a red splotch on the floor, and her heart raced. Had someone been injured?

She rushed over to the table and grinned. The

only injury seemed to have been to the drawing of Santa. Her gaze circled the room. Why would someone leave such a mess, unless it was a child who didn't want anyone to know what they'd done?

After setting down her armful of boxes, Jaycee surveyed the situation. A scan of the area told her there wasn't anything to clean up the mess. Perhaps, she could use some of the cardboard from one of the boxes to scrape up the worst of it.

She pulled her trusty Swiss army knife out of her coat pocket, sliced through the tape, and then cut off one of the flaps. The flap was too big for the job, so she cut a quarter off one end. *Perfect.*

As she closed up her knife, she heard a high-pitched voice. "Jay-ceeeee."

When she turned, Maddie was racing toward her. She carried a roll of paper towels almost as big as she was, but she still found a way to run. Jaycee feared she'd trip over the towels that had unwound as she continued her sprint.

Jaycee took several steps toward Maddie. "Maddie." Jaycee couldn't hold back her huge grin. So much for playing it casual.

Jaycee bent down as Maddie barreled toward her. A few steps from Jaycee, Maddie's feet got tangled in the paper towels, and she stumbled forward. Jaycee's reflexes took over, and she snatched Maddie from the air before she sprawled face first onto the hard surface.

Maddie squealed and laughed, apparently unaware of the possible danger she'd just been rescued from. Jaycee spun Maddie around before she set her on the ground. "Where were you going in such a hurry?"

Maddie shifted her gaze to the floor. "I had an

accident."

Jaycee smirked. "You mean that little paint spill over there."

"Yep." Maddie continued to stare at her feet. "I'd be happy to help you clean it up if you want me to."

Maddie looked up with a huge gap-tooth smile. "Would you?"

Jaycee started to nod, but movement out of the corner of her eye diverted her attention. She shifted her gaze and froze.

Piper froze, as well, and gaped with a slack jaw. "Uh, hi."

Jaycee had envisioned this moment for the last three weeks, and now that she was here, she wasn't sure what to say. Piper wore an oversized sweatshirt and a pair of jeans, but to Jaycee, she looked amazing.

"Hi back at ya," Jaycee said, hoping it came out more casual than she felt.

"Why are you looking so surprised?" Piper laughed. "I wasn't expecting to see you again, but I'm thinking you knew chances were that you'd run into me if you came in."

"True." Jaycee nodded. "I guess the…uh… the…" Jaycee pointed over her shoulder. She covered her mouth so Maddie couldn't see, and she mouthed, "the Santa massacre threw me off."

Piper laughed and held up her bucket. "We were just about ready to do cleanup on aisle four."

Maddie looked at Piper with a confused look. "Aisle four?"

Piper laughed again and put her hand on Maddie's shoulder. "It was just a silly joke."

"Ah, a grownup joke." Maddie looked up at

Jaycee. "I'm not supposed to listen to grownup jokes." She put her finger against her lips. "I won't say anything about aisle four."

Jaycee bit her lip and met Piper's gaze. Piper smiled, and Jaycee's breath caught. *What the hell?*

"Aisle four isn't grownup words. Mommy just made a joke that wasn't funny."

"It's okay, Mommy. You make lots of jokes that aren't funny."

Jaycee coughed to cover up her laughter. Piper shot her a dirty look, but amusement danced in her eyes.

Piper handed the bucket to Jaycee and winked. "Since you offered to help."

Jaycee took the bucket and smiled at Maddie. "Shall we?"

Maddie scuttled over to the puddle of paint and plopped down next to it. She started to put her finger into the red pool when Piper said, "Madelyn! Do not put your hand in the paint."

"I wasn't. Just this one." Maddie held up her index finger.

"No hands or fingers," Piper clarified.

Maddie's shoulders slumped. "Okay."

Jaycee knelt beside Maddie. "Can I have some of your towels?" Maddie held out the roll, and Jaycee pulled off a handful. The paint had begun to harden on the top, so she pushed through the shell. The first swipe smeared more paint than it picked up.

"I see you don't have a lot of practice with paint cleanup," Piper said as she squatted beside Jaycee.

Jaycee put on her best glare. "I might be a bit rusty, but give me a minute, and it'll come back to me."

"Oh, so you do have experience?"

"Nieces and nephews." Saying the words hurt. Not wanting to let the wave of sadness overcome her, she said, "Where's Paxton?"

"In the kitchen helping Sergio and Caleb. You know, the real kitchen geniuses that left me to drown on Thanksgiving." Piper ran the paper towel through the paint, and with a twist of her wrist, she scooped up a sizable portion. "He loves making pudding."

"Pudding?" She must not have heard Piper right. Who liked making pudding?

"Yep, pudding." Piper smiled as she ran another towel through the mess. With this swipe, she captured most of the loose paint. "He always has."

Jaycee shot her a sideways glance. "Always? How long has he been making pudding?" She remembered he was only eight.

"Since the first time we ever stepped foot into the shelter." Piper got a distant look before she focused on the stain. She glanced at Maddie. "Mommy's gonna spray the floor with cleaner. Then I want you to run a towel over it."

Maddie lifted her head high, smiled, and held up a paper towel. "I'm ready."

"How old was he when he first came to the shelter?" Jaycee asked once Piper had covered the floor with spray, and Maddie went to work scrubbing the spot.

"Four." Piper's voice came out low.

Even though Jaycee wanted to ask more, something held her back. Instead, she turned her attention to Maddie. "You do good work."

Maddie smiled and held up her paint-splattered towel. She pointed to herself. "I made the mess. I clean it up."

Jaycee smiled and met Piper's gaze. "Why do I think she's heard that phrase a time or two?"

Piper chuckled. "She might have heard me say it a few times." Piper's faraway look receded. "What brings you in tonight?"

"I brought a donation." Jaycee pointed over her shoulder at the boxes she'd brought in.

"Holy sh—uh, cow," Piper said. "That looks like a lot."

Heat rose up Jaycee's neck to her ears. "Coats. They take up a lot of room. I figured with winter coming on that coats might be a hit."

"Thoughtful." Piper saturated the floor with more spray and picked up a towel to help scrub.

Jaycee did the same. They scoured in silence for a bit before Jaycee said, "I bought a couple special ones for Mitzy and Donovan. Is that...uh...is it okay, or does it go into a general stash?" Jaycee held up her hands. "I understand if it has to. I don't want to break any rules, but if I can give the special ones to them, that would be cool, too."

"It's your donation. You can allocate it any way you want."

"Oh, good. As long as it wouldn't be insulting or anything."

Piper put her hand on Jaycee's knee. "Relax. We're grateful for any donations, so we certainly aren't going to turn away something for any of our patrons."

"Thanks." Jaycee continued to scrub. "So how has everyone been?" *Dumbass.* They were homeless. Was it even appropriate to ask such a question?

"Good. The colder weather is—"

"Except for Mommy," Maddie said. "She's been sad-angry."

Piper shot Maddie a mom look. "Madelyn!"

"But...but...that's what we were talking about," Maddie pointed over her shoulder, "right over there, before Jaycee came in."

Piper's face colored, and she suddenly got extremely interested in the spot she was cleaning. "Holidays."

Jaycee waited for her to elaborate, but she didn't. It made sense it was difficult to work at a shelter during the holidays. How hard it must be to leave every night and return to your warm house when you knew the people you served didn't have that luxury. Jaycee stood.

"Looks like we've done a good job with the floor." Jaycee grabbed the spray, and after moving Santa out of the way, she doused the table.

"Are you going to stick around for dinner?" Piper asked.

"No, no. I just wanted to bring by the donation."

"Oh, okay." Piper's face fell. At least Jaycee wanted to believe it did.

"I mean...I don't want to take a meal from someone here."

"I'll make you a deal." Piper pointed at Jaycee. "Five dollars and you can buy the meal."

"Twenty," Jaycee countered.

"Ten."

"Fifteen. And that's my final offer."

"Sold." Piper's smile was gigantic.

Maddie had crawled onto the chair and was furiously scrubbing the table. She leaned over toward Jaycee. "You make Mommy smile," she whispered.

"What?" Piper asked.

"Nothing," Jaycee said quickly. "Maddie and I were just chatting."

After they finished with cleanup, Piper patted Maddie's shoulder. "Why don't you work on a new Santa while I take Jaycee into the kitchen?"

"Are you gonna make me cook again?" Jaycee faked a groan.

"No." Piper crossed her arms over her chest. "They won't let me in the kitchen after that debacle."

"Debacle? I thought we pulled it off splendidly."

"We did." Piper grinned. "Will you be okay out here?" she asked Maddie.

Maddie's tongue stuck out of the side of her mouth as she concentrated. She managed to give a slight nod but kept her focus on her painting.

Piper reached toward Maddie's head but stopped. "I better not touch an artist at work."

"I advise against it." Jaycee grinned. She felt lighter than she had in weeks. Who'd have guessed that her new favorite place to be would be the homeless shelter?

As they walked toward the kitchen, Piper filled Jaycee in on how she'd fared on the classes that she'd finished last week. Two A's and a B.

"Congratulations," Jaycee said. "One more step closer to your master's."

"It's been a long haul, but I keep telling myself I'm almost there."

"You should be proud of yourself. It can't be easy with kids and a full-time job."

Piper slowed and glanced at Jaycee. "Thank you. I appreciate that you recognize that. I wish a few more of my professors would have understood."

"Do they give you trouble?"

"Sometimes." Piper sighed. "I thought I was going to flunk one class. I had to go to the dean. Professor Glenn still hates me to this day."

"What happened?"

"For our final project, he wanted the group to go into Chicago for the weekend. Not only was it expensive, but I also didn't have anyone to leave the kids with for an entire weekend. I tried to talk to him about it, but he said he'd have to give me an F for the assignment, which was twenty-five percent of our grade."

"Ouch." Jaycee's jaw tightened. "What an idiot."

"After the dean intervened, I got to write a paper instead." Piper shook her head. "Twenty-five pages that had to use at least ten sources."

"What a jackass."

"I did him one better. Thirty-three pages with thirteen sources."

Jaycee chuckled. "What grade did he give you?"

"An A." Piper winked. "When I submitted the paper, I cc'd the dean."

"That might explain why he hates you."

"Possibly." Piper paused outside the kitchen door. "Before we go in, I apologize in advance for anything Sergio and Caleb might say or do."

"This should be fun." Jaycee rubbed her hands together like a villain in a melodrama. She couldn't say for certain why meeting Piper's coworkers had her quite so nervous.

"You've been warned."

As soon as Piper pushed open the door, the soft strains of classical music filled the air. A slightly overweight, balding man stood in front of the stove with his back to them. His shoulder moved to the beat as he stirred what was in the large pot. Whatever it was smelled delicious. The scent of thyme and rosemary filled the air. *Beef stew?*

Paxton was seated at the table where Mrs. Akers had cut the pumpkin pies. His concentration was so focused on filling the foil containers with pudding that he didn't register their arrival.

A tall thin man with white blond hair raced into the kitchen from the pantry. "Found some," he called, holding up a jar. He stopped, and his gaze landed on her stocking cap. "Well, I'll be fucked, you must be Jaycee."

Jaycee gaped. *Shit.* They hadn't been here on Thanksgiving. Had they recognized her from her picture plastered all over town?

The man at the stove turned. "Holy hell, Jaycee?" He pulled the spoon out of the pot and laid it on the spoon rest. "I'll be damned."

Both men rushed toward her and Piper. Jaycee resisted the urge to press back against the door or possibly even run.

Paxton looked up from his task. "Jaycee." His face lit up, and he let the spoon clatter to the table, pudding splattering everywhere. Apparently, he was as messy as his sister.

Piper nudged her. "Evidently, everyone's happy to see you."

"And how do they know who I am?"

Piper gave her an innocent smile and shrugged.

The balding man was the first to reach her. He extended his hand, but before she knew what happened, he'd wrapped his arms around her. "It's so nice to meet the woman that saved Piper's ass." He clapped her on the back a few times before he released her.

By the time he had, the tall man had arrived and reached out his hand. She was fast to extend hers before this man grabbed her, too. He shook her hand. "Ignore him. He's Italian. He can't help himself."

"What can I say? We're friendly, unlike the Germans."

"For fuck's sake. I'm ten percent German at most."

The bald man flipped his hand. "That's enough to make you cold."

The tall man started to respond, but Piper whistled. "Would you two stop before you scare her away?"

They both looked contrite but continued to shoot looks at each other.

Piper pointed to the balding man. "This is Sergio. I apologize that he accosted you."

Sergio snorted. "Accosted. Ha. I bet it was the best hug she's had in a long time."

"Afraid not." Jaycee smiled, immediately feeling comfortable.

Sergio gave her a look of horror as the other man laughed.

"Maddie gave me a hug when I walked in."

"Damn it." Sergio slapped his hand against his knee. "No fair. Maddie's hugs are the best."

"And this," Piper said, "is Caleb."

"Nice to meet you," Caleb said. "We've been hoping you'd stop in, so we could thank you."

Paxton had been standing off to the side a few feet away with his arms crossed over his chest. "Where have you been?" His brow was furrowed, and his voice held a note of anger.

"Paxton James," Piper said. "Do not be rude."

He steeled his gaze at Piper. "But she said she'd come back, and she didn't."

Piper's eyes blazed. "She's here now," Piper said through clenched teeth.

Guilt flooded through Jaycee. How could she explain to an eight-year-old why it had taken her so long to return? She couldn't even explain it to herself.

"Yeah." Paxton shrugged and gave her a look of indifference.

"Apologize to Jaycee," Piper said.

"Sorry," he muttered.

"Paxton!" Piper moved toward him with a scowl.

Jaycee squatted so she was at eye level with him. "I'm sorry, too. It wasn't fair for me to make you wonder if I'd ever come back." She knew the feeling all too well, so she never wanted to make a child feel that way.

"It still doesn't excuse you for being rude," Piper said as she looked down on them.

Paxton finally met her gaze, but his eyes were still guarded. "Didn't you have a good time?"

"Paxton!" Piper put her hand on her hip.

Jaycee put up her hand, hoping that Piper didn't take offense. "I had the best time."

"Then why didn't you come back?"

She took in a deep breath. How could she explain?

Jaycee must have paused for too long because Piper said, "Jaycee has a busy life."

"That's true." Jaycee nodded. She leaned in toward Paxton. "But can I tell you something else?"

"Sure," Paxton said.

"I've wanted to come back every day since I last visited." Jaycee couldn't believe she was saying this, but there was something about talking to a child that made her want to tell the truth.

"Then why didn't you?" He scrunched up his face, obviously confused by her words.

"I was afraid." *Yep.* It must be the kid that made her want to be honest. She kept her gaze on Paxton, not wanting to look at Piper. Actually, she wanted nothing more than to see Piper's expression but was afraid of that, too.

Paxton's eyes widened. "Of us?"

Jaycee shook her head. "Not of you. That I wouldn't fit in like I did the first time."

Paxton studied her for a beat before he wrapped his arms around her. "I understand. We all feel like that sometimes."

Jaycee bit her lip. She would not cry.

"Well, damn," Sergio said. "Now you've had two hugs better than mine."

Jaycee laughed, grateful that Sergio had lightened the moment.

Paxton let go of her and pointed toward the table. "I've gotta finish my job, or people will be mad if they don't get pudding."

"Go." She patted him on the shoulder. "And thanks, Paxton. You're a good guy."

He smiled broadly before he raced off.

"Kids say the darnedest things, don't they?" Caleb said. "But now we want to hear all about how you pulled off the Thanksgiving meal."

Chapter Nine

Jaycee had survived Sergio and Caleb; in fact, Piper was pretty sure she'd enjoyed talking with them. They'd demanded a blow-by-blow replay of how Jaycee had pulled off Thanksgiving, working with someone as hapless as Piper. Piper pretended outrage, but the banter and having Jaycee here caused her mood to soar.

It had taken some doing, but she'd finally extracted Jaycee from Sergio and Caleb's clutches. Although, they could have stayed in the kitchen longer since Piper had been unable to convince Jaycee to get into the food line sooner.

Piper nudged Jaycee. "Everyone's gone through."

"Are you sure?" Jaycee gazed around the room. "Where's Mitzy and Donovan?"

Piper shrugged. "They're young. They don't always show up on time." She refrained from saying, *Sometimes they don't show up at all.* It might freak Jaycee out.

"But it's cold outside."

"Then they'll likely wander in soon. Let's go." They'd been standing off in one corner as the others had filled their plates. "Paxton won't be happy until you eat some of his pudding."

That must have been the magic phrase because Jaycee pushed herself off the wall and motioned for Piper to lead the way. They'd just about made it there when the door flew open. When Mitzy and Donovan pushed inside, Piper shot a glance at Jaycee, who sported a huge smile. Piper's gaze returned to the two young people, and she could sense right away that Jaycee wouldn't likely be smiling for much longer.

"Mitzy. Donovan," Jaycee called out over the din of the other diners. When they didn't respond, she waved her arm.

Mitzy looked in their direction, made eye contact with Jaycee, and then turned her back.

"Maybe we should go somewhere else," Mitzy said to Donovan loud enough for most everyone in the room to hear.

Jaycee started to say something, but Piper grabbed her hand. "Don't. Mitzy's looking to get a rise out of you."

"Me?" Jaycee said. "What did I do?"

"You said you were coming back, and it's been three weeks."

"They're pissed," Jaycee said as a statement not a question.

"Mitzy is. Donovan will be okay." Piper put her hand on Jaycee's shoulder. "They're young. You have to keep in mind many homeless youth feel abandoned, so they're extra sensitive."

"God, I'm such an idiot." Jaycee's jaw tightened. "What do I do?"

"You leave them be."

"Will they come around?" Concern registered on Jaycee's face.

"Probably." Piper motioned for Jaycee to continue in the food line. "Time will tell."

Jaycee's face dropped. "You're telling me that

I just need to leave it be, and they may or may not forgive me?"

"It's a trust thing. It just might take some time." Piper filled her bowl with stew and picked up a piece of bread.

Jaycee stopped mid-ladle and shook her head. "That's not right. There must be something I can do to apologize."

"Give 'em space." Piper's heart went out to Jaycee, but she couldn't do anything more. Jaycee would have to learn the patrons and how to deal with them. Piper couldn't do it for her.

Jaycee's shoulders sagged, but she finished filling her bowl. At the end of the line, she stopped. "You might want to go around me," Jaycee said to Piper.

"Why?"

"I have to find the perfect tin of pudding."

Piper laughed. "Paxton would approve."

๑ใ๑ใ๒๒

Even though Mitzy and Donovan's reaction had felt like a gut punch, Jaycee was determined not to let it dampen her mood. It had been easier than she thought since Sergio and Caleb had the table in stitches, talking about their disastrous Thanksgiving trip to Chicago. Just like her first time, she was amazed at the festive spirit and how much she'd laughed.

Jaycee ran her spoon around the foil container for what must have been the tenth time, scraping up the last drop of pudding. She made an exaggerated chef's kiss and turned to Paxton. "My compliments to the chef."

He beamed back at her, and a blotch of red

colored both cheeks. "It's my specialty. I've been making it for a long time, so I've got experience."

Jaycee bit her lip, so she wouldn't smile or worse laugh. With Paxton taking his job so seriously, she knew her demeanor needed to match his. "Maybe you could teach me."

His face lit up, but then it quickly fell. "Sure," he said, his enthusiasm gone.

His reaction broke her heart, but she was determined not to let it end at this. After spending so much time with her nieces and nephews over the years, she knew they could detect bullshit from a mile away. "I get it. I have to earn your trust back before you'll agree to teach me your special recipe."

He shot a glance at Piper, so Jaycee sneaked a peek herself. Piper's lips were drawn together in a neutral expression, but her eyes were warm. She gave him a slight nod as if to tell him to go ahead.

Good parenting. Some parents would have encouraged him to *be nice,* despite how he was feeling, but Piper had just given him permission to be honest. It would serve him well as an adult.

"I gotta make sure you're gonna stick around," Paxton said. "I like you and all, but I gotta be careful."

"Understood." Jaycee smiled at him. "No pressure." She glanced around the table and winked at Piper before she leaned toward Paxton. "I think learning how to make such delicious pudding is worth the wait."

Across the table, Piper's smile and soft eyes caused Jaycee's insides to warm. *Stop.* Ever since she stepped foot into the shelter, all the emotions she'd tried to bury the past nine months seemed to be lying just under the surface.

"Are you okay?" Piper asked.

Jaycee nodded, afraid that her voice would betray her.

"It's okay." Piper leaned over the table and talked softly. "This place can be a bit overwhelming in the beginning. Some volunteers can't handle it, and they never come back."

Jaycee's eyebrows shot up. "Is that what you thought? That I couldn't handle being here?"

Piper's head bobbed up and down, as did Sergio and Caleb's.

Sergio smiled. "We wash them out all the time."

"It's tough for some people to see," Caleb added. "Makes them uncomfortable."

Jaycee wasn't sure how to respond, so she looked from one face to the next, hoping for an answer, but her gaze kept returning to Piper. "I can see that." Without thinking, she added, "My emotions have definitely been churned up since I last visited."

Piper drew her lips together. "Care to elaborate?"

Jaycee held her hand up and wiggled her fingers. "It's all a jumble of emotions. Some good. Some bad." She diverted eye contact as she spoke the last line.

"No shame in that," Caleb said.

Piper patted Jaycee's hand. "I don't think you'd be human if you weren't feeling conflicting emotions."

"And it doesn't help that the first person you met was this lady." Sergio motioned toward Piper.

Jaycee's breath caught.

"I meant you met her kids," Sergio said and winked. "They'd steal anyone's heart."

Jaycee met Sergio's gaze and tried to read what he was saying, but he wasn't giving anything away. His comment might have been innocent, or it could have had an underlying meaning.

They all seemed to be waiting for her to answer, but she wanted to climb to safer ground. "It's both heartbreaking and heartwarming. I feel uplifted and guilty at the same time." Everything she said was true, and diverting the conversation away from Piper to the shelter was her smartest course.

"We get that a lot," Piper said. "Some of our volunteers struggle with what they have compared to what our patrons don't have."

"I can see that." Jaycee breathed a sigh of relief. This conversation was much safer. "I did the same thing when I went home the first night."

Piper smiled and pointed toward the boxes Jaycee had brought in. "That's not an uncommon reaction."

Heat rose up Jaycee's neck. If Piper only knew how many more boxes were sitting in her house. "So I'm not special?"

"Oh, you're special." Piper's cheeks reddened slightly. "It's not everyone that gets suckered into cooking Thanksgiving dinner."

Everyone laughed.

"I'm just bummed that I wasn't here to see it." Sergio snapped his fingers and pointed at Jaycee. "Christmas?"

"Christmas?" Jaycee said.

"Perfect." Caleb clapped his hands together. "But this time, we'll be here, so you won't have to do it all yourself."

Piper's gaze shifted between the two as she glowered. "You can't put her—"

"I'd love to," Jaycee said. *Damn.* Where had that come from? While it was true, she'd committed herself to returning to the shelter.

Paxton held his hand up for a high five, so she slapped his hand. Not to be forgotten, Maddie waved her hand, too. After Jaycee finished her round of high fives, Piper said, "Are you sure you want to do that? Or did these clowns pressure you into it?"

"I want to do it." Jaycee was surprised how true the statement was.

"It's actually on Christmas Eve," Sergio said. "I hope you can still make it."

"I can." Jaycee smiled. A wave of relief washed over her. Another holiday that she wouldn't have to wander her cavernous house.

Piper's expression was unreadable, but Jaycee had no doubt that Piper was studying her. Instead of trying to guess, Jaycee said, "What's that look for?" Sharing uncomfortable emotions seemed to be the way of the shelter, so she might as well join in.

Before Piper could answer, Sergio rose to his feet. "The kitchen isn't going to clean itself."

Piper started to rise, as well.

"Nope." Caleb put his hand on Piper's shoulder and eased her back down. "You've been working hard enough. Stay out here and talk with your friend."

Friend? Was Piper her friend? Wasn't it too soon? Probably, but over the past three weeks Jaycee had thought of Piper—a lot. Besides, why couldn't she make friends with someone who worked at the shelter?

Piper sighed and remained seated. She pointed at Caleb. "But I owe you."

He smiled. "I think I still owe you from Thanksgiving."

A broad smile lit Piper's face. "True. Hell, I think I can sit back and watch you boys clean for a good month."

"Don't push your luck, dearie." Sergio chuckled.

While Jaycee watched the exchange, an idea percolated in her mind. It was probably a bad one, but it niggled at her. Before she could convince herself not to ask, she blurted out, "Would you and the kids like to go see the Wild Lights tonight?"

Piper's face was a mask of indifference. Her eyes narrowed slightly as she gazed at Jaycee. There was something off in her reaction, and Jaycee immediately regretted that she'd asked.

ॐ ॐ ॐ ॐ

Piper felt her back stiffen at Jaycee's invitation. She struggled with how to respond, but the children didn't seem to have the same reservations.

"I wanna go," Maddie said, although Piper doubted Maddie knew what she was saying yes to.

"What are Wild Lights?" Paxton asked.

Jaycee shot Piper an apologetic look before she turned to Paxton. "The Milwaukee Zoo is decorated for Christmas." She threw her hands out wide. "They have lights. Everywhere."

"Zoo." Maddie was clapping her hands and bouncing in her chair.

"Cool." Paxton's face lit up, but then he glanced at Piper, and a serious expression replaced his joy.

Piper's insides churned. *Damn it.* The children were so excited, but what if Jaycee did another disappearing act? On the other hand, if she said no, it would be one more experience they wouldn't get.

Piper felt Jaycee's gaze on her, but she wasn't ready to meet it, so she focused on Paxton. "Why the long face?"

He shrugged.

"Do you really want to go?"

A smile tugged at the corner of his mouth, but she could tell he was trying to play it cool. "I think it would be fun." He pointed to his sister, who was still bouncing in her seat. "I think it would be good for Maddie."

"You do, do you?" It took everything for Piper to control her smile.

He bit his lip, an expression he'd picked up from her, and nodded. "She loves Christmas."

Paxton's words cut into Piper. Her earlier conversation with Maddie flooded her mind. *Sad-angry* was what Maddie had called it, and she hadn't been wrong. She didn't want them to grow up disliking Christmas because of her. That settled it.

Piper slapped both hands on the table, harder than she'd intended. She finally met Jaycee's concerned gaze. "We'd love to go."

Paxton and Maddie squealed, while a huge smile spread across Jaycee's face.

The children excitedly talked about what they'd see, so Piper took the opportunity to lean across the table. "Are you sure you want to do this?"

"Of course." Jaycee's brow furrowed. "Why wouldn't I?"

Piper knew it wasn't fair to say, but she was doing it for the kids. Wasn't she? "It'd be hard on them. Well, if you...um...if you—"

"Disappear?"

"Yes." Piper maintained eye contact, even though she wanted to look away. She wasn't being fair. "It's not like they haven't seen plenty of people come and go. It comes with the territory at the shelter. So I'm just being silly."

"Lots of turnover?"

"That's the goal." Piper smiled. "It's bittersweet when a regular moves on."

"Oh, wow, I hadn't thought of that." Jaycee's eyes filled with understanding. "Of course, you want people to leave the streets."

"Yep."

"But don't they come back and visit?"

"Some," Piper said. "But most want to leave this chapter of their lives behind. They come a few times, and then without a word, they never come back." Piper dropped her gaze to the table. "It's what we want for them." She patted her chest. "But still, it sometimes hurts."

"Just like that, they're gone?"

"We might get a thank-you card or an email, but others just fade away." Piper dropped her fist to the table. "But that's a good thing. We like to think they made it out."

"That's hard. So the kids are used to people leaving without a word." Jaycee pointed at the empty seats where the children sat before they'd run off to tell the others about their upcoming trip to see the lights. "How do they handle it at such a young age?"

It was a question that Piper didn't care to answer, but it was only fair. She thought about it for a couple of beats, but before she could speak, Paxton and Maddie returned with Mitzy and Donovan in tow.

"You thought you'd grace us with your presence, huh?" Mitzy's voice dripped with sarcasm.

Jaycee looked up and smiled as if she hadn't heard Mitzy's tone. Piper guessed she had but was feigning ignorance. "Mitzy. Donovan. Nice to see you."

Mitzy rolled her eyes, but a slight smile played on Donovan's lips. "Kids say you brought us something," Mitzy said. She adjusted her fedora as if it were a tiara.

Piper was used to Mitzy's flamboyant style, but by the look on Jaycee's face, Mitzy's outfit was a bit much for Jaycee. The purple fedora complemented her shocking pink jumpsuit and made quite a statement with her bubble gum pink platform tennis shoes. *Street chic.*

Recovering from the visual onslaught, Jaycee nodded. "I did. It's in one of those boxes." Jaycee pointed.

Mitzy lifted her eyebrow and looked toward the boxes. When she made no move for them, Jaycee jumped up and rushed to the pile. She returned with a large box marked MD.

Jaycee pointed at the initials. "Mitzy and Donovan."

Mitzy's icy stare thawed a bit when she saw the initials. Piper wanted to melt the expression further. "See, Jaycee shopped especially for you two."

The flush in Donovan's cheeks made him look much younger than his eighteen years. "That's awful nice of you." He smiled at Jaycee.

Mitzy elbowed him. "Let's find out what's in the box before you go saying that shit."

Donovan leveled his gaze at Mitzy. "It's nice regardless."

All right. Piper hid her smile beyond her hand as she faked a cough. Occasionally, Donovan would stand his ground, and today was the day.

"Whatever." Mitzy flicked her fingers into the

air, but she dropped the argument.

"Who wants the honors?" Jaycee asked.

"You open it," Mitzy said to Jaycee. A momentary look of disappointment shadowed Jaycee's eyes, but she clapped her hands together enthusiastically. "Okay." Jaycee pulled her keys from pocket and sliced through the tape. A twinkle danced in her eyes. "This one's for Donovan."

Mitzy's eyes widened, but then Jaycee burst out laughing. Mitzy narrowed her eyes, but she couldn't hide her grin.

Jaycee smiled at Donovan. "Ya know, this does match her hat. Do you think I should give it to her instead?"

Donovan pretended to ponder the question. "Let's see what else you got in there before I decide."

"Keep it up." Mitzy put her hand on her hip. "And both of you are gonna have to deal with the wrath of Mitzy."

Jaycee pulled out a puffy black coat that looked to be full of down.

Thoughtful. Piper couldn't believe how perfect the coats were. Jaycee had obviously given the selection thought.

Donovan snatched the black coat. "I'll take this one." He hadn't even finished the sentence before he was sliding it on.

Mitzy took a little longer to don hers. She held the coat out in front of her by the hood. With a flick of her wrist, she twirled it slowly, examining it from all angles. "Hmm. North Face." She met Jaycee's gaze. "You've got good taste."

"Thanks." Jaycee smiled. "Are you going to try it on?"

"In a minute." Mitzy glanced at Donovan, who was checking out the pockets and strutting around in his new coat. "I'm not a caveman like some people." Donovan smiled and winked but said nothing as he raised and lowered the zipper on the coat several times.

Maddie tugged on Piper's sleeve.

"What, sweetie?" Piper asked.

"Can Mitzy and Donny come with us?" Maddie asked.

"Go where?" Mitzy raised an eyebrow. With the children around, likely Mitzy already knew but wanted Piper or Jaycee to tell them.

Piper shot Jaycee a questioning look.

"Wild Lights at the Milwaukee Zoo," Jaycee answered.

Mitzy's eyes softened, but then a veil descended. "When you going?"

"In a little bit," Jaycee said.

Mitzy gave a nonchalant shrug. "I don't know."

"Okay. We'll be leaving in about fifteen minutes." Jaycee flipped her thumb in the direction of the door. "Meet us up front if you decide you want to go."

Slick. Piper fought her smile. Jaycee's time with her nieces and nephews paid off. Never push a teenager.

Piper put her hands together. "It's time for us to get ready." She pointed at the children. "Bathroom break. Wash your face and hands and get your coats."

Maddie jumped on her toes and squealed. "We get to go to the zoo."

"Honey," Piper said. "You know we probably won't see any animals."

"Lights. Pretty lights." Maddie continued to

bounce.

Paxton was a lot cooler, but even he couldn't stand still.

"Go." Piper made a shooing motion. She glanced at Jaycee. "You better wash up, too. And don't forget to pee."

Jaycee smiled. "Yes, ma'am."

Chapter Ten

Jaycee was shocked that Mitzy and Donovan waited for them by the door. Piper didn't seem nearly as surprised. As they piled into Jaycee's Range Rover, Mitzy seemed to be the only one who took any notice of the vehicle.

Mitzy lifted her eyebrow and said, "Nice."

The trip to the zoo was uneventful, except when the bus with her face plastered on the side pulled up beside them. Jaycee made an abrupt turn at the next light, but with the lively conversation that filled the vehicle, nobody noticed the unnecessary detour.

The children's chattering grew louder as they idled in the line of cars. Jaycee stifled a chuckle at the oohs and ahhs coming from behind her.

Piper opened her tiny purse and dug inside. "How much is admission?"

"It's on me." Jaycee crinkled her nose. "You don't invite someone to join you and then make them pay."

"Are you sure?" Piper fidgeted with her well-worn wallet.

"Positive." Jaycee flicked her wrist. "Put it away."

Piper's face reddened, but she put her wallet back in her purse. "Thank you." Her voice came out quiet, almost shy.

"You're welcome." Jaycee turned her gaze from the windshield and glanced at Piper. "You're helping me out. I love doing things like this, but I'd look like a creeper coming here on my own."

Piper smiled. "Glad to be of service."

The line moved faster than she expected, and soon they were parked. Jaycee couldn't keep her gaze off Paxton and Maddie. The look of wonder on their faces was priceless. The few times she glanced at the others, they too were watching the children.

Paxton tried to play it cool and casually strolled on the path, but it wasn't long before he hurried along with Maddie. Their jaws were slack and eyes wide.

"Okay, slow down," Piper called to the children as they approached the official entrance. She turned to Jaycee. "If they're this in awe before we even get inside, I can't imagine what comes next."

"It gives me hope that they'll enjoy it." Jaycee smiled and pointed to the sky. A light snow had begun to fall. "Looks like Mother Nature wants to enhance the effect."

"Good thing we have these fancy new coats," Mitzy said, wrapping it tighter around herself.

Jaycee smiled, but it soon faded when she looked at Paxton and Maddie. She wanted to kick herself. Their coats were worn. Hopefully, it wouldn't be too cold for them. Why hadn't she thought to get them coats, too? She should have known that Piper likely didn't make big money working at the shelter.

"Jaycee, are you listening?" Piper said.

"Huh? Sorry, I was gaping at the lights." Jaycee hated to lie, but in this case, she'd give herself a bye.

"Maddie asked if she could hold your hand while we walked through the lights."

Jaycee looked down at Maddie, who had a huge smile on her face. "Of course." Jaycee held her hand out.

Maddie snatched it. "Let's go."

Piper held up a map she'd picked up. "Where do we want to go first?"

Donovan leaned over and put his finger on the far side of the map. "We're here. I think we should just walk around this way."

"Lead the way," Piper said.

As soon as they entered the first area, *Have Yourself a Merry Little Christmas* filled the air. Jaycee shivered but not from the cold. The song always made her feel. Feel nostalgic. Feel family. Feel home. Those feelings were bittersweet tonight.

As if sensing her distress, Piper moved closer, and her shoulder rubbed against Jaycee's arm. "I've always loved this song."

Jaycee nodded, but the lump in her throat prevented her from speaking.

Piper chuckled as Maddie let out a squeal as she pointed at the lighted penguins holding hands.

Jaycee pulled out her cellphone and took the first picture of what she suspected would be many. Maddie had to get her picture taken with the penguins as did Paxton.

When they rounded the corner, Jaycee's senses were assaulted. "Holy cow. That's a lot of pink."

Mitzy threw her hands in the air. "Isn't it glorious?"

Piper pointed at the map. "Flamingle All the Way."

"Seriously, is that the name?" Jaycee chuckled.

Piper held the map up. "See for yourself."

"Oh, gawd, look at these names." Jaycee laughed, forgetting her earlier discomfort. "Jungle Bells. Fantasea."

"Oh. My. God. I think that one has fish," Donovan said. "I love *Finding Nemo*."

"Hello." Mitzy waved her hand. "Slow your roll. We've got glorious flamingos to explore." She held out her hand to Maddie. "Come on, sweetie. I know you'll appreciate them."

Maddie looked up at Jaycee with her big brown eyes. Jaycee let go of her hand. "Go ahead. Mitzy needs your help."

After an extensive pink photo op, they moved on to the sea area, which enthralled Donovan and Paxton.

"A seahorse," Paxton said with his eyes wide.

"Do you want your picture with it?" Jaycee asked.

He nodded and ran off toward the lights.

"I'll be back," Jaycee said over her shoulder. "Your son's spotted a seahorse."

Piper laughed. "Go. I'll catch up, but you better not leave Donovan behind."

"Coming," Donovan said as he hurried past.

The snow began to come down a little harder, which made it even more spectacular. It wasn't sticking to the paths because of the foot traffic, but the ground around some of the exhibits was covered in white.

Jaycee couldn't resist looking into the sky and putting out her tongue. It had been a long time since she felt this free. Happy. The last nine months had been hell, but as she walked around the zoo, she realized that it had been years since she'd felt like this. Things had been falling apart with Tessa long before the breakup.

No. Jaycee wouldn't let Tessa seep into her enjoyment of the evening. She steeled her jaw and shifted her gaze back to the kids, who had run over to the bear and moose lights. Duty called. She couldn't miss a picture because she was feeling sorry for herself. *Winter Wonderland* blasted from the speakers, and Jaycee caught herself singing softly to the familiar tune. Her gaze darted around. *Whew.* None of the others was near enough to hear her. It was foolish to be self-conscious of singing, even if she couldn't carry a tune, but Tessa always berated her when she did something embarrassing in public.

Enough. This was the last time she'd think about Tessa tonight.

Piper waved at her from in front of a moose. "I think I need my picture taken here. I love mooses. Meese?"

Jaycee laughed. "It's just moose."

A light danced in Piper's eyes, and in that instant, Jaycee suspected that Piper knew the proper plural of moose. Likely, she'd wanted to pull Jaycee out of the mood she was sliding into. After only being around Piper for a short time, Jaycee sensed that Piper saw more than she let on.

Jaycee snapped pictures as Piper pretended to do a modeling photo shoot with the moose. Paxton and Maddie soon joined in, followed by Mitzy and Donovan.

The poses got more outrageous, and as Jaycee tried to hold back a laugh, it came out as a snort, which sent the others into another fit of laughter.

It had been so long since Jaycee had laughed so hard. She wished the lights would go on forever, but they were well over halfway through the exhibit. *Stay in the moment,* Jaycee reminded herself.

"Look," Maddie said with her voice full of awe.

In the distance, a long tunnel of lights beckoned. Maddie grabbed Piper's hand and tried to pull her along.

Piper held up her hand and let her tongue loll out the side of her mouth. "You guys are pooping me out." She glanced at Mitzy and Donovan. "Would you mind taking them through? We'll be along behind you."

The four rushed off toward the tunnel of lights. Jaycee glanced at Piper from the corner of her eye. Somehow, she didn't believe that a dynamo like Piper had run out of energy.

As if reading her mind, Piper moved closer and said, "I'm not really tired, but I thought letting the kids get a chance to run a bit wouldn't hurt." She paused for a beat and then said, "Besides, I kinda wanted a chance to thank you for this."

"No, thank you for agreeing to come." Jaycee smiled. "I'm having a blast."

"Me too." Piper stopped and looked into Jaycee's eyes. "It's been a while since we've had the chance to just go out and have fun." Piper's eyes seemed to glisten, but it might have just been the lights. "I appreciate this more than you know."

Emotions welled inside of Jaycee, but she struggled with a response. "Do the kids have a dad in the picture?"

"Whoa. That was random." Piper's eyes widened, but Jaycee didn't sense any anger in them.

"Sorry. Wow. That was not only random but rude." Jaycee shook her head. "I shouldn't have asked."

Piper began walking again, so Jaycee slid in beside her, shortening her gait to keep in stride. After several steps, Piper said, "I don't mind you asking."

She turned and smiled. "They don't have a dad at all."

"Oh." She hoped her surprise didn't show on her face. Should she ask another question or leave it be?

Piper laughed. "Oh, god, that look was priceless."

"So much for a poker face," Jaycee said, hoping to redeem herself.

"They have a dad, but I don't know who he is." Piper held up her hand. "Before you give me another stunned look, sperm donors."

"Ah."

"Nope, still not going to win at poker." Piper winked.

"You'd think I was born in a barn." Jaycee shook her head. "I've known people who've used sperm donors. My wife and I even thought of it long ago."

It was Piper's turn to give Jaycee a sideways glance. "Wife?"

"Sorry. Soon-to-be ex-wife." Jaycee shrugged, trying to give the appearance of nonchalance but feared it came out as bitter. When Jaycee noticed the look on Piper's face, she forged on. "Does that make you uncomfortable? Me being gay?" Jaycee ran her hand in front of her body as if to display her physique. "Um, I just assumed you knew."

"No, I didn't know, but I guess I suspected." Piper shook her head hard as if trying to clear the cobwebs. And then unexpectedly, she laughed.

Jaycee stiffened. She wasn't sure what she expected, but laughter hadn't been it.

Piper grabbed Jaycee's arm and was still chuckling. "I'm not laughing at you. I'm laughing at how ridiculous my reaction must have seemed."

"Some people are more comfortable with queerness than others." Jaycee tried to sound supportive, even though the thought of Piper being homophobic stung.

"No. God, no. I'm more than comfortable with it." She pointed at herself. "That's why I had a sperm donor. The kids had two moms not a dad."

It wasn't lost on Jaycee that Piper said *had*. "Did something happen to your…um…wife?"

"We never married," Piper said.

They entered the light tunnel, and Jaycee caught a glimpse of Mitzy in the distance. "Did something happen to her? You said had."

"She didn't die, if that's what you're asking. Technically, they still have another mom." Piper's lip curled into a sneer. "But she wants nothing to do with them."

"But they're such good kids." Jaycee hoped her mouth hadn't fallen open. "I mean, what kind of person would just…" She glanced at Piper, who had a distant look in her eyes. "I should just shut up."

They walked in silence for a few steps. "This is beautiful," Piper said and moved closer to Jaycee again.

"It is," Jaycee answered, taking Piper's lead. "The snow makes it nearly perfect."

"It does, doesn't it?" There was no doubt that Piper's eyes were glistening. Piper seemed to hesitate for a second, but then she continued. "The kids don't get to do enough of this. Sometimes I wonder if I'm being selfish taking classes."

Jaycee's heart went out to Piper. In her career, she'd dealt with so many single mothers who were forced to sell their home after a divorce. Being one salary down must have been hard on Piper, but Jaycee wouldn't pry. "Bettering yourself is never selfish, it means you're a good role model. What do you want to do with your degree once you're done?"

"The director of DOTS is nearing retirement, so I'd love the opportunity to run the organization. I have so many ideas for it."

"Can't you implement them now?"

"Some, but the current director is pretty old school, and I really want to shake things up."

"I see." Jaycee smirked. "I wouldn't have taken you for a rebel."

"You might be surprised." Piper bumped Jaycee with her shoulder. "I've even thought of going bigger. After I get my degree, I'd love to change some of Milwaukee's policies on homelessness. Or maybe even Wisconsin's."

Jaycee bumped Piper back. "Who says you need to stop at Wisconsin? How about the United States?"

"Better yet." Piper smiled. "Maybe I can eradicate world hunger."

Jaycee couldn't help but smile down at Piper. There was something about her that touched Jaycee. Her spirit was contagious, even though Jaycee suspected she hadn't had it easy. Jaycee wanted to know what had happened with Piper's ex, but that would have to wait since the kids were barreling toward them with Donovan and Mitzy in tow.

The music changed, and *Run Rudolph Run* filled the air. "I love this song." Piper raised her hands over her head and danced toward the children as she sang along.

Jaycee grinned as she enjoyed the carefree way Piper moved her body. By the time Piper reached the others, they were all dancing.

Chapter Eleven

Jaycee scrolled through her email. Around the holidays, her business was normally slow, but her team of agents had brought in twenty-five new listings over the weekend, including another property on Lake Michigan. Now if she could only close the deal on the commercial property in Madison, she'd have one hell of a December.

A knock pulled her away from her computer screen. "Come in," Jaycee said.

Georgette strolled into the room with a smirk on her face. She casually waved a piece of paper as she walked.

"What's that shit-eating grin for?" Jaycee asked.

"I thought you might want me to bring this in right away." Georgette sat in the chair in front of Jaycee's desk and held the piece of paper against her stomach.

"Do you plan on showing it to me?" Jaycee knew if she acted too eager that it would only delay Georgette from sharing with her.

"Maybe."

Jaycee turned to her computer screen. "I'll just finish up a few more emails then."

"Fine." Georgette slammed the paper onto Jaycee's desk. "You'll want to see this."

Jaycee resisted snatching the page; instead, she deleted a few spam emails before she turned back to

Georgette. "What is it you have?" Jaycee picked up the piece of paper. "Holy shit. The full price?"

"Yep. Apparently, they want the property—bad."

"Damn. It's been a banner month." Jaycee pumped her fist.

Georgette leaned back in the chair and put her hand on her chin. "In more ways than one."

Jaycee looked at Georgette over the top of the paper she still held. Did she want to take Georgette's bait? Why not? "And what's that supposed to mean?"

"Ever since you burst in here this morning like you were auditioning for *Dancing with the Stars,* I assume you visited the shelter this weekend."

Jaycee scowled. "I did not burst in here, and I wasn't dancing." Well, maybe a little, but she wouldn't admit that to Georgette.

"Hmph." Georgette rolled her eyes. "Nobody shows up on Monday morning that bright eyed. And since when did you get into *Run Rudolph Run*?"

Jaycee's cheeks warmed. *Shit.* She couldn't let Georgette notice, so she dropped the paper and bent to pick it up. If she let a little blood rush to her head, Georgette wouldn't notice her blush. When she sat back up, she said, "It's a great song."

"Unless you're singing it." Georgette turned up her nose. "But I don't want to talk about your singing talent, or lack thereof. I want to hear about *Piper*."

"Why do you think it has anything to do with Piper? Maybe I'm happy because of all the new business we're bringing in."

Georgette rolled her eyes, then looked at her watch. "I ain't got all day. Just tell me."

"Fine." Jaycee crossed her arms over her chest.

"I took her and the kids to see Wild Lights."

"It's about time you pulled your head out." Georgette rubbed her hands together. "I want to hear all about it."

For about two seconds, Jaycee considered not telling Georgette anything, but the prospect of reliving the moment as she told the story won out.

Jaycee told her story, and in true Georgette fashion, she interjected several questions as Jaycee shared.

"Well, all right," Georgette said when Jaycee finished. "And when are you going to see her again?"

Jaycee tried to keep her huge grin at bay, but she likely failed. "I'm helping at the shelter on Christmas Eve."

Georgette clapped her hands together. "Perfect. And you're coming to my house on Christmas Day then?"

"I don't want to intrude on your family." Jaycee squirmed in her chair.

"Nonsense. The kids are coming Christmas Eve, so it'll just be me and Stanley." Georgette drew her brows together and pointed at Jaycee. "Besides, I don't want you to do something stupid like you did on Thanksgiving."

Jaycee leaned against the back of her chair and rubbed her hand across her face. "I know. But Christmas is going to be so hard."

"Exactly why you need to come. Between Piper and me, we'll keep you from making a fool out of yourself."

"But it hurts." Jaycee sighed. "I miss them so much."

A shadow crossed Georgette's eyes. "Did you hear what you just said?"

Jaycee shook her head. "I said I missed them."

"Them." Georgette leaned forward in her chair. "I don't believe I've ever heard you say you miss Tessa."

Jaycee frowned. What was Georgette talking about? Surely, Jaycee had said it.

"Well, do you?" Georgette pushed.

"Now you sound like Tessa." Jaycee snatched a folder off her desk. "I have things to do."

"Nice try." Georgette chuckled. "But we both know you and Tessa had been over for years."

Jaycee tossed the folder onto the desk. Sadness filled her. She wanted to protest, but she knew Georgette was right. "Maybe, but I don't get why the Wilsons tossed me out like yesterday's newspaper." Jaycee looked down at her hands. "Didn't I deserve better?"

"You did, honey." Georgette's voice softened. "I'm not sure why they did that or what Tessa said to them, but in my thoughts, you got two choices."

Jaycee glanced up. "Which are?"

"You either let them go, or you try fixing things—"

"But I—"

Georgette held up her hand. "No, you don't show up there like some raving lunatic on the holiday. You reach out like a normal person. Give Betsy Wilson a call."

"Go straight to the matriarch?"

"Exactly." Georgette grinned. "The matriarch wields great power."

"I can't." Jaycee's heart raced. "I can't take any more rejection."

"She texted you on your birthday, didn't she?"

Jaycee shrugged. "Just a happy birthday. No emojis. No *I love you*. Just happy birthday."

"And if I recall, all you said was thanks."

Jaycee nodded.

"It's a start," Georgette said.

"That was four months ago. Then since, nothing. No Happy Thanksgiving. No—"

"Did you send her anything?"

"No, but—"

"Did you text her on her birthday?"

"I thought about it."

"But did you?"

Jaycee put her head in her hand and leaned on the desk. "No."

"So I'll say it again. Either let it go or do something about it. Sometimes you have to risk being hurt to get what you want." Georgette clapped her hands together, causing Jaycee to jump. "But if I were you, I'd be careful not to mess up things with that little hottie."

"My god, we just met. Besides, Piper is *just* a friend."

"Just the same, I'm thinking you could use a friend, other than this sixty-five-year-old vintage model." Georgette swept her hand along her side. "As fabulous as I may be, you need other friends."

"I didn't when I had a family." Jaycee knew it came out as a pout, but she didn't care. She'd put so much of herself into the Wilson clan, and for what, just to be thrown out on the trash heap.

"And that's where you're wrong and how you got yourself into this situation. Now you have a chance to make a friend." Georgette wriggled her eyebrows. "And maybe something more."

Jaycee picked up the file folder again. "Can I work now?"

"Only if you agree to come have Christmas dinner with me and Stanley."

"Fine." Jaycee threw up her hands, but she was secretly glad she'd have somewhere to be on Christmas. She wasn't sure if she trusted herself not to do something stupid. "If you promise to leave. Now."

Georgette jumped to her feet. "Do you want me to make anything special?"

Jaycee's eyes lit up, and she made a big circle with her hands. "Those giant sugar cookies."

Georgette laughed. "I'll stop at the store this week and pick up those silver sprinkles that you love."

"Sold." Jaycee smiled. "Now let me get some work done."

Chapter Twelve

Jaycee checked herself in the mirror one last time. Maybe she shouldn't wear her new stocking cap. She adjusted it slightly, so Rudolph's red nose was slightly off to the left instead of in the middle of her forehead.

Just because Piper had said she loved Rudolph didn't mean Jaycee needed a Rudolph hat. The vision of Piper dancing to *Run Rudolph Run* flashed in her mind.

It had been a week since they'd gone to the Wild Lights, but she'd thought of that moment often the past week. The way Piper moved her hips and glided to the music caused Jaycee's heart to race. Jaycee shook her head. They were friends, nothing more. Or were they even friends?

Of course, they were becoming friends, Jaycee needed to stop overthinking. They'd exchanged phone numbers last week after the trip to the zoo, and they'd texted a few times since. Nothing major. Piper had sent a gif of Rudolph dancing, and Jaycee had countered with a chorus line of reindeer dancing. With each text that followed, they'd found another goofy Christmas gif. Stupid, but Jaycee had enjoyed searching for something ridiculous to send to Piper.

Jaycee adjusted her hat one last time and turned from the mirror. If she continued to hang out at the shelter, eventually she'd need to dye her hair. It would likely raise suspicions if she wore a stocking cap in the summer.

Wow. This was only her third time visiting the shelter, and she was already thinking six months ahead. She needed to get a grip.

When she descended the stairs, she was greeted by the pile of boxes lined up in the foyer. FedEx had dropped them off earlier. It was the Christmas decorations she'd ordered after seeing the ratty old decorations they had at the shelter.

She glanced at her watch. Still a half hour before she needed to head out. Plenty of time to pick out a few of her favorite things, so she could deliver them tonight.

❧ ❧ ❧ ❧

Piper leaned in toward the mirror and stared at herself. She noticed a few wrinkles around her eyes, and each year, she swore, the laugh lines around her mouth grew deeper. Soon they'd swallow up her whole face.

She started to smile at her idiocy but stopped because it would only make her laugh lines worse. Sergio and Caleb were always trying to pump her up, telling her how pretty she was. She didn't feel pretty. What she felt was haggard and ugly.

Piper put her hands over her face. *Knock it off.* It had been a while since she'd been so critical of herself, but it was back with a vengeance. Self-doubt always crept in when she least expected it.

Likely, it was just the holiday blues. This year, they'd been different, and she couldn't deny why they'd not haunted her as bad this past week. *Jaycee.*

Butterflies fluttered in her stomach at the thought. *Damn it.* She wasn't some hormonal teenager, so she needed to stop acting like one.

A knock at the door pulled her from her thoughts.

"Mommy," Maddie said. "Are you gonna come out? I have to pee."

Piper smiled. Maddie wouldn't give Piper time to dwell on her inadequacies. One of the many things she loved about her children. "Just a second. I'm about done." She looked into the mirror one last time and steeled her gaze. "You've got this," she said to herself.

As soon as she opened the door, Maddie rushed in.

"Once you do your business," Piper said, "put your shoes on. I told Sergio that I'd help get the kitchen set up tonight."

"Are the church people coming?" Maddie asked.

"Yep. They'll be here, and they're going to sing Christmas carols."

Maddie bounced on the toilet and clapped.

"Whoa." Piper laughed. "You're going to fall off. Finish your business." Piper turned toward the door. "I have to wrangle your brother."

"He's in his bedroom drawing pictures."

❧ ❧ ❧ ❧

When Piper entered the kitchen, Caleb and Sergio were singing to the Christmas songs that blared from one of their cellphones. "Putting on a Christmas concert," Piper yelled over the music.

Sergio snatched up the phone and cut the music, but he continued to shake his hips. "Sorry, I—" He stopped cold when he turned to look at her. "Holy hell. You clean up well."

Caleb turned and let out a loud whistle. "Girl. You're looking fine."

Piper scowled. They had no way of knowing about her earlier doubts. She brushed her hair away from her face. "Would you two stop looking at me like that?"

Sergio circled his fingers at her. "Honey, you've got it all going on."

"Careful," Caleb said. "You just might turn me straight if you keep looking so fine."

"That's it." Piper turned and walked toward the door. "I'm leaving."

Sergio and Caleb chuckled.

"All right, come back," Caleb said. "We'll stop talking about how gorgeous you look."

Piper turned back.

"And I won't mention that she's wearing make-up," Sergio said.

Piper pointed. "You're pushing it."

"Fine." Sergio stuck out his bottom lip. "Where are the kids?"

"Playing cards with Ole Freddie." Piper smiled. "I gave Paxton the night off since we aren't having pudding."

Sergio grinned. "When's our star volunteer arriving?"

Piper considered feigning not knowing who Sergio was referring to, but she shrugged instead. "I'm not sure. She didn't give a time."

"She'll show," Caleb said. "So you can stop your worrying."

"Who said I was worrying?"

"Okay. You're not worried," Caleb said as he stepped into the pantry.

"Has she told you that she's Jaycee Re-Ward yet?" Sergio asked.

"No." Piper sighed.

Caleb peeked around the corner of the pantry. "I can't believe she thinks she can fool us with that stocking cap. Not only is her face plastered all over the city, but the woman is downright handsome."

"Boyishly handsome," Sergio added.

They were both right, but Piper didn't plan on commenting. She picked up one of the boxes off the floor and started unloading the contents onto the countertop.

Sergio laughed. "No comment, huh?"

"I'm not sure why she hasn't told us who she is," Piper said, avoiding all talk of Jaycee's good looks. "But she deserves the same courtesy as the patrons."

"I know. I won't push it," Sergio said. "She'll tell us when she's ready."

Caleb emerged from the pantry with four large cans clutched in his arms. "She probably gets hounded by every charity in the city for donations, so it makes sense she'd want to keep it on the down low."

"That's what I figured, too," Piper said.

"You want to know what the biggest shocker is?" Sergio asked Caleb.

"What?" Caleb tentatively lowered the cans to the counter.

"She's got Piper breaking all the rules." Sergio winked.

"I don't break rules." Piper put her hand on her hip. "What are you babbling about?"

"Oh, you mean you had her fill out the volunteer

packet?" Sergio smirked.

"Why did I agree to help you two?" Without bothering to find a knife to break down the box, Piper ripped through the tape with her hands.

Sergio and Caleb both laughed. "Now look what you've done," Caleb said, "you've pissed her off."

Piper put on her best sneer, but the twinkle in her eye likely ruined the effect. She gathered more of the empty boxes littering the kitchen. "I'm taking the trash out."

⁂

Since Jaycee's arms were filled with packages, she kicked the Range Rover's door shut with her foot. After much debate with herself, she'd decided to only bring what she could carry in one load, although she'd been creative and piled them high.

As she walked the block to the shelter, she hoped a strong wind wouldn't blow up, or she'd likely drop everything. Despite being Christmas Eve, the weather in Milwaukee was pleasant. Temperatures had hovered just below freezing most of the day, but with the winds blowing off the lake, it felt much colder.

On her drive to the shelter, a light snow had begun to fall and had picked up considerably by the time she arrived. She stepped on a slippery patch on the sidewalk and nearly lost her grip on the packages.

"Holy shit," Mitzy called from the front of the shelter. "Donovan, go help Jaycee."

Jaycee couldn't see over the boxes in her arms, but she heard heavy footsteps coming her way.

Donovan's soft laugh filled the air. "Are you trying to break your neck?"

Jaycee laughed. "I hadn't planned for the snow."

"Do you want some help?"

"Please!"

Despite Donovan's small stature, he was strong and snatched three-fourths of the packages from her.

"My hero," Mitzy shouted from under the awning.

"She's a drama queen." Donovan shook his head. "But I still love her."

Jaycee smiled. "Thanks for the help."

"Did you buy out the store?"

"I wanted to make sure everyone had a nice Christmas."

Donovan stopped and met Jaycee's gaze. "You know you don't have to buy us off, don't you?"

Donovan's words were like a gut punch. Was that what she was trying to do? Was she one of those people who threw money around? How could she not be when these people had so little? Guilt gnawed at her.

Donovan's face dropped. "Hey, dude. I wasn't trying to be offensive. It's just…just…we like you whether you bring gifts or not."

Jaycee didn't trust her voice, so she nodded and kept walking.

Donovan hurried to catch up to her. "I mean, we had a blast the other night." He smiled and suddenly looked much younger. "Spending time with you and Piper is just as good as any present."

"What are you rambling about?" Mitzy said as they drew closer.

"Not telling since you didn't drag your ass out to help," Donovan answered.

Mitzy turned and stuck out her full backside.

"My booty is luscious, and you know it."

"That I do." Donovan laughed and raised his eyebrows.

Jaycee couldn't help but laugh with them. Donovan's earlier words still stung, but Jaycee knew she was being overly sensitive.

"Piper inside?" Jaycee asked.

Mitzy smirked and then winked at Jaycee. "She's been waiting for you."

❧❧❧❧

"Would you stop pacing?" Sergio put his arm over Piper's shoulder. "You're making me edgy, and I can't cook under these conditions."

"I'm not pacing." Piper leveled him with her best glare. "I'm checking to make sure everything is set."

"She'll be here soon," Caleb said from where he stood at the counter. He'd just about finished laying out the food prep stations for the volunteers.

"Who?" Piper said.

"Good try." Sergio laughed and dropped his arm from around her shoulder. He picked up the tray of pies and carried them to the table Mrs. Akers would soon use to cut them.

Caleb turned and said, "The woman you've been pining for since last weekend."

"I haven't been pining." Piper's protests sounded lame even to her own ears.

"You keep telling yourself that, honey," Sergio said as the kitchen door swung open. "Whatever helps you sleep at night."

"Who's having trouble sleeping?" Jaycee said as she entered the room.

Piper's heartbeat quickened. Jaycee sported an adorable Rudolph hat that accented her ruddy cheeks. Had that been on purpose? *Nah. Coincidence.* Deciding to play it cool, Piper said, "Jaycee, I'm glad you could make it."

Jaycee smiled. "You look well rested to me."

"That's because she's been having sweet dreams," Sergio said and put on a cheesy smile.

"Sweet dreams are made of these," Caleb sang as he danced around the kitchen.

Piper's face heated. "Ignore them. They're goons." She took Jaycee by the arm. "Why don't you go say hi to Paxton and Maddie?" Piper led Jaycee to the door. "I'll be out in a second. Oh, by the way, I love that hat."

As soon as Jaycee was gone, Piper spun and pointed at the two men. "I am so going to hurt you both if you ever do that again."

They both laughed and continued dancing around the kitchen.

❧ ❧ ❧ ❧

Jaycee sighed and checked the time on her cellphone. She'd been at the shelter for nearly eight hours, but the time had flown. Even though she should go, she didn't want to.

Everyone else had scattered. Most of the regulars had gone to the sleeping area, while a few had ventured out into the snow. Now that it was just her and Piper sitting at the table over a cup of coffee, she could ask the question that had been nagging at her. She pursed her lips, trying to decide how to raise the question without it coming out wrong.

"Whoa." Piper held up her hands in front of her. "Why so serious?"

"Don't you have enough beds here?"

Piper cocked her head. "What do you mean?"

"After the meal..." Jaycee pointed toward the door. "Um, you sent all those people out into the cold. Some had really little kids."

Piper laughed, but she must have seen the look of concern on Jaycee's face, so she cut off her laughter. "They went home."

"Home?"

"Yes. Not everyone that comes here for a meal is homeless. Especially during the holidays. A lot are barely holding on to their houses, and they could never afford a nice holiday meal like we prepare. Most are patrons of our food pantry, but some we've never seen before."

"Then how do you know they need the food? That they can't afford it."

"We don't." Piper lifted one shoulder. "If someone comes in wanting a meal, we give it to them. No questions asked."

"That's nice," Jaycee said. "What happens if you run out of room for people to sleep? Do you have to turn them away?"

"We never do."

Jaycee let out a sigh of relief. The thought of turning children onto the street made her sick to her stomach.

"We need more compassionate people like you." Piper smiled.

Jaycee was embarrassed by the compliment since she knew so little about the homeless situation in the city. Shouldn't she be more aware, considering her line of work? Sure, she'd read about it, but until now, she'd not given it much thought. "How do you make room?"

"There are other shelters in the city. First, we contact them to see if they have any space. If they do, we transport them there."

"If they don't?"

"In a pinch, we use this room." Piper pointed at the tables. "We'll fold some of those up and make it work, but it's not the best place to sleep."

"They don't seem to have any trouble sleeping here." Jaycee smiled and pointed at Paxton and Maddie, who were fast asleep on a pair of beanbag chairs.

Piper snorted. "Those two could sleep anywhere. Plus, they've fallen in love with those chairs."

"I can tell."

"It's the damnedest thing. We seem to have an anonymous benefactor. Every day this week, we've gotten a delivery. No name. No card. Just a ton of boxes."

"'Tis the season for giving." Jaycee hoped to move the conversation along for fear her face would give her away.

"That it is." Piper frowned. "Giving tapers way off after the holidays, so we can't get too comfortable." Piper slapped her hand on the table. "It's Christmas. No dwelling on the negative."

Jaycee took a swig of her coffee and let the warm liquid roll around her tongue before she swallowed. It wasn't the best cup of coffee she'd ever had, but for some reason, it was hitting the spot. "I think everything turned out pretty good tonight."

"Undoubtedly." Piper chuckled. "It was a touch less chaotic than Thanksgiving."

"Just a little." Jaycee crinkled her nose and smiled.

"I swear there's a Santa Claus." Piper put her hand on her chest. "My day was made when Ole Freddie walked in the door. He's had us all so worried."

"He looked a little rough."

"He's looked worse."

Jaycee cringed at the thought of his mangled face. "Where do you think he got the scrapes and bruises?"

"Who knows? He's unlikely to tell us." Piper sighed and suddenly looked tired. "He disappears like this two or three times a year."

"How come the homeless prob—" *Crap.* Jaycee knew it would be rude to call it a problem. "The homeless situation hasn't been solved?"

"Now that's a loaded question." Piper grinned.

"I'm sorry." Jaycee adjusted her stocking cap. "You must think I'm ignorant."

"No, not at all. I love that you want to know more. Too many people would rather turn their heads and act like it doesn't exist." Piper's hands clenched into fists, and her voice was strained.

"Never mind. I shouldn't have brought this up on Christmas. I didn't mean to upset you."

"I'm just passionate." Piper swept her hand around the large room. "People shouldn't have to live like this, not in a rich country like the United States." Piper's face was as red as the Santa hat she wore. "It pisses me off that there are so many people dripping in money, while some of the people who come here don't have enough to buy a loaf of bread."

Feelings of guilt bombarded Jaycee, so she looked into her coffee cup.

Piper continued. "Affordable housing is a huge problem. Most people who are down on their luck can't afford first and last month's rent and a security deposit. It's a vicious cycle."

Jaycee lifted her gaze. Piper's eyes blazed, and her jaw was clenched. "What about government assistance?" Jaycee asked.

"It's not bad, if they can get it. What people don't understand is there aren't unlimited housing vouchers. Then add on slumlords and how the deck is stacked against them. It's soul crushing."

Jaycee's guilt returned, but she vowed not to shut down. She wouldn't be someone who avoided uncomfortable conversations. "I once read that anyone living on the streets wants to be living on the streets."

Piper held up a finger. "You do understand that living on the street and being homeless are two different things, don't you?"

"Huh?"

"That's what I thought." Piper smiled. "It's rare for someone to completely live on the streets. Shelters give people a roof over their head, but they're still homeless. Without a home."

"Why would anyone choose to live on the street, instead of a shelter?"

"It's complicated." Piper sighed. "Some people have had bad experiences in the shelters, while others have been banned."

"Banned?"

"For repeated rule violations." Piper's shoulders sagged as if all her energy had left her body.

"I'm sorry." Jaycee chastised herself. She didn't

want to cause that look on Piper's face. "We can talk about something else."

"It's not you." Piper gave her a weak smile. "It's so hard when we have to kick someone out. It breaks my heart, but we must think of the welfare of everyone. And other times, it's a bit scary. When someone gets kicked out for aggression, you never know what they might do."

Why had Jaycee not considered the potential dangers? Probably because her visits had been so uplifting, the negative side had never crossed her mind.

"It's okay." Piper smiled. "Never play poker."

Jaycee laughed. "Was my reaction that obvious?"

"Afraid so. Seriously, it's not that bad since it doesn't happen that often, but when it does, it's hard on everyone."

"I shouldn't be quizzing you, especially on Christmas." Jaycee picked at the napkin sitting on the table.

"You're fine. I'd prefer people ask questions than just make assumptions. There is so much misinformation out there."

"It's cool to be able to ask an expert."

"I'd hardly call myself an expert."

"I would." Jaycee smiled. "Politicians are always talking about it, but it seems to me they should be doing less talking and more listening to people who actually work in the shelters."

"Hallelujah." Piper raised both hands over her head.

Jaycee smiled at Piper's exuberance. "Can I ask one more question?"

"Sure.

"I was always under the impression that most people who are homeless have mental health issues or problems with substance abuse, but now that I've been around here, I'm thinking that's wrong, too."

"It's a stereotype. You'd be surprised how many people end up homeless at some point in their lives. For instance, a disability or a lost job can send anyone spiraling."

"So that's just a myth for television and the movies?"

"Not exactly." Piper took a sip of coffee before continuing. "What you're talking about is the chronically homeless. A large percentage of the chronically homeless have mental health or substance abuse issues. Many times, both."

"This is starting to make sense." Jaycee went to rub her head in thought but stopped, afraid she'd dislodge her hat. Instead, she rubbed her chin. "Most of the people here weren't what I expected. The majority I never would have known were homeless. Just a few."

"Like Ole Freddie and Loretta?" Piper asked. Her brown eyes held even more compassion than normal.

"Yeah. Like them." Jaycee returned Piper's gaze, hoping she was able to relay her concern.

"It'll break your heart if you let it." Piper put her hand over her heart. She slugged down the last of her coffee and rose from the table. "Do you want another cup?"

"Sure." Jaycee said, even though she should be going. It had been too good of an evening for her to want it to end.

Chapter Thirteen

Jaycee smiled at herself in the mirror. She'd outdone herself with this stocking cap. It was a replica of the ball that dropped in Times Square. Fitting for a New Year's Eve celebration, if she did say so herself.

She'd been tempted to put on a bow tie, but she hadn't wanted to risk it. Instead, she'd purchased a brightly colored Jerry Garcia tie. The reds, yellows, and oranges looked like flames and popped against her black shirt.

Sharp. She might have to mix it up and add a few more long ties into her wardrobe. It was probably silly wanting to dress up; after all, Piper had said it was a casual affair. New Year's wasn't a big holiday at the shelter like Thanksgiving and Christmas.

As she turned off the bathroom light, she heard her phone vibrate on the dresser. *Ugh.* It was amazing when people decided to put offers on homes, but seriously, seven o'clock on New Year's Eve. It shouldn't surprise her; she'd had calls on Christmas in the past.

Over the years, she'd gotten better at setting boundaries with her clients, but after Tessa had left, she'd let her boundaries loosen, welcoming the distraction. It was time to reestablish them.

Jaycee picked up the phone and froze. *Tessa.* Her heart raced. Oh, god, maybe something had happened to one of Tessa's parents. "Hello."

"Hey, babe," Tessa's familiar voice came through the phone. Jaycee heard a loud murmur in the background as if Tessa was surrounded by a lot of people.

"Hi," Jaycee said, her voice full of caution.

"What are you doing?"

This was getting weird. Did Tessa really call to see what she was doing? *No.* Tessa must have an ulterior motive. "Um, I'm just getting ready to step out for a bit."

Tessa laughed. "Going out on the town?" There were definitely other people in the background. "I'll take another. Make it a double."

"Pardon?" Jaycee said.

"Nothing. Just ordering a drink."

"Ah." Jaycee didn't know what else to say. If she'd known this was a social call, she wouldn't have answered.

"So you're going out on the town, huh?" Tessa snickered. "I didn't think you liked going out on New Year's."

Jaycee refused to take the bait. Tessa was right, though. Jaycee preferred spending New Year's at home with the family, not in some crowded bar. But she certainly had no intention of telling Tessa where she planned to spend her evening. "Did you call about the divorce papers?"

"Wow. You're going to jump to that?" Tessa's voice held an edge.

"I just...I just assumed that's why you'd be calling. Isn't New Year's about making fresh starts? My lawyer sent the papers to yours last week."

"I got them." There was no mistaking the curtness in her tone this time.

"Oh. Did I mess something up?"

"You can't wait for it to be over?" Tessa asked.

Wow. Jaycee wasn't even sure how to respond. Had she entered an alternate universe? Tessa had been at her for months to sign the papers.

"Thanks. Keep the change," Tessa said.

Bartender. Jaycee needed to focus on what Tessa said previously, but her mind was mush.

"Are you planning on answering me?" Tessa asked. "Hey, buy a round for the bar. On me."

Ugh. "What is it you want me to answer? The conversation is hard to follow."

"Oh, Christ. Hold on." There was rustling on the other end of the phone. "Here's my card. I'll start a tab. I have to step out to take this call."

The din disappeared, and Tessa said, "Is this better?"

"Yeah."

"Like I was saying, are you that anxious to get rid of me?"

Jaycee sat on the edge of her bed and stared at the wall. *What the hell?* "I don't even know how you want me to respond."

"What's so hard? Answer the question."

Jaycee took a deep breath. She would not let Tessa upset her or ruin her evening. "If you don't remember, you're the one who asked me for the divorce, so I don't think the question's relevant."

"What if I changed my mind?"

No. No. No. This was not happening.

"My parents miss you," Tessa said.

Ouch.

"Josh and Megan were asking about you at Christmas."

Knockout blow. It felt like a dagger had been thrust into Jaycee's chest.

"Are you going to say something?" Tessa didn't try to hide the impatience from her voice.

"How much have you been drinking?" *Wow.* That was the best she had? Jaycee knew it would set Tessa off, but with the walls closing in around her, she didn't know what else to say.

A deep inhale came from the other end of the phone, but Tessa didn't speak for several beats. "Do you want to join me for a drink?" Tessa's voice came out upbeat, almost cheery.

When was the last time Jaycee heard anything but contempt in Tessa's voice? Tessa didn't exactly scream cheery. "Where are you?" *Shit.* Had that made it sound like she wanted to have a drink? *Damn it.*

"That's more like it." Jaycee could hear the smirk in Tessa's voice. "The Outsider."

"Uh...oh. I'm on my way out."

"So you're going to meet me?"

Fuck. Why did Tessa have this effect on her? She just needed to say no and get off the phone. As she struggled with a response, her phone vibrated. *Shit.* "Hey, Tessa. Hold on. Another call is coming in."

Before Tessa could respond, Jaycee tapped on the incoming call. "Hello."

"Hey, are you on your way?" Piper's perky voice came through the phone.

Should she tell Piper that something had come up? She could talk to Tessa face to face and see what she wanted. The thought of disappointing Piper made Jaycee uncomfortable. "I'm running a bit behind. I had a phone call."

"No worries. We'll be here." The sound of children laughing could be heard in the background.

"Sounds like the party has already started."

"A giant box of Lego was delivered this afternoon." Piper paused for a beat before she said. "Anonymous."

"Hmm," Jaycee smiled. "Sounds like it's a hit."

"Definitely. It's almost like the donor knows exactly what to send." Piper chuckled. "Plus, we got a box of snacks. That's why I'm calling."

"Something wrong with them?"

"No M&M's."

"But…" *Shit.* She couldn't say that. She'd ordered M&M's because she knew they were Piper's favorites. "But we can't have a New Year's celebration without M&M's."

"Exactly. It wasn't the donor's fault. The packing slip says they're on back order."

"You want me to stop and pick up M&M's, huh?"

"It would make my day."

"Well then, I guess I'm stopping." Jaycee smiled, imagining the twinkle in Piper's eyes and her playful smile.

Jaycee was pulled out of her thoughts when her phone beeped. *Shit. Tessa.* "Hey. I have another call. Can I let you go?"

"Sure. See you soon." Then the call dropped.

"Hello? Are you there? Damn it, Jaycee." Tessa's angry voice was loud.

"Um, sorry," Jaycee said. "I had to take that call."

"Always working. One of the things I loved about you."

Jaycee didn't feel the need to correct her on any of her points. In the brief time she'd talked to Piper, her head cleared. The contrast between how talking to

Tessa and talking to Piper made her feel was so clear, and she was back on firmer ground. "Listen. I have to get going, or I'm gonna be late."

"Late? Take your time, I'll be here."

"No!" Jaycee said it with more conviction than was probably necessary. "I'm not coming. I already have other plans, and I'm going to be late if I don't get moving." Jaycee smiled. Besides, she needed to stop for emergency M&M's.

"So that's it? You're going to blow me off?"

Jaycee bit down on her lip. Even though she wanted to say something angry, she wouldn't. It would only make Jaycee feel bad, and she wanted to have a good time tonight. "Since we didn't have plans, I think you characterizing it as blowing you off is a bit off base."

"Cancel them."

"I can't…No, I won't cancel." Jaycee steeled her jaw. "I have to go now. Have a happy New Year." Then she disconnected.

Her heart raced and her palms were covered in sweat, but she felt good. She felt…free.

Chapter Fourteen

Jaycee leaned in toward Piper and whispered, "Who are those people?"

Piper tried to focus on Jaycee's question, but it was hard with Jaycee being so close. Her cologne had a hint of masculinity, a mixture of sandalwood, vanilla, and leather. "Which people?" Piper asked, stalling for time to get her bearings.

"The group huddled around Mitzy and Donovan."

"Oh, they're regulars."

"First time I've seen them. Is this like an LGBTQ+ hotspot or what?"

"Unfortunately." Piper gave Jaycee a sad smile. "While it's hard to get accurate statistics on homelessness, some studies show that forty percent of homeless youths are LGBTQ+."

"Damn." Jaycee's eyes widened. "I'd read it was higher, but shit, forty percent."

"It's not really surprising." Piper watched the teens, laughing about something. If she didn't know better, they looked like they could be hanging around an arcade or movie theater, not a homeless shelter. "Many of their families threw them out when they discovered they were *different,* while some chose to leave on their own because they weren't accepted." Piper shook her head. "Abuse, both physical and sexual, sometimes comes into play, too."

"I feel like such a jerk. I never really thought about it," Jaycee said.

"Take a look at some of the information the Trevor Project puts out. It's eye-opening." Piper patted Jaycee's arm and looked away from the teens.

Jaycee pulled out her cellphone. "You said the Trevor Project?"

"Yeah, they do good work."

"I'm not Googling." Jaycee held up her phone. "Just putting it in my note app, so I can look it up later."

"Good, because if you started reading, it'll take you down a rabbit hole, and you have to help me get the bubbly ready." Piper bumped Jaycee with her shoulder.

Jaycee scrunched up her face. "We've still got an hour and a half."

Piper didn't think she'd ever get tired of all of Jaycee's expressions. "Nope. Half an hour."

"It's only ten thirty."

"Central Time." Piper winked. "We celebrate on Eastern Time when the ball drops in Times Square."

"Ah, so you go by the standard that it's midnight somewhere?"

"Exactly." Piper nudged Jaycee. "By the way, nice hat. We might have to have you stand on a chair and lower your head along with the ball."

"Be careful what you ask for, you never know what I might do."

Piper grinned. "That's what I'm bargaining on."

❧ ❧ ❧ ❧

"Five, four, three, two, one," the group called

out as Jaycee lowered her head all the way to the floor. "Happy New Year."

Jaycee grabbed for her hat, so she could throw it into the air when she remembered she couldn't. Instead, she straightened it and leapt to her feet. Everyone laughed, cheered, and hugged as they sipped sparkling grape juice from their plastic champagne flutes. Glasses that the *anonymous* donor had sent.

After Piper released Paxton and Maddie from her embrace, she shoved a glass into Jaycee's hand. Piper held up her own glass, and they made a silent toast since the room was too loud to hear anything over the uproar. *Auld Lang Syne* played in the background, and Mitzy and her crew threw confetti and streamers.

Jaycee's heart filled. It was perfect. Absolutely perfect.

It didn't take long after the ball dropped for the party to break up. Since the attendees were mostly regulars, they moved on to their sleeping quarters, while Mitzy and her crew slipped out into the night.

It made Jaycee nervous to see them leave, but Piper reminded her they had to make their own choices. Paxton and Maddie had begged Piper to go into the other room with some of the children to watch a Disney movie until she'd given in.

Several of the patrons had offered to help clean up, but Piper had waved them off. It suited Jaycee since her favorite time at the shelter was at the end of the evening when it was just the two of them. It gave Jaycee the opportunity to get to know Piper better.

It hadn't taken them long to find their groove. Cleanup took little time when they worked together, and soon they had the entire place cleaned up.

They'd sat at Mrs. Akers's table in the kitchen

with a full bottle of sparkling grape juice.

Piper twisted off the cap. "Are you sure we can handle it?"

Jaycee shook her head. "I don't know. You might get wild."

"Me? I'm not the one using my head as a ball." Piper gave her a huge smile.

Piper's smile made Jaycee's heart race. The bigger the smile, the deeper the laugh lines, the more she was drawn to Piper. "I believe it was your idea."

Piper laughed. "I'll have to remember that. You'll do anything I tell you to do."

There was an unmistakable flirtation to Piper's tone. Jaycee smirked. "Just about anything."

"Good to know." Piper looked away, her face flushed. "We cleaned up all the glasses. Are you opposed to drinking out of the bottle?"

"I'm good with that." To prove the point, Jaycee took a long pull from the bottle and passed it to Piper.

Piper grabbed it as if she were a drunken sailor and took a swill. Then she swiped her arm across her mouth. "Now if I could only burp on command."

Jaycee laughed. "I could never do it, either."

"Couple of lightweights."

"I can't believe how much fun this was with absolutely no alcohol."

"Did your family always have alcohol at events like this?" Piper asked.

"Mostly. Don't get me wrong. Nobody would get fall-down drunk, but I never thought it was the best thing to do in front of the kids." Jaycee snickered. "I guess I'm a prude."

"No." Piper put her hand on Jaycee's arm. "I think that's sweet. Kids see too much."

"Thanks. Tessa always thought I was being ridiculous." *Shit.* Why did she just say that? It wasn't a conversation she'd planned on broaching, and she couldn't even blame it on the bubbly.

"Is Tessa your ex?" Piper asked.

"Soon-to-be ex, yes."

Piper's eyes softened. "How long have you been split up?"

"Going on a year now." Jaycee sighed. "She waited until after the holidays last year to tell me." Jaycee rolled her eyes. "So thoughtful."

"Is that why you've been coming around here?"

Jaycee leveled her gaze at Piper. "It was the first time."

Piper pursed her lips. "Something happened that day, didn't it?"

Jaycee sighed before she relayed her humiliating Thanksgiving story and why she'd showed up at the shelter with macarons. Piper listened without interruption.

"I'm so sorry that happened to you," Piper said once Jaycee finished.

Jaycee shrugged. "In hindsight, I was asking for it."

"No." Piper frowned.

"Who shows up at a Thanksgiving dinner uninvited?" Jaycee steeled her jaw. "It was crazy. No wonder Tessa kicked me out."

"It sounds like grief to me. Not craziness." Piper's voice came out with conviction. "What about your family? Where are they?"

"I don't have one." Jaycee opened her eyes wide. She would not cry.

"None?"

"I was an only child, and...uh...my mom said she was an only child." Jaycee wondered if Piper would pick up on how she'd worded her response.

Piper paused for a beat. "What about your dad?"

Jaycee hoped the wince she felt inside didn't show on the outside. "I don't have a dad."

"Oh. Okay." Piper's poker face wasn't working, either. She tried to cover her initial look of surprise with a casual air.

"I never had one." Jaycee let out a humorless chuckle. "Well, obviously, I had to have one. I'm not a miracle baby. I just don't know who he is. My mom was working in a conference center. People from all over come in for those. It was a real estate convention. She said she never got his name."

"What aren't you saying?"

"Damn, you're perceptive." Jaycee grinned. "I never believed she didn't know his name, but no matter how hard I pressed, she wouldn't budge."

"Did she ever find someone else?"

Jaycee shook her head. "She said I was all she needed. Never dated. Nothing."

"Wow. That's a lot to put on a kid." Piper put her hand over her mouth. "Sorry, I shouldn't have said that."

"It's nothing I haven't thought. My friend Georgette says I'm naïve because I was so sheltered." Jaycee shrugged, trying to shake off the label that she knew was true. Over the years, she'd worked to become less naïve, more *worldly*, but according to Georgette and Tessa, she'd only had limited success.

"I like that about you." Piper patted Jaycee's hand. "Innocent."

"Ugh." Jaycee put her hand against her forehead.

"You're killing me."

Piper laughed. "How about pure?"

"If you say simple, I'm leaving," Jaycee teased.

"Don't change, Jaycee. I'm serious. You're genuine. Real." Piper gave Jaycee a warm smile.

Jaycee looked away, not able to handle Piper's intense gaze. "Don't get me wrong. My mom was the best, and I loved her dearly, but sometimes it was hard to have her sole focus on me."

"She's gone?"

"Been gone four years. She was only seventy. Massive stroke."

"Oh, Jaycee. I'm so sorry."

Jaycee couldn't dwell on her mother's death, or she'd spiral down another rabbit hole, but she couldn't just change the subject. "She was thirty-six when she had me. Never married or in a long-term relationship. She'd come from an abusive home. She wouldn't tell me much about it, but I think she was afraid of relationships. I've always wondered if she'd purposely set out to have me."

"Did you ever ask?"

"Plenty. But she always gave me her stock answer. Which was, *leave the past in the past*." Jaycee sighed. "Same answer she'd give whenever I'd ask about her family."

"You never met anyone in your mom's family?"

"Nope." Jaycee put her hand against her chest to quell the ache, but still tears welled in her eyes. "Tessa's family was the only family I ever had. Now they're gone."

"Oh, Jaycee." Piper's expression softened. "How long were you together?"

"A little over fifteen years." Jaycee bit the inside

of her cheek. She would not cry. "I watched the kids grow up. I loved them so much." She put her fist into the air and released her fingers. "Then poof, the only family I had was gone. Overnight."

"That's messed up." Piper must have registered the confused look on Jaycee's face because she added, "Sorry. I just mean that's not right. You don't stop being their aunt because you divorce."

"That's what I thought, too, but apparently, that's not how the Wilsons do things. I got a happy birthday text from my mother-in-law, but it felt forced, so I just said thank you. None of the others sent one."

"Didn't you reach out to them?"

"Tessa told me not to. That they didn't want to hear from me. Obviously, it was true because I never heard from them again." Pain twisted inside Jaycee, making it hard for her to breathe. "I thought I meant something to them." Jaycee shrugged, trying to appear nonchalant. "I guess the saying blood is thicker than water is true."

Piper scowled. "Didn't you say Tessa asked for the divorce?"

Jaycee nodded.

"I'm trying to understand." Piper paused and bit her lip. "Did you...uh...did you do something to make her ask for the divorce?"

Jaycee grinned slightly. "If you're asking if I cheated on her or did something equally horrible, no. It came out of the blue." Jaycee sighed. "No, not out of the blue. It died with a whimper, certainly not a bang." When Jaycee saw the puzzled look on Piper's face she added, "We didn't fight. Year by year, we just drifted apart."

"Did you try counseling?"

"After she asked for the divorce, I tried, but she declined." Jaycee looked down at her hands, no longer able to meet Piper's gaze. "She claims that I loved her family more than I did her. Says I checked out of the relationship years ago."

"By your reaction, is there some truth to that?" Piper's tone was gentle, yet the question still felt probing.

Afraid how her voice would come out, Jaycee nodded. She found it hard to breathe. "Enough about me," Jaycee said with a nervous laugh. "It's your turn."

Piper studied her for several seconds. "Thank you for sharing. It looks like you've had enough for tonight." Piper reached out and squeezed Jaycee's arm. "What do you want to know?"

Jaycee's insides warmed. No doubt, Piper knew she couldn't have this conversation any longer, so she easily pivoted without question. It was unlike Tessa, who was a bulldog and would come at Jaycee relentlessly without giving her time to think or reflect. One of the many things that derailed the relationship over the years.

Jaycee looked up from the table. "I'm assuming that Paxton and Maddie are both your biological children."

Piper laughed. "Good assumption. It always pissed off Emma that they looked so much like me." Piper's smile widened. "We even used a sperm donor that had her coloring. Lighter complexion, blue eyes, blond hair, but they both got my dark hair and eyes."

"Does she ever see the kids?"

"Nope. She cut and ran." Piper put on a smile, but pain danced in her eyes. She snapped her fingers.

"Just like that, she was gone."

Jaycee stared, knowing she should say something. "I'm so sorry." *Really?* That was the most cliched comment she could make. "Ugh. I don't mean to be so inarticulate. It's just hard to fathom how someone could do that to you and the kids."

"Trust me. I know." Piper shook her head. "People who supposedly love you don't do that."

"But she did."

"Yeah. She did." Piper's voice came out in barely a whisper.

Jaycee bit back saying, *I'm sorry,* again. "Do you even know where she's at?"

"Chicago. I guess I can't really say she cut and ran. She got offered a job at the Chicago Mercantile Exchange. It was too good to pass up, so she moved ahead of us to get settled in and said she'd send for us."

"When was that?"

"Four years ago."

"Ouch." *Wow.* Could she react any worse? "I don't know what my problem is. I'm stunned and certainly not saying the right thing."

"I think it's sweet." Piper grabbed Jaycee's hand. "It's genuine. Someone doesn't have to say the right words to know they feel for you." Piper patted her own chest. "And I can tell that you do."

"Oh, god, yes." Jaycee copied Piper and put her hand on her own aching chest. "I feel it right here. I'm angry. I'm sad. I just can't believe someone would be so horrible to you and the kids."

"Thanks." Piper smiled again, but this time, the smile touched her eyes. "She said she'd made a mistake. That she didn't want kids."

Jaycee wrinkled her nose. "I'm confused. In your

case, it's not like you can accidentally get pregnant."

"Exactly what I said." Piper chuckled. "She acted like I entrapped her with the kids. Revisionist history. She was the one that convinced me to have them, which took a bit of persuasion since she had no interest in carrying them." Piper slapped her hand on the table. "Enough of this." She held up her cellphone. "It's only a few minutes to midnight. We need to do a proper toast."

"How do we toast with one bottle?" Jaycee swirled the liquid around in the bottle they'd been sharing.

"That'll never do." Piper jumped from her chair and slid over to the water cooler and pulled off two paper cups. "This will work. Find a countdown while I pour."

Jaycee flipped through her phone and found a local station that was broadcasting from a nearby hotel. They were amid the crowd, many who looked as if they'd been partying for a while. Jaycee turned up the volume on her phone, so the music and sound of festivities filled the kitchen.

Piper had finished pouring the sparkling grape juice and held one cup out to Jaycee. Just as Jaycee was about to take it, Piper pulled it back. "You have to be on your feet for a proper toast."

Jaycee smirked. "Is that in the official rules?"

"Duh."

"If you say so." Jaycee stood, and Piper gave her the flimsy cup.

The crowd began their countdown. "Ten. Nine. Eight—"

"Seven. Six." Piper's voice rose and drowned out the sounds coming from the phone. She motioned for

Jaycee to join her.

"Five. Four. Three," they said in unison. Piper took a step toward Jaycee, so they were only a few feet apart. "Two. One. Happy New Year."

They both slugged their drinks. Piper smashed her cup down hard on the table as if she were in a bar, hinting to the bartender that her glass was empty.

Then Piper did something Jaycee wasn't expecting. Piper wrapped her arms around Jaycee and pulled her in for a hug.

The strains of *Auld Lang Syne* emitted from the phone. Jaycee wasn't sure who began rocking from side to side, but before long, they were dancing along with the crowd in the ballroom.

Piper lay her head against Jaycee's shoulder and swayed to the music. Jaycee couldn't be sure if the warmth she felt was from Piper's body heat or if it was coming from inside her own body.

As the song ended, Piper lifted her head from Jaycee's shoulder, and their gazes met. Piper's eyes were different, more intense. Even though Jaycee knew she should look away, she couldn't.

Piper put her hand against Jaycee's cheek, and her tongue circled her lips, wetting them.

Jaycee's heart raced. She leaned forward. Their faces were only inches from each other.

The kitchen door banged open. "Mom, Paxton woke me up singing that dumb song," Maddie said.

Jaycee jumped back and immediately missed the warmth of Piper's hand on her face. Piper stumbled backward, her cheeks crimson.

"Honey, what are you going on about?" Piper asked Maddie.

"What were you guys doing?" Maddie's gaze

traveled between Piper and Jaycee.

"Um…um…we were celebrating the New Year with a hug."

Maddie put her hand on her hip. "Huh-uh, we did that a long time ago."

Piper sighed and went into an explanation of time zones for Maddie.

The moment was broken.

Chapter Fifteen

The entire drive home, all Jaycee could think about was her dance with Piper and their near kiss. What would have happened if Maddie hadn't burst into the room?

It was better that they hadn't found out. Life was uncertain enough. After Tessa's earlier phone call, Jaycee had been off balance, but it was nothing compared to how she felt now.

After Maddie's arrival, she hadn't stayed much longer. When Jaycee said she needed to go, the look in Piper's eyes had been complicated. It had been a combination of disappointment and regret, twinged with what might have been relief.

Jaycee glanced down at the speedometer and eased her foot off the gas. The police would be out in force on New Year's Eve, and she certainly didn't need a ticket. She should focus on her driving and not what happened earlier.

At a slower speed, she was able to take in a bit more of her surroundings. Flurries swirled around her but not enough to stick on the road, but she suspected that would change. It was dark—very dark. The clouds blocked out the moon and stars and seemed ready to dump snow all over the city.

Traffic was surprisingly light. Maybe everyone had finally wised up and stayed put when celebrating New Year's, or maybe it was just too early. She glanced at the clock. It wasn't even twelve thirty.

She smiled to herself. *Life was strange.* If she'd been asked two months ago where she'd celebrate New Year's Eve, the homeless shelter wouldn't have made her top ten. Hell, it wouldn't even have cracked her top one hundred.

But now, DOTS was her favorite place to be. If she spent too much time analyzing that, she'd likely panic. Good thing she was nearly home.

Maybe she'd grab a glass of wine, a large one, hop in her Jacuzzi tub, light a few candles, and read a steamy book. *Dumb idea.* She'd noticed lately whenever she read a spicy sapphic book, one of the characters strangely looked like Piper.

"Ugh," she yelled. It felt good, so she yelled louder. "Shit. Fuck. Shit."

Mature! But it was oddly cathartic. The snow was coming down harder as she pulled into her driveway.

Hmm. She didn't remember leaving the lights on in the house, but between being rattled by Tessa's phone call and her excitement to see Piper, it was possible.

After she pulled her Range Rover to a stop in the garage, she looked over at the other bay at her baby all covered up for the winter. For a fleeting moment, she considered throwing caution to the wind and taking it for a spin, but a Porsche 911 convertible wasn't exactly the best car to drive in a snowstorm.

The thought of speeding down the highway, trying to outrun her thoughts did have an appeal, though. She slammed the Range Rover's door, stepped up to the covered car, and put her hand on the hood of her beloved convertible. *Maybe just a quick trip.*

No. It had been winterized. Besides, it would be

irresponsible to take it out on a night like this and potentially damage it. Her heartbeat quickened. *Shit.* She certainly couldn't drive it to the shelter. Guilt stung her like a bee. Suddenly, she felt greedy. Had she become one of those clueless people who didn't care about the suffering of others?

It wasn't like she bought it to showcase. She loved to drive it and feel the wind and sun on her face. One of her favorite things was to explore the shores of Lake Michigan on a beautiful sunny day.

Was she trying to justify her excess? She pulled back the cover until the bright yellow hood was exposed. She continued pulling it back until she could open the door. She slid into the driver's seat and gripped the steering wheel.

Maybe she should sell it. After all, it cost more than some people's homes. Guilt gnawed at her. With what it cost, she could probably feed everyone at the shelter for the year.

She wondered how Piper handled that every day, leaving everyone at the shelter and returning to her own home. As caring as Piper was with the patrons, it had to be a struggle not to want to take them all home with her. Jaycee would have to talk to Piper about how she handled the guilt.

Jaycee sighed and rubbed the dash. She stared at the bright yellow hood, the only color she'd considered, much to Tessa's chagrin. For as long as she remembered, she'd said when she made her first million, she'd get a bright yellow convertible. It was her splurge, but now she couldn't help but feel boastful and greedy.

She put her head down on the steering wheel, and Piper's face filled her mind. What would Piper think when she found out the truth about Jaycee? Would she be mad? Certainly, she wouldn't. After all, Jaycee hadn't lied, she'd just not revealed who she was, but on the other hand, no one had asked.

"What the hell are you doing?" a loud voice called out.

Jaycee screamed. Her heart raced as she watched the figure come through the door that led into the house. Her gaze darted around the garage, looking for a weapon, and it landed on her golf bag in the corner. Would she have enough time to reach it before the intruder sprang?

"Jesus, Jaycee. What are you doing sitting in the car?"

Tessa? Why was Tessa coming from inside her house? She must have fallen asleep with her head on the steering wheel, and now she was having a vivid dream.

"Are you going to say something?" Tessa marched to the car, but her gait was a bit unsteady, so it was more a weaving stomp.

"Tessa?" Jaycee finally said.

"Who the hell else would you think it was?" Tessa must have realized her harshness because she froze and put on a big smile. She wriggled her eyebrows. "I've been waiting for you to get home," she said in a sultry voice.

Jaycee wasn't sure if she wanted to laugh or vomit. Either way, Tessa's attempt at sexy wasn't having the desired effect. "You just about scared me to death."

"Well, if you hadn't been sitting in the garage forever, I wouldn't have." Tessa put her hands on her hips. "Is this the weird shit you do living alone?"

Now that Jaycee's racing heart had returned to normal, she studied Tessa. She wore a pair of tight black dress slacks that showed off her narrow hips and firm butt. Several buttons were left undone on her bright blue silk shirt, which accented her ample cleavage. Her short brown hair had the carefree tussle that Jaycee once found so endearing. It was the intense look in her piercing blue eyes that caused Jaycee to look away.

Tessa standing here with bare feet, looking this good should have sent her heart racing, but it caused Jaycee to shiver. There had always been a coldness about Tessa, but Jaycee hadn't given it much thought. Was it Piper's warmth that made it so evident now? Jaycee smiled. Piper's warmth was like a hug that enveloped Jaycee.

"I see you're happy to see me." Tessa skirted around the car door and stood over Jaycee.

Shit. Tessa thought the smile was for her. Jaycee fought against letting her gaze dart around the garage for an escape route. Tessa wouldn't react well if she caught on. Jaycee swung her legs out of the Porsche, forcing Tessa to take a step back. "Why don't we go inside?" That should buy her some time.

Tessa tilted her head toward the hood. "Or I could do you right there. On your baby."

Gross. Did Jaycee once find that talk sexy? The past year had turned so much of her life upside down that she couldn't remember anymore. Jaycee laughed, hoping Tessa would think she'd taken it as a joke, although she doubted it was. "I polished her up so much at the end of the season, anything on her would slide right off." Jaycee stood and shut the car door.

Tessa smirked and took a step toward Jaycee.

She put her hand on the roof of the car and pinned Jaycee against the side. "Sounds like it could be an adventure."

Jaycee ducked around Tessa's arm and picked up the corner of the cover that lay bunched on the ground. She wove the canvas around Tessa and draped it back over the hood. As she bent to secure it, Jaycee felt Tessa press in behind her. Tessa's pelvis ground against Jaycee's buttocks.

Tessa leaned in with her mouth only inches from Jaycee's ear. "Do you want to do it on top of the cover?"

A whiff of hard alcohol, probably whiskey, assaulted Jaycee. "Are you drunk?" Jaycee asked as she slithered away from Tessa.

Anger flashed in Tessa's eyes before the cool intensity returned. "I might have had a couple, but that doesn't change anything."

Jaycee finished securing the cover and walked toward the door. "Doesn't change what?"

"It doesn't change that I wanted to see you earlier, and I still want to." Tessa followed Jaycee inside.

Having gotten inside far enough to put distance between them, Jaycee held up her hands and turned from side to side. "There you've seen me. I think it's time for you to go home now."

"I like what I see." Tessa slowly licked her lips. "Nice tie. But why are you wearing that ridiculous stocking cap?"

Shit. Jaycee started to make a comment about her hat but thought better of it. By the way Tessa was twisting every comment, Jaycee would be better served to keep the conversation on Tessa, not Jaycee.

"It's time for you to go home."

"I can't." Tessa smirked.

Jaycee wasn't sure if she should take the bait, but she needed to keep the focus on Tessa. "Why not?"

"I don't have a car."

Dumb. How had she missed it? Probably because Tessa had nearly scared her to death. "Where's it at?"

"The bar. Did you think I'd drive after I'd been drinking?" Tessa turned up her nose.

One point for Tessa, but Jaycee wasn't ready to give her any more. "You took an Uber then?"

Tessa nodded and moved toward Jaycee. "I guess I'll have to spend the night." Tessa undid the top button of her blouse. "Do you want me to do this myself, or do you want to?"

Jaycee stiffened. This couldn't be happening. She'd longed for a reconciliation with Tessa for the last ten months. Now that Tessa stood in front of her, she wanted Tessa to go away. "Stop. Why are you doing this?"

"I've missed you. Why else?" Tessa's eyes filled with sadness. "I didn't realize what I had until it was gone."

Jaycee took a step back. Could she believe Tessa, or was the sadness a put on, a way to play on Jaycee's sympathies? "Why now?"

Tessa paused for a few beats before she said, "The holidays."

Could it be true? Had the holidays been hard on Tessa? After all, they had spent the last fifteen years together at every family gathering.

Even though Tessa had started a fire in the fireplace, the room seemed colder. Jaycee walked to the fire and held her hands out toward the flames that licked at the log. She still didn't know how to respond, so she said nothing.

Tessa moved up beside her and put her hands out as if to warm them. "I remembered how you always loved to have the fire going when it got cold. That's why I got it started for you."

"That was nice. Thank you." *Really?* That was the best response she could come up with?

"You're welcome." Tessa moved closer so their shoulders were touching. "We could pull out some blankets and rediscover each other by the light of the fire."

Jaycee cursed herself when a tingle ran through her body. It had been a long time since she'd had sex. She'd pleasured herself, but it hadn't been the same without a partner. She longed to be touched. As she considered it, Piper's face flashed into her mind, and Jaycee's breath caught.

Tessa turned to face Jaycee. By the smirk on Tessa's face, she must have thought she'd caused Jaycee's sharp inhalation. With Tessa being nearly the same height as Jaycee, they stood face to face.

Tessa's ice blue eyes chilled Jaycee, so she broke eye contact and moved toward the couch.

"You want me over there?" Tessa smiled, obviously mistaking Jaycee's reaction.

"I need to go to the bathroom," Jaycee said over her shoulder as she rushed out of the room.

Tessa laughed. "I'll be waiting for you."

Jaycee hurried to the bathroom, and closed and locked the door, something she normally didn't do. She needed to think, so she rested her back against the barrier between her and Tessa and closed her eyes. During the entire encounter, Piper kept invading her thoughts.

Piper was a friend, regardless of what nearly happened earlier. There was nothing between them, so why should she have any bearing on what Jaycee decided to do?

If she crossed the line with Tessa, somehow it would feel as if she were cheating on Piper. She put her hand against her forehead with such force it stung and made a loud pop. What the hell was she thinking? *Misplaced loyalty?*

She took a deep breath and turned toward the mirror. When she looked into her own eyes, she laughed. "Dumbass," she said aloud. "What kind of moron worries about cheating on someone they aren't dating?"

Jaycee shook her head. Even though it was illogical, she couldn't shake the way she felt. When had her thought process become so convoluted? Nobody would say having sex with the woman who was still her wife could be cheating on the woman she'd never had a relationship with.

Maybe she should just do it, to prove she hadn't lost her mind. She'd almost convinced herself of that when her gaze landed on her stocking cap. Piper's soft brown eyes and wide smile flashed in her mind.

"Damn it." She plopped onto the lid of the toilet and put her head in her hands. She pulled her phone out of her pocket, feeling guilty that she was even having this internal struggle.

Tessa had a way of twisting her in knots, and she knew when she went back into the living room the onslaught would continue. Would she be strong enough to resist? After all, she would have done anything to get Tessa back only a few short months ago.

That was until everything changed on Thanksgiving. Remembering Thanksgiving solidified her decision. She scrolled through her apps until she landed on the one she was looking for.

Jaycee was still a bit shaky inside but drew on her professional experience to appear at ease as she walked into the living room.

Tessa was sprawled on the couch and had unbuttoned her shirt the rest of the way. Her lacy bra left little to the imagination. Not that Jaycee had to imagine Tessa's body since she knew it like her own.

"I sent for an Uber. It should be here in fifteen minutes," Jaycee said.

"You did what?" Tessa cocked her head.

"An Uber will be here soon." Jaycee pointed toward Tessa's stomach. "You probably want to button that up, so you don't give the driver a shock." The time in the bathroom must have done her good because her self-doubt was in check. *Good.* She'd been afraid she'd crumble in Tessa's presence, but the unbuttoned shirt had been almost laughable.

Tessa sprang from the couch, and Jaycee saw the anger that raged under the surface. An anger that had never been a part of their relationship until Tessa filed for divorce. Not that she'd ever been violent, but in the past nine months, her words had wounded more times than Jaycee cared to admit. Jaycee braced for the verbal attack.

Only a few feet from Jaycee, Tessa stopped, and a mask came down over her face. "Oh, come on, babe. We can send them away."

Unbelievable. Was Tessa still trying to seduce her? Doubt niggled in Jaycee's mind. Maybe Tessa sincerely missed her to go to such lengths.

As if reading Jaycee's mind, Tessa said, "I can't help that I missed you. We were together a long time." Tessa was right about that. She'd spent most of her adult life with Tessa. Jaycee's jaw tightened. "You should have thought of that a year ago." Jaycee hoped her words came out more confident than she felt.

"I know. I screwed up."

Jaycee stared at Tessa slack-jawed. Had Tessa just admitted she'd been wrong? How many nights had Jaycee cried to Tessa that she didn't understand how she could walk away without trying, and how many emails had she written that went unanswered?

"Christmas wasn't the same without you." Tessa took Jaycee's hand. "The kids were heartbroken when nobody brought a silly game. It felt like something was missing. There wasn't near the laughter without you." Tessa squeezed her hand. "We wrapped up by eight o'clock."

Eight? The Wilsons' parties normally went to at least midnight. "How are the kids?" Jaycee knew she shouldn't ask, but she'd missed them so. It was as if a piece of her heart had been torn out.

Tessa smiled. "The twins are doing great in school. I think they were made for college. Especially Megan. She's thinking about pledging a sorority."

Jaycee smiled and shook her head. "They better be careful. She'll be leading it if they let her in."

"Right." Tessa laughed and took Jaycee's other hand. "Josh is a starter this year."

"Did he finally master his free throws?" Jaycee's heart soared. For the past three years, he'd practiced so hard. She'd spent hours in the driveway with him, retrieving balls and watching his shooting form.

"Um, yeah…sure. I guess," Tessa said.

"He had the mechanics down. It was always his nerves that got in the way."

Tessa squinted as if she were trying to make sense of what Jaycee said, but she recovered and said, "And Barty and Sylvia are growing like weeds."

Ouch. It was the young ones who changed the most. After nearly a year, they'd likely grown a few inches.

"What do you say? Should we cancel the Uber?" Tessa asked.

It was as if a bucket of ice water was thrown on Jaycee. She let go of Tessa's hands and stepped back. "No," she practically shouted. "You need to go." How had she almost fallen for it?

Tessa's eyes turned to steel. "What the fuck is wrong with you? Just cancel the damned ride already."

Jaycee shook her head, hoping to clear the rest of the thoughts that Tessa had tried to weave into her mind. Part of her couldn't believe that Tessa would stoop so low to use their—no, Tessa would say her—nieces and nephews. "Why are you really here?"

"I told you. I miss you."

A thought grenade went off in Jaycee's mind. "Oh, my god, she dumped you. That's why you're here."

"What are you going on about?" Tessa scowled, but Jaycee could tell that her words landed a blow.

"Son of a bitch. She dumped you, and you couldn't stand to be alone, so you show up here."

"Like you have room to talk," Tessa shouted. She motioned toward her still open shirt. "I offered all this to you, and you didn't bite, but as soon as I mentioned the kids, you get all dewy-eyed. I thought you were going to rip your clothes off and do me right here after I mentioned them."

"Don't be so crude." Jaycee turned up her nose.

"Oh, does it offend you?" Tessa sneered. "It just reinforces why I left you in the first place. You were in love with my family, not me."

It was an argument they'd had before. Could Jaycee deny it? Before Tessa could respond, Jaycee's phone dinged. "Your ride's here."

Tessa's jaw tightened, and her nose flared. She pointed at Jaycee's tie. "I don't know who you were all dressed up for, but she's obviously not that into you since you were home so early." Tessa shrugged. "Your loss. You had your chance."

"Don't forget to button up," Jaycee said as she gestured toward Tessa's shirt.

Chapter Sixteen

Piper kicked the garbage can but still couldn't pull the overstuffed bag out. Grasping it tighter, she swung her leg back again.

"Whoa." Sergio rushed across the kitchen. "You're either going to hurt yourself or mess up my clean kitchen. Neither would make me happy."

She let go of the bag and muttered a string of curse words under her breath.

"Aren't you a ray of sunshine? Want to tell me what's bothering you?" Sergio pulled the drawstring and cinched the bag closed.

"I hate that stupid trash can. You have to be a bodybuilder to get the bag out." Piper glowered for emphasis.

Sergio pulled it out with one hand and spun it around a few times before he tied a knot. "Or maybe you just need to be taller than five-foot-nothing."

"I'm five-foot-two and three-quarters," she snapped. She turned and started toward the door.

"Oh, no, you don't," Sergio called. "You can't just assault my garbage can and then waltz out of here like nothing happened."

Piper stopped and turned. She knew Sergio only wanted to lighten the mood, but she didn't want her mood lightened. "I'd hardly call it an assault."

He pointed at her shoe print on the side of the can. "Evidence says otherwise."

"Send me a bill for the damages," she said without humor. It wasn't fair to Sergio, but she just wanted to get the rest of the chores done and go home. She still had a few things to clean up in the main room before she could call it a night, so she continued toward the door.

"Piper. Please, stop."

"What do you want from me?" Piper hated that her voice came out in a whine, so she steeled her jaw and added, "I've got things to do."

"Does this crappy mood have anything to do with a certain hottie in a stocking cap?"

Piper glared. "Why would it have anything to do with her?"

"Let's see." He rubbed his chin. "You were buoyant on New Year's Eve and practically giddy the next day, but then every day after, you've become more and more sullen. Don't think I haven't noticed that Jaycee hasn't been around since, either."

"It shouldn't surprise me." Piper dismissively flicked her wrist, trying to convey a casualness she didn't feel.

"Why's that?"

"She disappeared after Thanksgiving, too. It's starting to be her pattern."

He pursed his lips. "I see. And have you reached out to her?"

"Well...no, but she knows where I am. I don't know where she is."

"Ah that's right." He grinned. "Apparently, she didn't give you her phone number."

"You know I have her number, so don't be a smartass."

"Is there a reason you're choosing not to use it?"

"Like I said, she knows where I am." It even sounded absurd to her own ears, but she didn't have anything better to go with, so why not double down? "The holidays are over. She did her good deed for the year. Alleviated her guilt, so now she can go on with her life. Forget us until next season."

Sergio wrinkled his nose and snorted. "Do you really believe that?"

"How else do you explain it?"

He shrugged. "I'm not sure until you give me the rest of the story."

Her eyes widened. How had he known she wasn't telling him everything?

Sergio laughed. He approached her and put his arm across her shoulders. "How about you finish cleaning up in the other room, and I'll finish up in here? Then I'll pour you a stiff drink, and we can talk."

"Coffee?"

"What else?" He winked. "Unless you have something stronger in your purse."

She smiled slightly for the first time. "Sorry, I'm afraid I left it in my other purse."

"Coffee will have to do then."

"But I should get the kids home. It's after eight."

"And it's Saturday, so they don't have to get up for school. Besides, they were having a blast with the arcade basketball game that came yesterday."

"Our mysterious donor strikes again."

"Yep, sure, it's a mystery." He chuckled. "It's almost like our donor is trying to send a message. Perhaps an offering."

Piper glowered and headed toward the door with the garbage.

It hadn't taken long for her to finish up. As she

worked, she debated with herself. Should she tell Sergio what had happened? Normally, she'd keep things like that to herself, but lately, something inside of her had shifted. Since Emma left, she'd been guarded with her feelings. She'd stayed closed off and focused on Paxton and Maddie.

By the time she sat down with the steaming coffee in front of her, she'd convinced herself to be honest with Sergio. She breathed in the floral scent of the brew. She absentmindedly ran her spoon around her cup as she waited for Sergio to return to the table.

"I know these aren't macarons." He set a plate of scones on the table. "But they'll have to do."

"They look amazing. Are they for tomorrow's breakfast?"

"Yep. It's a new recipe. I hope you like them."

She put one of the scones on the napkin in front of her and tore off a piece. "Oh, god, this is delicious." She moaned as she chewed.

He clapped his hands. "Marvelous. I wanted to surprise Caleb with them. They're his favorite."

"Mmm," she said through a mouthful. "You've outdone yourself."

His cheeks reddened slightly as he grinned. He waved off her compliment and said, "Are you ready to talk?"

She nodded but stuffed another bite into her mouth to buy more time.

He sat across from her and took a bite of his own scone. He didn't try to goad her into talking; instead, he patiently waited.

She ate nearly half her scone before she decided it was time to speak. "You were right earlier."

"About what?" He smiled. "I'm right about lots

of things, so I'm afraid you'll have to narrow it down a bit."

"Hmm, that's not what Caleb told me."

"The scoundrel. What does he know?"

She knew Sergio was letting her stall and suspected he knew that should he push she'd likely bolt for the door. "You're right about Jaycee causing me grief."

"What happened? You seemed to be getting along great." He nodded. "There was some serious chemistry oozing off the two of you."

"Huh-uh, we're just friends." She shot him a warning look.

He held up his hands. "My bad. I just thought... oh, never mind. I need to let you tell your story."

She took a sip of her coffee before she continued. "We had a really nice time on New Year's Eve. Jaycee stayed around to help me clean up, and we were sitting in here." She pointed to the spot where Jaycee sat. "Drinking our sparkling grape juice and talking. Then she found the Milwaukee countdown on her phone."

He nodded and took another bite of his scone.

"I'm not sure what happened." She let out a long breath. "We were dancing to *Auld Lang Syne* and then..." She took another sip of her coffee.

He leaned forward. "And then what?"

"I don't know." She shook her head. Her pulse quickened as she remembered the moment. "I think... uh...I think we almost kissed."

"It's about damned time." He slapped his hand on the table in front of him, causing the coffee in his cup to splash over the rim and run down the side.

"The key word was—almost." Piper sighed again. "We didn't, but I thought we were going to.

Then Maddie burst into the room."

"Ugh." Sergio stopped wiping up his spill and put his hand against his forehead. "Kids sometimes have the worst timing."

"Or the best." Piper crossed her arms over her chest. "I don't need that kind of complication right now. Not ever."

He tilted his head and raised his eyebrows. "And why is that?"

"I'm too busy. Working. Raising two kids. Trying to finish school. Besides, I'm not looking for a relationship."

"Sometimes those things have a tendency to find us when we're not looking." Sergio waved his hands in the air as if in celebration. "We'd be so happy if you found someone."

Piper intentionally narrowed her eyes to slits and glared.

"Apparently, that wasn't the answer you wanted to hear."

"No. I wanted you to talk some sense into me."

"She's adorable and sweet. And I haven't seen you smile that big since I've known you. Plus, you're always taking care of everyone else, maybe it's time to let someone care for you for a change." He sat up straight and drew his lips together. "Oh. By the look you're giving me, I got it wrong again."

"Shit. I don't know." Piper put her hands over her face. "It doesn't matter, anyway. She ran off and hasn't come back."

"Ran off?" He scrunched up his face. "I can't see her running off."

"Right after Maddie interrupted us on New Year's Eve, Jaycee practically bolted." Piper's shoulders fell.

"And I haven't heard from her since."

He grinned. "Except we got that huge anonymous grocery delivery on Wednesday, complete with five big bags of M&M's. And then the arcade game that came yesterday."

"We don't know for sure she's the one sending them." Piper crossed her arms over her chest. "It could be anyone."

"Okay, if it helps you sleep at night."

"Don't be an ass." She tried to glare at him, but she couldn't sustain it. She didn't have the energy. The last few days, she'd been drained. What she normally breezed through took all her will to finish. She knew it had to do with Jaycee, but she hated it. "I can't, Sergio. I don't want to feel like this."

"Like what?"

"Scared. Hurt. Angry. Confused. Like I'm on a roller coaster." She put her hands on top of her head. "Ugh. But…damn it…I miss her." She slammed her hand on the table. "There I said it."

"Then what are you going to do about it?"

"Do?" Piper pulled back as if a snake had shot out of Sergio's mouth. "Nothing," she said with conviction. "She's made her choice."

"Did you ever think she might be freaking out, too?"

"Who's freaking out?" Piper put on her best stoic face but then laughed. "Fine. I'm freaking out, but why would she be?"

"Isn't she going through an ugly divorce?"

"Well, yeah."

"Didn't you go through an ugly breakup four years ago?"

What was he getting at? "You know I did."

"And you're still feeling the effects, and hers is a lot more recent."

Duh. Why hadn't she considered that? Because she was so wrapped up in her own insecurities that she couldn't think clearly. She pursed her lips and nodded. "You might have a point."

"Then call her. Tell her you're crazy about her."

"Stop." She held up her hand. "Neither of us is ready for that. I just want my friend back."

"Then you better do something about it."

Chapter Seventeen

Piper stared at her cellphone. *Ten o'clock.* Was it too late to call? It was Saturday night, so probably not. She set the phone on the end table and stood up from the couch. She should check on Maddie and Paxton. *Ridiculous.* Still, she made her way down the short hallway. They were likely sound asleep after how much they'd played with that silly basketball game.

She opened Paxton's door a crack. Since he no longer slept with a nightlight, she had to let her eyes adjust before she could make out his form on the bed. Piper resisted going farther into his room for fear of waking him. He groaned in his sleep, rolled over, and pulled the covers over his head. Apparently, he'd sensed the light from the hallway. Quietly, she shut his door.

Next, she turned the knob to Maddie's room. When Piper pushed open the door, Maddie's nightlight made it much easier to check on her. Maddie's arms were wrapped around her large teddy bear, and her head rested on its chest. Piper's heart filled. Just like Piper had been at her age, Maddie was so tiny that sometimes Piper wanted to wrap her up and protect her from the world.

Piper sighed. Who was she kidding? Maddie might be small, but she was scrappy just like her mom. These two were her heart—her life. Did she have any room for anyone else? Sergio thought so.

Stop. Jaycee was simply a friend. That was what Piper needed. Nothing more. Besides, the kids didn't need that kind of complication, either. Another adult to disappoint them. *No.* That wasn't fair. Maddie didn't remember Emma, and Paxton only had a vague recollection of her, so it wasn't as if they were traumatized. It was only Piper who had been.

Piper glanced at the sleeping Maddie one last time before she slowly closed the door. She made her way back into the living room and sat. She glanced at her cellphone. Should she? The longer she sat here and thought about it, the less likely it would be that she'd do anything.

She snatched the phone off the end table. An idea flashed in her mind. She could open the door and then see if Jaycee walked through it. Piper's thumbs flew over the screen.

She hit send before she had time to chicken out. *Hi. Can you talk?*

It couldn't have been more than ten seconds before Piper's phone rang.

~ · ~ · ~ · ~ · ~

Jaycee's pulse raced as she waited for Piper to answer the phone. Maybe she'd been impulsive calling, instead of answering Piper's text. *Shit.* Should she hang up? Before she could decide, the ringing stopped.

"That was quick," Piper's voice came through the speaker.

Jaycee's pulse raced at the sound of Piper's voice. "Is everything okay?"

"Yeah...uh...I just hadn't heard from you, and I, well I—"

"I'm so sorry," Jaycee said. "I should have called."

"I could have called, too."

"Hey, yeah, you could have." Jaycee laughed, but she feared it came out as a nervous giggle. "Oh, fuck."

"I shouldn't have called so late."

"I called you."

"That's right. You called me." Piper laughed, and it came out as unnatural as Jaycee's had. "But I texted."

"Yes, you did." Since they'd met, they'd had an easy rapport, so this was painfully awkward. "I've missed you," Jaycee blurted out. *Oh, god.* Why did she say that?

"I've missed you, too."

The tightness in Jaycee's chest lessened. She almost said, *you did?* but that would send them down another weird path.

Before Jaycee could respond, Piper said, "Jaycee, I want you to know I really value your friendship."

Friendship. Why had her heart just sunk? Because she was being an idiot. She'd obviously imagined the near kiss. She valued Piper's friendship, too, and certainly didn't want to screw it up. "I feel the same."

"Good. I'm glad we cleared that up."

"Me too." Jaycee wanted to move on from this conversation, so she said, "What have you been up to this week?"

"Maddie's about to lose a tooth."

"Her first?"

"Yep."

"Uh-oh, is she traumatized?"

Piper laughed. "Hardly. I have to keep telling her not to mess with it. Paxton's told her all about the tooth fairy, so she's approaching it like an entrepreneur."

Jaycee laughed, imagining Maddie trying to pull it out. "Priceless."

"That child is going to test me in ways that Paxton never did."

With the ice broken, their conversation flowed. Nearly an hour later, Jaycee was shocked when she glanced at the clock. "Shit, do you know what time it is?"

"Holy hell, it's nearly eleven thirty," Piper said.

"How'd it get to be so late?"

"You're a motormouth."

"Me?" Jaycee laughed. "I think there were a few times you went a good three minutes without taking a breath."

Piper laughed. "Maybe. Hey, before we went off on a tangent, you were going to tell me what happened when you got home on New Year's Eve."

"Oh, yeah." *Shit.* Jaycee had been relieved when their conversation had been sidetracked. She'd chalked it up to the universe sparing her. Not that it should be a big deal since nothing happened, and Jaycee and Piper were just friends. "I had a visitor when I got home."

"Visitor? That late at night?"

"An unwelcome one."

"A skunk?" Piper guessed.

Jaycee stifled a laugh. She'd never liked it when someone name called their ex, so she bit back the joke she could have made at Tessa's expense. "No. Tessa."

"Tessa?" Piper's voice rose an octave. "What did

she want?"

"She was drunk." While Jaycee wouldn't lie to Piper, she'd prefer not to get into all the ugly details of the evening, either. "Her girlfriend broke up with her."

"Oh, I see," Piper said. Was there an edge to Piper's voice, or was Jaycee imagining it? "Does she want to get back together with you?"

"She was drunk."

"Yeah, you already said that."

Oh, crap. Jaycee was making a mess of this. By the tone of Piper's voice, she thought something had happened between her and Tessa. *Damn it.* Why should it matter if it had? Jaycee closed her eyes and took a deep breath. It did matter, and she needed to get this right. "She started out flirtatious. When I wouldn't bite and called her an Uber, she got angry."

"Oh, so she didn't stay?"

"God, no!"

"Okay. I just asked."

"Sorry, I wasn't yelling at you. I just didn't want you...uh...I mean, I wouldn't want anyone to think that something was going on with us." *Wow.* Could she come off any more obvious and ridiculous? "I just...it's over, that's all."

"Oh, okay. You didn't want to try and salvage anything?"

"No. It was just uncomfortable. Unpleasant." Jaycee couldn't tell Piper that it was Piper's face that kept invading her thoughts.

"You said she got angry. Did she do anything to you?" The concern was evident in Piper's voice.

"No. Just yelled a bit. Nothing major."

"Did she get angry a lot when you were together?"

Piper asked.

Jaycee was taken aback by the question. "No, actually, no. Her anger is something new. Tessa has always been stoic—a little cold—so being fiery and angry isn't like her. The divorce brought out the worst in her."

"But she wanted it?"

"She asked me for it, so she must have. No, she definitely wanted it," Jaycee responded. "It's just strange after living with someone for that long to see a side in them you've never seen before."

"Maybe it's more common than you think. I thought I knew Emma, too, but I was wrong."

"True." Jaycee sighed. "We were having such a nice conversation. Can we talk about something else?"

"Actually, I wanted to see if you wanted to go bowling with me and the kids tomorrow."

"That sounds perfect."

Chapter Eighteen

Jaycee pulled off her bow tie and unhooked her suspenders. She couldn't show up for lunch with Piper looking so much like Jaycee Re-Ward. Every time she saw a bus with her picture on it, she cringed. She'd always hated the gigantic image that made her look like King Kong, but she hated it more now that Piper had come into her life.

She pulled a stocking cap from her top desk drawer. She'd bought several and had a stash at home, work, and in her Range Rover. Even though she knew it was ludicrous, it was her security blanket in case she stumbled upon someone from the shelter. The charade would have to end eventually, but she couldn't think about it today. She didn't want to keep Piper waiting.

Things had been good between the two, and they'd fallen back into their easy friendship. While they saw each other frequently, they'd not had a repeat of their near kiss on New Year's Eve. In the month since, things had evolved. Jaycee volunteered at the shelter twice a week, but they'd begun to get together away from DOTS, mostly with Paxton and Maddie. Yesterday, after they'd taken the kids to the movies, Piper proposed they meet for lunch while the kids were in school. Jaycee had jumped at the chance. She adored the kids, but it would be nice to have the chance to talk—just the two of them. Jaycee snorted. It wasn't as if they never talked. Piper called nearly every night once she'd put the kids to bed, but there was something different about being face to face. Jaycee adjusted her cap and stepped out of her office. Georgette was at her desk, pounding away on her keyboard. Jaycee had never met anyone who typed louder. As Jaycee started to make a joke about the keyboard, she thought better of it. She didn't have time for a sparring match with Georgette or she'd be late.

"I'm heading out for lunch," Jaycee said.

"Uh-huh." Georgette continued to pound on the keys. "Punxsutawney Phil saw his shadow today. So you've got six more weeks to wear that silly hat that fools nobody."

"Happy Groundhog Day." Jaycee wouldn't bite at the hat comment. "I'm not sure when I'll be back."

Georgette's attack on the keyboard stopped, and she looked up for the first time. "I see. Meeting Piper?" she asked, drawing Piper's name out.

"In fact, I am."

"You're not going to ask how I know?"

"Wasn't planning on it." Jaycee stifled a grin. She knew it drove Georgette crazy when Jaycee didn't take her bait.

"You probably think I figured it out because you stripped down and put on that beanie."

Jaycee wrinkled her brow. "Don't say it like I took off all my clothes, and it's a stocking cap—not a beanie."

Georgette shrugged and rolled her eyes. "It's not the way you're dressed. It's that look in your eyes. Gives you away every time. How that woman doesn't know you're hot for her, god only knows."

"Stop," Jaycee said. She almost said, *I'm not hot for her,* but didn't. Hot for her sounded so crude, but she'd be skating the truth if she denied it. "I'm gonna be late if you keep yammering at me."

"I'll see you tomorrow." Georgette smirked.

"I might be back before you leave."

"Sure you will. If someone calls about a showing, what do you want me to do?"

"Schedule them for tomorrow."

"Will do." Georgette snickered. "Yep, you'll be back."

Jaycee glared on the way out the door but didn't say anything other than *goodbye*.

ৠৠৠৠ

Jaycee was already seated at the table when Piper arrived. Piper muttered under her breath. She hated being late, but she'd gotten tied up on a phone call with one of the organizers of the Poverty Summit.

Jaycee smiled and waved when she saw her. As Piper approached the table, Jaycee got to her feet.

"I'm so sorry," Piper said. "I got stuck on a phone call."

"No worries," Jaycee said as they hugged.

If Piper was being honest, the beginning and end of their meetings were some of her favorite times since she was wrapped in Jaycee's warm embrace.

"Did you order yet?" Piper asked as she sat.

Jaycee smiled. "I might have told them to bring out some poutine when they saw you arrive."

Piper groaned and grabbed her stomach. "You're going to be the reason I gain a hundred pounds."

"You don't have to eat it all." Jaycee winked.

"Don't swear at me." Piper pointed at Jaycee and pretended to glare.

"Hey, not to change the subject from your massive weight gain, but did I hear Sergio say you were preparing to speak at a conference?"

Shit. The Poverty Summit was something Piper hadn't wanted Jaycee to find out about. "It's no big deal." *Wow.* That was an outright lie, and it immediately made her feel uncomfortable. She didn't lie, and she certainly didn't lie to Jaycee.

A puzzled look passed over Jaycee's face, but then she shrugged. "Oh, okay. I must have misunderstood. When I heard Sergio telling one of the other volunteers, he sounded pretty stoked."

"You know Sergio. He gets excited when he tries a new laundry detergent."

Jaycee laughed. "He does get rather...um... flamboyant."

"Exactly." Piper felt guilty for leading Jaycee down this path, but she didn't want to talk about her speaking engagement.

The waiter arrived with a heaping plate of poutine, which ended any talk of the conference.

"Holy hell." Jaycee stabbed two french fries with her fork. A large cheese curd clung to one of the fries. "Look at that cheese."

Piper had already speared her own bite, so she nodded in response. The flavors erupted in her mouth, and she closed her eyes. "Mmm, this is so good," she said through her bite.

"Are you going to pull a *When Harry Met Sally*?"

Piper opened her eyes and grinned when she saw the twinkle in Jaycee's expressive brown eyes. "You mean the orgasm scene?"

"Yep. With the sounds you're making, I was starting to worry." Jaycee nodded to an older woman several tables over. "I don't want her asking the waiter what we're eating."

Piper gathered up another bite, making sure it had the right proportion of all the ingredients. When she brought the bite toward her mouth, she moaned a bit louder. "Uh-oh, I think it's starting to happen."

Jaycee's gaze darted around to the nearby tables.

Piper put her fork down and burst out laughing. "You really thought I was going to do it, didn't you?"

With an exaggerated gesture, Jaycee clamped her hand against her chest. "Jesus. You had me worried for a minute."

Piper winked and picked up her fork. "I like to keep you on your toes."

જી.જી.ૐ.ૐ

Jaycee wasn't sure how the time had disappeared. It was the first they'd sat across the table from each other at a restaurant without Paxton and Maddie. It felt like a date, but she quickly pushed the thought aside. Thinking like that could only lead to trouble or heartbreak.

She'd laughed so hard that at one point tears ran down her face. Here she was worried about Piper causing a scene, but it was her laughter that had garnered stares from nearby tables. The only time things had almost gotten awkward was when a client had recognized her and approached the table. While she'd told Piper she sold houses for a living, she worried the client might give her full identity away, so she excused herself and went to his table. It was a relief when she returned, and Piper hadn't questioned her.

"I know you probably can't answer this, but I have to ask," Jaycee said. "Is everything okay with Mitzy? Things seem off with her."

Piper let out a deep breath. "Off the record, I'm worried about her."

"I've noticed that Donovan's been solo quite a bit the last few weeks, and he doesn't look good." Jaycee paused and measured her words.

Piper caught the hesitation and said, "Just say it."

"I don't want to come off wrong." Jaycee's heart rate accelerated. "But Donovan was always put together, but he's starting to look...um—"

"Homeless?"

"Thank god you said it." Jaycee let out the breath she'd not realized she'd been holding.

"Yeah, he's struggling. They've always been the dynamic duo, so he's lost without her, but I can't get him to say much."

"Where's she been?" Jaycee knew Piper would likely not answer the question, but she had to ask.

Piper shot a glance at the nearby tables and leaned in. "I don't know. She won't talk, either, but usually when someone stays away for long stretches, it's never good. It makes my heart hurt."

"I'm sorry. I know how much those two mean to you." There wasn't much more she could say, and she wanted to erase the worry lines in Piper's forehead. "It was great seeing Ole Freddie again. Rehab agreed with him."

"Doesn't he look amazing?" Piper clasped her hands together. "Let's just hope this time it sticks."

Jaycee knew the likelihood was slim, but she wanted to hold on to hope along with Piper.

Piper glanced at her watch. "Ugh, I have to get home before school lets out."

Jaycee didn't want the day to end. It had been nearly perfect. "I have an idea."

"About?"

"After the big snow last night, I bet the sledding hills are perfect. Would you and the kids like to join me?"

"Going by yourself if we can't make it?" The laugh lines in Piper's face deepened.

"I just might." Jaycee jutted out her jaw. "I don't have to have an entourage for sledding."

"But it's much more fun with one."

"Exactly."

Chapter Nineteen

The snow was coming down heavier as Jaycee parked on the street near DOTS. Hopefully, it would keep some people away from the sledding hills, or possibly, it would lead to more people. She shrugged. They were going regardless of the crowd size.

Jaycee was giddy as she jumped out of her Range Rover. It had been a few years since she'd been sledding. Memories flooded her mind. *No.* She wouldn't let the past bring her down—not today. She loved sledding and knew Paxton and Maddie would have a blast. That was what she needed to focus on.

When she got inside the shelter, Jaycee stomped the snow off her boots. Dinner was over, and only a few stragglers remained in the dining area. She scanned the room, but Piper and the kids weren't there. Of course, in her excitement, she'd arrived twenty minutes early.

Donovan was sitting at a table by himself, so she made her way over to him. He looked up when she approached and gave her a half-smile. His eyes were red and puffy. Had he been crying?

"Hey, Donovan. What's up?" Jaycee said.

"Hey," he answered.

"Are you busy?" Jaycee pointed to the chair across the table from him. "Mind if I sit down?"

"Sure."

"Sure, you mind, or sure, sit down?" Jaycee put her hand on the back of the chair but didn't pull it out.

He gave her another half-smile. "Sure, sit."

With his one-word answers, this conversation would be short. On the other hand, it might be long if she had to get at what was bothering him one word at a time. There was no doubt that something was wrong.

Jaycee sat. Should she ask about Mitzy? Something told her to save that question for later, so she said, "What are you reading?"

He held up a book. *The Outsiders.*

Ugh. Now she wasn't even getting one-word answers. "Great book. I didn't realize young people were still reading it today."

"Piper gave it to me."

Ahh. An improvement. A whole sentence. "Are you enjoying it?"

"It's all right."

"I remember how much it touched me." Jaycee put her hand over her heart. "It spoke to me as someone who felt like I was an outsider."

"Yeah. That part is pretty cool."

Progress. "I don't want to spoil it for you, so I won't say too much until you've finished. Maybe we can discuss it more once you're done."

"Okay."

Shit. Backslide. It was time to hit the issue head-on since this didn't seem to be working. "I can't help but notice you're not quite yourself. Is everything okay?"

Donovan shrugged.

"Do you want to talk about it?"

He shrugged again.

Jaycee would take not getting a *no* as a win. "I'm

a good listener. Would you mind if I took a guess at what's going on?"

"Go for it." He looked down and fanned through the pages of the book. Jaycee suspected he wasn't really seeing them, but it gave him something to do with his hands.

"I've noticed Mitzy hasn't been around as much. Is something going on with her?"

He nodded.

"Did you have a fight?"

"Kinda."

Shit. She hated *kinda* as an answer. It meant that she'd have to play twenty questions, but at least he was talking. "Did you break up?"

Donovan shook his head.

Good. With her pending divorce, she tried to avoid talking about breakups whenever possible. "Did she do something to upset you?"

Donovan nodded.

Yes or no questions were getting her nowhere. Where was Piper when she needed her? Piper was the social worker and would know better what to say. What did a Realtor know about these things? "I can tell you're hurting. Sometimes it helps to talk things out. Would you tell me what happened?"

Donovan stopped rifling through the book and looked up. His eyes held a world of pain and sadness. Jaycee wanted to hug him, but she knew that would likely scare him off.

He didn't say anything for several beats, but Jaycee let the uncomfortable silence between them build.

"She wants to get off the streets," Donovan said.

That sounded like a good thing, but Jaycee wouldn't interrupt, so she nodded.

"I want that, too, but we have different ideas about how to get it." He looked down at the book again, but he didn't fan the pages. "I've been trying to find a job. A legit job. Piper says I'm smart and could make it in college. I want to do that, too." He held up the book. "I love to read and learn shit."

"That sounds like a great plan." Jaycee's thoughts spun. She employed a lot of people. Maybe she could hire him. *No.* That would likely be a bad idea, but she knew plenty of people and could probably help open some doors for him.

"Mitzy doesn't think so. Says she doesn't want to work some dead-end minimum wage job."

Jaycee's heart sank. This didn't sound good. "Is that what you've been arguing about?"

Donovan nodded.

Jaycee knew she needed to choose her words carefully. "Is she doing something that makes you uncomfortable?"

Donovan nodded again.

"Would you tell me what it is?"

He looked up and glanced around the room before he met her gaze. He couldn't hold it and looked down. "You can't tell anyone."

Damn. She hated making a promise like that. What if it was something Piper needed to be involved with? As much as she wanted to know, she wouldn't trick him. "How about I say this? I won't tell anyone unless I think I have to."

Donovan looked up again and studied her. Their gazes locked for several seconds before he nodded. "That's fair enough."

She breathed a sigh of relief. "Tell me, what's going on?"

The floodgates opened, and monosyllabic Donovan suddenly found an entire litany of words. "She's been hanging with a different crowd. We met them at a party on New Year's Eve. I don't like the shit they're into, but Mitzy likes the money they flash around."

Donovan wrinkled his nose in a look of disgust. "They were buying drinks and passing around weed vapes like they were candy."

Weed vapes? Jaycee didn't want to interrupt but assumed he meant marijuana. She'd have to Google it later.

"They've got their hands in all kinds of shit, and they started recruiting Mitzy. Hardcore." He shook his head. "They was all over her. Telling her how beautiful she was and shit. She is and all, but it pissed me off. She's mine and they knew it, but they sure didn't act like they cared. Mitzy's a good woman, but she's insecure. She was eating up all their attention, and I got pushed to the side.

"I know what I am." Donovan met Jaycee's gaze and framed his face with his hands and then let them trail down his body. "I'm a short pudgy dude that still don't have all my parts right. I'm average at best, while Mitzy's a knockout."

Mitzy was a head turner, but Donovan wasn't giving himself enough credit. Jaycee debated with herself whether she should interrupt his story. Donovan liked people who shot from the hip, so she doubted he'd respond to platitudes. She could, however, state the truth. "I've seen the way Mitzy looks at you. She adores you."

Donovan gave Jaycee a slight smile. "Love only goes so far on the streets. Mitzy came from money. As she always says, she wants to live the lifestyle she was accustomed to. Says she wants to get us better hormones, not the black market shit we've been taking. I got long-range plans to get us there, but it ain't fast enough for her."

"She wants to take a short cut?"

"You got it. Fast and easy money. And when you look like Mitzy, there's more opportunity for that."

Jaycee's stomach roiled. She didn't like the turn the conversation was taking and wanted to shout out questions, but she bit them back. If she pushed, Donovan may snap out of his chatty streak.

"They've been after her to turn tricks. She keeps telling me that she ain't doing it. But then she disappears for a day or two and comes back bearing gifts. Last time, she gave me vintage T."

Jaycee assumed Donovan meant testosterone. She wondered how Donovan could tell the difference between black market and vintage, but now wasn't the time to ask.

"The first time she disappeared was New Year's Day. She came back with a wad of money. Said it could be our seed money for us to get a place." Donovan huffed. "Fucking seed money. Right."

"Have her...um...disappearances increased?" *God.* Did that come out sounding as ignorant as it felt?

Donovan didn't seem to notice. "Yep. Still says she ain't doing it. But where the hell else would she be? So now she's lying to me on top of everything else." Tears welled in Donovan's eyes.

Jaycee tried to hide the look of surprise on her face. How much call was there for a prostitute like Mitzy in a small city like Milwaukee?

"Dude. You need to control your expressions." Donovan pointed at Jaycee's face. "Market's hot for someone like Mitzy. Guys that want to pretend they're straight and still get their di....um..." Donovan fidgeted with his book. "I mean...uh...they still want a piece of what Mitzy's still packing...if you get my meaning."

Jaycee did. Loud and clear. She hoped her face wasn't as red as it felt. She wanted to come off worldly, not like someone who'd been as sheltered as she'd been her entire life. "Yeah, yeah. I understand."

"Then last night, I figured out she's been working off the clock."

Jaycee squinted. "Off the clock?"

"After hours." Donovan must have seen the look of confusion on her face, so he continued. "Staying overnight with a customer. She'd said she was crashing with one of the other girls from the party on the nights she wasn't at the shelter." He frowned. "It was warm the other night, so I decided to surprise her. Went to her friend's house, where she said she'd been staying. They hadn't seen her. They wouldn't tell me anything else. Course they're gonna cover for her."

Donovan rubbed the stubble on his chin and frowned before he shook his head. "That ain't true. I've been thinking something was up for a bit, so I was spying on her."

Jaycee's heart went out to him. She gave him a nod, encouraging him to go on.

Tears welled in his eyes. "I hung out near her friend's house, and I saw this big fancy car pull up. I just about vomited when Mitzy gave the guy a peck on the cheek before she got outta the car. A fucking peck on the cheek. That's just weird.

"She said she wants to make a better life for us." Donovan ran his hand through his short, disheveled hair, and his gaze bore into Jaycee. "But I don't want that. I don't want her to do those things for me. That's why I gotta get a job and make her stop."

Jaycee caught Piper out of the corner of her eye. She and the kids had just walked in. Piper must have seen the look on Donovan and Jaycee's faces since Piper grabbed Maddie as she started to make a dash toward them.

"What kind of work are you looking for?" Jaycee asked.

"I dunno." Donovan shrugged. "I want to go to school to be an architect. Build things." He pointed toward the ceiling. "I could design a much better shelter than this." He smiled. "Maybe one day I could work with Piper. She's learning how to run this place, and I could build her a better one."

Jaycee smiled. Statistically, she wondered how likely it was for someone living on the streets to achieve Donovan's dream. *No.* She couldn't think that way. Piper certainly didn't. A wave of guilt washed over her.

She'd been coming to the shelter for nearly three months, but she still clung to her biases about homeless people. The saying, *know better and then do better,* flashed in her mind. That was what she needed to remember. "Would you want to find work in construction?"

Donovan's eyes sprang to life for the first time. "That would be awesome." Then his face fell. "But there's no way I could get into something like that. From what I've heard, most times you gotta know someone. Besides, construction crews aren't exactly open to guys like me." He fanned the book again. "A year or so ago, I looked into what it would take to be an electrical or plumbing apprentice, but…" He shrugged. "It was just a dumb dream."

Jaycee's mind raced. She knew a female-owned handyman service that she'd thrown lots of business to over the years. Jenny owed her a favor or two. "I might know someone."

Donovan's eyes lit up. "Really?"

Jaycee wanted to kick herself. The last thing she wanted to do was get his hopes up. "No promises. But let me make a few calls and see what I can find."

"That'd be awesome." He smiled, and then his jaw tightened. "I'm gonna make it. The street ain't gonna get me."

"I know you will. You've got grit," Jaycee said and meant it.

"Piper's been an inspiration." He glanced toward where Piper and the kids stood talking with Sergio. "She's inspired lots of us."

It warmed Jaycee to see how much respect Piper garnered from everyone at the shelter. It was a testament to how much of herself Piper gave to everyone there. When Jaycee glanced toward Piper, her pulse quickened, so she quickly looked away and met Donovan's gaze.

"She's pretty special." Donovan gave Jaycee a knowing smile, which told Jaycee that her reaction to Piper hadn't gone unnoticed.

"She is that." Jaycee's cheeks were still warm.

"We're all so proud of her, speaking at a national convention and all." Donovan's smile widened. "She says she's gonna represent us well."

Jaycee's breath caught. *National convention?* Piper had told her that it was nothing special. The last thing she wanted was for Donovan to notice her reaction, even though it felt like a gut punch. Part of her wanted to question him about the conference, but he would be too astute for that. He'd figure out that Piper had told her little about it and clam up. "Speaking of, we're getting ready to hit the sledding hills. Care to join us?"

Donovan's eyes flashed before he slumped in his chair. "Mitzy might come back. I better stay here."

Something told Jaycee that Mitzy wouldn't be showing up tonight, but she knew Donovan would hold vigil anyway. "I got an idea. We can leave Mitzy a note with my cellphone number. If...uh...when she comes back, she can call me. She can either join us, or you can come back here to be with her."

Donovan shook his head. "We won't be able to get back and forth."

"I'll spring for an Uber."

"You sure?" Hope danced in his eyes.

"Positive."

His huge grin transformed his entire face, and Jaycee knew she'd made the right call.

Chapter Twenty

The snow was perfect for sledding, and the kids were having a blast. Piper had bowed out of the last round and sat on a bench by herself. It was movie snow—magical—the large flakes landed on her eyelashes and melted. She tilted her head to the sky but struggled to keep her eyes open as the flecks hit, so she closed them and enjoyed the feeling of the wet landing on her cheeks.

Piper's eyes popped open, and she glanced at the hill. Paxton would never forgive her if she missed what he was calling their epic run. *Whew.* They were still in line awaiting their turn. Even though it was getting late, she'd agreed to let them take one more turn on the hill since the crowd was finally dwindling. She was shocked at how many fools came out on a night like this.

Piper laughed. Obviously, she was one of those fools. Today had been perfect. Of course it was, she'd spent most of it with Jaycee. Their time together was becoming her favorite, and as soon as they parted, she couldn't wait for the next time. Jaycee was so good with Paxton and Maddie and the people at the shelter. She had such a pure heart, and her naivety was so endearing. At first, Piper had thought it was an act, but she'd soon discovered it wasn't.

A shiver ran through Piper's body, and it wasn't because of the cold. Piper was scrappy, a street fighter who'd found a way to take care herself, so Jaycee's ways were foreign, always looking out for her and the kids, checking in on her just to make sure she was all right. It felt amazing and scary all at once.

Piper was pulled out of her thoughts by yelling from the top of the hill. Jaycee, Paxton, Maddie, and Donovan waved their arms at her. They were next in line. She smiled and gave them a thumbs-up. She wasn't sure they could see it through the heavy snow, so she waved back.

Her heart filled as she watched Jaycee get the kids settled on their sled before she jumped on her own. Jaycee held up her hand and dropped it as if she were a flag person starting a race. The sleds careened down the hill, and the sounds of Maddie's happy screams filled the air. As they neared the bottom, Jaycee turned her sled hard to the left and went into a skid. A plume of snow shot into the air toward the other three. Piper couldn't see them any longer, but she heard the squeals and laughter. Jaycee rolled off her sled into the deep pile of snow.

Piper laughed and stood from the bench. She better go save Jaycee since the others had piled on her in retaliation for the snow shower Jaycee had sprayed on them. Maybe Piper should be cautious and protect her heart, but tonight, she just wanted to enjoy.

By the time Piper arrived, Jaycee was hopping around, trying to get the snow out from inside her jacket, while the other three laughed. Paxton, who was her serious child, laughed so hard that tears streamed down his face. It was good to see him being a kid.

"I hope you've learned your lesson." Piper pointed at Jaycee as she approached.

"Me? I was attacked by these savages." Jaycee

continued to jump around as snow fell from her coat.

"I saw it all. You started it." Piper grinned.

Donovan high-fived Paxton, then Maddie, who waved her tiny hand in the air.

Jaycee finally took off her coat and shook it out but continued to jump up and down.

"For god's sake, what are you doing?" Piper asked.

Jaycee put on an exaggerated glare at Donovan, Paxton, and Maddie. "One of these monsters put snow down my pants. And I'm not going to take my pants off to get it out."

Piper laughed.

Donovan shrugged and looked between Paxton and Maddie. "I didn't see who did it, did you?"

The kids giggled and shook their heads.

"I didn't see anything," Piper said. "The snow was coming down too hard."

"It's a conspiracy." Jaycee shook the leg of her pants and a clump of snow fell to the ground. "You're all in on it."

Piper threaded her arm through Jaycee's. "Come on, I'll buy you a hot chocolate to warm you up."

⁂

Sweat beaded on Jaycee's forehead as she took the last gulp of her hot chocolate. It was so good that she ran her tongue around the rim of the cup.

"Whoa, slow down." Piper held up her own cup of hot chocolate. "You're beet red."

Jaycee fanned her face. "I do feel a bit overheated."

"No duh. You just inhaled a steaming vat of liquid."

"Vat? I think that's an exaggeration." Jaycee blew out a breath. "Although I feel a bit like a fire-breathing dragon."

Piper shook her head. "I'm glad the kids are preoccupied." Piper motioned toward Paxton and Maddie, who were building tiny snowmen with Donovan on the next picnic table over. Their hot chocolate cups sat next to them. From the looks, they'd only drank about a quarter of theirs. "I taught them how to properly drink hot chocolate, so I don't need your bad influence leading them astray."

"I never claimed to be a hot chocolate drinking expert." Jaycee grinned.

"Do you drink your coffee that way?"

"I hate coffee."

"Tea?"

"Don't like that, either."

"Ah, that explains it. Amateur." Piper picked up her cup and brought it toward her lips. "You sip a hot drink, not chug it."

Jaycee turned her empty cup upside down. A few drops dribbled onto the snow. "I'll have to practice next time." Jaycee shrugged. "I'm out."

"I'd buy you another one for practice, but I'm afraid you'd scorch your insides if you screwed up again."

Jaycee patted her stomach. "Yeah, I don't think my tummy wants any more for a while."

Maddie bounded over with a huge smile on her face. She crawled up next to Piper and whispered in her ear.

Jaycee watched as Piper listened intently. It was these natural moments, when she was being fully present with her children, that took Jaycee's breath away. Piper had such a calm presence about her. Her eyes held wisdom beyond her years, and compassion radiated from her.

Piper smiled. She patted Maddie's back and said, "Go ahead."

Maddie gave Piper a huge toothless smile since she'd lost another tooth last week. Then Maddie slid off the bench next to Piper and ran around the table to where Jaycee sat. When Jaycee met Maddie's gaze, Maddie stood up to her full height.

"Jaycee," Maddie said.

"Yes."

"Would you like to come to my Valentine concert?"

"Tell her when and where," Piper coached.

Maddie stood up straighter and put a serious expression on her face. "It's at my school. It's on the twelfth, not the fourteenth, but it's still for Valentine's Day."

"You might want to tell her what time," Piper said.

"It's at seven o'clock," Maddie said and finally smiled.

Jaycee pulled out her phone and pretended to check her schedule. If anything was on it, she'd change it. Jaycee pursed her lips and nodded. "It looks like I can make it. I'll put it in my calendar now."

Maddie clapped and hopped on her toes. "Yea! I told Paxton you'd want to come." With those words, she was off to tell Paxton the news.

"Why wouldn't Paxton think I'd want to come?"

"He's more cautious than Maddie. It takes him a little longer to trust than it does her." Piper sighed. "I'm not sure if that's a good thing or a bad thing."

Jaycee considered Piper's words. "It's likely a little of both."

A sad expression passed over Piper's face, but then she smiled. "I suppose it is. He guards his heart more and tries to do the same for Maddie, but I know she drives him crazy when she throws caution to the wind."

Jaycee wasn't sure how to respond. She wanted to tell Piper that she'd never let Paxton and Maddie down, but she'd told her nieces and nephews the same and look how that turned out. Instead, Jaycee decided a change of subject was in order. "Hey, I've been meaning to ask you, Donovan mentioned that conference you were speaking at. I thought you said it wasn't a big deal."

An odd look flashed in Piper's eyes, but it was gone as quickly as it had come. *Panic?* No, that didn't make sense. Piper waved her hand. "It isn't."

"But he said it was a national conference." Jaycee probably shouldn't push, but Piper's reluctance to talk about it piqued Jaycee's curiosity.

"A small one." Piper pointed. "Look at the cute snowmen they made. They're adorable."

It wasn't lost on Jaycee that Piper was changing the subject, again. For a moment, Jaycee felt hurt that Piper didn't want to talk to her about it. Maybe Piper was just nervous about the presentation; judging by her reaction earlier, that was probably it.

Jaycee had gotten used to public speaking with her business, so she'd forgotten how anxious it made some people. That was probably why Piper kept avoiding talking about it. Jaycee's shoulders relaxed, and she switched her attention to the tiny snowmen lined up like little soldiers.

Chapter Twenty-one

"What the hell did you do to yourself?" Georgette said as soon as she walked into Jaycee's office.

"Do you like it?" Jaycee ran her hand through her short brown hair that was no longer her signature white blond.

"No! I hate it." Georgette turned up her nose as she walked toward Jaycee's desk. Slowly, she circled Jaycee, taking her in from all sides. "Nope, looks hideous from all angles."

Jaycee chuckled. "Please, tell me how you really feel."

Georgette reached out toward Jaycee's hair. As soon as her fingers made contact, she pulled her hand back as if she'd been burned. Georgette turned up her nose. "Child, why did you do something like that to yourself?"

Jaycee rolled her eyes. "Would you stop being so dramatic?"

Georgette pretended to fan herself, and her gaze darted around the room, and then she made a beeline for the couch.

"Jesus. You are not seriously going to—"

"I'm getting light-headed. I think I can make it." Georgette rushed across the room and threw herself onto the couch. Her high heels flew off as she fell. She put her arm across her forehead, covering her eyes.

"The nineteenth century called and wants its fainting couch back," Jaycee said as she stood. She walked over to where Georgette lay on the sofa softly moaning.

"You don't understand." Georgette kept her eyes covered as she spoke. "It's too much for a refined Southern woman to see such depravity."

"Oh. My. God. I colored my hair. I wasn't having sex with Lucifer on my desk."

"You might as well have been. It couldn't have been any more horrific than that." Georgette removed her arm from her eyes and pointed. She pretended to swoon and lay back against the pillow.

"And you're not Southern, either." Jaycee knew that would get a rise out of her.

Georgette lifted her head. Fire flashed in her pale blue eyes. "Bite your tongue. I am a Southern lady through and through." If anything, her accent was heavier than usual.

"You've been in Milwaukee most of your life." Jaycee shook her head, not wanting to engage in the conversation they'd had many times before, so she returned to her desk. "Let me know when you're ready to talk like a civilized human being."

Georgette moaned and snorted while Jaycee leafed through the files for their newest listings. With each passing year, she landed more and more high-end properties. Her reputation for closing the deal had served her well and allowed her to build a team of dedicated agents. Beyond that, she'd like to believe she could attribute much of her success to her honesty and being a straight shooter.

"Jaycee," Georgette called out in a weak voice.

Jaycee had to hand it to Georgette. She had

stamina once she decided to take a stand, but Jaycee wouldn't fall into her trap. The next file was her favorite property. She'd considered buying it herself. It was a much smaller house than her own, but it was quaint. It screamed family to her. The house she and Tessa had purchased never felt like a home. It was more like a museum or a hotel.

"Jaycee." Georgette's voice was louder this time.

"Yes, Georgette." Jaycee sighed and looked up from the file.

"I think I'm ready to discuss this. Your transgression."

Now it was a transgression. Jaycee shook her head, but she refused to take the bait. "Okay."

"Could you come sit over here with me?" Georgette rose to a sitting position.

Jaycee considered refusing, but it would only prolong the conversation. Reluctantly, she rose, went to the couch, and sat in a nearby armchair.

Georgette stared at her for what felt like an eternity, shaking her head and tsking.

"Come on. Hit me with it. Give me your best shot."

"No, no." Georgette fanned herself again. "A lady doesn't stoop to insults. What's done is done. I just don't understand why you'd do something like that to your gorgeous hair." Georgette narrowed her eyes. "You look ordinary."

"Perfect." Jaycee clapped her hands, knowing it would irritate Georgette.

"And why in God's name would you want to look ordinary?"

"I was going for incognito, but I'll take ordinary."

"And why would you want to be incognito? You

have a brand to maintain."

"Haven't you been paying any attention?" Jaycee scowled. Not that it was Georgette's job to listen to all her ramblings, but Georgette was the only person she had left to confide in. At least now that her family was gone.

"Of course I've been listening. You've been mooning over that homeless woman for nearly three months now."

Jaycee was about to respond when Georgette waved her off. "Okay, so I know she's not homeless, but still, you go from a doctor to someone that runs a homeless shelter. Don't you think that could, um, hurt your brand?"

Jaycee leveled Georgette with a glare. Georgette had come from humble beginnings, so Jaycee was stunned to hear her talk this way. After all these years, she'd never known Georgette to be an elitist. Sure, she played up her Southern charm, but she'd never looked down on people. Jaycee tried to push back her disappointment.

"Okay, fine. That came out way wrong." Georgette crossed her arms over her chest. "Truth be told, I'm worried about you. Tessa almost broke you, and you're still not healed. And now, poof, that Piper woman comes along, and you're hooked."

"I'm not hooked." Jaycee scowled in protest. "We're friends."

"How long have I known you?"

"What's that got to do with anything?" Jaycee crossed her arms over her chest to match Georgette's posture.

"Just answer the question."

"I suppose around eighteen years."

"Exactly." Georgette pointed at Jaycee's face. "I saw you 'fall' in love with Tessa." She made air quotes as she said fall. "And I can tell you that I have never seen the look you get on your face when you talk about that Piper woman."

"For one," Jaycee said, raising her finger. "You can simply call her Piper, not 'that Piper woman.' And second," Jaycee put another finger in the air. "You have just proved my point. You watched me fall in love with Tessa, and you are not seeing me have the same look with Piper."

"No. It's deeper."

"What the hell are you blabbering on about?" Jaycee rose from the chair and paced her office.

"You never fell in love with Tessa."

"Seriously, is that why we were together for fifteen years, married for ten?" Jaycee could feel her heart racing and took several deep breaths to try to slow it.

"You were in love with the idea of Tessa. And her family."

"Jesus. Now you sound like her." Jaycee threw her arms in the air. "That's what she said when she asked for the divorce. Said that I'm in love with her family, not her."

"Wow, it's a first." Georgette smiled. "For once, I agree with Tessa."

Jaycee shook her head. "No. I loved her. Still do. Piper is just a friend."

"Tessa was your dream." Georgette's eyes softened. "Successful. Driven. Ambitious. Plus, she has a large tight-knit family. She was everything you thought you wanted."

"I see." Jaycee continued to pace around her

desk. "Did you get a psychology degree when I wasn't looking?"

"But this Piper woman...I mean Piper is different. You like *her*. Just her. And that must be scary as hell for you."

"I think you've watched too many Hallmark movies."

"I didn't hear you deny it."

"Deny what?"

"Come on, Jaycee." Georgette moved to the edge of the couch and sat up straight. "Tell me that Piper hasn't crawled into places that you weren't even aware were there."

"I've not known her that long."

"Long enough." A twinkle danced in Georgette's eyes. "And I'll bet you felt it the first time you met her."

Jaycee flipped her wrist at Georgette, trying for dismissive but feared it came out as anger. *Oh, well.* She would be angry soon if Georgette kept it up. "And you came to all these conclusions because I dyed my hair?"

"Why now? Obviously, you want to show her more of yourself." Georgette stood and walked toward Jaycee.

"Ha. That's where you're wrong." Jaycee shot Georgette a condescending smirk. "Maddie's Valentine concert is tonight, and I couldn't wear a stocking cap to it, could I?"

"You keep telling yourself that." Georgette smiled and put her hand on Jaycee's arm. "If that's what you need to believe to get through."

Chapter Twenty-two

Jaycee brushed the lint off her shirt. Navy blue seemed to show everything. Maybe she should change into a lighter colored shirt. She groaned. Last night, she'd picked out her outfit but had already changed it five times this morning.

Why was she so damned nervous? It wasn't as if she was giving the speech. No, it was more than that. No matter how many openings Jaycee gave Piper to tell her more about the conference, Piper hadn't.

It hurt. Since Maddie's Valentine concert three weeks ago, they'd talked daily, but for some reason, Piper remained closed-lipped about her presentation. Those three weeks would have been perfect if the lingering doubt about Piper's motives hadn't constantly been at the back of Jaycee's mind. But even with that, Jaycee had found a level of happiness that she didn't believe possible after Tessa had dropped her divorce bomb.

Of course, her heart still ached for the family she'd lost. The Wilson clan was never far from her mind, but there was nothing she could do about it, short of giving into Tessa's seduction. Although, that was likely off the table since she hadn't heard from her since New Year's.

Jaycee shook her head. Now wasn't the time to think about unpleasant things. She wanted to focus on Piper's accomplishment. It wasn't every day that someone was asked to speak at a national conference on homelessness. It also wasn't every day you hid it from your best friend.

Best friend. Just last week, Piper had introduced Jaycee to another volunteer as Piper's best friend. It had left Jaycee giddy for two days. Who was she kidding? The goofy grin she stared at in the mirror told her she was still giddy.

Day by day, their friendship deepened, but it had been two months since they almost crossed the line. Their *near* kiss played on Jaycee's mind, but she'd convinced herself that it was better that they remained best friends and didn't complicate things.

Jaycee pulled her colorful tie tighter and straightened it. She'd been wearing more long ties than bow ties lately, even at work. Georgette scowled every time she didn't have on her signature bow tie, so it was a bonus.

Her brown hair would still take some getting used to. She'd never admit it to Georgette, but she liked the white blond color better, too. Before she turned from the mirror, she ran her hand through it to give the waves more body.

The night of the concert, the first time Piper had seen her without a stocking cap, Piper had done a double take. Jaycee worried that Piper was disappointed in her looks and wanted Jaycee to put the cap back on. *Stop.* They were friends. Nobody cared what their friend looked like. She could be bald, and it shouldn't matter.

Jaycee grabbed the gift bag from the coffee table as she made her way to the garage. She'd bought Piper a card and a few of her favorite treats as a congratulations gift. Jaycee paused at the door. Maybe this was a bad idea. She should leave it here or maybe stop along the way and buy a more substantial gift. A gift card or something. She'd intentionally chosen a gift that was less expensive but loaded with meaning since she'd been careful not to throw money around. Now she wondered if it would make her look like a cheapskate.

She could have flowers sent to the shelter tomorrow as a congratulations. Jaycee frowned. Did friends send each other flowers? *Oh, fuck it.* This was the same circle she'd been running herself in for the past week. If anything, it had gotten worse.

Still undecided, she peeked into the gift bag. She'd take it with her and leave it in the vehicle. That way, she'd have the option whether to give it to Piper later or not.

࿐࿐࿐࿐

Piper paced the green room, at least that was what she and her peers had been calling it, even though the walls were tan. The Poverty Summit had been a success thus far. She'd networked with a plethora of experts and had come away with so many new ideas. It had exceeded her wildest dreams, but now all she could think of was her looming speech.

She chuckled. *Looming.* That about summed it up. Everyone had been so nice the last two days, telling her they were looking forward to her closing keynote address, but still her nerves threatened. Since Jeff had taken the stage, she was the only one left in the green room.

She glanced at the clock. Ten minutes until showtime. Her speed increased as she circled the room. There were nearly one thousand attendees, by far the largest group she'd ever told her story to. Today, someone had said that both Channel 6 and 12 might cover the event. She'd frozen when she'd caught wind. What if Jaycee watched the local news?

It was doubtful she'd have anything to worry about. The news programs normally covered such a small snippet of a speech nobody could decipher it anyway. Besides, there were prestigious leaders in the field from around the country, so the media would focus on them.

Piper's stomach lurched. That meant the experts in the field would soon be listening to her. Why had she agreed to this?

Her stride lengthened. She'd worn sensible heels, or she would have risked falling. Her skirt billowed as she walked. Thankfully, it wasn't a pencil skirt, or she'd never be able to move this quickly.

As honored as she was for the opportunity, she was relieved it was nearly over. The last few days, the hurt in Jaycee's eyes was becoming harder for her to ignore. It wasn't that Piper wanted to keep things from Jaycee, but she wasn't ready to let Jaycee in on this part of her life.

No, that wasn't the truth. Piper was terrified of how Jaycee would react, and she couldn't risk a negative reaction right before the biggest moment of her professional career.

The door opened, and Piper froze. She didn't want anyone to see her racing around the room like a track star. Piper adjusted her skirt and ran her hands down the front of her sweater, hoping she was more put together than she felt.

Shit. She probably should have checked her hair

before she went on stage. Thinking about Jaycee had distracted her from making sure everything was in order.

Her notes. She shoved her hand into the pocket of her dress and immediately calmed when her fingers brushed the note cards. It was unlikely she'd need them, but it was a good safety net. After all, she didn't know how she'd react staring out at so many people. She could freeze up, and then her notes would be a lifesaver.

Norma, the chairperson of the conference committee, strode in with a large smile. "Are you about ready?"

Piper nodded. She needed to speak, but she was afraid her voice would betray her.

Norma put her hand on Piper's shoulder. "I know such a large crowd can be intimidating, but I've seen you present in smaller venues, and you've never failed to grab the audience. The same will happen here."

Piper smiled. "You're too kind, but thank you."

"Can I share a piece of advice that I was given many years ago?"

"Of course. I can use all the help I can get."

"Pick out three people in the audience. One in the center, one to the left, and one to the right. Find friendly faces. I gravitate toward nodders, while some prefer smilers, or you might want to find someone with compassionate eyes considering the nature of your talk. Whoever you choose, you only talk to those three people."

"Wow. That's great advice."

"I thought you might like it. That's why I came for you early. I normally pick the people out before

I go on stage. You can check out the audience from backstage while Dr. Enzo is finishing up his remarks."

"How thoughtful." Piper put her hand against her chest, truly touched by the gesture. "I appreciate your thinking of me."

"It's my pleasure." Norma leaned in and said in a stage whisper, "Besides, I have selfish motives."

"Oh?"

Norma squeezed Piper's arm and winked. "If you knock it out of the park, like I know you will, then I look like a pretty smart chairperson."

Piper laughed, happy to release some of the tension bubbling just under the surface. At least she didn't feel like she was going to throw up anymore.

Norma put her hand gently on the small of Piper's back. "Are you ready?"

"As I'll ever be."

They walked in silence to the auditorium. Dr. Enzo's booming voice filled the air as soon as they pushed open the doors. *Yikes.* Would she sound that loud, or would her voice sound like a squeaky mouse? Worse yet, would she be able to speak in complete sentences, or would her words pour out in an incoherent jumble?

That kind of thinking was self-defeating. She refused to do this to herself. Her fingers wrapped around the index cards in her pocket, and immediately, a sense of calm washed over her. She could do this; she had to.

When they arrived behind the curtain at the rear of the stage, Norma pointed to the side. "If you peek out over there, nobody should notice, but you'll get a pretty good look at the audience." Norma's eyes softened. "You've got this."

"Thanks." Piper took a deep breath before she peered through the tiny opening in the side curtain. Time to pick her anchors, as Norma had called them.

Piper's heart raced as she scanned the crowd. It looked more like a rock concert than a symposium. She chuckled. *Exaggerate much?* It took her eyes a moment to adjust to the lighting.

She'd decided she'd look for people who smiled a lot since they were the type who made her feel most at ease. Her attention immediately landed on a middle-aged gentleman sitting a few rows back on the right-hand side who was smiling and nodding. *Good. A twofer.* In the center, her gaze was drawn to a striking black woman with a beautiful smile. *Done.*

This was easy. All she needed was someone on the left, which might prove more difficult since it was on the opposite side from where she stood. She'd just find the person with the brightest smile.

She scanned the crowd. Her breath caught, and she struggled to breathe. *No.* It couldn't be, but she'd recognize that face anywhere.

Dr. Enzo was still talking, so she could make her escape. Slip out the side door, and she'd be gone before anyone realized. *No.* She wouldn't do anything to jeopardize her career. This certainly wasn't the way she wanted Jaycee to hear her story, but it was too late now.

She'd been through worse, much worse. At least she could pick someone other than Jaycee as the anchor on that side of the room. She snorted. Who was she kidding? Every time she looked to her left, Jaycee would be the only person she saw. Besides, Jaycee had become her anchor in many ways.

Just last week, Piper had accidentally called

Jaycee her best friend. Although it was true, she hadn't meant to say it, but in a way, she was happy she had. The look on Jaycee's face had been priceless. Every time she glanced over at Jaycee on the food line, the grin hadn't left her face.

Piper's stomach did a flip-flop. She couldn't think about that right now, or she wouldn't be able to walk on stage.

It sounded as if Dr. Enzo was making his closing remarks. Piper peeked through the opening one last time to see Jaycee, and then she turned away. The audience was on their feet clapping and cheering for Dr. Enzo. Piper didn't have any more time to dwell on things. She gripped the notecards in her pocket. It was showtime, and she wouldn't blow it.

Piper hurried to the back of the stage where she was expected to enter from. Norma was already there and greeted her with a smile. "Did you pick your anchors?"

"I did."

"Excellent. I'm up," Norma said as she slid between the curtains.

After Norma's glowing introduction, Piper walked onto the stage. Her face was still warm from Norma's kind words. Piper stepped up to the podium and smiled out at the crowd. "Thank you so much for having me today." Piper picked up the tiny mic from the podium and held it up. She hunkered down behind the podium. "I'm going to use this lapel mic and get out from behind this thing." She thumped the lectern. "It's a cruel joke that tall people have bestowed on the vertically challenged." She hunkered lower, and the crowd laughed.

Good start. It took her a few tries to get the mic

attached to her sweater since her hands shook so badly. She couldn't say whether it was her nerves at making a speech in front of so many people or at having Jaycee in the audience. She suspected it was likely the latter.

When she stepped from behind the podium, she hadn't expected the wave of panic that washed over her. The podium had offered her cover, but she felt exposed now. She immediately looked toward Jaycee, and their gazes met.

"Okay, that's much better she said." She smiled. "And this way, I can pace."

❧❧❧❧

Jaycee's attention had been riveted on Piper from the moment she walked onto the stage. Her long navy blue skirt elegantly rippled as she made her way to the podium. The cream-colored cable sweater was oversized and draped around Piper's hips. Her hair was pulled into an updo, but it was her smile that Jaycee's gaze was drawn to. With her hair pulled up, her smile lines were even more pronounced and attractive.

Stop. Jaycee needed to listen to her speech, not drool all over herself. When the crowd laughed at Piper's joke about the podium, a burst of air shot out of Jaycee's mouth. It was loud enough for the man beside her to give her a side eye. Apparently, she'd been holding her breath, and her palms were covered in sweat.

All of Jaycee's nervous energy disappeared when Piper looked her way, and their gazes met. She had no doubt that Piper saw her, so she gave Piper her biggest smile and winked.

Piper walked the stage and spoke without notes. She rattled off an impressive number of national statistics before she drilled into the state of homelessness in Milwaukee.

"Milwaukee has the distinction of being the city featured in one of the most influential books on homelessness in recent times," Piper said as she moved across the stage. "Most of you know of Dr. Matthew Desmond's work and his subsequent book *Evicted: Poverty and Profit in the American City.*"

"His ethnography examined the core of what it was like to live in poverty in Milwaukee during the Great Recession in 2008 and 2009. It's my hope that my city learned from his work. I believe we have, but there is still much to be done."

Piper paused in the center of the stage and stopped for a beat before she continued. "A big part of Dr. Desmond's work revolved around the devastation caused by housing instability. Our homes are where we go to feel safe. A place to hang our hats, so to speak. Without that stable home base, everything else becomes more challenging.

"Today, I'm here to tell you about a transitional housing program that DOTS has been piloting since 2018. When DOTS moved to its current location, there were rundown apartments on the floors above the shelter. Through the ingenuity of the board and generous grants, the apartments were turned into transitional housing. It gave families a way to get help without having to live inside the shelter. It's the first step to independence."

Piper stopped at the podium and took a drink from the water glass. She walked back to the center of the stage and moved in Jaycee's direction before she spoke. "Some of you here today have heard my story." Piper's gaze locked on Jaycee. "While some of you will be hearing it for the first time."

Piper held Jaycee's gaze for a few beats before she turned.

Jaycee gaped at Piper's back as she walked away toward the center of the stage. Something had just happened, but Jaycee wasn't sure what. There had been a message in Piper's words, and the intensity of her gaze had caused goose bumps to rise on Jaycee's arms.

Once back at the center of the stage, Piper said, "I know a lot about the transitional housing program because I'm one of the success stories, or at least I hope to be."

Piper's gaze landed on Jaycee. As much as Jaycee wanted to look away to collect her thoughts, her instincts told her to stay steady and maintain eye contact with Piper. It was the only way to convey that no matter what Piper said, nothing changed their friendship.

Piper's eyes held a mixture of sadness and fear, so Jaycee smiled and mouthed, *You've got this.*

Piper blinked several times before she continued. "I won't go into all the gory details about the relationship that started me on the downward path I found myself on." Piper smiled. "It would qualify as TMI."

The crowd laughed.

"My partner left me with two young children, two and four, with no means to support myself. I was a stay-at-home mom and a student. I had three thousand dollars in my bank account, and the rent paid up for a month. It was June 2019."

Piper moved behind the podium. It wasn't lost on Jaycee that it likely offered her imagined protection.

"I did what any mother would do, I went out and found a job. It was a good job, an office job." Piper shook her head. "I lost that job after only a month when my baby girl came down with the flu. I wouldn't leave her when she was so sick, and even if I wanted to, no babysitter would want to sit for a kid who was vomiting everywhere."

Piper paused and took another sip of water. "My next job was more flexible, but I wasn't nearly as well paid. I became a waitress. I found if I smiled just right, I could make good tips. Sometimes I didn't feel like smiling, but I did anyway, or I wouldn't make rent. I had to quit school. I wanted to get a second job, but I'd bartered as many hours of child care as I could." Piper shrugged. "I have no family in Milwaukee, and I couldn't afford the rates at a licensed day care center, which by the way is called *day care* for a reason. The better tips were normally at night, but finding child care was tricky."

Jaycee listened, mesmerized by Piper's story. Her heart ached for Piper. She wanted to rush the stage and wrap Piper in a hug. Even though Piper remained stoic as she talked, Jaycee could only imagine the emotions churning inside.

"I was hanging on by a thread. I knew any turbulence could cause my world to crash down around me." Piper smiled. "But hey, what could go wrong? At least, that's what I thought as the calendar flipped to March 2020."

Piper laughed, which allowed the crowd to laugh along with her.

"I'd hit my stride, waitressing was going well,

and I was making it work. And then..." Piper put her hands over her head. "And then, COVID hit. Waitressing wasn't the best *career* to be in at the start of the pandemic, so I lost my job. And two months later, I was evicted."

Piper held up her hand. "I know, I know. They shouldn't have been able to do that, but people don't always follow the rules, and I was too ignorant to know any better. I didn't know then what I know now. I was just trying to survive. I ended up having to move to a sketchier neighborhood since that was the only place I could afford. I could have been one of the stories in Dr. Desmond's book."

Jaycee's jaw tightened. What kind of asshole would evict a mother with two children? Who was she kidding, she'd done business with assholes like that, but she'd never truly considered the human consequences.

"I quickly learned the meaning of the word slumlord. Our heat and air only worked part of the time. The toilet backed up so often that I took to having to use a strainer to hold back some of the... uh...the excrement, so too much wouldn't go down the pipes at one time. The lock on my front door didn't work, so I had to push a dresser in front of the door every night."

Piper put her fists on each side of her head near her temples and pretended to scream, but no sound came out. "The conditions were horrible, but at least we had a roof over our heads."

Piper pointed her finger toward the ceiling. "But that was about to change. Nobody told me the unspoken rule that you should never complain about the condition of the building if you wanted to have a place to call home. I complained. I got evicted, again. It wasn't a formal eviction because, of course, they couldn't do that. It was a *suggestion* that I leave before I got blackballed. It was made clear that two evictions wouldn't look good on my record and that the landlord community is tight knit. I got his message loud and clear. He could have been blowing smoke up my ass, but I wasn't in a position to call his bluff."

Piper wrung her hands and met Jaycee's gaze. Jaycee hoped she was able to convey the affection she felt for Piper.

"That's when we moved to our car," Piper said. "It was either that or beg my parents for help. Since they hadn't wanted anything to do with me once I came out as gay, I chose my car. I can tell you that one doesn't sleep well in a car. Every sound, every noise might mean someone's trying to break in. I had my kids to protect, so I was always on guard." Piper continued to look at Jaycee. "My lowest point came one night in early December as we were settling in the backseat to go to sleep. My then nearly six-year-old son looked at me with a worried expression."

Jaycee leaned forward in her seat, waiting for Piper's revelation.

It appeared that Piper was fighting back the emotions that she'd kept in check during her presentation. "He asked me if Santa would be able to find us since we never stayed parked in one place for more than a few days." Piper put her hand against her chest and paused. "It hurt. I was so ashamed. At that moment, I felt like the biggest failure as a parent. Not just as a parent but as a person."

Piper scanned the crowd before she made eye contact with Jaycee again, but she didn't hold Jaycee's gaze for long. "No child should ever have to wonder if Santa could find them." Piper's eyes glistened. "That evening, I did something stupid." Piper shook her head. "I drove to Walmart, and while the kids slept, I slipped inside. I bought them both a small present. I spent less than twenty dollars, but it was a lot when I had so little cash left."

It wasn't just Jaycee who sat on the edge of her seat. The entire crowd was silent as they listened to Piper's story.

"You might wonder why I did it. What possessed me to spend our food and gas money." Piper let out a half snort. "I've asked myself that question often." She shrugged. "I've heard similar stories and seen it played out many times. Desperation, shame, hopelessness sometimes leads people in those situations to make *bad* choices."

Piper stared out at the crowd for several beats. "I consider myself a practical person, but in that moment, all I could think of was that no matter what happens Santa will come to our car. My children will not learn there is no Santa in such a cruel way." Piper shook her head and gave the crowd a half smile. "I know it sounds crazy. I'm embarrassed to tell this story, but I want you to understand what homelessness can do to someone's psyche."

Jaycee wished Piper would look back in her direction, but it was as if Piper was purposely avoiding her side of the room. Subtly, Jaycee rubbed her chest, hoping to loosen the tightness that gripped it.

"I hid the presents in the trunk. A week before Christmas, we ran out of food and money. We ended up at the Dreams of Tomorrow Shelter...DOTS. We spent about a year living in the shelter while I tried to get on my feet. The transitional housing pilot came at just the right time. I was one of the first who got an apartment through the program."

Piper moved from behind the podium and stood in front of the crowd. She looked so small, but she held her head high, which exuded a sense of confidence. "DOTS and the transitional housing program saved my life and my children's. The program not only saved me, but the board of directors had the courage to *bend* the rules, so I could one day give back to the community. You see, I know how horrible it feels. How helpless it makes someone. It's become my life's work to prevent someone else from feeling the way I did in my car that night.

"I once read that nobody thinks the homeless are less deserving than the homeless themselves." Piper hung her head. "It's true."

When Piper looked up, she gave the crowd one of her wide smiles. "But Santa found my kids at the shelter on Christmas."

The crowd collectively cheered as Piper stood in front of them in all her vulnerability. Jaycee swallowed the lump in her throat, and her heart went out to Piper. Finally, Piper turned and met Jaycee's gaze. An unexpected surge of emotions coursed through Jaycee. All she wanted was to wrap Piper in a hug, but instead, she smiled through her tears.

Piper went on to talk about her experiences at the shelter and her role there. The entire time, Jaycee sat on the edge of her seat, taking in every word.

"Once you fall into that cycle...the cycle of poverty, it's hard to climb out without help." Piper pounded her fist into her palm. "As a society, we must do better and not throw away people who are down on their luck."

Piper returned to the podium. "I'd like to end my remarks by saying the shame, guilt, and self-loathing were something I could never imagine until I lived it. The stigma is real. The pain is real." Piper flashed a huge smile. "But I'm committed to do everything that I can, so nobody ever has to feel as badly as I did. Thank you."

The applause was deafening, and Jaycee was one of the first to rise from her seat as the entire room stood. Piper's gaze locked on Jaycee. There was no mistaking the mist that clouded Piper's eyes.

Chapter Twenty-three

A surge of attendees pressed toward the stage. Piper stood with a smile, looking a bit shell-shocked at the attention. The woman who had introduced her moved in beside her. Many of the conference goers made their way to the exit, but the group surrounding the stage must have been at least twenty deep.

Jaycee had been so thunderstruck by the presentation that she'd remained rooted to her spot for too long. Now she would have to fight the crowd to get to Piper, which was all she wanted to do. There were so many things she wanted to say. The most pressing one was to tell Piper how proud she was of her.

The woman standing next to Piper had restored some semblance of order, and Piper was taking comments from the galley of people pushing in around the stage. Some had questions, while others simply wanted to tell her how inspiring her remarks had been.

Piper was even more breathtaking than usual. Her cheeks were slightly flushed, and her eyes shone bright. She made eye contact with each participant who asked her a question and rewarded them with her easy smile.

Jaycee needed to move. She needed to get to Piper. The need drove her forward. When she got to the edge of the crowd, she turned her body sideways and pressed between them. Some grumbled as she slid through, but all gave way.

She'd nearly made it to the front of the pack when Piper noticed her, and their gazes locked. Jaycee hoped Piper could read the admiration on her face.

Piper's eyes brimmed with tears. She shook her head at Jaycee and mouthed the word *no*. Jaycee froze in her tracks at the rebuff. Piper didn't want her to come any closer. How could that be?

Jaycee's shoulders slumped when Piper looked away. Piper whispered to the woman beside her, and the woman nodded several times and smiled. Piper pointed to another well-wisher and leaned forward as she listened to the question being asked.

Jaycee's gaze never left Piper, even through the pain of knowing Piper wanted her to stay away. As Jaycee listened to Piper speak, she felt a body press up beside her. *Damn.* Piper's reaction had left her on edge, so someone standing so close made her skin crawl. She shifted to get away, and the person moved with her.

Wanting to be calm before she confronted the innocent bystander, Jaycee took a deep breath. The person was likely intent on hearing Piper's answer and oblivious that they were violating Jaycee's personal space. The poor soul didn't need Jaycee going off on them because of her mood.

As soon as Piper finished her answer, Jaycee started to turn to ask the stranger to step back, when the stranger grabbed her arm. *What the hell?* She turned and recognized the middle-aged woman immediately. The woman from the stage.

"Hi," the woman said with a large smile. "I'm Norma. Ms. Marsden, Piper, asked me to come talk to you."

Jaycee's heart sank. Was this going to be like one of those bad high school scenes? One where the girl breaks up with a guy but sends her friend to tell him. *Seriously?* They weren't dating, so that was an erroneous analogy, but it certainly felt like a slap in the face.

When Jaycee didn't respond, Norma leaned in, "You are Jaycee, aren't you?"

Jaycee was jolted out of her thoughts at the sound of her name. "Yes. Yes. Sorry, I was caught up in the moment."

"Of course." Norma patted Jaycee's arm. "Piper's story has that effect. Both heartbreaking and uplifting."

"Yes." Jaycee nodded, not sure what else she should say. Norma just needed to get it over with. Tell her to leave so this didn't get any more awkward.

"Piper would like you to come with me."

And there it was. Jaycee's face burned. "Uh, okay."

Norma led Jaycee through the crowd without speaking. Jaycee was grateful for that. Besides, it would have been nearly impossible to talk in the throng anyway.

As soon as they were free from the crowd, Norma said, "I'm going to take you to the green room." She chuckled. "Well, it's not really green, but we wanted the Hollywood feel."

Green room? What was Norma talking about?

"The green room's backstage." Apparently recognizing Jaycee's confusion, Norma said, "It's where Piper wants to meet you after she's done."

Jaycee's heart soared. Piper wanted to talk to her. Jaycee knew her broad smile would likely seem overblown for the situation, but she didn't care. Piper wasn't kicking her out. "Wonderful."

As they made their way out of the auditorium and wound through the hallways, Norma talked about Piper's inspirational story. Jaycee tried to listen, but her thoughts were loud in her head. What would she say? What would Piper say to her?

They arrived at a large door, and Norma paused with her hand on the handle. She smiled at Jaycee and said, "I have to ask, why in the world did you dye your beautiful hair?"

Shit. Norma knew who she was. "Uh, um… change of pace," she lied.

"You're still stunning." Norma smiled. She studied Jaycee's face. "Not that you asked, but I loved it the way it was."

"Thanks."

Norma clapped her hands together. "Well, I should get back to Piper. I might have to shoo the crowd away if they don't disperse on their own." She pushed open the door. "You might have to wait a bit, though. I hope that's okay."

"Absolutely." Jaycee wasn't going anywhere. She'd wait here for Piper no matter how long it took.

✺✺✺✺

Piper walked slowly down the corridor, happy to have shaken Norma, who'd wanted to walk with her. *No.* That sounded too negative. Norma was an amazing woman who'd championed Piper every step of the way.

It was just that she was overwhelmed. Her hands trembled. She wasn't sure if it was caused by the adrenaline rush from her speech and overwhelming response afterward, or if it was fear of what awaited her in the green room. Likely both.

She'd stopped in the restroom on her way and embarrassingly sat in the stall for some time, hoping that she could get her emotions under control. Every nerve ending felt raw, and she feared what would happen if anyone touched her in such an exposed state. Not just anyone but Jaycee.

Piper continued to walk slowly but knew she couldn't put it off forever. Would Jaycee be angry? Hurt? She couldn't blame her. Piper had wanted to tell Jaycee for the past month but kept putting it off. She'd convinced herself that she couldn't tell Jaycee until after she delivered her speech. Her reasoning— she couldn't handle such an emotional topic while she was preparing for her biggest professional moment. Now the choice of when to tell Jaycee was out of her hands.

She reached into her pocket and grasped the note cards she hadn't needed, hoping they'd make her feel as centered as they did while she was on stage. It didn't work. Her heart raced as she got closer to the green room.

Having been so wrapped up in how Jaycee would react, she'd not taken the time to process how she felt. Should she be mad that Jaycee had shown up without an invitation? Piper snorted. It was a public event, so Jaycee could go wherever she wanted. Besides, it was Piper's own fault for zigging and zagging every time Jaycee tried to bring up the subject.

What would it do to their friendship? Would someone as successful as Jaycee want to hang out with a homeless woman? Doubtful. Although, it was a good sign that she'd stuck around, but maybe it was just to tell Piper off.

Piper's stomach churned. Her thoughts were doing nothing to calm her, in fact, quite the opposite. Like everything else she did in life, she just needed to tackle it head-on.

She picked up her pace. It was time to get this over with.

❧❧❧❧

Jaycee had counted every swirl on the carpet—twice. She'd come up with two different numbers, so she started again. Anything to stop her from imagining what would happen when Piper arrived.

Who designed this carpet? The pattern practically made her dizzy. She already felt like she might throw up, but this was making it worse.

Her obsession with discovering the accurate number of swirls won out, so she moved to the far-left corner. This time, she'd approach it more methodically. *One. Two. Three.*

The door rattled. Jaycee froze. Her pulse quickened as she stared at the door. She swore it opened in slow motion, but it was likely just her nerves.

Piper entered. She stopped just inside the door and closed it. Neither moved as they stared at each other across the room.

Jaycee took a step forward, followed by another. Piper stayed rooted in place, so Jaycee stopped.

There was no smile on Piper's face, and her beautiful brown eyes were full of fear. It broke Jaycee's heart. Piper's eyes welled, and Jaycee felt her own doing the same in response. Piper took a tentative step toward Jaycee.

Jaycee wasn't sure what happened next, but they met in the middle of the room. Jaycee grabbed Piper, or maybe Piper grabbed Jaycee. It was all a blur. But they clung to each other, holding on tight as if they would never let go.

The tension that had been building inside Jaycee released, and tears streamed down her cheeks. Jaycee suspected Piper was crying, too, by the way her body shook, but Jaycee wasn't willing to loosen her grip to see. All she knew was having Piper in her arms was the only thing that mattered. If she let go, she feared that somehow it would all have been a dream and Piper would disappear.

When they finally separated, Piper swiped at her eyes. "God, I must look a mess. Here I got all dressed up and put makeup on, and I'm ruining it."

Jaycee reached out and put her hand on Piper's cheek. She wiped away an errant tear. "You look beautiful."

Piper blushed. "Maybe not beautiful, but I at least felt pretty earlier. But now I'm a hot mess."

"No." Jaycee gazed into Piper's eyes. "You've never been more radiant."

Piper smiled.

Jaycee ran her thumb along Piper's smile line. "I've been wanting to do that from the moment I met you."

"Why?" A crease appeared on Piper's forehead. "They're ugly."

"Are you kidding?" Jaycee's voice rose an octave. "I find them irresistible."

Piper wriggled her eyebrows. "What stopped you then?"

"Pure terror." Jaycee grinned.

"Why aren't you afraid now?"

Jaycee took Piper's hand and laid it against her chest. "Feel that?" Jaycee's heart raced.

"Uh-huh."

"I'm still terrified."

"What can I do to calm you?" Piper smirked.

"Is that an offer?"

"I believe it is."

"In that case." Jaycee returned her hand to Piper's cheek and gazed into her eyes. "Are you as afraid as I am?"

"Uh-huh." Piper's voice came out low. She held up her shaking hand.

"Maybe I can do something to fix that."

"Please."

Hearing Piper's voice so full of longing accelerated Jaycee's pulse. Why did she feel like an awkward teenager who had never kissed a woman before? For Christ's sake, she'd been in a relationship for fifteen years, so this was far from her first kiss.

Something in this moment felt different. Monumental. *Oh. My. God.* Is this what happens when someone has been out of the dating scene for so long?

"Are you okay?" Piper asked; her eyes filled with concern.

How could Jaycee explain all the emotions rushing through her? Piper would likely think she was crazy. Jaycee gently ran her hand along Piper's cheek, wishing Piper's hair was down so she'd have something to brush off her face. "I will be. If I can work up a little more courage," Jaycee admitted.

"We're quite the pair." Piper grinned. "We better get on with this kiss before one of us passes out."

"Or both." Jaycee laughed. "It wouldn't be very

romantic."

"But it would make for one hell of a first kiss story."

Oh, shit. This was their first kiss. The one they'd refer to for years to come. *Whoa.* Call off the U-Haul.

Piper cocked her head. "What's that look about?"

No way could she tell Piper what she'd been thinking, so instead, she slid her hand to the back of Piper's neck and leaned forward.

Jaycee closed her eyes as she inched toward Piper. When their lips met, a charge raced through Jaycee's body. Piper's lips were as soft as she'd expected. Even though Jaycee wanted to devour every part of them, she held back. Piper had been through a lot the last few years, as had Jaycee. Piper needed tenderness, not raging hormones.

Piper nibbled on Jaycee's lower lip, threatening to shatter Jaycee's restraint, so Jaycee ran her tongue over Piper's lip to slow things down. Piper moaned, and the sound further lessened Jaycee's control.

Jaycee gasped and pulled back. Piper's eyes were unfocused. Jaycee suspected hers reflected the same stupor.

Piper grabbed Jaycee's collar and pulled her in. Jaycee didn't resist. Instead, she put her hand on Piper's lower back as their bodies pushed against each other.

"Mmm," Piper said before she thrust her tongue between Jaycee's lips.

Another shock wave coursed through Jaycee's body. She sucked Piper's tongue farther into her mouth, eliciting another soft moan.

A kiss had never made her feel so charged. There was no time to reflect when Piper pressed her breasts against Jaycee. *Jesus.* They were larger and firmer than Jaycee expected. Being winter, Piper was always in loose-fitting sweatshirts and jackets that hid her body.

A mental image took shape in Jaycee's mind. *No!* She couldn't allow herself to think of Piper's body, or she would likely lose any semblance of restraint she had left.

Jaycee gently parted Piper's lips with her tongue and then retreated. Piper's breath caught as Jaycee repeated the gesture several more times, putting her tongue in slowly and then pulling it out even slower.

When Jaycee licked the corner of Piper's mouth, her breath quickened. Jaycee kept it up, moving from one corner of her mouth to the other, until Piper's breathing became so rapid Jaycee feared she'd hyperventilate.

Piper pulled back and fought to catch her breath, but she didn't release her hold on Jaycee. Emboldened by Piper's reaction, Jaycee lowered her head to Piper's shoulder. Jaycee's mouth was only inches from Piper's slender neck. A vein that was normally covered by Piper's hair throbbed.

Jaycee couldn't look away, so she moved in closer. Her warm breath touched Piper's shoulder, causing her to shudder. That was all the encouragement Jaycee needed. She brought her lips to the tiny vein, and her tongue traced it along Piper's neck.

A loud moan escaped Piper, and her knees buckled. Jaycee pulled Piper to her and supported her weight, as she continued to kiss her way up Piper's neck. Once she reached Piper's hairline at the base of her neck, Jaycee ran her fingers through the wispy hairs that had escaped from the updo.

Piper moaned again. The sounds of pleasure

coming from Piper caused Jaycee's heart to race. She wanted to keep doing whatever she could to hear her moan.

Being so attuned to Piper, Jaycee had disconnected from her own body. That changed when Piper kneaded Jaycee's back. With each pass, her touch moved lower.

Jaycee had just reached Piper's earlobe, when Piper hit the sensitive spot right above Jaycee's buttocks. Jaycee gasped.

It must have sounded loud in Piper's ear because she chuckled and said, "I think I found an erogenous zone."

"Uh-huh," Jaycee said, still trying to catch her breath. It proved difficult since Piper continued to massage the area. It was as if there was a direct line that connected it to her clitoris. She shifted, hoping the sensation would pass.

"Two can play at that game." Piper chuckled.

"You win," Jaycee said breathlessly.

"I think we both do." Piper's voice was sultry, a tone Jaycee had never heard from her before, which only intensified her excitement.

Piper gently guided Jaycee's lips to hers. This time, the kiss started out more urgent. Less sweet. Full of need.

Jaycee's mind was screaming for her to stop, but her body had other ideas. Piper's lips were too delicious to willingly abandon. Just as Piper pushed her tongue into Jaycee's mouth, a loud knock came at the door.

"Shit," Piper said and jumped back. She unconsciously smoothed her sweater and reached for her hair. "Who is it?"

"Piper, it's Norma. I wasn't sure if you were still here."

"Fuck," Piper said under her breath. "Ah, come in. Jaycee and I were just talking about the conference."

Jaycee took two giant steps back before the door swung open. She wanted to laugh. Piper looked like a guilty schoolgirl, and Jaycee suspected she looked the same. Piper's clothes were slightly askew and her lips swollen.

Her lips. Jaycee had to force herself to stop staring at Piper's lips when Norma strode into the room.

Norma's gaze darted from Piper to Jaycee before she settled her sights on Piper. Norma let out a nervous giggle and said, "The cleaning crew wanted to get in here and finish up, but...um...they said they thought there was someone still in here."

Piper gave Norma a large smile. "I'm so sorry. Jaycee had so many fascinating..." Piper shot Jaycee a look that sent shivers down Jaycee's back, "she had so many interesting questions that we lost track of time."

"Of course, of course." Norma's head bobbed up and down. Jaycee suspected that Norma sensed more than she let on, especially since she'd knocked before entering the room. "I understand. What would you like me to tell the crew?"

"Tell them we'll be out of here in five minutes." Piper smiled again. "And thank you again for inviting me to be your keynote speaker." She glanced at Jaycee out of the corner of her eye. "It was life-changing."

Jaycee bit her lip, so she wouldn't break into an enormous smile. "It was enlightening," Jaycee said to Norma.

"Piper is an inspiration." Norma smiled.

"That she is." Jaycee rubbed her lower back.

Piper's eyes twinkled, and she let out a half-laugh that came out more of a snort. When Norma's head whipped around, Piper feigned a cough. For good measure, she coughed again. "Sorry. I must have swallowed wrong. I'm not used to all this praise."

"It's well deserved." Norma smiled. "I better get out of here, so you can finish up." When she got to the door, she said, "It was a pleasure having you."

"It was my pleasure," Piper said, loud enough that only Jaycee could hear her.

Once the door closed behind Norma, Jaycee laughed. "Wow. I feel like a couple kids caught making out in their parents' basement."

"No doubt." Piper adjusted her clothes. "So what happens next?"

"When do you have to pick up the kids?"

"I don't."

Jaycee's eyes widened. "Come again?"

"They went to Chicago with Sergio. He wanted to give me a weekend to myself since I've been so wound up about my speech."

"Then you have to work?"

"Nope. Caleb stayed back to cover."

"Wow. You have some amazing friends."

Piper smiled. "That I do."

Jaycee smirked. "So you have the entire weekend free?"

"Possibly."

"No plans?"

"None that can't be changed."

"I see." Jaycee nodded, pretending to contemplate. "Could I interest you in dinner? To celebrate your success."

"Where do you have in mind?" Piper's eyes

danced.

"The Sapphire Inn."

"What? It's Friday night. I heard on the news that reservations need to be made three months in advance."

"I have a few connections." Since Piper's revelation, Jaycee planned on telling her the truth tonight at dinner. It was only fair.

"By the way, we need to talk about that."

"About what?"

"You know about what." Piper scowled and pointed at Jaycee's head. "And you need to get rid of that horrible dye job."

Jaycee's mouth fell open. "You knew?"

Piper touched Jaycee's chin. "How could I not with a face like this?"

"How long have you known?"

"Since the first day Sergio and Caleb met you. They knew right away. I can't believe I'd missed it."

"But that was...holy shit...that was almost four months ago."

"Yep."

"Why didn't you say anything?"

"Shelter creed. You tell your story when you're ready."

"Oh."

Piper snickered. "You sure screwed up our paperwork."

"Paperwork?"

"All volunteers are supposed to fill out volunteer packets." Piper shook her head. "But since you obviously wanted to remain anonymous, we let you slide."

"Rulebreaker." Jaycee smirked.

"I had accomplices. I talked it over with Sergio and Caleb. We didn't know your story and thought maybe you'd had a bad experience with another nonprofit. We didn't want our *anonymous* benefactor to run away. We figured we'd broach it with you once you'd gotten comfortable."

"But it's been four months."

"It got complicated." Piper winked. "I might have gotten a tad bit attached, and I was afraid you'd bolt if we pushed it."

"Your accomplices agreed."

"Yep."

"So am I gonna have to fill out paperwork now?"

"Yep."

"Damn."

"Come on." Piper motioned toward the door. "Let's let them clean up the room. We can talk about it over dinner."

Chapter Twenty-four

Are you sure this outfit is good enough?" Piper said as they pulled up outside of the Sapphire Inn. Though she was excited about the restaurant, she'd started to feel self-conscious during the drive. She had no business in a place like this.

"You look amazing," Jaycee said. "More than amazing. Stunning."

"Stop." Piper scowled.

"Get used to it." Jaycee pushed open her door as the valet rushed toward them. "I'm going to keep telling you that all night."

The valet stopped and opened Piper's door. "Thanks," she said as she stepped out.

Jaycee hurried around the Range Rover and held out her arm. "Shall we?"

Piper smiled and threaded her arm through Jaycee's. She glanced at the people bustling around outside the restaurant and felt self-conscious all over again.

Men dressed in expensive suits escorted women whose purses likely cost more than Piper's entire wardrobe. Undoubtedly, they were designers, but Piper couldn't tell the difference between a Coach purse and a Louis Vuitton, if Louis Vuitton even made purses.

Ugh. She didn't belong here. It was too late now, Piper thought as Jaycee led her into the building.

There was something different about the way Jaycee moved through this world. A confident, almost cocky aura surrounded her, something Piper hadn't seen from Jaycee when they were at DOTS.

Jaycee must have sensed Piper's discomfort because she leaned down and whispered, "None of these women could hold a candle to you."

"Right." Piper rolled her eyes. "I am completely underdressed in my Goodwill sweater."

"I don't care where you bought it. It looks amazing on you." Jaycee smiled. "If you're truly not comfortable here, we can leave. But Mary Ann is saving a table for us."

"No, it's okay," Piper said. She was just being silly. It wasn't fair to let her insecurities interfere with their evening. "I'm looking forward to the meal." They just needed to get to their table, and she'd be fine.

Several people said hi to Jaycee as they passed. Jaycee smiled and called each person they met by name, but she kept moving through the throng. They'd nearly made it to the hostess stand when a tall man with graying temples clapped Jaycee on the back.

"Jaycee, it's been a while," the man said.

Jaycee turned. "Hank. Good to see you."

"Have you met my wife?" He pulled a woman who was at least half his age toward him.

"I've not had the pleasure," Jaycee said, her delivery smooth as if she had these types of conversations all the time, which Piper realized she probably did.

"Sarah, I want to introduce you to Jaycee Ward." He gave his wife a sleezy smile. "She's the one responsible for our bedroom."

Sarah's brow creased, and she shot him a look.

Jaycee laughed. A laugh Piper knew was put on.

"He's fooling with you. I sold him the house you're living in."

Sarah laughed and grabbed Jaycee's arm. "Oh, my gawd. I'm obsessed with our bedroom." She turned to Piper. "Third floor, overlooking the lake. I practically live in that room."

"I knew what I was doing when I bought it." Hank's leer intensified. "It's the best place in the house for you."

They all laughed, but the exchange made Piper want to vomit.

"Well, Hank and Sarah, I need to get to our table before they give it away."

As soon as they were out of earshot of Hank and Sarah, Jaycee leaned down. "I'm sorry I didn't introduce you. He left his wife of thirty years for a newer model, so I didn't think he was someone you'd want to know."

"You weren't embarrassed by me?"

"God, no." Jaycee's brow creased. "I didn't make you feel that way, did I?"

Piper shook her head. "No. I make myself feel that way."

"I can take you back and introduce you if you'd like."

Piper laughed. "I think I'd rather impale myself on that unicorn statue." Piper pointed. "At least I think it's a unicorn."

Jaycee tilted her head and looked at the sculpture. "A Picasso unicorn, maybe?"

"The artwork in here is something else." Piper pointed at a series of paintings spanning the length of one wall.

"Reminiscent of Dali, if he were a meth addict."

"I thought he did LSD."

"Exactly. And those paintings were clearly not done by someone on LSD."

Piper playfully elbowed Jaycee. Her joking was starting to put Piper at ease, which she suspected was Jaycee's intention.

As soon as Jaycee gave her name to the hostess, they were led into the expansive dining room. The décor was done in blues and silvers. Of course, the Sapphire Inn. "This place is beautiful," Piper said.

"It is," Jaycee agreed.

As they traversed one of the newest hotspots in Milwaukee, Jaycee strode through as if she belonged, while Piper fought against running for the exit or hiding under a table.

Piper expected the hostess to stop, but she continued through the restaurant until they came to a large silver door. She pulled it open and motioned for them to enter a corridor. The artwork here was even wilder. The paintings were all nudes, at least Piper thought they were.

"I know I'm a lesbian, but I thought I knew a little more about the male anatomy," Jaycee whispered.

Piper gave Jaycee a sideways glance.

"I don't think the penis belongs on his forehead."

"Oh, god." It did look as if a penis was growing out of the man's forehead, but the women's anatomy was no better. "I'm pretty sure women aren't supposed to have six breasts, either."

Jaycee stuck out her lip as if thinking. "I'm okay with that."

The hostess looked over her shoulder. "Your table is in here." She reached for the wall and pulled open a door that Piper hadn't realized was there.

"Mary Ann said she'll stop in and see you later."

The square room looked to be the size of an average bedroom. A table for two sat in the middle of the room. The walls were decorated in bright reds, yellows, and oranges.

Jaycee laughed and turned to the hostess. "She decided to give me the fire room, huh?"

"She did." The hostess smiled and indicated a bottle chilling on the table. "She also ordered one of our finest champagnes. On the house, of course."

"Thank you," Jaycee said.

Piper muttered a *thank you*. She was too in awe to say anything more.

"The menus are on the table, and," the hostess reached under the table, "you'll find a button under each side. Please push it when you would like to call your waiter. He won't disturb you unless summoned."

Jaycee nodded and thanked the hostess again before she left.

As soon as the door clicked shut, Piper said, "Good lord. What is this place?"

"Private tables," Jaycee answered. "There's four. This is the fire room. There's also the earth, air, and water rooms."

"Wow" was all Piper could muster. Could she sound more clueless?

Jaycee pulled out one of the chairs. "Would you like to sit?"

When Piper hesitated because she was so busy examining the walls, Jaycee said, "Or we could make out."

Piper finally registered Jaycee's words. "Would you stop? This is a classy restaurant, not the back row of a sleazy movie theater."

"She said the waiter wouldn't come in unless we called him." Jaycee wriggled her eyebrows.

"You're going to be dining alone if you can't behave yourself."

"Fine." Jaycee motioned to the chair she still held. "Please, have a seat."

❧❧❧❧

"That may have been the best meal I've ever eaten," Piper said.

Jaycee had eaten at many five-star restaurants through the years, but she'd have to agree with Piper. "It was exquisite."

"And the champagne." Piper licked her lips. "I can still taste it."

"Hey now, you can't do that." Jaycee stuck out her bottom lip, making sure to convey her pout.

"Do what?"

"You said I have to behave, and then you go licking your lips like that."

"Really? I was pointing out I could still taste the champagne."

Jaycee chuckled. "I know, but it was still sexy."

Piper rolled her eyes. "That's what you said when I dropped my spoon on the floor."

"You had to bend over to pick it up."

"And when I got crumbs all over my sweater."

Jaycee made a motion as if wiping crumbs off her own shirt. "I saw the way you wiped them off."

"You did, huh? And how exactly did I wipe them off?"

"Sexily."

Piper's laughter filled the room. All evening,

Jaycee had done whatever she could to hear the sound that filled her heart with joy.

"I don't think you realize how beautiful you are," Jaycee said.

"Remember what I told you." Piper pointed her finger at Jaycee. "You can't keep telling me that."

"Why?"

Piper folded and then unfolded her napkin. "It makes me uncomfortable."

Jaycee studied Piper before she spoke. "Because you don't like it or because you're not used to it?"

Piper crossed her arms over her chest and scowled. "I refuse to answer."

"On what grounds?"

"That you'll continue to do it when I admit I like it, but I'm not used to it."

Jaycee smiled and put her hand on top of Piper's. "I'm sorry your ex hurt you so badly."

"It's ancient history." Piper shrugged. Jaycee suspected she was trying to appear carefree, but she didn't pull it off.

"No. A breakup is one thing, but leaving you in such a bad spot that you ended up homeless...that's fucked up."

"She didn't know that's what would happen."

"I don't care. Leaving you and those two amazing kids with no means of supporting yourself is not acceptable."

Piper sighed. "No, it's not, but I need to let it go, so it doesn't burn a hole in me. A hole that could destroy me if I let it."

"I understand." Jaycee rubbed the back of Piper's hand with her thumb.

"Besides, it led me to where I am today, sitting

across the table from you." Piper smiled. "If Emma hadn't pulled her shit, we never would have met."

"I withdraw what I said earlier. Emma is my new hero."

Piper laughed. "I'm not sure I'd take it that far." She pointed at the table. "Dinner's over, and you know what that means."

"Dessert?" Jaycee knew that wasn't the answer Piper was looking for, but Jaycee couldn't give in too easily.

"Nice try. You said we'd talk about why you felt the need to hide your identity from me all these months."

"I didn't know I was going to become a regular at DOTS." Jaycee smiled. "Remember, I just wanted to drop off my macarons when this little dynamo put me to work."

Piper returned Jaycee's smile. "There was that, but when you became a regular, why didn't you come clean?"

Jaycee sighed. How could she explain it to Piper? Instead of speaking, Jaycee shrugged.

Piper's eyes softened, and she took Jaycee's hand. "I know we both kept things from each other, so I'm not trying to call you out. I just want to understand."

As much as Jaycee wanted to change the subject, it wasn't fair after Piper had laid herself open earlier. "I thought if you knew, you wouldn't want me around," Jaycee said in a rush.

"Are you serious?" Piper squinted. "Or are you just messing with me again?"

"I'm not messing with you." Jaycee looked away. "You're doing good things for the world, for people, while I've been selfishly going about my life making money. I figured you'd think I was superficial and not want me around."

"No. I don't judge people for having money or for not having money. What makes you think that?"

How could she explain it to Piper without sounding ridiculous? Jaycee spread her hands out in front of her and motioned to their surroundings. "I have all this. But nothing else."

"I'm afraid I'm not following."

"I have nothing but a lot of money. I lived my life for the Wilsons, and poof, they're gone. I was so busy with them, I never took the time to develop meaningful friendships. So all I have is casual acquaintances, mostly tied to my business."

Piper took Jaycee's hand and squeezed it.

"Family is supposed to be forever." Jaycee fought back her tears. "If I was worth anything, they'd still be around. They wouldn't have left me."

"Oh, honey." Piper's eyes filled with tears. "Is that really how you feel?"

"How could I not? I'm thirty-eight years old, and regardless of my money, until I wandered into the shelter, I was completely alone. Well, except for my assistant Georgette, but your life, on the other hand, is full of people. People who love you."

"I'm having trouble wrapping my mind around this," Piper said. "After getting to know you, I don't understand how anyone could just walk away from you."

"Imagine how I feel." Jaycee didn't want the pain to come back, not now. The day had been magical, but she was afraid this conversation could put a damper on it. "It hurts, but there's nothing I can do about it."

"I don't believe that." Piper put her hand on the

table with force. "This isn't making sense."

"Trust me, I've run through it in my mind a million times. I still can't figure out what I did wrong. But

Tessa made it clear that in their family blood is thicker than water. That's just the way they did things. It's true. When her sister got divorced, Kyle wasn't welcome. Granted, he was a douchebag and was cheating on her."

"So that's a completely different situation."

"At first, that's what I thought. I figured Tessa was just blowing smoke up my ass and someone in the family would reach out to me. Her mom or sister, or one of my...uh...the nieces or nephews. Well, the twins reached out, they wanted to say goodbye. I didn't return their text. I couldn't."

Piper shook her head and scowled. "That's just shitty."

Despite the pain their conversation was causing her, Jaycee couldn't help but smile at Piper's attempt at outrage. "You're kinda cute when you're angry."

Piper tried to give Jaycee a stern look, but her upturned mouth gave her away. "I'm trying to be all big and bad and protective, and you're looking at me like I'm a fuzzy little kitten."

Jaycee reached out and touched Piper's hair. "You are awfully soft...just like a kitten."

"Seriously?" Piper's voice held a hint of irritation.

Jaycee dropped her hand to the table and averted her gaze. "Just trying to lighten the mood. I can't cry anymore. That's what I did for too many months. Half the time, it hurt so bad that I could barely breathe. Then on Thanksgiving, I walked into DOTS."

"I'm sorry, Jaycee." The compassion in Piper's

eyes nearly brought Jaycee to tears. "I'm just trying to understand your experience, not bring you pain."

"I know. Early on, I tried to explain it to a couple of my...uh...acquaintances, but they didn't seem to get it." Jaycee took a long drink from her water glass. "It's grief, and not just for the relationship, but for the loss of an entire family. I don't think most people get that. They only focus on the relationship itself. I'm not sure normal people experience a breakup like I did."

Piper squeezed Jaycee's hand as if encouraging Jaycee to go on.

Jaycee swallowed hard. "Probably because normal people have their own family and friends to cushion the blow. But the Wilsons were the only people I had. Nobody seems to comprehend how devastating it was...still is. It's like a huge tornado came along and swept them all away. Can I tell you something horrible?"

Piper nodded. "I want you to feel free to tell me anything."

"Don't get me wrong, I didn't want any harm to come to them, but in my darkest moments, I thought it would've been easier if they'd actually been swept up by a tornado. How horrible is that?"

"No, you're not horrible," Piper said with conviction. "Losing someone is hard. Even harder to lose that many people all at once. And had they been swept up by a tornado, you wouldn't be stuck in a constant loop of asking what you did wrong. What you could have done to prevent it. And why."

Jaycee's breath caught. Maybe Piper did understand. "That's exactly it. How did you know?"

Piper gave Jaycee a sad smile. "Because I've asked

myself a million times how Emma could have left me. Not just me but Paxton and Maddie, too, knowing we would struggle, but obviously not caring. Who does that? How could she have hated me that much?"

"How insensitive of me." Jaycee squeezed Piper's hand.

"No. It's nice knowing we can relate to each other's pain. You have to process how an entire family let you down, while I have to process why someone let down an entire family."

Chapter Twenty-five

Piper laughed. As they'd been waiting for the valet to bring Jaycee's Range Rover, Jaycee had been sharing stories about some of the eccentricities of her clients.

"Stop," Piper said, trying to catch her breath from laughing so hard. "Now you're just making shit up."

Jaycee raised her right hand. "I swear. He stole a giant carrot out of their refrigerator."

"Carrot?"

"Yes. Carrot."

"Why?"

"I have no goddamned idea." Jaycee's mortified expression made Piper laugh harder. "I was showing him around the grounds, and the fucking carrot fell out of his pants leg."

"He shoved the carrot in his pants?" Piper asked. It was good to be laughing with Jaycee again after the heavier conversation they'd had at the end of dinner.

"Where else would you hide a carrot?"

"I don't know. How big was this carrot?"

Jaycee held up her hands about a foot apart. "It was enormous. It wouldn't have fit in his pocket, so I figure he must have shoved it in his pants."

"When this carrot fell out, what did you do? Say, 'excuse me, sir, is that your carrot?'" Piper laughed at the thought.

"At the time, I had no idea he'd taken it from inside the house, so I'm thinking, *what the hell*, has he been walking around with a carrot in his pants the entire time? Eww."

"Oh, my god." Piper pointed. "You thought he had it in…um…unmentionable places."

"What would you think if an enormous carrot fell out of someone's pants?"

"So what did you do?"

"What anyone would do. I acted like I didn't notice. I pretended to be checking out the landscaping. When I turned back, the carrot was gone."

"Wait." Piper wrinkled her nose. "How do you know it came from the house?"

"The homeowners called and told me their carrot was missing."

"You are so full of shit." Piper put her hand on her hip.

Jaycee started to protest, but the valet arrived with the Ranger Rover. Jaycee tipped the driver and opened the door for Piper. "I'm telling you the truth. Apparently, it was their daughter's prized carrot. The one she planned on entering in the county fair."

"Did you tell them what happened to it?" Piper asked when Jaycee climbed into the driver's seat.

"No! How could I explain that shit? I played dumb."

Piper smiled. "Thank you."

"For what? Lying to those poor people?"

"No, for making me laugh when I needed it."

"I think we both needed it." Jaycee smiled. "And thank you for getting me to talk about hard things. Things I needed to get off my chest for a long time."

"Good thing we had a private room."

"No doubt. Rumors would have been flying if my customers would have seen us bawling in the middle of the restaurant."

"It felt good, though. Didn't it?"

"It did. But you know, we got so caught up in the moment that we didn't talk about what we'd do next."

"What would you like to do?"

"I'd like to spend the weekend with you," Jaycee said without hesitation.

Piper's eyebrow shot up. *Bold.*

"Oh, god. That came out wrong."

Not so bold. Piper couldn't see by the light of the streetlights if Jaycee had turned red, but she suspected she had. A twinge of disappointment ran through Piper. Had she wanted Jaycee to be bold? *Yes.* Who said Piper couldn't be the bold one? "Bummer. I was about to say yes."

"You what?" Jaycee said with her voice full of surprise.

Damn. Piper wished it was light outside, so she could see the look on Jaycee's face. "I was hoping you wanted to spend the weekend with me."

"I do. I do. I definitely do." Jaycee's words came out in a rush. "I just didn't want you to think I was propositioning you."

"Why not?" Piper wasn't sure where her daring was coming from. Perhaps the dark gave her courage.

"Uh...uh...um," Jaycee stammered.

Piper bit back a laugh. She wasn't sure what had gotten into her, but this was too much fun. Seeing the calm and confident Jaycee rattled made her even more appealing. "Is that a yes or no?"

"Oh, shit. It's a yes. A definite yes. If you're sure

that's what you want." Even though Jaycee's words tumbled out, her voice held a note of confidence.

"It is what I want. I think it's what I've wanted for a long time."

Jaycee pulled to a stop at the red light and turned to Piper. In the dim lighting, their gazes met. "I have, too." She reached out and touched Piper's cheek. "But I don't do one-night stands."

"Neither do I." Piper smiled.

"I don't play the field or date more than one person at a time."

"Are you saying, if we do this you want us to be exclusive?"

"Yes. I can't do it any other way." Jaycee's voice trembled as she delivered the line.

"I can't, either."

Despite the lighting, there was no mistaking the huge smile that broke out on Jaycee's face. "Your place or mine?"

"It'll have to be yours. That's if you want privacy. I'd prefer the shelter patrons not be up in our business."

"My house it is," Jaycee said as the light turned green. She hit the gas a bit too hard, and the tires squealed as they pulled from the stoplight.

"That's a first. I've never had a woman lay down rubber to get home, so they could get into my pants."

"That...I mean...my foot just...it slipped. I don't want you to think..."

Piper burst out laughing. "Something tells me this is going to be a great weekend."

❧❧❧❧

Jaycee had stayed in the Range Rover when they'd stopped at Piper's, so Piper could pack a bag. They needed to wrap their minds around what this meant before they let anyone else in on it. As a courtesy, Piper had let Caleb know where she would be so nobody would worry, but she'd sworn him to secrecy.

They'd kept the conversation light on the drive, but Jaycee had felt the tension boiling just under the surface. When they'd arrived at her house, Piper's eyes widened as she took in the enormity of Jaycee's house. Jaycee had fought the urge to apologize, feeling ashamed of the abundance in her life.

Now Jaycee only had a few minutes to get herself under control while Piper changed into her swimsuit. Jaycee perused her wine rack. What was a good hot tub wine? She settled on a bottle of merlot that she'd had imported from France. It was one of her favorites, so she hoped Piper would like it.

She pulled down two wine glasses and set them on the counter. *Food.* She should put out something to snack on. *Shit.* Hosting wasn't her forte, especially for a date. She'd not dated in over fifteen years. How the hell was she supposed to figure it out now?

Jaycee threw open the refrigerator and scanned its contents. *Oh, good.* She had some grapes and strawberries. And cheese. Cheese was always good. She pulled out a package of gruyere and smoked gouda. *Shit.* Did she have any crackers? Surely, she must.

She rummaged through the pantry and found a box of unopened table crackers. Hmm, the expiration date was last month, but maybe they'd be okay. She ripped into the box. Everything needed to be nicely plated by the time Piper returned, but she didn't want to serve stale crackers.

Jaycee shoved a handful of crackers in her mouth to make sure. She heard a rustle behind her, so she turned and nearly choked on the crackers.

Holy fuck. Piper stood in the middle of Jaycee's kitchen wearing a very small yellow and black two-piece bikini. Jaycee hoped her eyes weren't as large as they felt. "My god, you're beautiful," Jaycee said before she remembered she hadn't swallowed the crackers.

Jaycee clamped her hand over her mouth and hoped that none of the dry dusty crumbs had spewed out when she'd spoken. She swallowed hard without chewing more and practically choked as the jagged pieces scraped the back of her throat.

A smile played on Piper's lips. "What in god's name are you doing?"

Jaycee grabbed a bottle of water from the refrigerator and slugged it until she felt the cracker dislodge from her throat. "Um, sorry." Her voice came out in a croak, so she coughed. She held up the box of crackers. "I was just testing to see if they were stale."

"Were they?"

Crap. Were they? After seeing Piper in the swimsuit, Jaycee had no idea what the crackers tasted like. She needed to relax and not let the change in their relationship get in the way of the connection they'd built. "I have no clue." Jaycee smiled.

"I see." Piper smirked. "Why not?"

"I wonder." Jaycee took a step forward and locked gazes with Piper. "Something might have distracted me."

Piper's face reddened. She crossed her arms over

her chest and seemed to close in on herself. "Sorry, I feel a bit self-conscious. I haven't needed a swimsuit where we live. This is the only one I have." She glanced at the ground. "It's ten years old. I had it BC. Before children."

"No. You look amazing." Jaycee looked away. "I mean, I don't want to be all leery and make you uncomfortable."

Jaycee rushed from the room without explanation. *Jesus.* Could she be any more awkward? Too late now, it would look even more ridiculous if she hurried back in and explained why she'd left.

When she returned, Piper was still standing in the same spot with a puzzled look on her face. Jaycee thrust out her hand. "Here. I got you a towel. I apologize that I didn't think about it before. I want you to feel comfortable here."

Piper took the towel with a smile and wrapped it around herself. "I do. I'm just not used to...to someone looking at me like that."

Jaycee flinched. She'd blown it. "I apologize again. I was being lascivious."

"Lascivious? I'm not sure I've ever heard a real person use that word in conversation." Piper grinned, and a twinkle danced in her eyes. "But I don't think I'd call you lascivious. Maybe just a little pervy."

Jaycee threw up her hands, happy to be on firmer ground. "Is pervy really any better?"

Piper shrugged. "I'm not sure, but it's easier to pronounce."

Jaycee laughed. She moved a step closer to Piper and said, "All kidding aside, I never want to make you feel uncomfortable."

"You didn't. It's been a long time since anyone

has looked at me like that." Piper shook her head. "I'm not sure Emma ever did."

"Then she was a fool," Jaycee said with conviction.

Piper gave Jaycee a slight smile. "It was nice, just a bit overwhelming."

"It's winter, so I didn't know."

Piper tilted her head, and creases lined her forehead. "Wow. Now you've lost me. What does winter have to do with anything?"

Jaycee's face heated. "You're always wearing hoodies, sweaters, and baggy clothes, so I didn't... um...I didn't realize," Jaycee gestured toward Piper's body, "what was underneath."

"You mean you decided to date me before you even knew what I had underneath the hood, or should I say hoodies?" Piper laughed.

The heat in Jaycee's cheeks intensified. "I guess I'm not as superficial as my earlier reaction may have indicated." Jaycee brushed a strand of hair off Piper's cheek. "I fell for the smile and the person behind the smile. The body is just a bonus."

Piper shook her head. "Beware. You only got a glimpse. I've had two kids, so I don't fill out the bikini quite the way I used to."

"Doesn't matter," Jaycee said. "I think you're beautiful."

"Would you stop talking and kiss me already?" Piper pressed against Jaycee.

Jaycee's heart raced as their bodies melded together. She bent and their lips met. The kiss was different than the one at the conference. Less urgent. Maybe because they both knew they had all weekend, or maybe Piper was as terrified as Jaycee was.

After several minutes of soft kisses, Piper pulled away. "I'm standing here half naked, and you're fully dressed. Do you plan on getting in the hot tub like that?"

"Oh, shit. I forgot." Jaycee pointed at the food spread out on the counter. "I was putting together a little snack when you *distracted* me."

"Little? Didn't we just eat a ten-course meal?"

Jaycee laughed. "It wasn't ten courses. Besides, I thought I was supposed to offer food."

"Holy cow." Piper picked up a strawberry. "This is gigantic. Paxton would be so jealous."

"He likes strawberries?"

"His favorite food. Where'd you get these?"

"The Public Market." Jaycee snapped her fingers. "That's right. He practically inhaled the strawberry macarons."

Piper shook her head. "Ever since he was a little kid, he's loved them. For a few years, he didn't get them much, so now I try to get them for him whenever I can."

Jaycee's chest ached at the thought of everything Piper and the kids had to do without. She couldn't keep feeling guilty about it. "Have you ever been to the Public Market?" Jaycee asked as a plan formulated in her mind.

"A long time ago."

"We could go this weekend. Get him some fresh ones." She held up the bowl. "He's welcome to these, but fresh ones would be better."

"He'd like that." Piper smiled and took the bowl from Jaycee. She set it on the counter and pressed against Jaycee. "But for tonight, I'd like your focus on me."

"Public Market? What's the Public Market?" Jaycee grinned. She was joking, but Piper being so close was making it difficult to think. "I want to kiss you again, but we'll never make it to the hot tub if I do."

Piper stepped back. The fire burning in her eyes nearly took Jaycee's breath away. "You better go get your swimsuit on. Now. Or I won't be responsible for what happens on your kitchen counter."

Without thinking, Jaycee glanced at the counter, and heat crawled up her neck.

Piper laughed. "Apparently, you're imagining it."

"Okay. Okay." Jaycee held up her hands and took several steps back. "But you need to stop flirting."

"Fine." Piper slowly licked her lips. "I will."

"No. No. Not fair." Jaycee moved farther away from Piper. "I'm going to change." Jaycee closed her eyes for emphasis. "I'm not going to look at you, or you'll try to distract me again."

"Do you want me to throw together a *sensible* snack plate while you change?"

"Yes," Jaycee called over her shoulder. She wasn't going to make the mistake of looking at Piper.

⁂

When Jaycee hurried from the room, Piper chuckled. What had gotten into her? Piper was never good at flirtation and overt sexuality normally made her squirm, but something about Jaycee made her bold. Or maybe it was because Jaycee made her feel sexy, something Emma had never done.

Emma had approached sex much like a mathematical equation that needed to be solved. Touch here. Push there. Rub that. Orgasm. Go to sleep. Granted, her formula usually worked, but it always seemed so mechanical.

The feelings she was having now were hard to explain. She squeezed her legs together. *Yep.* Her body was reacting, but it was more than that. There was a lightness in her, a feeling of playfulness and humor. Plus, a bit of mischief since she relished causing Jaycee to turn red.

Piper put a few strawberries and grapes into a bowl and returned the rest to the refrigerator. She didn't want to overanalyze what was going on with Jaycee; instead, she wanted to enjoy everything. All the feelings. All the fluttery butterflies in her stomach. Even the niggling of fear.

She found a cheese slicer in the drawer and cut off a few slices before putting the large wedges away. After she lined the cheese up around the fruit, she grabbed the box of crackers.

As soon as she had the box in hand, she giggled. The stunned look on Jaycee's face played back in her mind. *Priceless.* She'd hoped she looked okay in her swimsuit since it'd been so long since she'd worn it. Jaycee's reaction told her she didn't look half bad.

What if her performance didn't measure up? She'd only slept with one other woman since Emma left, and it had been a disaster. It hadn't been the other woman's fault. *Crap.* She couldn't even remember her name. *Karla? Cari? Fuck.* This wasn't what she should be thinking at a time like this.

Piper took two deep breaths as she put crackers on the plate. Her walls had been so high that Karla, or whatever her name was, didn't stand a chance. Would the same thing happen with Jaycee?

No. Why was she letting so much self-doubt in at the worst possible moment? She closed the box of crackers. Not wanting to rummage around in Jaycee's pantry, she left the box on the counter.

Two wine glasses and a bottle of merlot sat on the island. She picked up the bottle. *Hmm.* She'd not heard of it before, but by the look of the label, it looked expensive and French. Certainly not the Barefoot brand she was used to drinking. She should wait for Jaycee to open it.

She set it down, and as if on cue, Jaycee entered the kitchen. Jaycee had a towel wrapped around her. "No fair. I don't get a show like I gave you?"

Jaycee blushed. Her ruddy cheeks made her even more adorable. "You'll get to see plenty later. I mean…if that's still what you want. If not, it's okay, too, we can—"

"Take a breath." Piper smiled. "I think you're more nervous than I am."

Jaycee held up her sweaty palms and then swiped them down her towel. "I'm a bit rusty." Jaycee snorted. "Rusty is an understatement. It's been over fifteen years."

"You haven't had sex in fifteen years?" Piper's eyes grew large.

"No." Jaycee laughed. "I mean yes, I've had sex in the last fifteen years, just not with someone…"

Piper knew what Jaycee was trying to say, but she couldn't resist messing with her. "Ah, lots of masturbating then?"

"No!" Jaycee practically shouted.

Piper burst out laughing.

"You knew what I meant, didn't you?" Jaycee

glowered.

"Yes. You've only slept with Tessa in all that time."

Jaycee nodded.

"I couldn't help myself. You're just so damned sexy when you're flustered."

Jaycee continued glowering, but humor danced in her eyes. "I'm glad you find my discomfort sexy."

"Trust me. It is."

Jaycee snorted and then pointed at the wine. "Do you like merlot?"

"Love it."

"Then let's pour ourselves a glass and hit the hot tub."

"Holy shit," Piper said when Jaycee pushed open the doors. "This is amazing." She looked around, trying to take it all in at once.

The large hot tub sat in the middle of a mostly glass room, which was nearly as large as Piper's entire apartment. Off to the left and right, windows started at waist level and spanned to the ceiling, which must have been at least twelve feet high. She gazed up and looked through two large skylights over the hot tub.

"Those are retractable." Jaycee pointed skyward as she set the food and wine on a large wrought iron table that sat off in one corner. "But I think it's a bit cold for that today." She smiled. "Although, I sometimes open them when it snows."

"That would be so perfect. You could pretend you were in Aspen." Piper motioned toward the large bank of floor-to-ceiling windows in front of them. A sliding door opened onto a small patio that was surrounded by tall trees. "This is so secluded."

"That was the idea." Jaycee threw open the doors.

"I usually open these up when the weather permits."

A stiff breeze blew into the room, causing Piper to shudder. "And you call this weather that permits?"

"No." Jaycee chuckled. "I just wanted you to see it."

Piper wrapped her towel tighter around herself and followed Jaycee onto the patio. "This is gorgeous. I can't imagine what it would be like with leaves on the trees."

"You'll feel like you're in a tree house." Jaycee pointed. "The only good thing about not having leaves on the trees is if you look really hard, you should be able to see the moon shimmering off Lake Michigan." She motioned Piper forward, so they were standing against the far railing.

Piper strained forward and caught a glimpse of the shimmer. "Oh, my god. There it is."

"Was it worth the risk of being frozen to see it?"

"Absolutely." Piper slid over next to Jaycee. "You could warm me up."

Jaycee jumped at Piper's touch. "Let's go inside. The hot tub will warm you up."

Piper felt a hint of disappointment that Jaycee didn't take her bait, but she needed to be patient. Probably for both of them. Even though part of her longed to be touched by Jaycee, the other part wanted to take this slow.

Back inside with the doors closed, the air still held a chill. Jaycee busied herself preparing the hot tub. She pulled back the cover and punched buttons on the panel on the front of the tub. Soft lights began to cycle, turning the water various shades of blue and green. All around the inside, jets sent bubbles in all directions.

"Any preference for music?" Jaycee asked. "I've got a little of everything."

"Surprise me."

"Romantic shuffle it is."

Speakers were mounted in each corner, so the music filled the room. A sultry R&B song that Piper couldn't place was the first offering. Her hips swayed to the music.

"Obviously, I made a good choice. Why don't you go ahead and get in? All I need to do is shut off the lights."

Piper climbed the stairs, being careful with her wine glass. The last thing she wanted to do when she was trying to exude sex appeal was to trip and spill her wine in the water.

She'd just settled into her seat when the lights went out. Now she'd have to see by the lights of the hot tub. *Damn.* She was hoping to get a good look at Jaycee in her swimsuit, but the lighting would likely stymie her.

Jaycee dropped her towel and climbed the stairs. Piper could make out that Jaycee also wore a two piece, but her suit had much more material than Piper's. The top was more like a sports bra and the bottoms were briefs.

Even in the dim lighting, Piper could still see Jaycee's muscles ripple as she lowered herself into the water.

"Nice view," Piper said.

"Notice I shut the lights off first."

"I noticed."

"Is the music too loud?"

"Maybe a touch." Piper didn't want to have to talk loudly to be heard over the music.

Jaycee grabbed a large remote control mounted to the side of the tub, and the music lowered.

Piper slapped the water. "You can shut the lights off from in here, can't you?"

Jaycee laughed. "Busted."

"No fair." Piper stuck out her bottom lip. "I was half naked in your kitchen."

Jaycee rolled her eyes. "Half naked is a bit of an exaggeration."

"Maybe. But still."

"Fine." Jaycee made her way to the stairs and climbed out of the hot tub. "Let's try this again."

When she flipped on the lights, Piper blinked so her eyes would adjust.

Jaycee stood next to the light switch. "Are you ready for my grand entrance?"

"Hold on." Piper took a sip of her wine and pretended to get situated in her seat. "Okay. Bring it on."

"I feel so cheap," Jaycee said with a laugh.

"Just pretend you're a Victoria's Secret model."

"Ick. Are you kidding?" Jaycee flexed the muscles in her arms and shoulders. "Do I look like a Victoria's Secret model?"

Piper stared at Jaycee's sculpted shoulders. "Yummy."

"Did you just call me yummy?"

"Uh-huh."

Jaycee sighed. "I suppose that's a little better."

Jaycee arrived at the top lip of the hot tub and paused. She looked down at Piper. "May I get into the water now?"

"Hmm, do you think you could turn around?" Piper did a turning motion with her finger.

"No. Why do you think I waited to turn on the light after I got out?"

"Why?"

"Because I didn't want you staring at my ass."

Piper laughed. "Buzzkill." She'd never been one for sexual banter, so this was strange. At the same time, it felt so natural. It was both playful and sexy at the same time. Normally, it would make her uncomfortable, but with Jaycee, it felt different.

Once Jaycee was seated, she used the remote to turn off the lights. "Satisfied?"

"For now."

"For now?"

"I might want to see a little more—later."

Chapter Twenty-six

aycee glanced down at her empty wine glass, willing it to refill. It didn't. It was probably better that way. She wanted to be fully sober for whatever might happen next with Piper.

They'd been in the hot tub for over an hour, talking about nothing and everything. The conversation had moved on from the sexual innuendo from earlier. They'd shared stories of their childhoods and discussed their dreams.

Jaycee couldn't remember the last time she'd been so comfortable talking to someone. Sure, she talked to people all the time in her job, but that was different. It was business—nothing intimate or personal. Normally, when conversations got too deep, she found herself rushing for the door.

With Piper, it was different. Jaycee wanted to share her life, her thoughts, and even her feelings.

"So why did you get into real estate?" Piper asked.

Jaycee shrugged. "I could give you my standard answer. The one I give to everyone else."

"Which is?"

"It was the best way I could find to make a lot of money."

"But it wouldn't be entirely true?" Now that Jaycee had adjusted to the lower lighting, she could see the compassion in Piper's eyes.

Jaycee shook her head. "No. It wouldn't be." She looked down at the water and let her hand graze over the surface. "It's silly." Jaycee suddenly felt self-conscious. She checked her glass again. Still empty.

"Would you tell me about it?"

Jaycee sighed. "Growing up, I always wanted a big house full of family, but it was only me and my mom. Don't get me wrong, my mom was an amazing lady, but it was always just the two of us." What was it about Piper that made her want to tell her things? Things she'd never said to anyone else. "I suppose a therapist would say I'm trying to compensate for something I didn't have."

"Are you?"

"I suppose. In some ways, but then I feel guilty. My mom gave me everything I ever needed and more." Jaycee looked down at the water again and let her hand trail through the bubbles. "After she had the stroke, I felt even more like a terrible person." Tears welled in her eyes. "You want to hear something stupid?"

"I wish you wouldn't say things like that." Piper's eyes softened. "I want to hear what you're thinking."

"I blame myself sometimes."

"For your mom's stroke?"

"Yes." Jaycee willed herself not to cry. "I thought maybe I was being punished. Karma. Because I wasn't grateful enough. I didn't appreciate her enough since I was always longing for something more."

"Oh, Jaycee." Piper glided through the water to where Jaycee sat and crouched in front of her. She reached out and put her palm against Jaycee's cheek.

The touch was almost too much for Jaycee, so she closed her eyes. She put her hand over the top of Piper's, enjoying the warmth. "I've asked myself a million times why my mom wasn't enough, so when she died, I couldn't help but blame myself. Maybe I broke her heart."

Piper slid onto the seat next to Jaycee and took her hand. Under the water, Jaycee could only feel the pressure of Piper's touch, so she lifted their hands out of the water.

"I'm afraid I don't understand. I thought you'd said you were always close with her. Were you estranged?"

"No, no." Jaycee shook her head vigorously. "No, never estranged. But she was content with it being just her and me. Then I met Tessa and the Wilsons. I brought other people into our world."

"That's what happens when our kids grow up." Piper swept their clasped hands across the water, creating ripples. "Paxton and Maddie will one day start their own family. Sure, it'll be a change not having them all to myself, but I would never want to hold them back."

"Do you think my mom felt the same way?"

"Absolutely. All the stories you've told me about your mom, how much she loved you, I can't believe she'd have been anything but happy." Piper paused, turned, and met Jaycee's gaze. "Did something happen to make you think otherwise?"

"No." Jaycee tapped on her own head. "It's all up here. It was hard when she died. It still is. And then when I lost the Wilsons, I was positive I was being punished."

Piper let go of Jaycee's hand and lifted her arm out of the water. She turned slightly, and a frown etched her brow. "I'm afraid I didn't think that through."

"What?"

Piper lifted her arm higher. "I was going to put my arm around you, but the logistics are all wrong." Piper's arm remained suspended in air.

Jaycee smiled. "You'll never get it over my shoulders."

"Don't you think I already figured that out?" Piper flung the water dripping from her arm toward

Jaycee.

"I could slide forward a bit, so you can put it around my waist."

"That'd be good, so I'm not sitting here looking like a fool." Piper shook her arm for emphasis.

Jaycee chuckled as she moved forward and put her arm over Piper's shoulders. Piper put her arm around Jaycee's back and snuggled against her side. "Better?"

"Better," Piper answered. "Back to our conversation. Please, don't think you're being punished."

"I know it's illogical. It's just been a tough year, and all my old demons are rearing their ugly heads."

"It's okay. We all have demons that we let kick our ass every now and then."

"Thanks." Jaycee tightened her hold on Piper. "So to answer your question. I got into real estate because I wanted to help people find a house they could turn into a home."

"That's beautiful."

"I love stopping by my clients' houses on moving day to drop off a housewarming gift." Jaycee smiled. "The big loud families are my favorite. But enough about this." Jaycee lifted her foot out of the water. "I'm turning into a prune."

"How long have we been in here?" Piper asked.

"Well over an hour."

"Shit." Piper jumped to her feet beside Jaycee. "Isn't that dangerous?"

"Not at the temperature I keep it." Jaycee turned and was at eye level with Piper's scantily clad breasts. Her breath caught in her throat.

"Did you just gasp?"

Shit. Did she? Jaycee looked up at Piper guiltily. "Um, maybe. I don't know."

Piper laughed. "You're full of all kinds of firsts for me."

Firsts? She studied Piper, trying to figure out her meaning.

"First, you squeal away from the stoplight so you can get me home, and now you're gasping when you look at me." Piper waved her hand in front of her face as if fanning herself. "A girl could get used to that kind of attention."

"I hope so."

⁂

Piper leaned against the back of the couch. Her body was so relaxed it was rubbery. After her shower, Jaycee had given her a large terrycloth robe, so not only was she relaxed but warm.

When they'd gotten out of the hot tub and dried off, Piper had expected Jaycee to make a move. She hadn't. Was Jaycee waiting for Piper?

Piper stretched her leg out on the couch and let her foot brush against Jaycee's thigh. "What happens next?"

Jaycee was slumped on the couch, but she sat up straighter at Piper's words. "What do you want to happen?"

Piper grinned. "Question with a question. I see how this is going to work."

Jaycee pulled at the neck of her robe, as if it were too tight. "This is just weird."

The comment was like a slap to the face. Piper wrestled with how to respond.

By the pained look on Jaycee's face, she must have caught Piper's reaction. "Wow. That came out so wrong."

"How was it supposed to come out?" Piper said tentatively, still feeling the sting from Jaycee's comment.

Jaycee ran her fingers through her drying hair.

"Normally, the first time people sleep with each other, it's an accident."

"Accidental sex?" Piper smirked. "You'll have to enlighten me."

"Jesus. Not accidental. I mean the first time people have sex…uh…it's like animalistic passion." She shook her head violently. "No, no. Not animalistic. That sounds gross."

Piper pursed her lips, trying to keep from laughing.

"I mean, like in the movies or in books, if we were really into each other, one of us, as soon as we walked in the door tonight, would have pushed the other against the door."

"And what? Had sex on the living room floor?"

"Yeah. I suppose."

Was Jaycee trying to tell her something? "So you're thinking we're not really that into each other? Maybe better off friends?"

Jaycee nodded. An unreadable expression settled on her face, but she didn't speak.

"Oh. Okay." Piper fought against the heaviness that descended. Staying friends with Jaycee was truly what mattered. Piper knew she was out of practice, but how had she misread things so badly? "We can still hang out together, can't we?"

"Sure." Jaycee hung her head and picked at a loose thread in her robe.

Although Piper felt as defeated as Jaycee looked, she still wanted to save the evening. "There's no shame in not wanting to rip my clothes off."

Jaycee's head snapped up. "Huh? I want to rip your clothes off." Jaycee put her hand over her mouth. "Shit. I didn't mean it like that." Her face reddened. "What is wrong with me?"

"Hold on." Piper waved her hand. "I think we're having a major miscommunication. Do you still want to do what—" *Crap.* How was she supposed to say it? "What we came here for?"

"Um, what do you think we came here for?"

Ugh. Another question with a question. Piper took a deep breath. "Have sex."

Jaycee nodded. "Um, yes, I want that more than anything."

"Then why are we having this conversation?"

Jaycee shrugged. "I don't know. I thought maybe you weren't interested anymore. We've been hanging out and chatting," Jaycee checked her watch, "for over two hours, and nothing's happened."

Piper stood and reached her hand out to Jaycee. "Well then, I think you better take me to your bedroom."

Jaycee was on her feet before Piper had finished her last word.

"Impressive reaction time." Piper chuckled. "I think that was the equivalent of ripping away from the stoplight."

Jaycee took both of Piper's hands, stood in front of her, and gazed into Piper's eyes. Piper's heart rate accelerated. Jaycee drew Piper's hands up, so they were resting against Jaycee's chest. Their gazes remained locked. "Piper?"

"Yes?" Piper was surprised when her voice came out in a near whisper.

"I don't just want to be friends. I want you to feel everything I'm feeling inside. I want to explore every inch of your body."

Piper's knees weakened. She wasn't sure if it was Jaycee's words or her intense gaze that caused it, but she wanted Jaycee. "Then you better get me to your bedroom before I tear your robe off."

"Now that's more like it," Jaycee said with a smirk.

꙰ ꙰ ꙰ ꙰

Jaycee paused just inside the bedroom door. Even though her entire body tingled with anticipation, there was still something she wanted to do. "Can I make a request?"

"Uh, okay. And then can we get to the clothes-ripping part?" Piper asked.

"Most definitely." Heat rose up Jaycee's neck and settled on her cheeks. "I want to see you...all of you. Even though that swimsuit didn't leave much to the imagination, I want to get a good look before we get all tangled up in the sheets."

Piper stared back at her.

"Oh, shit. Do you think that's a creepy request?"

"No. Not at all." Piper smiled. "I've just never had anyone ask it before. I guess I'm just a bit self-conscious."

"You don't have to do anything you're not comfortable with." Jaycee took Piper's hand. "Let's get in bed."

Piper didn't move forward when Jaycee took a step toward the bed. Jaycee spun around. "I want to," Piper said. "I just need a little time."

"Would it help if I dropped my robe first?"

"Yes." Piper's eyes shone. "I'd like that." She licked her lips.

Jaycee let go of Piper's hands and took two steps back. She undid the drawstring around her waist and let the robe fall to the floor. Maybe it was all the years she'd spent in locker rooms, but she'd never been overly self-conscious about her body.

Piper took a step forward and ran her hand up Jaycee's arm to her shoulder. Then she swept her hand across Jaycee's chest, above her breasts, before her hand trailed down Jaycee's other arm. The sensation sent shock waves through Jaycee's body, but she stood stoically.

Next, Piper lightly brushed Jaycee's stomach. "You have gorgeous abs." Piper ran her hand up the crease running the length of Jaycee's stomach.

Jaycee stepped back. "And ticklish."

Piper grinned. "My bad."

"How come I don't think you're too sorry?"

"Maybe this will help you forgive me." Piper let her robe slip to the floor.

"Oh, Jesus," Jaycee said.

"Calling out to Jesus already before I've touched you. This could be a wild night." Piper winked.

"May I?" Jaycee held out her hand but didn't touch Piper.

"Please."

"Do I have to keep it PG-13?"

"You better not." Piper licked her lips.

Jaycee took in a breath, louder than she'd intended. She started at Piper's collarbone, keeping her palm flat, and she ran her hand across Piper's chest just above her breasts.

Piper let out a soft moan. "That feels good. Your hands are so warm."

With Piper's encouragement, Jaycee made several more passes across Piper's body. With each sweep, Jaycee's hand edged nearer to Piper's firm breasts.

Piper closed her eyes and let her head fall back as Jaycee continued her exploration. Jaycee moved behind Piper and pressed her naked body against Piper's back. She reached around and gently cupped Piper's breasts.

Piper let out another throaty moan.

Jaycee gently kneaded Piper's breasts, taking her time before she centered on Piper's nipple.

When Jaycee flicked Piper's nipple with her thumb, Piper leaned against Jaycee, and her breath quickened. Piper ground her buttocks against Jaycee's pubic mound. When Piper slowly rotated her hips, she brushed Jaycee's clitoris.

Jaycee couldn't hold back her moan. As her excitement mounted, she increased the intensity in which she rubbed Piper's breasts. Piper joined Jaycee and contributed to their chorus of moans.

"Oh, shit. You better stop that, or I'm gonna come before we get into bed," Jaycee said.

"That's okay." Piper continued to rotate her hips. "I don't plan to stop at one."

"You don't, huh?" Jaycee whispered in Piper's ear as she leaned in to kiss her neck. "All right then." Jaycee snaked her hand around Piper's hip and moved toward her sweet spot.

Jaycee slid her finger between Piper's folds, and Piper let out a loud moan. Piper was wet. Really wet. Apparently, she didn't want to be just friends after all. Jaycee grinned and then put all her focus on bringing Piper pleasure.

Chapter Twenty-seven

Shit. We can't stay in bed all day," Jaycee said. Although, she wasn't sure she meant it. As satiated as she should have been, Piper's breath against her neck caused Jaycee's pulse to quicken. The room had begun to darken as the light waned, casting shadows across the curves of Piper's body.

"Why not?" Piper rested her head on Jaycee's shoulder, still panting from their last round.

"It's nearly five o'clock. We've literally spent our entire Saturday in bed."

"Uh-uh." Piper lightly brushed her fingers across Jaycee's chest. "You ran downstairs to bring us up some sustenance."

"Cheese and stale crackers don't exactly count as sustenance."

"Don't forget the grapes and strawberries."

"Shit, we never made it to the Public Market for Paxton's strawberries." Jaycee put her hand against her forehead. "And we ate all the strawberries I had."

"There's always Sunday."

"True." Jaycee stretched. "But we should get up and do something. Go see a movie or at least grab dinner."

"Dancing."

"Ugh. You have the energy for dancing? I'm not sure if I can even walk." Jaycee accented her point with a groan.

"Nice try, but you just told me that moving would do me good. Which is it?"

"Moving is one thing, but dancing is like, I don't know, like running a 5K after just finishing a marathon."

"Are you saying that having sex with me is as painful as running a marathon?" There was no mistaking the grin in Piper's voice. "Should I be offended?"

"I'm not going to win this argument, am I?"

"Not a chance."

❧❧❧❧

It was nearly eight o'clock when they'd finally climbed out of bed. Piper was applying the last of her makeup when Jaycee wandered into the bathroom naked.

"Oh, no, you don't." Piper pointed. "You're taking me dancing, so don't even try to distract me."

"Relax." Jaycee held up a shirt in each hand. "I wanted to see which you think would look better."

"What pants are you wearing?" Piper ran lipstick across her lips and pursed them. She glanced into the mirror and wiped off a tiny spot that had gotten onto her teeth.

"You mean I have to wear pants?"

Piper laughed and turned away from the mirror. She let her gaze travel the length of Jaycee's body. "Although, I might enjoy you going pants-less, the Milwaukee PD might have other ideas."

"Fine. I'll wear black pants."

Piper pointed to the purple shirt. "Then I'd choose this one."

"Purple it is." Jaycee turned to leave the room but stopped. She reached out and touched Piper's face. "You're beautiful."

Piper's face heated. She looked at the ground. "Thank you." She wasn't sure how long it would take to get used to Jaycee's compliments or the way Jaycee looked at her. Piper lightly slapped Jaycee on the butt. "Now get outta here, so I can finish getting ready."

Jaycee chuckled. "If you keep spanking me like that, I might not want to get dressed."

Piper crossed her arms over her chest and put on her best glare. "Jaycee Ward, go get dressed. Now."

"Going." Jaycee hurried out of the room, chuckling as she went.

Once Jaycee was gone, Piper turned back toward the mirror and straightened her necklace. She stared at her face and ran her finger along her smile line. Piper had always hated the deep lines, but Jaycee apparently found them irresistible.

She ran her hand down the front of her black dress to smooth it. When was the last time she'd worn it? She couldn't recall, but it had to have been before Emma left. There wasn't much call for a dress like this at the shelter. She turned sideways and looked in the mirror. It would have to do.

Piper wandered into the bedroom where Jaycee was tucking her shirt into her pants. *Damn.* Jaycee's butt looked good. Piper smirked. "You're bringing out the beast in me."

Jaycee turned and raised her eyebrow. "Why do you say that?"

"I should be satiated. Then I walk into the room and see your ass, and I'm drooling all over myself. What is wrong with me?"

Jaycee laughed. "Do you need me to scratch that itch before we leave?" Jaycee took a step toward Piper.

Piper took a step back and held out her hand. "No. You stay right there, or we will never get out of this house."

"Is that such a bad thing?"

"Yes." Piper tried to put on a scowl, but it was difficult with Jaycee grinning at her. "We're acting like horny teenagers. I've never had so much sex in a twenty-four-hour period in my life."

The expression on Jaycee's face went from playful to contemplative. "Would it make you uncomfortable if I said it doesn't feel anything like teenage sex?"

Piper wasn't sure why the comment would make her uncomfortable, unless Jaycee was trying to insinuate that Piper's body had seen better days after having had two children. *No.* Piper didn't think that was it, but she was puzzled by Jaycee's meaning. "You'll have to explain."

"My body certainly felt everything you did to me." Jaycee's cheeks reddened. She thumped her hand against her chest. "But it's what I felt in here that was different."

Piper knew exactly what Jaycee meant. During one of her many orgasms, Piper's heart felt as if it had opened, and all her emotions threatened to pour out. "I felt it, too," Piper said, knowing her words came out barely over a whisper.

"It's a good thing, isn't it?"

"Oh, definitely." Piper moved toward Jaycee, wanting to erase the worry lines that had formed on Jaycee's forehead. "Come here."

Jaycee covered the distance between them in two steps but stopped a few feet from Piper. It was almost as if she were afraid to touch Piper.

"Are you okay?" Piper asked.

Jaycee nodded. "I just don't know what to do with all these feelings churning inside of me."

Piper stepped up and placed her hand on Jaycee's chest. "It's okay. We'll figure it out together."

Hope filled Jaycee's eyes. "You feel it, too?"

Piper took Jaycee's hand and placed it against Piper's chest, so they stood with their hands over each other's hearts. Jaycee's hand was hot, and it was as if the warmth penetrated Piper's skin and heated her insides. The insecurity Piper felt earlier evaporated and was replaced by peace. "I feel it."

They stood in that position for several minutes, neither speaking as they gazed into each other's eyes. Several times, Piper wanted to look away, but she couldn't. Finally, Piper stepped back and shook her hips. "I'm ready to dance."

ᔕᔕᔕᔕᔕ

"Piper," Jaycee said and lightly shook Piper's shoulder. "Piper," she said louder.

Piper stirred but didn't awaken.

Jaycee smiled. Piper had kicked her shoes off as soon as she'd climbed into the Range Rover and curled her legs under her in the large leather seat. They'd barely driven three blocks when Piper had slumped against the back of the chair and fallen fast asleep. Now that they were home, Jaycee hated to wake her.

Jaycee pulled into the garage and turned off the vehicle. Quietly, she opened her door and climbed out of the Range Rover. She went around to the passenger side and slowly opened the door. Piper murmured in her sleep.

"Piper," Jaycee said, this time a bit louder. She put her hand on Piper's arm. "We need to go inside."

"Huh?" Piper said, opening her eyes. She squinted at the light from the garage. "Where are we?"

"Home. My house."

"Did I fall asleep?" Piper blinked.

Jaycee bit her lip so she wouldn't laugh. Piper was adorable. "Practically as soon as we got into the car."

Piper groaned and stretched. "I'm sorry. I was supposed to keep you company on the drive."

Jaycee reached out her hand, and Piper took it. "All that dancing wore you out."

Piper swung her legs around and slid from the seat. When her feet hit the garage floor, she said, "Oh, crap. I lost my shoes."

Jaycee picked them up from the floorboard and held them up. "I've got them." She closed the door and held out her arm.

Piper leaned against Jaycee as they walked across the garage. "God, you'd think I was drunk."

Jaycee laughed. "I was thinking the same thing, but unless someone else was slipping you drinks, you only had three all night."

"What time is it?"

"Almost two."

Piper held up her fingers. Her eyes were still slits, so she put them close to her face and moved one finger at a time as if she were counting. "We were there for five hours. I doubt I'm drunk then."

Jaycee opened the door and stepped back, so Piper could enter first.

Once inside, Piper ran her hand through her hair, causing it to splay out in all directions. "I should take a shower after all that dancing." Her eyes were still unfocused as she blinked at the light Jaycee turned on.

"I don't think that's in the cards." Jaycee led Piper toward the bedroom.

"But I promised if you took me dancing that I'd—" Piper yawned.

"That's not in the cards, either." Jaycee put her hand on Piper's back as they entered the bedroom.

"I'm sorry." Piper yawned again.

"No. You never have to apologize for that."

"You'll give me a raincheck, won't you?" Piper smiled.

"Definitely."

Chapter Twenty-eight

Jaycee glanced at Piper's overnight bag sitting on the counter. Their time together was almost over. When had Jaycee become such a drama queen? Just because their weekend was coming to an end didn't mean everything was crumbling. Then why did it feel that way?

It had been an amazing weekend, possibly the best of her life, and not just because of the phenomenal sex. Her cheeks hurt from laughing so hard, and her legs were sore from dancing. But what happened next?

"Why so glum?" Piper asked as she entered the room.

Jaycee shrugged, not wanting to admit the doom and gloom racing through her mind. She pointed toward the window. "Mother Nature can't decide if she wants to hold on to winter or bring on spring. I hate sleet."

Piper went to the window and looked out. "It is rather gloomy, isn't it?" She stayed at the window for some time before she turned back. "Seems pretty gloomy in here, too."

Jaycee sighed. They'd let themselves be completely open with each other this weekend, so Jaycee needed to be honest now. "I'm scared."

Piper leaned back with a puzzled look on her face. "Scared? That's not what I was expecting. I thought you were gonna say something about missing me."

"I will." Just the thought of Piper going home

made Jaycee sad. Sergio would be back from Chicago with Paxton and Maddie, so Piper needed to be there to greet them. "This weekend has been magical. Beyond anything I could have imagined, but now it's back to the real world. What does that mean for us?"

"Aww." Piper came to Jaycee and put her arms around her. "It means we're going to build on the amazingness. The journey is just beginning."

Jaycee didn't know what to say, so she hugged Piper tighter, hoping it would quell her fears.

When Piper let go, she took a step back and looked into Jaycee's eyes. "I'm not sure what's going on. I feel as if I could climb Everest after this weekend, but you look like you might collapse walking to the refrigerator."

Damn it. Tears threatened. What would Piper think if Jaycee burst into tears? How could she explain to Piper that she'd gotten so caught up in the moment that she'd pushed aside her terror, but it was back full force? Jaycee needed to say something. "I'm just being stupid."

"Do you really think I'm going to let you get away with that lame response?" Piper grinned and put her hand on her hip.

There was the dynamo who Jaycee had been falling for since the first day they met. The look of determination on Piper's face penetrated Jaycee's morose. "Probably not." Jaycee smiled inwardly, but she wasn't going to give in quite so easily.

"Ya got that one right." Piper smiled and took Jaycee's hand. "What do I need to do to assure you that things will be fine?"

Jaycee smirked.

"We don't have time for that."

"But I have a raincheck." Jaycee held up an imaginary paper.

Piper pretended to snatch the paper from Jaycee.

"Which you cashed in multiple times this morning."

"I thought it had unlimited redemption."

"Nice try." Piper playfully smacked Jaycee on the shoulder.

Even though Jaycee didn't want to dampen their playful banter, fear still gripped her. "I want to believe this is real." Jaycee looked down at the floor, no longer able to meet Piper's gaze. "It feels like the most real thing I've ever felt, but what if I'm wrong?"

"First, if you're wrong, then so am I. Second, if we're both wrong, then we brush ourselves off and keep on going."

Piper's words were like a gut punch. Jaycee clenched her teeth together.

"Crap," Piper said. "That came out wrong, didn't it?"

Jaycee nodded. "That one hurt."

"I didn't mean for it to be hurtful." Piper put her hand on Jaycee's chin and lifted her head, so their gazes met. "If this doesn't work out, I'd be devastated. Maybe being homeless changed me. Regardless of what happens in my life, I will survive, and so will you. I love the meme, *Congratulations you've survived 100% of your worst days.* But what it doesn't say is that we can ruin our best days if we allow ourselves to worry about how it will end."

Jaycee nodded. She knew Piper was right. The last thing she wanted to do was put a damper on her time with Piper.

"What's that song by Garth Brooks?" Piper asked.

"Well, hey, that narrows it down." Jaycee grinned. "He has like a million."

"It's the one about not wanting to know what the future holds. Shit." Piper closed her eyes and began swaying, which Jaycee assumed was to the song playing in her head. "The one where he would miss—"

"*The Dance*," Jaycee said.

"Yes!" Piper's eyes popped open. "That's the one. He didn't want to know how the story would end." Piper frowned. "When I got together with Emma, I wouldn't have wanted to know I would end up on the street— homeless."

"But if you'd known, you could have done things differently, or maybe you wouldn't have done it at all."

Sadness shone in Piper's eyes. "Do you realize what you just said?"

Jaycee studied Piper. Something she'd said upset Piper, but she wasn't sure what. "Uh, I said that you could have avoided the pain."

"I think you better listen to the song again." Piper turned away. "I need to get my purse."

Shit. This conversation couldn't end this way. "Wait. Please."

Piper turned back. The sadness in her eyes had turned to steel. "I'm listening."

"I've said something wrong. I just don't know what. Please, tell me."

Piper inhaled and then let out a deep breath. "If I hadn't been with Emma, I wouldn't have Paxton and Maddie."

Dumbass. Apparently, Jaycee's fears had clouded her judgment if she missed something so obvious. "I'm such an idiot." Jaycee moved toward Piper and was relieved to see the anger in Piper's eyes had softened. "I need to pull my head out of my ass."

"Ya think?" Piper said with a grin.

"You're not gonna let me get away with anything, are you?"

"Nope. It's not the way I'm built." Piper crossed the kitchen and stood in front of Jaycee. "I can't force you to dance with me, but I'm going to tell you one thing, I plan on dancing. I have no idea what happens next or how this ends, but by god, I'm going to enjoy every minute of the fucking dance. So what's it going to be, Jaycee? Are you going to dance with me or not?"

"Are you always this fearless?" Jaycee asked.

"Who said I'm not afraid? I'm terrified."

Jaycee held out her hand. "Waltz or tango?"

Piper took Jaycee's hand. "I prefer to tango."

"I should have known." Jaycee smiled and pulled Piper against her.

Chapter Twenty-nine

Jaycee propped her feet on her desk and leaned back in her chair as she read through the report. Business had been good—very good. With numbers like these, she should be able to spread into northern Illinois within the next year. She scanned the report, identifying agents who would be good to target for the expansion.

A knock sounded at her door.

"Come in," Jaycee said.

Georgette breezed in. She stopped and stared at Jaycee's feet before she said, "Well, aren't you comfortable?"

Shit. Jaycee wasn't one to sit around the office so casually. Subtly, she pulled her feet from her desk and sat up. Jaycee held up the report. "Great numbers. I think we're about ready to tackle Illinois. Maybe shoot for July."

"Seriously? It's early March, and you think we can be ready by July?" Georgette smirked. "What the hell, why not tackle California and New York, too?"

There was meaning behind Georgette's words, but she didn't know what precipitated Georgette's sarcasm. "Did I miss something?"

"Do you really think we can be ready for Illinois by July?"

"Why not? The numbers are good."

"And the infrastructure?"

Jaycee shrugged. "We'll have to work on that, but it's doable."

"Or you're walking on cloud nine, so you're delusional."

Jaycee gaped at Georgette. "What's up with you?"

Georgette sat in the chair across from Jaycee with a sour look on her face. "You waltzed in here this morning, you're sprawled all over your desk when I come in, and you've got delusions of grandeur. So my question is, when are you going to tell me what happened this weekend?"

"First, I tangoed in here, not waltzed." Jaycee tried not to laugh at her own joke. "Second, I was not sprawled. This is what sprawled looks like." Jaycee threw herself onto the top of her desk and lay there for several seconds before she returned to her seat. "And third, wanting to expand the business is not delusional."

"And still, you haven't told me about your weekend and why you have everyone whispering in the hallways."

"Whispering? Who's whispering and about what?"

"Oh, for god's sake, Jaycee, you practically have a neon sign flashing over your head saying, *I had sex...lots of it.*"

"I do not have a neon sign." Jaycee sat up taller and jutted out her chin.

Georgette laughed. "But you didn't deny having lots of sex."

"I will not have this conversation with you."

"I'm not asking for the gory details." Georgette scrunched up her face. "But I do want to hear about how Piper's presentation went. I thought you'd at least text me this weekend with an update."

Jaycee grinned. "I was kinda busy."

Georgette bounced in her chair and pointed. "I knew it. The neon sign is never wrong."

"Let's just say that Piper and I have decided to

date."

"About damned time."

"Oh, now you're for it?"

"I always was."

"I call bullshit," Jaycee said. "You were lecturing me about being careful the other day. That's why I didn't tell you about it this morning."

"That doesn't mean I didn't want you to date her. I just wanted you to go in with your eyes wide open." Georgette sighed. "If you recall, after Tessa left, you said you would only date a woman with no family attachments."

"I do recall." Jaycee rolled her eyes. "And you said you'd sign me up on an only child dating app."

"I was being facetious."

"Duh, I know that." Jaycee crinkled her nose. "What was the point of this conversation?"

"You wanted someone with no attachments. Instead, you found someone with two kids. That's far from no attachments."

Jaycee's heart sank. She'd been trying to push it from her thoughts, but hearing it from Georgette brought it to the forefront of her mind.

"Hey," Georgette said. "Don't look so glum."

"How can I not be?" Jaycee put her elbows on her desk and rested her head in her hands. "I'm setting myself up for more heartbreak."

"Or for the best thing that's ever happened to you."

Jaycee looked at Georgette through her fingers. "But what if she dumps me?"

"Then you pick yourself up and go on."

Jaycee's head snapped up. "Jesus, that's exactly what she said."

"Smart woman." Georgette chuckled. "I like her already."

"She said we shouldn't miss the dance just because we're afraid."

"I love that song." Georgette swayed in her chair and sang the lyrics in her exaggerated Southern drawl.

Jaycee covered her ears. "Please, stop, you're gonna make my ears bleed."

"I'll stop singing under one condition."

"I won't negotiate with terrorists." Jaycee pushed her palms tighter over her ears.

Georgette sang louder and more off key.

"Fine." Jaycee slowly lowered her hands. "Name your condition."

"Fight your fear," Georgette said. "In all the years I've known you, I've never seen that look in your eyes. I think she might be the one."

Jaycee fell against the backrest of her chair. "I can't think that way, or fear is gonna paralyze me."

"Fine, fine." Georgette nodded. "Then take it one date at a time and enjoy every moment you have with her."

"One date at a time. I can do that." Jaycee smirked. "So you think we should hold off our business expansion in California and New York?"

"And Illinois. At least for the time being."

"All right." Jaycee let out a heavy sigh, feigning disgust, even though she knew Georgette was right.

"You never told me how the conference went," Georgette said.

"Oh, god, I can't believe I didn't tell you that part." Jaycee thought back to Piper's speech, and tears welled in her eyes. "It was the most touching speech I've ever heard."

Georgette cocked her head. "Do tell."

Chapter Thirty

The overpowering smell of cabbage hit Piper as soon as she walked into the kitchen. *Yuck.* "That may be the most repugnant smell in the world."

"What?" Sergio turned away from the large pot he stood over and inhaled deeply. "Nothing beats the smell of corned beef and cabbage on St. Paddy's Day."

"The only thing worse might be a dirty diaper."

"Did you hear that, Caleb? She's insulting our cooking." Sergio fanned himself. He was dressed in a hideous green sweater that had little pots of gold emblazoned on it. Piper bit her lip to stop herself from laughing.

Caleb turned. He held a knife in one hand and put his other hand on his hip. *Oh, god.* His sweater was worse. A giant 3-D leprechaun protruded from his chest. It resembled the creature from the movie *Alien.*

"Well, aren't you two festive?" Piper said.

Caleb and Sergio beamed, apparently taking her remark as a compliment.

Sergio cocked his head and stared at her. "What's up with you?"

Shit. Was she glowing? Piper gave a nonchalant shrug. "Nothing."

"Bullshit," Caleb said. "You've been gooey-eyed for the last three weeks. Ever since your *weekend* with Jaycee." He drew out the word weekend. He waved his hand around her face. "But that look is something else."

Piper tried for a stern look but knew she was failing at it. "Fine. I'm happy today."

"No kidding? We already figured that out." Sergio put his hand on his chin. "Sex was obviously involved, but there's something else."

"Good call," Caleb said.

"Ugh. Tell me again why I'm friends with you two."

"I'm sure it's my charm," Sergio said.

"And my personality," Caleb added. "But don't think you can distract us from the original question. What's up with you?"

Piper wrestled with herself. Part of her wanted to shout from the rooftops, while the other part wanted to hold on to her secret as if it were a delicate rose that would perish if she let anyone else touch it.

"We have a meal to finish cooking." Sergio turned back to the large pot and stirred it a few times. "So would you stop standing there with that lovesick look on your face and tell us what's going on?"

"How did you know?"

"Know what?" Sergio stared at her for a beat before he turned to Caleb. "I think she's had so much sex that it's scrambled her brain."

Piper realized her error. Sergio hadn't known. "Jaycee told me she loved me last night."

"Before or after sex?" Caleb asked.

"Or during?" Sergio chimed in.

"During doesn't count," Caleb said.

"True." Sergio nodded. "I hope it wasn't during."

"I'll have you know that no sex was involved. So there." Piper jutted out her chin for emphasis. "We were at McDonald's, so the kids could go to the PlayPlace. We were just sitting there eating french fries." Piper smiled at the memory. "Then she took my hand, looked into my eyes, and said, *I love you.*"

"I'm surprised it's taken her this long," Sergio

said.

"We've only been dating for like three weeks," Piper said defensively.

Caleb and Sergio both laughed.

"Try four months," Caleb said.

"I think I know how long I've been dating."

"Honey, the two of you've been dating since you met on Thanksgiving, but neither of you knew it," Sergio said.

He had a point, but Piper wasn't going to admit it. It certainly felt as if they'd been dating for much longer. "Whatever." Piper knew it was a weak response, but she couldn't come up with anything better.

The guys chuckled again.

"Tell us more," Sergio said.

"Not if you're going to keep laughing at me."

"Oh, sweetie." Caleb set his knife on the countertop before he approached her and draped his arm over her shoulders. She just hoped he didn't turn toward her, or the dreadful leprechaun would poke her in the boobs. "You know we're just teasing. We love you, and it warms our hearts to see you so happy."

Piper wrapped her arm around his waist and lay her head against his chest. "Oh, god, I'm in love."

"You say it like it's a bad thing," Caleb said.

"Not bad." Piper sighed. "Just bad timing."

Sergio raised a ladle over his head and shook his hips. "There is never a bad time for love."

Piper laughed at his antics, which she supposed was his point.

"There's no one in the world that deserves love more than you." Caleb pulled her tighter against him. "And Jaycee's a keeper. She'll take good care of you."

Piper stiffened. "I don't need anyone to take care of me."

"Whoa. Calm down, tiger," Sergio called from across the room. "Don't take poor Caleb's head off."

"Sorry." Piper slumped against Caleb.

"We know what you've been through, sweetie," Caleb said. "And we know you've taken care of yourself and those kids beautifully, but sometimes having someone solid like Jaycee to lean on and help carry some of that weight isn't a bad thing."

"I know." How could she tell them how tired she was after years of fighting to survive and make a better life for Paxton and Maddie? But what if she let Jaycee take some of the weight and it didn't work out, would she have the strength to carry it all on her own again? Or was it better not to let anyone carry it in the first place? Plus, the kids had been through so much, was it fair to them? Piper sighed. "For now, I just want to enjoy the moment. One *I love you* doesn't exactly translate into marriage."

"You heard the lady, Sergio." Caleb squeezed her one more time before he let her go. "Let's leave Piper be to enjoy the moment."

"Certainly." Sergio stirred the corned beef and cabbage, turned, and did a chef's kiss. "And the corned beef."

"Yuck." Piper crinkled up her nose. "I'm not eating that repulsive stuff."

"She wounds me." Sergio clutched his chest. "I guess you'll just have to starve."

"Wrong again." Piper smirked. "Jaycee's bringing me and Mitzy sushi."

Caleb's eyes lit up. "Mitzy's coming tonight? What about Donovan?"

"They should both be here later."

Caleb clapped.

"Save Donovan and Jaycee a plate. Jaycee has a meeting and won't be here until later, either." Piper glanced at her watch. "The volunteers should be here soon, so I better get to it."

Jaycee wiped her mouth with her napkin. "Oh, my god, was that good." She leaned back in her chair and put her hands on her stomach. She'd always loved Betsy Wilson's corned beef and cabbage, but this was even better.

"Don't expect me to kiss you tonight." Piper turned up her nose.

"You didn't think that one out, did you?" Mitzy wagged her finger at Jaycee. "No sugar for you."

Jaycee smiled. It had been a while since she'd seen Mitzy, so she was more than happy to take the ribbing. Mitzy looked good. "I'm so glad you two made it tonight," Jaycee said to Mitzy and Donovan.

Donovan held up his last bite of corned beef. "No way would I miss this meal. It's one of my favorites."

"Uh-huh." Mitzy rolled her neck. "Somebody else ain't gonna get any kisses tonight, either."

Jaycee pointed at Donovan and laughed. "Looks like we're in the same boat."

Donovan leaned in toward Jaycee. "Do you think it was worth it?" he asked in a stage whisper.

Jaycee shifted her gaze from Donovan to Piper and then back to Donovan. "Man, I don't know. Her kisses are pretty damned sweet, but that corned beef was to die for."

Piper elbowed Jaycee.

"I meant to say, absolutely not worth it," Jaycee said and took Piper's hand.

Once the laughter stopped. Piper said, "I want to hear all about your apartment."

"And Donovan's job," Jaycee added.

"Oh, crap, I don't think I'm gonna be able to talk about it," Mitzy said. "I promised the little ones I'd play their arcade basketball game with them after I finished eating."

"Looks like Maddie's on a mission." Jaycee pointed at Maddie, who marched toward them.

Mitzy held up her hand. "What was I thinking? I might break a nail."

Donovan laughed. "By the look on Maddie's face, I doubt she'll take that as an excuse."

"Ugh." Mitzy put the back of her hand against her forehead. "I'm not gonna argue with that Lil Miss. I know when I can't win." Mitzy slid from her seat. Jaycee had almost forgotten her bright green pants until she stood. There was something to be said for confidence, and Mitzy had it in abundance to wear those pants out in public. "I'm coming." Mitzy trotted across the floor in her high heels.

"She looks good," Jaycee said as soon as Mitzy was out of earshot.

Donovan smiled. "That she does."

"Have things gotten better?" Jaycee asked tentatively.

Donovan shifted his gaze between Piper and Jaycee and nodded. "I think so."

"You think so?" Piper said.

"We've been in our apartment for a little over a month, and she's been home every night when I get home from work."

"Thank god. We've been so worried about her."

"About both of you," Jaycee said.

"Yes." Piper reached out and patted Donovan's hand. "Both of you."

Donovan's face reddened at Piper's touch. "Thanks. Things are looking up, thanks to you and Jaycee."

"Nope," Jaycee waved her hand. "You did it yourself. I ran into your boss the other day, and she was raving about how well you were doing. Asked me if I had any more just like you."

Donovan's face turned redder, and he let out a

small chuckle. "You're gonna embarrass me."

"We're so proud of you," Piper said.

Jaycee didn't think it was possible for Donovan's face to get any redder, but it did.

He jumped from the table. "Uh, I gotta go save Mitzy. It looks like the kids have her on the ropes." He started to walk away but turned. "I just want you guys to know how much I appreciate you."

Before either could respond, he'd turned away. Jaycee blinked back tears. Donovan and Mitzy had gotten into her heart. Piper squeezed Jaycee's hand.

Jaycee swallowed down the lump in her throat before she turned to Piper. Piper's intense brown eyes were filled with compassion and love. Jaycee said the only thing that came to her mind, "I love you so much."

Piper smiled. "I love you so much, too."

Chapter Thirty-one

"I cannot believe we're doing this," Piper said as she exited the Range Rover. "It could be a game changer for the shelter."

The valet handed Jaycee a ticket before she joined Piper under the awning outside of the Sapphire Inn. At Piper's insistence, they'd arrived early, which was a good thing judging by Piper's demeanor.

"Are we ever going to see the sun again?" Piper glowered at the sky.

"April showers bring May flowers," Jaycee said, reciting what her mom always told her.

Piper turned up her nose. "Then it's a damn good thing tomorrow's the first of May because I'm getting tired of all this rain."

They'd only had two days of rain the past week, but Jaycee decided it was better not to correct Piper when she was this uptight.

Piper ran her hands down the front of her dress smoothing it. *Nerves.* At least Jaycee assumed it was since her charcoal gray suit was impeccable. Despite Piper's protests, Jaycee had insisted on buying Piper a couple of high-quality business outfits. A couple was accurate. Piper had drawn the line, allowing Jaycee to purchase two. The only reason she'd agreed was to give her a more professional appearance when she did business for DOTS.

"You get more beautiful every day," Jaycee said,

hoping to distract Piper from her nerves.

"Would you stop that?" Piper frowned. "This isn't a nightclub."

Jaycee grinned. "It's not my fault you're so hot in a business suit."

Piper shot Jaycee a look. "This meeting is important to me. You understand that, don't you?"

Yep. Piper was nervous. She rarely lost her playful side, but she had today. "Don't think I'm making light of it. I'm just trying to get you to relax."

"Relax? How can I relax when so many people are counting on me?"

"Note to self. Never tell someone to relax when they're freaking out. It's never a good idea."

Jaycee got the first genuine smile out of Piper. "I've been a tyrant these last few days, haven't I?"

"Well." Jaycee tilted her head. "I wouldn't exactly say tyrant. More like despot."

Piper laughed. "That's why I love you. You always keep it real."

Warmth spread across Jaycee's chest. She wasn't sure if she'd ever tire of hearing Piper say the words *I love you.* It had been two months since Jaycee learned the truth about Piper's past. And two months since they'd spent their magical first weekend together. Since then, their relationship continued to get better, exceeding anything Jaycee thought was possible.

"I still love you, even if you are a despot." Jaycee winked.

"And I'll still love you, even if you're a slob." Piper reached up and straightened Jaycee's tie. "Did you dress in the dark this morning?"

"Why?" Jaycee put her hand over Piper's and felt the tie knot. "Oh. That's bad."

"Come here." Piper pulled Jaycee away from the front doors to a secluded area next to the restaurant. "We're going to have to retie it."

Jaycee pulled at the tie to undo it. "I was better with bow ties," she grumbled.

"But you look cuter in long ones." Piper grinned. "That is, if it doesn't look like a third-grader tied it."

"Here." Jaycee pulled the tie from her neck and held it out to Piper. "You do it."

"Gladly." Piper stood in front of Jaycee and threw the tie around Jaycee's neck. Since Piper was in heels, she didn't have to reach up as far as she normally did. "And don't forget to fix your suspenders. They're all twisted in back."

Jaycee snorted. "I'm not sure how I managed to dress myself before I met you."

"Neither am I," Piper said as she continued to tie Jaycee's tie. After she finished, Piper flicked her fingers in Jaycee's hair. "I'm so glad you have your natural color back."

"The brown was hideous, wasn't it?"

"Hideous might be too strong of a word." Piper screwed up her face. "After all, I ravished you for two whole days when you had that brown mop."

Jaycee's face heated.

Piper laughed. "It's almost too easy."

⁂

Piper took a deep breath and smoothed the front of her dress. She knew it wasn't wrinkled, but doing it helped keep her calm. They were standing outside the largest private room at the Sapphire Inn. The others had already been seated, but Mary Ann, the owner of the restaurant, had insisted on making a formal announcement for their entrance.

Despite having to wait, her nerves weren't nearly as bad as they'd been earlier. Jaycee always had a way of soothing her, usually with humor. Piper couldn't imagine doing this without Jaycee at her side. Maybe this was what Caleb and Sergio meant about sometimes letting Jaycee help carry the load. It still felt foreign, but if she were being honest, it felt good, too.

"You're going to crush it," Jaycee said into Piper's ear. "Mary Ann can be a bit long-winded." She leaned in toward the door. "Sounds like she's still going on about something."

"I just hope I'm well enough prepared."

Jaycee snorted. "Jesus. How much more preparation do you think you need?"

"I don't know." Piper shrugged. "I've seen you get ready for an open house, and it just seems more thorough."

"Let's see. I do *one* thing." Jaycee held up one finger. "That's it. And you," Jaycee waved her hands in the air and wiggled her fingers, "you do everything."

Piper wrinkled her nose.

"Don't give me that," Jaycee said. "You run a shelter, go to school full time, are raising two kids, and now you're taking on this project. While all I do is run one business, so stop selling yourself short."

It wasn't the first time Jaycee had told her this, but it was good to hear as her self-doubt crept in.

Just as the door started to swing open, Jaycee leaned in with a glint in her eyes. "Plus, you keep your girlfriend well satisfied in the bedroom."

"Piper. Jaycee. We're ready for you," Mary Ann said as she opened the door wider.

Piper shot Jaycee a look. Jaycee laughed and winked. "Go get 'em."

Mary Ann collapsed into the chair across from Jaycee and said to Piper, "You were amazing."

"Wasn't she?" Jaycee sported a proud smile.

"I couldn't have done it without the two of you. Thank you."

"It was my pleasure," Mary Ann said. "What was the final tally?"

Piper flipped open her notebook and ran her finger down the page as she counted. Piper still couldn't believe that the project had gained so much momentum. How amazing it would be that once a week the patrons of DOTS would get a meal prepared by the best chefs from some of the finest restaurants in Milwaukee. "Eighteen, with five who said they'd get back to me."

Mary Ann flicked her wrist and turned up her nose. "Those cheap bastards won't budge until they see how much publicity it generates. I say you don't let them in on principle."

Piper smiled at Mary Ann's flamboyant disgust. "I'd probably be remiss if I turned down free meals for the shelter."

"Yeah, I suppose." Mary Ann shook her head. "I can't believe some people."

"I can't worry about them," Piper said. "There's too much to be done in the next three months."

"Shit." Mary Ann pulled her cellphone from her back pocket. "I need to put it in my calendar. The first Tuesday in August, right?"

"Yep."

"Got it." Mary Ann turned to Jaycee. "Hey, I almost forgot, how's your golf game?"

"That's random," Jaycee said.

Mary Ann grinned. "I'm in a golf league, Thursday evenings. One of our foursome broke her leg. I thought you might want to join us."

Jaycee shook her head. "I volunteer at the shelter on Monday and Thursday."

"You should do it," Piper said. "We can change your day to Wednesday."

"Are you sure?" Jaycee asked.

"Positive. It'd do you good to get out with friends." Since she and Jaycee had been working with Mary Ann on this project for DOTS, Piper had been encouraging Jaycee to deepen her friendship with Mary Ann.

"It's been a while, but I'm not half bad," Jaycee said.

"Sold. I'll email you the details." Mary Ann stood. "I need to get my ass back to the kitchen. Are you two going to stay for dinner?"

Jaycee turned to Piper and raised an eyebrow.

"The kids are staying with Caleb and Sergio tonight."

"Seriously?" Jaycee's eyes lit up.

Mary Ann cackled and pointed at Jaycee's face. "If that wasn't a booty call expression, I don't know what the hell is."

"Shut up." Jaycee glared.

Piper laughed. "She's right, honey."

Jaycee's face reddened, and she groaned. "I don't know why I hang out with you guys. You're both mean."

Mary Ann clapped her hand on Jaycee's shoulder. "You've got this room for another half hour, then I'm gonna have to move you to a table in the main dining room. We need to get ready for the party that's coming in at seven."

"No worries," Jaycee said. "Just make sure you give us a good table."

"For Piper, of course." Mary Ann winked at Piper. "And don't forget, Margot and I are having a party at our house next Saturday."

Jaycee crossed her arms over her chest. "I might not be able to make it."

Mary Ann smiled and looked to Piper. "Then I'll see you there? Your kids are welcome, but maybe you could bring a date that's less surly than this one."

"Absolutely," Piper said. "And thanks again for everything you've done to get this project off the ground."

"No, thank you for including me." Mary Ann smiled. "I've been blessed with an abundance. It makes me feel good to be able to give back in some small way. It's truly an honor." Mary Ann turned to the door.

"Maybe she isn't all bad," Jaycee said loudly.

"I heard that, Realtor. Keep it up, and I might not have a table for you tonight."

Jaycee grinned. "That's okay. Then I can get to my booty call early."

Piper swatted Jaycee's arm. "Keep that up, and there will be no booty call."

Mary Ann laughed as she slipped from the room.

"So dinner and then..." Piper licked her lip and then bit it.

"About that." Jaycee stood and reached out her

hand to Piper. "Why didn't you tell me I had you all night?"

Piper rose from her seat and stood facing Jaycee. "I wanted to surprise you."

"It's a nice surprise." Jaycee pulled Piper to her. "A real nice surprise."

It was rare they got the opportunity to spend the entire night together. Caleb and Sergio were the only people Piper trusted to leave the kids with, but she didn't want to impose on their generosity.

Jaycee swayed to imaginary music and soon had Piper dancing with her. Piper rested her head against Jaycee's chest.

"Do you realize this will only be the second time we've spent the night together since we started dating?" Jaycee asked. "That's twice in two months."

"Uh-huh," Piper said into Jaycee's shoulder.

"It wouldn't have to be that way."

Piper stiffened. They'd had this conversation before. It never ended badly, but she knew each time how hurt it left Jaycee. "Do we have to talk about this now?"

"I guess not." Jaycee pulled her closer.

"But you want to?"

"I suppose, but I don't want to ruin our one night together, either."

Piper looked up at Jaycee. "What do you say we make a deal? Mary Ann said we're going to have to clear out of here soon. We talk about it now. Once we leave this room, the conversation about it is over."

"I can live with that." Jaycee smiled down at her.

Piper raised her head and pursed her lips. Jaycee picked up on her cue and bent farther. Their lips met. The kiss started out slowly but soon grew in intensity. Their bodies pressed against each other as they continued to dance as they kissed.

After some time, Jaycee pulled away. She had an unfocused look in her eyes, and her face was flushed. "Holy shit. You did that on purpose, didn't you?"

Piper shot Jaycee an innocent look.

"Don't give me that." Jaycee smiled. "You agreed to talk about the problem of our stolen moments, and then you went and kissed me."

"Hey. That's all on you." Piper smiled. "You're the one that wanted to talk, so I guess you should have controlled your lips better."

Jaycee chuckled. "I still have a few minutes left, so I'll jump straight to the point. Can't we revisit you and the kids spending the weekend with me?"

"We can revisit it, but I won't change my mind."

"I just don't understand. What's the harm?" Piper could tell that Jaycee was trying to keep the frustration out of her voice, but it was there.

"The shelter and transitional housing are all they've ever known. Paxton doesn't remember much of our time with Emma, and Maddie doesn't remember any."

"What's wrong with introducing them to something different?"

Piper sighed. "They know other people live in nicer places. I let them visit friends, and they stay with Sergio and Caleb."

"Exactly, so you're making my argument for me."

They'd stopped dancing, and Piper stepped out of Jaycee's embrace. She took a few steps back.

"You don't want to be close to me now?" The hurt was evident in Jaycee's eyes.

Piper smiled. "It's not that. I don't want to keep

craning my neck looking up at you."

"Okay." Jaycee gave her a tentative smile. "They've seen other places, why not mine?"

"I don't want them to be confused."

"How would that confuse them?"

Piper threw up her hands. "Fine. Do you want to know the entire truth?"

"Please." Jaycee's voice came out barely over a whisper.

Tears welled in Piper's eyes. "I don't want them to hate going back to our apartment every Monday."

"Then move in with me."

Piper took another step back. During all their past discussions, Jaycee had never asked Piper to move in with her. Anger replaced her tears. "No. That's not the way this works. Just because you don't get your way doesn't mean you throw something like that out without any thought. That was callous." Piper's gaze darted around the room. All she wanted was to escape.

"Whoa." Jaycee held up her hands. "I'm sorry. I wasn't trying to be callous. Please. I don't want this argument to interfere with our time together."

Piper focused on relaxing her shoulders. She didn't want their evening to be ruined, either. "Then you need to think before you speak. You can't just casually throw out something like that." Piper smoothed the front of her dress. "You don't know what it's been like for the kids...and me."

"I'm being insensitive." Jaycee took a step toward her. "I know your story and how courageous you've been."

"I'm no hero. I'm just a mother trying to do right by her children." Piper sighed. "I've been doing it all myself for so long, I'm not sure how to rely on anyone else."

"I know that." Jaycee gave her a sad smile. "But one day you will, and I hope it'll be me."

Jaycee's words tugged at Piper's heart. "I think it could be."

"Good." Jaycee's smile was broad. "Can I ask you one more question?"

"Okay." Piper hoped she wouldn't regret her answer.

"If I had a smaller house, a more normal-sized one, would it make a difference? Would you be comfortable with you and the kids spending the night?"

Would it? Piper already knew the answer, but she took several seconds before she answered. "Yes."

"That's what I thought." Jaycee bit her lip and appeared to be deep in thought.

"No." Piper pointed at Jaycee as she took a step back. "Don't even think about it."

"About what?" Jaycee failed at her clueless act.

"You will not buy a second home that's smaller."

"Okay." Jaycee's shoulders sagged.

Piper wanted to be mad at Jaycee's audacity, but how could she when Jaycee's only offense was wanting to spend more time with her? "I love you, Jaycee. I really do." Piper closed the gap between them and reached out for Jaycee's hand. "I just need you to understand how it feels to not be able to provide for my kids."

"How can you say that?" Jaycee's jaw tightened. "How can you think that you haven't provided for them? You are the best damned role model any kid could ever have."

"I try to make the right decisions and protect

them the best I can, so I need to take this slow so I know they won't be hurt again." Piper's eyes filled with tears, and her heart ached. "Do you want to hear something horrible?" Piper didn't wait for Jaycee to respond. "There was a point, when we were living in our car, that I wondered if the kids would be better off if I gave them up. Let someone better raise them."

"Oh, Piper." Jaycee's eyes brimmed with tears. "You have more spirit and grit than anyone I know. That's one of the things I love most about you. But I hate that you allow the hand you were dealt to make you feel lesser."

Piper could no longer hold back her tears, so she let them flow.

Jaycee wiped a tear from Piper's cheek. "I didn't mean to make you cry."

Piper shook her head. "You didn't. I'm making myself cry."

Jaycee wrapped her arms around Piper and drew her in. "It's okay. Sometimes the pain needs to come out."

Piper allowed the tears to flow freely and hoped she wasn't ruining Jaycee's shirt, but she needed to feel Jaycee's arms around her. Jaycee gently ran her hand down Piper's back. It was a comforting gesture that only served to make Piper cry harder.

"I'm sorry," Piper said. "I just need to get through my last semester of school and get this project for DOTS off the ground before I can think about this or take on anything else."

"You're right. I never want to make you feel pressured or backed into a corner. Sometimes I forget how much you're juggling."

"I wish I could be a better person for you." Tears

started up again as Piper delivered the line.

"No. Never say that." Jaycee hugged her tightly. "You're perfect."

Piper laughed. "Now you've gone too far." It felt good to laugh.

"Well, you're perfect for me." Jaycee lifted Piper's chin.

Just as their lips met, a knock sounded at the door. Piper took a step back as Jaycee said, "Come in."

One of Mary Ann's workers peeked her head in the door. "Um, Ms. Mary Ann said that you'd be done in here by six, so we can get this room set up."

"Yes, of course," Jaycee said. "We were just on our way out when you knocked."

"Great." A look of relief crossed the woman's face. "Ms. Mary Ann said to show you to a table."

"Could you please thank Mary Ann for us," Piper said, "but we won't be able to stay for dinner."

Piper felt Jaycee's gaze boring into the side of her head.

"Very well," the woman said as she backed out the door.

"Really?" Jaycee smirked. "We won't be staying for dinner, huh?"

Chapter Thirty-two

"You look beautiful, Mommy," Maddie said. Her eyes were wide as she looked up at Piper.

"Aww, thanks, baby girl." Piper twirled around so her dress flared out at the bottom.

She did feel pretty today. Yesterday, Jaycee had taken the day off work, and they'd taken the kids to the zoo. Being outside all day had given her a hint of color. It was still early June, so she wouldn't call it a suntan yet, but it gave her a healthy glow.

"Doesn't Mommy look pretty?" Maddie asked Paxton.

"I guess." He crossed his arms over his chest.

"Are you still mad?"

"I don't know why we can't go, too." Paxton's lip trembled.

"Because Jaycee and I are going on a date. We haven't had one in nearly three weeks."

"But I want to hang out with Jaycee, too."

Piper tried to hide her smile. The kids had taken to Jaycee from the start, but lately, they'd wanted to include her in everything.

"We spent the entire day at the zoo yesterday," Piper said.

"I loved the hippos," Maddie said.

"The hippos are stupid," Paxton snapped.

"They are not!" Maddie stomped her foot and glared at Paxton.

"They are so. They're big and fat just like you."

"Paxton! That is enough." Piper scowled. "Just because you're mad, you will not take it out on your sister."

"Sorry," Paxton muttered to Maddie, who'd already moved on and was cramming books into her overnight bag.

"You love spending time with Sergio and Caleb." Piper knew she was missing something, but she couldn't figure out what. She glanced at the clock. She had enough time. "Why don't we go in the kitchen and finish this talk?" She glanced at Maddie, hoping Paxton would get the hint.

"Okay," he said and marched across the room.

Piper glanced over her shoulder as she followed, but Maddie was deep into her packing and didn't seem to notice.

"Okay, mister," Piper said once in the kitchen. "Spill. What's bothering you?"

Paxton flopped onto the kitchen chair, and it wobbled under his weight. Lately, she'd been noticing more of those things. She doubted the apartment was getting any worse, but spending time at Jaycee's made the dinginess of their surroundings more evident.

She pushed the thought from her mind and focused on Paxton. He hadn't spoken yet, but by the way he rubbed his chin in thought, he was about ready to.

"Does Jaycee like us?" he asked.

Whatever question Piper was expecting, that wasn't it. "Of course she likes you. Why do you say that?"

He shrugged. "I dunno."

Piper sat on the rickety chair across from him. "I think you do."

He shrugged again.

"Jaycee takes us all kinds of fun places. Just because she and I have a date tonight doesn't mean she doesn't like you."

"I know." He ran his hand over the rough surface of the table. "Is she embarrassed by us?"

Whoa! Piper prided herself on being an aware mother, but she had no idea what Paxton was getting at. Her stomach roiled. "Did Jaycee say something to make you feel that way?"

"No."

Piper glanced at the clock. This conversation could take a while if he kept beating around the bush. "Sweetie. I want to understand what's bothering you. Jaycee and I have tickets, so I can't be late. Do you think you could just tell me what's the matter?"

"She doesn't want to come here." He kicked at the empty chair where Maddie normally sat.

"Do not kick the furniture," Piper said in her sternest mom voice.

"It's why she won't come here, isn't it? All our broken-down stuff."

She needed to get her emotions under control before she answered. She wavered between shame and anger. Neither a good place to dwell. Piper searched her mind for an answer but settled on the truth. "You're becoming a big boy, so I'm going to be honest with you."

He sat up straighter in his chair and looked at her expectantly.

"It's Mommy not Jaycee." Piper sighed. "Jaycee wants to come here, but I tell her no."

Paxton's eyes widened. "Are you embarrassed of us?"

"No, sweetie. Never." Piper brushed his bangs out of his eyes. "We don't have as nice of things as Jaycee does, so it makes me uncomfortable."

A groove formed on his forehead. "But Jaycee doesn't care about those things. She just wants to be with us. With you."

Piper blinked back tears and smiled. "When did you get to be so wise?"

"I'll be in the fourth grade next year, so I know things."

Piper wanted to wrap him in a hug, but she knew he'd take offense. "How about we invite Jaycee for dinner next weekend?"

His eyes lit up. "Do you think she'd come?"

In a heartbeat. Instead, she said, "Jaycee's picking me up downstairs today, and since you'll be helping Sergio and Caleb, how about you ask her when she comes?"

"Really?"

"Yep. And you better find out what she'd like to eat, too."

"Awesome." His smile transformed his face, but then a shadow crossed his eyes. "Can I tell you the other reason I think she's embarrassed by us?"

"Of course."

"She doesn't want us at her house, either. Just you."

Ugh. She'd brought this on herself. Trying to protect them, she'd done the opposite. "That's my fault, too. I told her no."

He frowned. "Why?"

Piper had always been as honest as she could with the children, so she needed to practice it now. "Jaycee has a lot more money than we do."

"Yeah," he said, as if it were obvious.

"You knew that?"

"Duh. Even Maddie knows that."

"I don't want you kids feeling bad because we don't have as much."

"Just because we don't have lots of stuff doesn't make us poor."

Piper narrowed her eyes and studied him.

"Don't you remember?" He looked at the ceiling and sighed. "You always told us there's lots of things money can't buy. Like love. We got lots of love, so we're rich, too."

"That we do." Piper smiled. "You're—"

"Jaycee was really sad when she came to the shelter on Thanksgiving. She didn't have much love."

"Did she tell you that?"

"No." He drew out the word as if he were exasperated with her. "I could just tell. But now that we all love her, she's happier." He smiled. "You're happier, too."

"I am." Piper smiled. "But I was happy before."

He nodded. "I know. We make you happy, but she makes you happy in a different way."

Wow. Where had she been when he'd been growing up right under her nose? She pushed back tears.

"All of you fill my heart."

He jumped from the table. "Can I go tell Maddie we're gonna invite Jaycee for dinner next week?"

"Sure, but I think I need a hug."

He cocked his head. "Okay." He walked to where she sat and wrapped his arms around her neck.

Piper hugged him with all her might.

Chapter Thirty-three

Jaycee jabbed at the elevator button for the third time, as if it would make the doors close quicker. *Relax.* If she arrived at Piper's door with this frenetic energy, she'd set the wrong tone for the evening. When Jaycee had talked to Piper on the phone earlier, Jaycee could hear the nervousness in Piper's voice, so Jaycee didn't need to add to it.

The doors whooshed closed, and the elevator began its ascent to the third floor. Jaycee closed her eyes and took a deep breath. So much was riding on how things went tonight. If it went well, Piper would likely invite her over more often, but if it bombed...

No. She couldn't think that way. It put too much pressure on the outcome of tonight. Even if things went badly, if it was uncomfortable, nothing would change between the two of them. She needed to stop worrying, or she'd jinx herself. Her relationship with Piper had exceeded her wildest dreams.

Jaycee had never been able to communicate with Tessa like she did with Piper. Sometimes they were still tentative when a tough issue arose, but eventually, they'd find a way to talk it out. Time after time, Jaycee discovered, or maybe Piper showed her, it wasn't scary to open up and be vulnerable.

The loud ding pulled Jaycee out of her thoughts. With a jolt, the elevator came to a stop, and the doors slid open.

Showtime. She clutched the bags she carried tighter as she approached the door at the end of the hall. The corridor was narrow but well lit. What had she expected, twenty-watt or broken bulbs? She watched too many movies.

She stopped outside the door. Apartment 304. There were only four apartments on the floor. For some reason, she'd expected more. It seemed quaint. A television blared from the apartment next door. She hoped the walls between the apartments had better soundproofing.

She lifted her hand to knock but stopped; instead, she took two more centering breaths. Before she could finish letting out her last breath, the apartment door flew open.

Jaycee jumped back in surprise. "Shit."

Maddie looked up at her with big brown eyes and laughed. "I scared you."

Jaycee slapped her hand against her chest and staggered around the hallway, exaggerating her fright.

The more Maddie laughed, the more Jaycee played it up. Before long, Paxton had joined Maddie. The sound of the children's laughter made it easier to put her nerves aside.

Piper appeared at the doorway. "What are you three carrying on about?" She graced Jaycee with a smile.

Blood pounded in Jaycee's ears. Piper looked beautiful. Her simple sundress was the color of mustard, and the cut showed off her well-defined shoulders. Jaycee detected a hint of makeup, but it was subtle and most pronounced around her eyes. It was her smile, as always, that made Jaycee's heart race.

"Do you want to come in, or are you just going

to stand there staring?"

Heat rose in Jaycee's cheeks. "You're beautiful."

Piper scowled. "Stop. And get inside before all the neighbors hear you. If they do, they'll tease me mercilessly about how bea-ut-i-ful I am."

Before Jaycee could respond, Maddie wrapped her arms around Jaycee's waist and hugged her. Jaycee laughed and hugged Maddie back. "Hi, Munchkin."

"I helped make dessert," Maddie said.

Jaycee shot a questioning glance at Piper, who gave her a confirmational nod. "Well, I bet it will be extra yummy then."

Paxton stood behind Maddie and shuffled from foot to foot. "Hey, Paxton," Jaycee said. "How are you?"

"I'm okay," he answered.

"Just okay?"

He nodded and looked down at the floor. "I'm glad you came."

"Are you nervous?" Jaycee wasn't sure if it was the right approach with Paxton, but she'd found straightforward was always better with her nieces and nephews.

He looked up at her wide-eyed. "How'd you know?"

"Because I'm a little nervous myself."

"Really?"

"Uh-huh." Jaycee smiled. "Do you know what usually helps me when I'm feeling nervous?"

He shook his head.

"A hug. Do you know anyone that might give me a hug?"

"Me." Maddie jumped up and down before she launched herself at Jaycee.

"You already gave her a hug," Paxton protested.

"But she asked who'd give her a hug." Maddie jutted out her bottom lip.

Paxton pointed at himself. "She wanted a hug from me."

"Oh." Maddie let go and started to step back.

"Actually, I wanted one from both of you." Jaycee wrapped the arm she carried her bags in around Maddie and opened her other one to Paxton.

Paxton slid into her embrace and hugged her tighter than she'd expected. She caught a glimpse of Piper's surprised expression out of the corner of her eye. She squeezed them once more before she let go and held up the bag. "I almost forgot. I brought presents."

Maddie squealed. "I love presents."

"Let Jaycee get all the way inside before you tear into them," Piper said. "Besides, Mommy wants a hug, too."

Jaycee smiled. "I'd hoped you'd say that." Jaycee opened her arms wide, and Piper moved into them. Something about holding Piper in her own apartment made the embrace more special, or maybe it simply served to push Jaycee's edginess away. For whatever reason, the hug filled Jaycee with warmth, and she didn't want to let go.

Piper must have felt the same since she didn't break the embrace, either.

"Are you ever going to stop hugging?" Maddie whined. "I want to see what's in the bags."

Jaycee laughed as she let go of Piper. "I think we've been called out." Jaycee winked at Piper.

"Young lady," Piper said in a stern voice, but Jaycee saw the amusement in her eyes. "Jaycee is a guest, and we will not be rude."

Maddie dropped her gaze to the floor. "Sorry," she mumbled.

"Okay." Piper clapped her hands. "Let's take Jaycee into the living room, so we can see what kind of goodies she has in those bags."

The kids raced ahead. Piper took Jaycee's hand, and Jaycee was surprised at how warm it was. Piper's hands were normally cold. *Nerves?* Jaycee decided not to ask. There was no sense drawing attention to it.

It took only two steps away from the door and a left turn for them to arrive in the living room. Jaycee tried to take it in without a reaction, but it was difficult. Piper wasn't kidding when she said her entire apartment could fit into Jaycee's bedroom.

The living room couldn't have been any bigger than ten by ten. A threadbare love seat sat against one wall and faced a coffee table with one of the smallest televisions Jaycee had ever seen. Guilt rose as she thought of her seventy-five-inch screen.

The only other furniture in the room was a La-Z-Boy with a small end table beside it. Despite the sparseness, there was a warmth about the room. The décor consisted mostly of family pictures covering the walls. Jaycee was drawn to them like a moth to a flame.

"These are great pictures," Jaycee said as she circled the room.

Piper smiled. "Lots of memories on these walls. After dinner, we'll give you a tour of them."

Jaycee pointed at one picture that looked to be the kids covered in mud from head to toe. "I can't wait to hear the story behind this one."

Piper laughed. "It's a classic."

Jaycee turned away from the pictures and held

up one of the bags. "Anyone ready for presents?"

The kids both crowded in around her. "I'm taking that as a *yes.*" Jaycee reached in and pulled out Maddie's present.

Maddie squealed and took the die cast motorcycle from Jaycee. "Mommy, look." She waved the toy over her head. "It's purple. My favorite color."

Piper leaned in. "Wow. That's pretty." She pointed at the logo on the packaging. "And it's a Harley-Davidson."

"Of course," Jaycee said. "They're the best."

Maddie had already ripped open the package and was pushing the motorcycle around the floor.

"What do you say?" Piper asked.

Maddie jumped to her feet and went to Jaycee. "Thank you." Her sparkling brown eyes and joyful smile warmed Jaycee's heart.

"You're very welcome." Jaycee reached into the bag again and pulled out a large container of strawberries. "I think these might belong to Paxton."

Paxton stepped forward, his eyes wide. "Wow. Look at how big they are." He held up a berry that was nearly as large as a tennis ball. He glanced at Piper. "Can I eat one before supper?"

"Just one since those are as big as your head," Piper said.

"Can I give one to Maddie?" Paxton asked Jaycee.

"I think that's a wonderful idea, and it shows what a gentleman you are."

Paxton beamed. "Come on, Maddie." He held out his hand to her. "We need to wash these before we eat them."

Maddie shoved her motorcycle into her pocket

and took Paxton's hand.

He got to the door and stopped. His eyes were wild with excitement when he turned back. "Mom, can we ask Jaycee if she would go with us?"

Piper smiled. "Go get the flyer."

Paxton ran from the room and returned with a wrinkled paper and thrust it into Jaycee's hands. "Do you wanna go?" he asked. "It's next weekend."

Jaycee looked down at the flyer, and her heart skipped a beat. *Not Cedarsburg.* How had she forgotten the town's Strawberry Festival? "Um...uh, this looks like fun."

"Are you okay?" Piper asked. "All the color drained from your face."

Jaycee shook her head. "It's nothing. I'd love to go." Jaycee wasn't going to dampen Paxton's enthusiasm because of her insecurities. So what, the Wilsons lived in Cedarsburg. Over twelve thousand people lived there; besides, the Wilsons never went to things like the Strawberry Festival anyway.

Jaycee felt Piper's questioning gaze on her. Not wanting to discuss her foolish insecurities, Jaycee held up the other bag. "I think I have one more present," Jaycee said with a little more gusto than she'd intended.

The kids joined in her enthusiasm, while Piper eyed her suspiciously. Jaycee handed the sack to Piper. "I'll let you do the honors."

"Mommy, can I help?" Maddie asked.

"Certainly." Piper squatted between Paxton and Maddie. "What do you think is in here? I think it's a giraffe."

The kids laughed.

"Maybe it's a hamster," Maddie said.

"Or a snake," Paxton added.

Maddie jumped away from the bag. "Gross."

Piper pulled out a large package wrapped in floral paper. "If this is a bouquet, it's the biggest I've ever seen."

"Open it." Jaycee smiled.

Piper tore a corner of the paper off and gasped. "Oh, my god, they're beautiful."

"Let me see." Maddie stood on her tiptoes and peered over Piper's shoulder.

Piper ripped the rest of the paper away to uncover a dozen red roses. "Jaycee, they're gorgeous. Thank you so much."

"Beautiful flowers for a beautiful woman," Jaycee said.

Piper stood, and when she did, Jaycee could see Piper's eyes were misty. "I better get these in water." She pointed to Paxton. "Will you grab the pitcher you make lemonade in?"

❧❧❧❧

Piper dried the last plate and placed it in the cupboard. The night had gone well. After they'd sat down to eat, her nervousness had disappeared as she and the kids fell into the easy interaction they always had with Jaycee.

"She finally fell asleep," Jaycee said as she entered the kitchen. "Sorry I didn't get back here to help."

"Sure you are." Piper grinned. "Pretty convenient you show up right after I'm done."

"But I—"

Piper laughed. "Relax. I'm just messing with you. I know Maddie's stubborn streak." Maddie had insisted that Jaycee read her a bedtime story.

"The kid has stamina. I'm pretty sure if she had toothpicks, she'd have propped her eyes open, so she'd get one more story out of me."

"How many times did you try to leave?"

"Four." Jaycee shook her head. "No matter how quietly I tiptoed, as soon as I got to the door, she'd call me back."

"Get used to it." Piper put her arm around Jaycee and gave her a quick kiss.

"Does that mean I'll get invited back?"

"Maybe." Piper winked. "Unless you keep throwing draw twos on me in Uno."

Jaycee grinned. "The kids thought it was funny."

"I didn't realize the object of the game was to see how many cards you three could stick me with." Piper chuckled. "I don't remember the last time I've heard Paxton laugh so hard."

"Has he always been that intense? Serious?"

Piper nodded, and her eyes clouded. "He saw too much." Piper waved her hand around the kitchen. "This is paradise compared to the lean years."

Jaycee shuddered but tried to cover it with a cough.

"Would you like to have a nightcap?" Piper asked, deciding not to comment on Jaycee's reaction.

"Sure."

"I have Coke, orange juice, tea, or water."

"Party animal. I'll have a Coke."

In the living room, Piper pointed to the love seat. "Care to join me?"

"I'd love to. Is this the make-out couch?"

Piper elbowed Jaycee. "There will be no making out with the kids in the next room."

"Oh, yeah."

Piper grabbed Jaycee's hand. "I might let you steal a kiss or two, though."

They'd been sitting on the couch for some time, talking about nothing and sneaking a kiss here and there when Jaycee said, "I need to tell you something."

Piper groaned. "That is one of the cringiest statements ever. Right up there with *we need to talk*."

Jaycee laughed. "It's not that bad, but I wanted to tell you this earlier, just not in front of the kids."

"Did something happen?"

"No. No, not really. I just want you to know that my in-laws live in Cedarsburg."

Piper wondered why Jaycee would bring up where her in-laws lived.

"The Strawberry Festival. Cedarsburg."

"Oh." Piper drew the word out. "Did you want to cancel?"

"No, not at all. They normally don't go to things like that, but in case I'm a little jumpy, you'll know why."

"We don't have to go."

Jaycee shook her head. "Did you see the look on Paxton's face? I won't be responsible for ruining his day."

"Okay. I've been thinking...um...you had your pool opened last week, didn't you?"

"Yeah?" Jaycee's voice held a questioning note.

"I thought maybe after the festival, I doubt it will take all day, maybe we could stop at your house for a swim."

Jaycee's eyes lit up. She threw her arm around Piper's shoulder and hugged her. "Really? You're going to let them visit?"

"I thought, maybe. Nothing overnight. Just an occasional visit."

"What changed your mind?" Jaycee's smile was enormous.

"Tonight didn't go too bad." Piper held back a smirk, knowing she was goading Jaycee.

"Wow. Not too bad." The twinkle in Jaycee's eyes told Piper that she was playing along with the game. "What a ringing endorsement."

"I thought so." A vision of when Jaycee first arrived flashed in Piper's mind. Her mood sobered. "Are you sure this doesn't bother you?"

"Bother?"

Piper suspected Jaycee was stalling for time, but Piper answered anyway. "Disgust you. Make you uncomfortable. Make you like me less."

"No. No. And no!" Jaycee said the last no with emphasis. "First, I admire you for your grit and determination. And second," Jaycee pointed to the wall where most of the family photos hung, "I might have a fancy house, but it doesn't have half of what this home has."

"Sure." Piper glanced around the room and rolled her eyes. "Such ambiance."

"But it has love." Jaycee's eyes were full of sadness.

Piper snuggled closer to Jaycee. "And it has even more love now that you're here."

Chapter Thirty-four

"Are we really going to try a strawberry corn dog?" Jaycee said. Just the sound of it made her want to gag.

"Or a strawberry brat," Piper answered.

Jaycee turned to Paxton. "Whose idea was it to come here?"

Maddie pointed. "Paxton."

Paxton beamed. They'd been at the Strawberry Festival for nearly three hours, and the kids had been having a blast. Who was she kidding, Jaycee was having just as much fun as they were.

They'd circled the streets twice, checking out the vendors. But it was the park that drew them back. There was a wide array of games and activities for the kids. It didn't take long for Jaycee and Piper to join the fun.

As they left the park in search of the food court, Piper pointed at the strawberry on her cheek. "I think we all look badass."

"Mommy," Maddie said, her eyes wide.

Paxton giggled.

"Um, I mean tough." Piper winked.

Jaycee grinned. They all sported matching strawberries on their faces. Paxton's was the coolest. When the woman doing the face painting had discovered his love for strawberries, she'd added leaves and runners to his. The greenery ran from his cheek down his neck.

Jaycee patted her stomach. "Can't I just have strawberry shortcake for lunch?"

"Absolutely not," Piper said. "You need to experience everything the festival has to offer. Which means strawberry corn dogs."

"Stop." Jaycee held out her palm. "Don't remind me."

Paxton rubbed his tummy. "Yum. Strawberry corn dogs." He smacked his lips together.

Jaycee put her hand against her throat and let her tongue hang out of her mouth. "You're gonna make me sick."

᪣᪣᪣᪣

Jaycee wasn't ready to admit it, but the strawberry corn dog hadn't been half bad. It wasn't something she'd want to eat often, nor would she encourage Mary Ann to put it on the menu at the Sapphire Inn, but still it hadn't been as repulsive as she thought it would be.

Of course, Paxton loved it. He used his teeth to pull the last bite from the stick. Jaycee was surprised he could chew with the big grin he sported.

"You won't need any food for a week," Jaycee teased.

His smile faded. "Don't we get strawberry shortcake?"

"You still want dessert?"

"Yep.' He nodded vigorously.

"Okay. But don't come crying to me when you get a stomachache." Piper turned to Jaycee. "Why don't Paxton and I go get the shortcake, and you can sit with Maddie while she finishes up her food?"

After Piper and Paxton had left the table, Jaycee pulled out a festival map and studied it.

"Why is that lady staring at you?" Maddie asked.

"Huh?" Jaycee looked up.

"That lady over there." Maddie pointed.

***

A dollop of whipped cream fell off the enormous strawberry shortcake and landed on Piper's finger. She grinned and put the whip cream on the tip of Paxton's nose.

They were both laughing when they returned to the table. She set the dessert down and slid into the seat next to Jaycee. Paxton had his fork at the ready as soon as his butt hit the chair.

"Slow down, mister. There's plenty for everyone."

For the first time since she'd arrived back at the table, Piper glanced at Jaycee. *Oh, my god.* "Are you okay? Are you allergic to strawberries?"

"No. Why?" Jaycee's gaze was fixed in the distance, and she never looked at Piper.

"Your face is beet red. Sergio's face looks like that if he gets too much MSG." Piper touched Jaycee's cheek.

Jaycee flinched.

Piper drew her hand back. *Ouch. That hurt.* Jaycee had never reacted to her like that before. "What's wrong?"

Jaycee turned to Piper and took a deep breath. "It's—"

"That lady's coming this way," Maddie said.

Jaycee's eyes filled with panic, and her gaze darted toward the exit.

"What lady?" Piper looked between Jaycee and

Maddie. "What's going on?"

"The lady that's been staring at Jaycee."

"Betsy," Jaycee whispered under her breath.

"Betsy?" Piper said.

"My soon-to-be ex-mother-in-law."

Shit. A tiny woman, Piper assumed was Betsy, marched toward the table. When she was within a few yards, she said, "Well, if it isn't Jaycee Ward." Her voice held an edge. From everything Jaycee had ever told her about Betsy, Piper wouldn't have guessed her tone would hold so much venom. Jaycee had practically anointed her with sainthood.

"Hello, Betsy," Jaycee said and then turned to the man who'd been rushing to keep up with her. "Hi, Chuck."

They both muttered a hello when they arrived at the table.

Piper's gaze shifted between Jaycee and the Wilsons. The tension between Jaycee and Betsy was evident, while Chuck appeared more uncomfortable than angry.

"You're the last person we'd expect to see here," Betsy said. "In our town," she added. The lack of welcome was evident.

Jaycee looked up at the Wilsons but didn't smile. She inhaled slowly and then pointed at Paxton. "He loves strawberries, so we couldn't pass it up."

To her credit, Betsy smiled at Paxton and said, "I see you have a special strawberry on your cheek. It's very nice."

Paxton smiled. He'd been studying the Wilsons, and Piper suspected he sensed the tension. Even as a young boy, he'd been observant and vigilant in assessing a threat.

"Paxton," Piper said. "Why don't you take the shortcake and your sister over to that table with the umbrella? He opened his mouth to speak, but Piper held up her hand. "You don't want the sun to melt the whipped cream, do you?"

Paxton held Piper's gaze for a few beats before he nodded. "Come on, Maddie, we don't want the dessert to be ruined."

Once the children were out of earshot, Betsy looked Piper up and down before she said, "Replacement family?"

Jaycee's face reddened, and her jaw clenched.

Piper tried not to gape but was finding it hard not to. Betsy's hostility didn't match the person Jaycee had described. Maybe Jaycee had been blind to her true character all these years.

Chuck put his hand on Betsy's arm. "I think you need to reel it back to about a five."

"But here she is flaunting her new family in our town." Betsy glared down at Jaycee and Piper.

"Flaunting? What the hell is that supposed to mean?" Jaycee kept her voice low. Piper suspected it was to keep from shouting.

Piper put her hand over the top of Jaycee's and gave it a slight squeeze.

"It means you have some nerve coming here," Betsy said.

"It wasn't enough to kick me out of your family?" Jaycee raised her voice. "But now I can't even come to your goddamned town? Would you like me to leave Wisconsin, too?"

"Kick you out?" Betsy's eyes flashed in anger. "You couldn't get away from us fast enough."

"What the hell are you talking about?" Jaycee

began to rise from the table, but Piper gently tugged at her arm to keep her seated.

"Mr. and Mrs. Wilson, maybe you'd like to sit down." Piper glanced around at the other festivalgoers, hoping that Jaycee and Betsy would get the hint.

It was Chuck who responded. "I think this young lady has a good idea."

"She has a name," Jaycee spat. "It's Piper."

"Jaycee!" Piper said with a little more volume than she'd intended. "Mr. Wilson wasn't being insulting."

"Chuck," he said. "Please, call me Chuck."

Betsy shot him a dirty look but allowed him to pull out a chair for her so she could sit. Once she was seated, he took the chair next to his wife.

Betsy crossed her arms over her chest. "You made it quite clear that you didn't want anything to do with us, so I'm surprised you'd come here."

"I don't know what game you're playing with me, but I don't find it amusing." Jaycee's nostrils flared. "Couldn't you have just left us alone? We weren't doing anything to bother you." Jaycee's voice cracked.

Shit. Piper's heart went out to Jaycee. From the look on her face, her anger was turning to hurt. "I'm not sure what's going on here," Piper said. "But as an outside observer, it seems as if you're both upset with each other."

Betsy snorted. "I see you found yourself a rocket scientist."

Piper pursed her lips and counted to ten. Sparring with this acerbic woman would do no good.

"Leave her alone," Jaycee said between clenched teeth.

"Maybe I should leave both of you alone." Tears

welled in Betsy's eyes.

After her performance so far, it surprised Piper. In desperation, Piper looked at Chuck. Their gazes met. She recognized the same helpless look on his face that was likely on hers.

Chuck cleared his throat. "Jaycee…" He waited for Jaycee to turn to him before he continued. "Betsy's really hurt, especially when you didn't reach out after her diagnosis last month."

"Diagnosis?" The crease in Jaycee's forehead deepened. "What diagnosis?"

Betsy swiped at her cheek. "Like you don't know."

Jaycee shook her head. "I don't."

"Her cancer's back," Chuck said.

Jaycee's face dropped. "What? No!"

"Her other breast," Chuck said.

"Oh, my god." Jaycee put her hand against her forehead. Her eyes filled with tears.

"You didn't know, did you?" Betsy asked.

Piper was stunned how much Betsy's features had softened.

"No. How would I have known?" Jaycee asked.

"Tessa said she told you." Betsy's arms were still crossed over her chest, but she shifted them as if she were hugging herself. "But you never reached out to me."

"I haven't talked to Tessa since New Year's Eve when she showed up at my house drunk."

Betsy shot Chuck a look. Chuck nodded and then said, "That's after Avery broke up with her."

Jaycee shrugged. "Figures, but I haven't talked to her since."

"Oh, honey, you really didn't know, did you?" Betsy said.

With the kindness in Betsy's voice, tears streamed down Jaycee's cheeks. "I had no idea. I'm so sorry. Is it...has it...um..."

"It's treatable. They caught it early." Betsy shook her head and looked down at her hands. "I should have made them take both the first time." Betsy sighed, and her shoulders slumped. "I hear the treatment has improved since the last time, though."

Tears continued to stream down Jaycee's cheeks, and Piper wondered if Jaycee was even aware of it. Piper wanted to hug her, but without getting in the way, all she could do was squeeze Jaycee's hand.

Betsy stood and came around the table. Piper let go of Jaycee's hand, so she could stand. Jaycee and Betsy fell into each other's arms.

Chuck glanced at Piper and said, "Apparently, my daughter's made a mess of things. I love her, but right now, I want to shake her."

Once Jaycee and Betsy separated, Betsy said, "Tessa told us you wanted a clean break from the family. She said it was too hard for you to be around us, knowing you couldn't have her."

Jaycee's face turned crimson, and her hands trembled.

Piper stood. She rubbed Jaycee's back and faced Betsy. "Um, why don't we all sit back down?"

"Unbelievable," Jaycee finally said as she sat. "Her ego knows no bounds, does it?" The vein in Jaycee's neck throbbed. "Sorry. I shouldn't talk about your daughter that way, but I'm pissed."

"I am, too." Betsy glowered. "But what about the twins?"

"What about them?"

"They said they texted you, but you wouldn't see

them."

"That's true." Jaycee groaned. "They texted that they wanted to meet to say goodbye. I couldn't do it. I didn't think my heart could take it."

Chuck snorted. "Damned kids. They didn't tell us they said that to you. They'd planned on asking you to reconsider."

It was hard not to get up and wrap her arms around Jaycee. Piper stood and glanced at the kids who sat a few tables over. "I should go check on Maddie and Paxton. It looks like they might have polished off that entire shortcake."

Jaycee clutched her midsection. "Oh, god. That makes my stomach hurt. That strawberry corn dog is sitting in it like lead."

Chuck wrinkled his nose. "You ate one?"

Jaycee made a face. "Yes." She motioned toward Piper. "She made me."

The Wilsons laughed.

"Well, it was nice to meet you," Piper said to the Wilsons.

"No," Betsy said.

Piper's eyes widened.

"Oh, my gosh." Betsy put her hand over her mouth. "That came out all wrong. I meant, we'd like to get to know you and don't want you rushing off."

Jaycee looked at Piper. "The kids were loving the park area. Maybe we could go back there, so they have something to do, and we can visit with Betsy and Chuck for a bit." Jaycee turned to the Wilsons. "That is, if you have the time."

"We'd love to," Betsy said.

Piper smiled. "I'd like that, too."

Chapter Thirty-five

Jaycee looked at the caller ID and groaned. *Shit.* Did she want to answer it? Maybe she should get it over with. "Hello."

"Hi, Jaycee," Tessa said.

Jaycee leaned back in her office chair. Good start. Tessa hadn't started off screaming. "What can I do for you?" Jaycee put on her most pleasant business voice.

"I hear you ran into my mom and dad on Saturday."

"I did." It was best not to offer any additional information.

"I just got done talking to Mom," Tessa said. "No, that's not true. I just got done being lectured by Mom. I didn't do much talking."

Jaycee smiled. She could only imagine what Betsy had to say. "Uh-oh. It's Monday. It took her that long?"

"She said she needed to cool down before she talked to me." Tessa snorted. "I'd have hated to see her when she was fired up."

"She's a spitfire." Jaycee had no idea where this conversation was going, but she'd keep it light until Tessa showed her hand.

"That she is. Uh...the reason I'm calling—"

Jaycee clenched the arm of her chair. *Here it comes.*

"I just wanted to...uh..." Tessa took a deep breath. "I wanted to apologize."

"For?" Jaycee hoped her voice didn't come out as tentative as she felt.

"Everything. I was an asshole to you, and I'm sorry."

What the hell? Jaycee needed to respond, but she had no words. *Think.*

Tessa laughed. A carefree laugh that Jaycee hadn't heard from Tessa in a long time. "I know. Not fair to hit you with that out of the blue."

"No. I...um...I appreciate it. I do. You caught me off guard."

"I'm sure you think Mom put me up to it, but that's only partially true. I've been wanting to reach out for nearly six months. Since my performance on New Year's Eve."

"Why didn't you?"

"I was embarrassed." Tessa cleared her throat. "And I haven't particularly liked myself."

"Divorces are hard," Jaycee said, wanting to throw Tessa a lifeline. Despite what had happened, they'd still spent fifteen years together. There were once good memories.

"I've just been so angry at you." Tessa's tone didn't hold any anger.

"Me?" Jaycee kept her voice level. "You asked me for the divorce."

"You pushed me into it."

Jaycee's jaw tightened. She wouldn't lose her temper.

"Wait," Tessa said. "That wasn't fair. Our relationship, or lack of one, pushed me to it. Do you remember what you said when I asked for the divorce?"

"No," Jaycee admitted. "It was all such a blur, but I likely asked you why."

"You said okay. In the calmest voice. No tears. No anger. Just okay." Tessa sighed. "Then you started asking about the logistics."

"I'm sorry. You have to understand I was blindsided."

"The funny thing is, I didn't really want the divorce." Tessa let out a half chuckle.

"Then why did you ask for it?" Jaycee's voice rose.

"Because you wanted it."

Could Jaycee deny it?

"I was so angry that day," Tessa said. "You probably don't remember this, either. You and Mom had been out shopping for the twins' birthday party, and you were rambling on and on about what you'd bought for them. And I realized I didn't even know what the hell to buy my own family, but you did. And you were laughing and happy. And it hit me. I'd known it all along, but it was like something in my brain opened, and I had clarity. You were in love with my family, not me." Pain had crept into Tessa's voice but still no anger.

"I do remember that day. You seemed irate the moment I walked in the door," Jaycee said in a soft voice.

"I never told you this, but I'd lost a patient on the operating table that day. A little girl. She was five."

"Oh, god, Tessa, I'm so sorry. Why didn't you tell me?"

"I was pissed off at the world. You were there and so happy having spent the day with my mom. So I lashed out." Tessa sniffed. Was she crying? Tessa didn't cry. "*I want a divorce* fell out of my mouth. I was shocked. I started to tell you that I didn't mean it."

"But why didn't you?"

"I went to, but I looked into your eyes. Do you know what I saw?" Tessa didn't wait for Jaycee to respond. "Relief. I saw relief."

Tessa's words stung.

"Damn it, Jaycee. I wanted you to stop me. To fight for me. To scream. To cry. Something."

"But I did," Jaycee said, finally finding her voice.

Tessa let out a breath. "A week later."

"But it took me time to process. I was a wreck. I spent so many months crying and begging you to go to counseling."

"After I cut you off from my family." Still Tessa's tone remained calm. "It's taken me a while to accept. If you had a family of your own, I doubt if we'd have made it for more than five years."

Bile rose in Jaycee's throat. She wanted to tell Tessa she was wrong, but thinking about it now, she couldn't. "I'm so sorry, Tessa. I never meant to hurt you. You must think I'm a monster."

Tessa chuckled. "I did for a while. My family's great. Who wouldn't have fallen in love with them?"

Even though Tessa's laugh held no mirth, Jaycee still felt terrible. *What had she done?* The lump in her throat made it impossible to speak.

"Hey," Tessa said. "Are you okay?"

"I don't know what to say. How to apologize," Jaycee croaked out. "I hope you know I didn't realize that's what I was doing."

"I know. I know it wasn't on purpose. You're one of the purest souls I know. I was so hurt. In the moment, I just wanted to hurt you back."

"So you took away your family," Jaycee said. "I got what I deserved."

"No. That was cruel, and I am so sorry. You weren't aware of what you were doing, but I did what I did intentionally." Tessa's voice came out in a whisper. "That's why I went to your house on New Year's. I wanted to apologize."

"Um, it didn't seem like that was your motive."

"I got drunk. I was a mess. I felt so guilty about what I was doing to you and to my family. Avery broke up with me right before Christmas because I had *unresolved issues.* It took a few more months for me to hit bottom. I started seeing a counselor in March."

Jaycee's mouth dropped open. "Counseling?"

Tessa laughed. "Don't act so shocked. I needed it. Avery's been there with me every step of the way."

Jaycee waited for a reaction in her body, but none came. "I'm glad you found someone," Jaycee said and meant it.

"Thanks," Tessa said with a smile in her voice. "Mom said you found someone, too."

Jaycee's cheeks warmed. Could she have this conversation with Tessa? "Yeah, I have."

"Can I ask you something?"

"Sure." Jaycee was hesitant, but so far, Tessa had been nothing but kind.

"What do you think happened to us?"

Jaycee sighed. It wasn't what she expected Tessa to ask. "I'm not sure. I guess we just grew apart."

"Were we ever really together?" Tessa's voice held a note of sadness.

Shit. Jaycee didn't want to hurt Tessa again, but she'd wondered the same thing, especially since she met Piper. The way she felt about Piper was unlike anything she'd felt for Tessa. "We were young, trying to build our careers and our life."

Tessa let out a humorless laugh. "Diplomatic answer, but I guess it says it all, doesn't it?"

What else could she say without inflicting any more damage? "We had some good times. Some real good times."

"We did." Tessa's voice softened. "But we wanted different things, didn't we?"

"I think so." Jaycee felt on firmer ground. "You were always wanting something bigger and better."

"And you were content in this little corner of the world." Tessa chuckled. "All you wanted was a little house, a family, and a white picket fence."

Jaycee smiled. It was true. "And you wanted out of here. To travel the world. To move somewhere exotic."

Tessa laughed. "I would have settled for Chicago."

"I held you back." Jaycee suddenly felt sad.

"No. I've got plenty of living left to do, and so do you."

Thirty minutes later after several tears and plenty of laughs, Jaycee stared at the phone. *What the hell is this?* They'd talked like two old friends who hadn't seen each other in a while. As surreal as it was, it also put Jaycee at ease.

"I better let you get back at it," Tessa said.

"Thank you so much for calling and talking."

"And hey, any time you want to hang out with my family, it's all right by me."

A lump caught in Jaycee's throat. "Thank you. And, Tessa, I love you."

"I love you, too, Jaycee."

Chapter Thirty-six

ow much farther do we have to go?" Sergio complained. His forehead was covered with beads of sweat.

"We're almost there," Piper said. "I want to find the perfect place."

"I'll take this." Caleb swept the picnic basket out of Sergio's hand and passed the blanket he'd been carrying to Sergio. "Holy hell, how much food did you bring?"

Piper smiled. She'd watched Sergio pack and had wondered the same thing. "I figured he must have invited twenty of his closest friends."

"Keep it up, and I'm not going to share with you two. Me and the kids will have a feast."

"Maybe he's smarter than we think." Caleb motioned to Paxton and Maddie, who ran ahead on the trail. "Those two are going to need to refuel as much as they've been running today."

"Or they're going to crash as soon as we finish eating and miss the entire fireworks display." Piper shook her head. "God knows they could sleep through it."

"It's probably good we've kept them so busy this afternoon," Caleb said. "Since Paxton was so disappointed earlier."

"He's not the only one," Sergio said.

"I don't think you should go there," Caleb said.

"Agreed." Piper had stopped the conversation earlier, but she'd known Sergio wouldn't let it go that easily. "We want to have a good time tonight."

"I can be pissed off for you and still have a good time," Sergio said.

Caleb shot Sergio a look, but by Sergio's reaction, he had no intention of letting it go.

"Fine. Get it out of your system," Piper said. "Because we won't have this conversation in front of Paxton and Maddie."

"How about over there?" Caleb said. "We'll be able to see the reflection of the fireworks off the lake."

Piper glanced at the shoreline up ahead. Lake Michigan was calm today, but they still should be able to hear the sound of the water from the site Caleb had chosen. "Perfect."

"And look." Sergio motioned to the sparse clusters of people who'd already staked out their places. "We could have come an hour later and still found a good spot."

"You don't know that," Piper said.

"And stop being so damned cranky," Caleb added.

"I'm pissed, and Piper said I could talk about it."

Piper sighed. She'd worked hard all day to be upbeat for the kids. "Just say it, for fuck's sake."

"Now look what you've done." Caleb frowned at Sergio. "You've made Piper drop the f-bomb."

"Paxton. Maddie," Piper called. "We're setting up over there by that clump of trees. Do *not* go any closer to the water."

"I'm not the one that stood her up," Sergio said.

Piper's jaw clenched. "I was not stood up."

"You might as well have been," Sergio countered.

"How do you figure?" Piper slid out of her backpack and dropped it to the ground. It was best she stayed busy to keep Sergio's comments from stinging.

"You've only celebrated every holiday together since Thanksgiving."

"So this time Jaycee had plans. It's not a big deal." But it was. At least it was to Piper. Today, no amount of ice cream or cotton candy had soothed the ache in her chest, not that she hadn't tried.

"Honey, I'm on your side and think Sergio should drop it." Caleb put his hand on her back. "But even I don't believe you think it's no big deal."

"What do you want from me?" Piper dropped to her knees, unzipped the backpack, and pulled out a blanket. "I won't be that girlfriend."

"Did you tell her you were hurt?" Sergio asked.

Did she? Not exactly. She might have hinted, but Jaycee was so excited to be invited to the Wilsons' Fourth of July party that she hadn't noticed. "Why should I be hurt? We hadn't made any plans for today."

"That's because it should have been a given," Sergio said. "At least in my book."

Piper stood and shook the blanket out and let it flutter to the ground. "She just reconnected with the family she'd been mourning for the past year. Of course, she'd want to see them." Piper knew it was true, but still she missed Jaycee. There was more laughter with her around, even for the kids. When had she allowed herself to become so attached to Jaycee that her absence created such a dark hole?

"She could have seen them some other day," Sergio said. "They haven't been around while you've been picking up the pieces of Jaycee they'd left behind."

Sergio's words cut into her, and she winced. She wanted to say something in Jaycee's defense, but the words stuck in her throat. Piper sat on the blanket and kicked off her shoes. Her feet were sore from all the walking they'd done today.

"Jesus, Sergio." Caleb set the picnic basket on the blanket. "Can't you see she's upset? Why don't you leave well enough alone?"

"I'm sorry." Sergio sat across from Piper with the picnic basket between them. He flipped open the top and reached inside. "I want better for you."

"Come on, don't say something like that." Piper met Sergio's gaze. "Give her a break. One mistake doesn't mean she's not good for me."

Sergio clapped his hands together. "Finally, you admitted it. She made a mistake."

"You did that intentionally." Piper looked up at Caleb, who still stood. "He did it on purpose, didn't he?"

Caleb glanced at Sergio. "He did." Caleb finished spreading the other blanket and sat. "Perhaps it's good he did. Now maybe you can tell us the truth about how you feel."

Piper wrapped her arms around her knees and hugged them to her. "Okay. Yes, I'm hurt, and I miss Jaycee. But I'm also pissed at myself for being so selfish. I want this for her. She deserves this, so she certainly doesn't need me making her feel bad about it. I love her. And if I love her as much as I say I do, then I need to be happy for her."

Sergio patted her hand. "Very mature of you, but it doesn't mean it doesn't hurt."

"This is the first time I've brought the kids here to see the fireworks. I wanted her with us." Piper shrugged. "Hopefully, we'll have plenty of fireworks in our future."

Sergio laughed. "We don't need to hear about your sexcapades."

"Get your mind out of the gutter." Piper drew her eyebrows together. "You know that's not what I meant."

"Did you tell her this was their first?" Caleb asked Piper, ignoring Sergio's comments.

Piper shook her head. "I wanted to surprise her. Let her see the kids' reaction without her knowing how awed they'll be. Stupid, I know."

"Are you going to talk to her about it?" Sergio asked.

"No. I need to give her space. You should have seen her. It was both heartwarming and heart-wrenching." Piper smiled as the movie of Jaycee reconnecting with the Wilsons ran in her head. "She's been a raw nerve since. Then add the phone call from Tessa and—"

"Whoa, back the train up," Sergio said. "She reconnected with Tessa, her ex?"

Shit. Piper had decided not to tell anyone, but now she'd opened the door. She felt both men's gazes boring into her, so she busied herself with setting the plates and cups out on the blanket.

"We're waiting," Sergio said.

Caleb smacked his leg. "Don't push."

Piper finished laying out the dishes before she looked up. "Tessa called to apologize. They had a nice talk. It was cathartic for Jaycee." Piper didn't intend on telling them more.

"And that's it?" Sergio asked. "No talk of reconciliation?"

"No!"

"And that was it? An apology, short and sweet," Sergio said.

"They talked for a while."

"What else did they talk about?" Sergio asked.

"Other things," Piper said.

"In other words, you don't know," Sergio said, ignoring Caleb's scowl.

"No, I do know." Finally, Piper felt on firmer ground. "Jaycee told me everything, but that doesn't mean I'm going to tell you guys her private business."

"As it should be." Caleb pulled baguettes from the picnic basket, followed by an assortment of meats and cheeses. He glanced at Sergio from the corner of his eye. "And we shouldn't be asking her to break Jaycee's confidence."

Sergio held up his hands. "All right. As long as you're not worried."

"I'm not worried about Tessa." Piper hoped Sergio and Caleb wouldn't catch what she'd said or, more accurately, what she hadn't said. She wasn't worried about losing Jaycee to Tessa, but she wasn't sure she could say the same about the Wilsons.

"We can't forget these." Sergio waved a container of strawberries.

Piper's shoulders tensed. *Seriously?* It was Paxton's love of strawberries that had reconnected Jaycee with the Wilsons, but Piper's reaction was ridiculous. *Damn it.* She needed to be happy for Jaycee. Piper steeled her jaw. No way would she ruin the kids' fireworks experience, nor would she begrudge Jaycee for spending time with the Wilsons.

"Paxton. Maddie," Piper called. "It's time to eat."

The kids looked up from where they'd been playing in the grass and were on their feet in seconds. They raced toward Piper.

"Apparently, this conversation is over," Sergio said.

"Good," Caleb said. "It's time we leave Piper alone."

Chapter Thirty-seven

The media coverage was insane. It was still three hours before the meal would be served, but news trucks were already lined up around the block. Never in a million years would Jaycee have expected this much interest. Every local news station was covering the event as were a few national news outlets.

The only downside was the temperature in Milwaukee had climbed to ninety, which was above average for early August, but at least it wasn't raining like the forecast had called for. Jaycee couldn't help but smile when several of the regular patrons came early and served water and ice cream to the news crews. It surprised the crews, but not Jaycee, who had witnessed firsthand the generosity of the patrons.

In true Piper fashion, she'd tackled the project with gusto, and her hard work paid off. At every turn, she'd scored another victory. The volunteer list for this evening read like a who's who of Milwaukee. The interest in helping had been so great they couldn't accommodate everyone who wanted to participate on the first night, so Piper had volunteers lined up through September. Two full months' worth.

Mary Ann had arrived with her kitchen staff about ten minutes ago. All wore *Chefs with a Heart* T-shirts. When the media had gotten wind of the project, they'd dubbed it Chefs with a Heart, and the name had stuck. From the start, Mary Ann had hated the moniker and grumbled to Jaycee about it at every opportunity, but apparently, Mary Ann had given in, judging by their shirts.

Jaycee knew to stand back when Mary Ann was on a food mission, so she'd greeted Mary Ann briefly before she introduced her to Sergio and Caleb. They'd swept Mary Ann and her crew up and escorted them to the kitchen.

Piper hurried into the room carrying a clipboard. Jaycee's heart soared. Piper looked adorable in her summer dress. Casual yet elegant. Piper spotted Jaycee and made a beeline to her. Piper stopped abruptly when she got closer. "Tell me you have a change of clothes upstairs in my apartment."

"Okay. I have clothes upstairs."

"Is it true?"

"You didn't say it had to be true. You just said I needed to say it."

Piper groaned. "We can't have you dressed like that for our interview." Piper glanced at her watch. "You have time to run home."

Jaycee chuckled. "My clothes are upstairs." Jaycee had become a regular guest at Piper's apartment. From the first day Jaycee had dinner with Piper and the kids, Piper's apprehension had dissolved.

"How did you manage to get so dirty?" Piper brushed dust off Jaycee's jeans and picked a cobweb off her shirt.

Jaycee pointed at the far row of tables. "We had to pull extra tables out of the basement. I don't think anyone has been down there in months."

"Probably more like years," Piper said.

"Well, it's clean now." Jaycee shook her head.

"All the schmutz is stuck to me."

Piper smiled. "Why don't you clean up now? I'm gonna need reinforcements to deal with Mary Ann."

Jaycee groaned. "Now what did she do?"

Piper held up her hands. "She didn't do anything wrong. She's got the kitchen humming. I'm just worried that I won't be able to get her to come out for the interview."

"I'll get her out," Jaycee said with more confidence than she felt. When it came to Mary Ann, Jaycee never knew.

"Get going. I'll have Donovan and a couple of the guys finish up."

"Is Mitzy here?" Jaycee glanced around the room.

"Shh." Piper leaned in. "Don't mention Mitzy. Donovan came in upset. He only worked half a day today, so he could help here. When he got home, Mitzy wasn't there. She showed up around an hour later. She was dropped off by a man in a fancy car, as Donovan said. When Donovan pressed her, she stomped out."

"I don't like this." Jaycee's stomach churned. "Last week, Donovan said he found a wad of cash hidden in her dresser. I'm worried sick."

"Me too. But there's nothing we can do about it right now. You need to go make yourself look presentable."

"Speaking of presentable, where's Ole Freddie?"

Piper smiled. "He's in his Sunday finest and ready to charm the press."

❧❧❧❧❧

Piper flopped into the chair next to Sergio. There were only a few stragglers left after a wildly successful evening. Piper should mingle, but she needed a few minutes to take a load off her feet. "We did it."

"No. You did it." Sergio smiled. "It was one hell of a night."

"I cannot believe the turnout." Piper held up her clipboard. "And you won't believe how many donations we got tonight. And I'm not talking small ones, either. There are so many things we'll be able to do with the money."

"Thanks to you."

Piper shook her head. "No. It took everyone. Without Jaycee, I never would have made any of these connections. And Mary Ann, of course."

"She's amazing." Sergio smirked. "If I wasn't gay, I might just go after that woman."

Piper laughed. "And if she wasn't a lesbian."

"Ah, there's that, too." Sergio shrugged. "I suppose Caleb wouldn't be too happy with it, either."

Piper spotted Betsy and Chuck Wilson talking with Donovan. She'd gotten little time to interact with them, or anyone else for that matter, since she'd been so busy making sure everything ran smoothly. "I should go over and say hi to Betsy and Chuck."

"Ah, the Wilsons," Sergio said.

"Knock it off." Piper pointed at him. "They're wonderful people."

"That are taking up most of Jaycee's time."

"Stop." Piper glared. "It's not like we never see each other."

"What about once a week since the Fourth of July?"

"It's more than that," Piper said, but she wasn't sure if it was true.

Sergio met her gaze and held it for several beats.

"Do you miss her?"

"Horribly." Piper's gaze dropped to the floor. "But I'm just being juvenile. Now that she has her family back, I have to share her."

"Just promise me you'll talk to her if you start feeling left behind."

"I will. But right now, there's nothing to discuss." Piper looked up and met Sergio's gaze. "For eight months, it was just me, her, and the kids, so it's taken some adjustment. But we'll be fine." Piper hoped she was right.

⁂

Piper was exhausted, but she was doing her best to follow the conversation. Betsy had taken to Donovan, and the two were chattering like old friends.

Betsy hung on Donovan's every word as he described the construction project he'd finished at work this morning. Piper stifled a yawn. She wanted to fall into bed and sleep for three days. The past few weeks, she'd been lucky to get five hours, and it had finally caught up with her.

The event had been a huge success, so hopefully, she wouldn't keep waking up in the middle of the night. Piper pushed aside the other reason she was having trouble sleeping. She would *not* be *that* girlfriend.

Betsy's face lit up, so Piper turned to see what had caused it. Mary Ann and Jaycee walked toward them. *Damn.* Jaycee looked good tonight. Piper wished she could get everyone to leave, so she could curl up in Jaycee's arms and fall asleep.

"Betsy, Chuck," Jaycee said as she pulled to a stop in front of the group. "I want to introduce you to our chef for the evening and the owner of the Sapphire Inn."

Piper tried to concentrate on the introductions and the conversation that proceeded, but she found her thoughts drifting. She focused on the joy on Jaycee's face. The heaviness and grief that once was there was completely gone. Had it begun to change because of Piper, or was it simply because she'd reconnected with the Wilsons? Piper hoped she'd played a role in Jaycee's recovery, but when she was this worn out, she began to doubt it.

"Piper?" Jaycee said.

Piper jumped when she heard her name. "Huh, what?"

Jaycee smiled and put a protective arm over Piper's shoulders. "I told you she's run herself ragged," Jaycee said to the others. "As much as we'd love to join you for a cup of coffee, I don't think Piper will be awake much longer."

"I'm sorry," Piper said. Maybe it was silly, but Piper's spirits rose when Jaycee turned down the invitation. "Jaycee's right. I'm exhausted." She put her hand on Betsy's arm. "I'd wanted to ask you how you're feeling but hadn't got the chance."

Betsy smiled. "I'm healing." Betsy twisted and raised her elbow up to shoulder level. "I still feel it at times if I move wrong."

"Honey," Chuck said. "I don't think you need to demonstrate when it hurts."

"Oh, yeah." Betsy put her arm down.

"Radiation starts soon?" Piper asked.

Jaycee was nodding as Betsy said, "In a few weeks if everything continues to heal well." Betsy smiled at Jaycee. "I'm just happy my story buddy has agreed to help out and stop by to keep me company."

"Story buddy?" Piper said.

Chuck and Betsy both laughed. "Jaycee kept me sane the last time I went through treatment. She read the entire Sookie Stackhouse series to me."

"*True Blood*?" Mary Ann turned to Jaycee. "That's racy. You read that to your mother-in-law?"

"Racy?" Betsy's eyes narrowed, and she stared at Jaycee. "I don't recall any PG-13 moments, let alone anything R-rated."

Jaycee's face reddened. "Uh...well, um...you know, I wasn't planning on reading them to you." Jaycee turned to Mary Ann and Piper. "I was reading them in the waiting room, and she insisted that I read aloud."

"Jaycee Ward, did you cut out the steamy parts?" Betsy put her hand on her hip.

Jaycee shot Chuck a pleading look.

"Don't look at me." Chuck laughed. "I know that expression. Give up now. You won't win."

Betsy smiled. "It's settled. You'll read me the entire Sookie Stackhouse series over again, but this time, you leave the good parts in."

"What the hell?" Jaycee said. "Maybe I should just read *Fifty Shades of Grey*."

"Oh, are those good books?" Betsy glanced at Piper and winked.

"Ugh," Jaycee said. "I'm going to keep my mouth shut."

࿔࿔࿔࿔

"Stay," Piper said.

Jaycee's head whipped around. Had she heard

right? "What?"

"I said, stay. Please."

Jaycee pointed at the floor. "Here?" All the guests had left, and Piper and Jaycee had just about finished cleaning the kitchen.

"Well, not here." Piper smiled. "Upstairs. In my apartment."

"Really?"

"I didn't mean it that way. I'm too tired for that."

"I didn't mean it that way, either." A wave of affection ran through Jaycee. "You look wiped out."

"I am."

Jaycee fixed her gaze on Piper. "You've always said that I can't stay over."

"I know." Piper sighed. She looked more tired than Jaycee had ever seen her.

"Why the change of heart?" Jaycee held up her hand as if to stop Piper from answering. "I mean, yes. I want to stay. I'm just curious why you're asking now."

"I don't know." Piper's eyes glistened. "I've always been like a three-year-old when I get super tired. Cranky and emotional."

"You want me to stay because you're cranky and emotional?"

"Uh-huh." Piper nodded, and tears welled.

"Okay." Jaycee couldn't think of anything better to say.

"I just want to curl up in your arms and have you hold me until I fall asleep."

"I'll do you one better." Jaycee took the paper towel from Piper's hand, threw it into the trash, and put her arm around Piper. "I'll hold you all night if it will make you feel better."

"It would." Piper gave her a weak smile as she

blinked back tears.

Jaycee brushed a drop from the corner of Piper's eye. "Let me tell you what I'm going to do." Jaycee led Piper from the kitchen into the dining room. "First, I'm—"

"Are you done in there?" Sergio pushed a broom around the table legs as Maddie followed behind with a dustpan. Caleb and Paxton were doing the same on the other side of the room.

"Yep. We're done," Jaycee said. "Are you?"

"Just about. We have a few more things to finish up."

"If you don't mind, I'd like to get Piper upstairs. She's dead on her feet. Then I'll come back down for Paxton and Maddie."

"Fine by me." Sergio smiled. "Take care of our girl. She's been running herself into the ground for too long. We'll keep the kids busy until you come back."

Piper managed to mutter a good night before she let Jaycee steer her to the elevator at the back of the building.

"You were telling me what you were going to do," Piper said, "but you got interrupted."

"Right." Jaycee put her arm around Piper as they waited for the elevator. "I'm gonna get you upstairs. Do you want to take a nice warm bath?"

Piper shook her head. "Too tired."

"Okay. Shower?"

Piper nodded.

"Okay." Jaycee smiled. "Do you want something to eat? I don't think you sat down long enough to eat, did you?"

"No, I didn't."

"What would you like?"

"Chicken noodle soup. Campbell's."

It wasn't what Jaycee expected, but she'd accommodate whatever Piper wanted. "It'll be waiting for you as soon as you get out of the shower." They entered the elevator, and Jaycee pushed the button for the third floor. "Then I'll run down and get the kids. They'll want to say good night to you before you go to bed."

Piper smiled. "I'd never go to bed without saying good night to them."

"After I get them tucked in, I'll be in to hold you while you fall asleep."

"Mmm, that sounds nice." Piper's eyes were only half open by the time the elevator stopped on the third floor.

"Tomorrow you're going to stay in bed for as long as you want." Jaycee took the keys from Piper and unlocked the door.

"I can't."

"Yes, you can." Jaycee shut the door after she entered the tiny apartment. "I'll take the kids to their program at the YMCA and pick them up."

"But you have to work."

"I'll rearrange my schedule." Jaycee followed Piper into the bedroom. "Then the kids and I will stop by the Public Market and pick up something for lunch."

Piper turned and wrapped her arms around Jaycee. "You're too good to me."

Warmth spread across Jaycee's chest, and she hugged Piper tight. "You do so much for everyone else. You deserve to be taken care of sometimes."

Piper sniffled, but Jaycee couldn't see her face since it was pressed against Jaycee's chest. Was Piper crying? Piper squeezed Jaycee, so Jaycee tightened her hold on Piper.

"Are you okay?" Jaycee asked.

Piper's head bobbed up and down. "I will be."

Jaycee ran her hand down the back of Piper's head several times, enjoying the softness of her hair. Jaycee had never seen Piper quite like this. Her little dynamo was struggling. Was it just because she was tired? It had to be since there was nothing else going on. Jaycee took a deep breath, relieved that nothing else could be wrong with Piper.

"Let's get moving." Piper smiled up at Jaycee. "The sooner we get done, the sooner we can curl up in bed together."

Chapter Thirty-eight

"Come in," Jaycee said.

Georgette hurried in with a stack of folders. "I need your signature."

"Holy shit," Jaycee said. "Did we sell that many properties?"

"Yep." Georgette dumped the folders onto Jaycee's desk. "Now that you're not being a workaholic, business has never been better."

Jaycee shook her head. "That still doesn't make any sense."

"Sure it does. For someone so smart, you can be dumb sometimes." Georgette plopped down into the chair in front of Jaycee's desk, which meant she planned on staying a while.

"Care to elaborate?"

"You've not been putting your hands in the middle of everything since you've been off gallivanting. No matter how good you are, your entire team will outsell you every time."

"So in other words, I just needed to get out of their way."

"You said it, I didn't." Georgette flashed her a cheesy smile. She pulled a piece of paper out of her pocket. "And what is this?" Georgette slid the paper across Jaycee's desk.

"Oh, that's the list of things I need for you to send someone to buy." Jaycee pushed the page back toward Georgette.

"A dozen long-stemmed roses, six cases of water, the fourth book in the Sookie Stackhouse series..." Georgette droned on, but Jaycee knew she wouldn't stop until she finished, "...four packages of Titleist golf balls, two gift cards from Ikea for two hundred fifty dollars each, and twenty-four mini-cups of Ben and Jerry's ice cream. You expect me to get all this today?"

"The book and golf balls can wait." Jaycee closed one file and opened another.

"Seriously?" Georgette's voice rose. She gave Jaycee a stern look. "And who is all this for?"

Jaycee looked up at the document and glared. "Aren't you my assistant? Should you really be asking me that question?"

"Tell me, or I'm not getting any of it."

"Fine." Jaycee signed two more documents before she continued. It was a moral victory, making Georgette wait. "The roses are for my niece's recital, I have to drop the water off to my nephew's soccer coach, the book is for Betsy, the golf balls are for Mary Ann and the other women I golf with, the gift cards are for the twins, and the ice cream is for Paxton's last baseball game tonight."

"And you're planning on doing all that this afternoon?"

"Except for the book and the balls."

Georgette shook her head. "That's a lot of running. Do you really think you'll make Paxton's ball game?"

"I'll make it."

"When was the last time you saw Piper?"

Jaycee looked up from her desk. "Why?"

"Seems like you've gotten too busy for her."

"That's ridiculous." Jaycee scowled.

"You didn't answer my question."

Jaycee did not want to have this conversation with Georgette, but by the way Georgette had hunkered into the chair, she had no intention of leaving. "Last Friday."

"You taking her out somewhere nice this weekend?"

"You know I have a golf tournament."

"Next weekend?"

"You also know I'm helping the twins move back to college in Chicago...Evanston."

"You're such an idiot."

"Wow. Tell me how you really feel." Jaycee set her pen on the desk and leaned back in her chair. Suddenly, Jaycee was tired. "What has you so worked up?"

"You're going to blow the best thing that's happened to you if you're not careful."

"Why would you say that?" Jaycee scowled. "I'm not going to screw anything up."

Georgette snorted and rolled her eyes.

"What was that for?"

"You're looking like hell lately."

"Gee, thanks. Is that why I'm going to blow it with Piper because I look bad?" Jaycee knew she wasn't getting enough sleep, but she wouldn't admit that to Georgette. Summers were meant to be busy. Things would slow down now that September was just around the corner. The kids would start school, and so would Piper.

"How did your volunteer work at the shelter go this week?"

Jaycee knew she was being baited, but she was too tired to care. "I didn't go."

"Oh, really?" Georgette feigned surprise. "Why not?"

"Piper has more than enough volunteers after all the publicity from Chefs with a Heart." Jaycee felt bad about cutting back at the shelter, but the past month and a half getting reconnected with the Wilsons had kept her busy. "And I had other engagements."

"Seems like you've had lots of other engagements with the Wilson clan. Do you think Piper is going to put up with it forever?"

"What's there to put up with?" Jaycee's ire rose. She didn't need Georgette making her feel bad. She felt bad enough as it was.

"You spent nearly every day with Piper until the Wilsons came back into the picture. The last month and a half, you barely see her."

"That's not true."

"Is that the best you've got?" Georgette's brow furrowed. "How many times did you used to see her each week?"

Jaycee looked down at the papers and shuffled them. "Five or six times a week." She knew where Georgette was leading her, but she couldn't think of a way to stop it.

"Now how many times do you?"

"Three or four."

"Try again." Georgette tapped her fingers. "How many times did you see her this past week?"

"Once, but I'll see her tonight at Paxton's baseball game."

"That's if you make it in time."

"These are all done." Jaycee picked up the pile of

signed documents and threw them hard onto the desk for Georgette. "I'll make it on time."

The challenging look in Georgette's eyes softened, and she gave Jaycee a smile. "I'm only saying these things because I love you. I don't want you to lose her."

Jaycee dropped her head into her hand and closed her eyes. "I don't want to mess things up. But I need her to be patient with me. I can't lose the Wilsons again."

"Have you told her this?"

"Piper understands." Jaycee sat up and pushed her chest out. "She wanted me to reestablish my relationship with the Wilsons. She's not only supported it, but encouraged it."

"What's really going on, Jaycee?"

"What do you mean?"

"Don't play dumb with me. I've known you too long."

Jaycee looked down at her fingernails. Could she tell Georgette the fear that nagged at her from the back of her mind since she'd talked to Tessa?"

"Stop thinking about it," Georgette said. "And say it."

"What if I'm doing the same thing to Piper that I did to Tessa?"

Georgette leaned back, and a look of confusion fell over her face. "You've lost me."

A crushing heaviness lay on Jaycee's chest. She'd been feeling it off and on since she'd talked to Tessa. Maybe if she spoke it aloud, then the pain would dissipate. "I fell in love with Tessa's family, not really her. What if I fell in love with Paxton and Maddie and all the others at the shelter and not really Piper?"

Georgette burst out laughing.

Whatever reaction Jaycee was expecting, this wasn't it. Heat rose up Jaycee's neck, and the tip of her ears burned.

Georgette's eyes widened. "You're serious? Sorry, I thought you were joking."

"Why would I be joking about something like that?" Jaycee didn't try to hide her hurt.

"Oh, sweetie, I'm sorry. But I can tell you there is *no* way that's what's going on with Piper, so you can scrub that from your brain."

The tightness in Jaycee's chest loosened enough that she felt as if she could take a full breath. Was Georgette right? "How do you know?"

"For starters, I see how you are whenever you're going to see her. In all my years, I've never seen a look like that on your face. It's sickening." Georgette winked. "It's all dreamy and lovesick."

Jaycee gave Georgette a half smile. "Go on."

"Then when I met her at the Chefs with a Heart event, it warmed my heart." Georgette smiled as if remembering the moment. "Any lingering doubts I had were gone when I saw the two of you together. She's the one."

"I know." Jaycee sighed. "As long as I don't blow it."

Chapter Thirty-nine

Despite Jaycee's best effort to make conversation, Piper had been unusually quiet on their drive to the Sapphire Inn. The restaurant was busy. They were the sixth car in line for the valet.

"Looks like Mary Ann must be down a valet," Jaycee said as one of what appeared to be only two parkers ran past.

"Uh-huh," Piper said.

"I've missed you." Jaycee smiled, hoping to break the ice. It had been over a week since they'd seen each other. When Piper didn't respond, Jaycee said, "I can't believe how busy we've both been."

"You more so than me," Piper replied. "But that's about to change."

Jaycee stared at the steering wheel not wanting to make eye contact with Piper for fear of what she'd see there. "I can't believe you started your last semester. Where did the summer go?"

"I'm not sure." Piper gave Jaycee a half smile. "As much as I love learning, I'm ready to be done."

"I don't blame you." Jaycee pulled ahead one car length. "At least things have calmed down at DOTS. Sorry I couldn't make it this week."

Piper shrugged. "We have more than enough volunteers."

Piper's words stung, which wasn't fair. Piper was right, the reason they hadn't seen each other was largely due to Jaycee's schedule or, more accurately, the Wilsons' schedule. "I'm sorry about last weekend, too." *Ugh.* Her apologies came out sounding hollow.

Piper shrugged again. "How do the twins like their new apartment?"

Jaycee had spent the weekend helping the Wilsons move the twins back to Northwestern. "They were ecstatic with their new apartment. I still can't believe they're juniors already."

"Time flies." Piper sighed.

"Unless you're in a line for valet." Jaycee chuckled.

Piper smiled but didn't laugh.

Why did the conversation seem so stiff tonight? Jaycee thought they'd talk nonstop since they'd barely spoken all week. She was wrong. "We're the next one up," Jaycee said, trying to find anything to fill the silence.

Jaycee jumped out of the Range Rover when the valet approached at a jog. She quickly went around the passenger side and helped Piper from the vehicle.

Piper was stunning tonight. The short midnight blue dress clung to her curves, and her three-inch heels drew attention to her shapely legs.

"Have I told you lately how beautiful you are?" Jaycee said.

"Thanks." Piper gave her a shy smile. After all these months, Piper still seemed self-conscious whenever Jaycee complimented her. "Thank god we have an in." Piper tilted her head toward the crowd gathered outside the restaurant.

Jaycee put her hand on Piper's hip as they made their way through the throng of people. The crowd was too loud to hear over, so they walked without talking.

When they got to the door, the maître d' recognized them and motioned them in.

At the hostess stand, Jaycee asked for Mary Ann. Despite Saturday being their busiest night, Mary Ann insisted on having a drink with them before dinner.

"I'll let her know you're here," the hostess said without asking their names. She pointed to an area off to the right. "You can wait over there if you'd like."

Jaycee searched for a space to stand that wouldn't have people crushing in around them. She couldn't find one, so she settled on where the hostess had pointed.

They had only been there for a few minutes when a booming voice called out, "Well look-ee here, if it isn't Jaycee Re-Ward."

Ugh. Jaycee gritted her teeth. She'd know that obnoxious voice anywhere. *Tom.* Her greatest rival in the real estate business. She turned and plastered on a smile. "Tom. How are you?"

"That's a loaded question, isn't it?" Tom shifted his gaze from Jaycee to Piper and let his gaze wander the length of Piper's body, then slowly back up.

Jaycee bristled. Seeing Tom leer at Piper made her stomach churn. She didn't want to cause a scene in Mary Ann's restaurant, but she couldn't let this asshole look at Piper like that.

With a subtle step forward, Jaycee blocked Tom's view of Piper.

"I saw you on the news the other day." He raised his voice, so that several other people around them turned and stared. "Apparently, I'm hanging out in all the wrong places. Who knew you could pick up a hot piece of ass like that at the homeless shelter?"

Jaycee saw red and took a step toward Tom.

Most of the people nearby had stopped talking and gaped at the drama unfolding around them. Jaycee raised her index finger and pointed it at his face. "You asshole. Don't you ever—"

"Tom Kelson," Mary Ann said from behind Jaycee. "Your reservations have been canceled."

"What? Why the hell for?"

"I won't serve a misogynistic asshole here that doesn't know how to talk to ladies."

"The food here is average at best," Tom said to those standing nearby. He turned on his heel and stomped toward the door. A murmur went up in the crowd as he marched across the floor.

"I'm sorry there's always an asshole in the crowd," Mary Ann said. "Don't pay him any mind."

"Thanks," Piper said. "I've had much worse said to me. Remember I lived on the street for a while."

Jaycee cringed. "I should have knocked that disgusting grin off his face."

Piper shrugged. "Relax. He was just trying to get to you."

"Nobody should talk to you like that." Heat rose up Jaycee's neck, and her collar suddenly felt too tight.

"Come on," Mary Ann said. "Let's get a drink."

≋≋≋≋≋

Piper clenched the sheet and let out a loud moan as Jaycee brought her close to another climax. A surge raced through Piper's body, and she called out, "Oh, god, right there." Piper shuddered, and her body pulsated around Jaycee's tongue.

Jaycee crawled from between Piper's legs and collapsed on the bed next to her.

"Damn, I needed that," Piper said as she ran her hand through Jaycee's hair.

"Me too." Jaycee inhaled deeply. "Fuck. I can't catch my breath."

Piper smiled. "That's what happens when we go two weeks without sex."

"No shit. Let's not go that long again." Jaycee threw the covers over Piper and snuggled against her side.

"That was nice," Piper said.

"Nice? That's all I get?"

Piper laughed. "How about spectacular?"

"That's better."

"I'm sorry I wasn't myself earlier." Piper kissed Jaycee's head. "And for the record, I missed you, too."

Jaycee lifted her head and met Piper's gaze. "Thank you. For the record, I noticed."

"I figured. You looked like someone kicked your puppy when I didn't say it back. Then the valet showed up, and everything got turned upside down when we went inside."

"It wasn't the best night we've ever had." Jaycee wriggled her eyebrows. "Well, until we got back here. That was pretty extraordinary." Jaycee grinned. "Notice, *I* didn't say nice."

"Good thing."

Jaycee's expression turned serious. "Do you want to tell me why you weren't yourself earlier?"

Piper shrugged. "Not really."

"Let me rephrase that. Will you tell me?"

"I was having a moment. Sometimes life is overwhelming. This is overwhelming."

"This?" Jaycee rose on her elbow, so she no longer had her head on Piper's shoulder. "Us?"

Piper pushed the pillows against the headboard, sat up, and pulled the sheet over her. This conversation was best had when they were looking at each other. Jaycee grabbed a pillow, turned sideways, and propped herself up on her elbow, so they faced each other.

"Yes, us. It's been amazing. You've been amazing." Piper smiled. "And I love you so much."

"And I love you so much, too." Jaycee put her hand on Piper's leg. "If everything is amazing, what was bothering you earlier?"

"I'm embarrassed to tell you and mad at myself for it." Piper shifted and adjusted her pillow, so she could break their gaze for a beat.

"Come on. It's me. Just say it."

When Piper looked back at Jaycee, the look of concern in Jaycee's eyes broke through Piper's shield. "It's the first time since we've been together that we've gone that long without seeing each other, and it didn't seem to bother you." Piper clapped her hand against her forehead and shook her head. "That sounds so pathetic and needy."

"No. I'm flattered."

Piper sat up straighter and shifted so Jaycee was no longer touching her. "So that's what happened. But I'm over it now."

Jaycee's face fell. "Oh, okay."

Damn it. Piper needed to say what was on her mind before this spiraled again. "I don't think you meant for what you just said to come out the way it did, or maybe I'm just overly sensitive."

Jaycee looked at her puzzled. "I don't know what I keep saying wrong."

"You said you were flattered. Not that you felt the same way."

"Oh, god, of course I feel the same. I adore you. Sometimes it scares me how much I love you."

"I don't want to be one of those clingy girlfriends, but I'm afraid that's how I'm acting." Piper put her hand down hard on the bed. "I should be able to go a week without missing you this bad."

"I hope not. I plan on missing you every day that I don't see you. I never want that to stop. If that makes me clingy, so be it."

"Really?" Piper's eyes lit up.

"Of course. I hate it when I don't see you." Jaycee smiled. "You know there's a way to fix it?"

No. Piper was finally feeling better, and she didn't want to have to turn Jaycee down again.

Before Piper could find a way to stop Jaycee from asking, Jaycee said, "You and the kids could move in with me."

Piper bit the inside of her cheek as she searched for the right words.

Jaycee held up her hand. "You don't have to respond. It's written all over your face. I should have known better." There was no anger in Jaycee's words, just hurt.

"Please, I need you to understand." Piper reached for Jaycee's hand. It was a good sign when Jaycee reached back. "As much as I love you, I can never put the kids or myself in that position again. Not until I'm sure." As soon as the words were out of Piper's mouth, she knew they'd come out wrong.

"So you don't trust me?" Jaycee's tone was measured, but her jaw tightened.

"It's not like that." Piper sighed and leaned back against her pillow.

"Then what's it like? You're not sure about us—

me?"

Piper squeezed Jaycee's hand and looked her in the eyes. "Since I met you, I've never been happier. It was amazing to fall in love with someone I was friends with first. It had never happened that way for me before."

Jaycee nodded and gave Piper a slight smile as if she were remembering their beginnings.

"And then it got better." Piper grinned. "The first weekend I spent here with you was like a fairytale. I was so raw from the conference, and you healed parts of me that I didn't even know needed to be healed." Piper paused and lay her head back and stared at the ceiling.

"You're telling me all good things." Jaycee's voice held a note of frustration.

"And they are, but then the world crept in, and I'm trying to—"

"You mean the Wilsons crept in?"

Piper studied Jaycee for signs of anger, but she didn't see any. "Yeah, and that's what has me so messed up—confused. I want you to have your family back, and I support you in that, but I'd be lying if I said that I haven't felt pushed aside the last two months since the Fourth of July."

"But—"

"Please, may I finish?" Piper said.

Jaycee nodded.

"We're walking this fine line. You need to have your family, and I never want to interfere with that. Yet I need to feel like you're all in. Maybe if I was on my own, it wouldn't be so hard, but I must think of Paxton and Maddie, too."

"And I'm letting everyone down," Jaycee said as

a statement not a question. Tears welled in her eyes.

"No." Piper shook her head. "You're trying to keep all the balls in the air. You're trying to keep everyone happy."

"But the most important person I'm making miserable."

Piper's insides fluttered. Jaycee had just called her the *most important* person. It felt good since Piper had begun to question if she was. "Not miserable." Piper weighed her words. She needed to be honest, without being hurtful. "Just sad, sometimes. I can't help but miss you. Then I remind myself, it's not like you're partying, you're reconnecting with the family you lost, so I shouldn't be so selfish."

Jaycee waited a few beats before she said, "Can I respond now?"

Piper nodded.

"First, you're not being selfish." Jaycee took Piper's hand between both of hers. "Georgette has been all over me lately. She says I'm either going to blow it with you, or I'm going to collapse from exhaustion."

Piper reached out and ran her thumb along the bags under Jaycee's eyes. "You do look tired most of the time."

"I am."

"Are you happy?"

Jaycee shrugged. "I'm grateful to have my family back. I thought that was all I needed to be happy again, but lately, I realize that's not true. The less I see of you, the less happy I am."

"Then we need to work on finding a way to spend more time together. Make us a priority." Piper smiled and pulled Jaycee toward her. Jaycee slid up beside Piper and rested her back against the headboard. Piper turned and lay her head against Jaycee's shoulder.

Jaycee hugged Piper tightly. "I'm going to prove to you that I'm all in."

A tear rolled down Piper's cheek. The fear and pain from the past two months threatened to overtake her, so she said, "Enough of this heavy talk. Caleb and Sergio took the kids this weekend, so we'd have time alone. We better not squander it."

"Agreed. Do you want to take a dip in the hot tub?"

Piper groaned. "My legs are too wobbly from earlier."

Jaycee smirked and ran her fingers across Piper's stomach. "How about I make your legs a little more wobbly?"

Chapter Forty

Jaycee threw open the doors to the walkout balcony. Since her clients were so enthralled by Lake Michigan, she knew this would be the hook. Nine times out of ten, she could accurately guess whether the clients would make an offer on the home. Once she saw their reaction to this view of the lake, she'd be ready to make her prediction.

She stepped back and motioned for the pair to walk out before her. The woman smiled and stepped outside. Her sudden intake of breath and gasp told Jaycee all she needed to know.

She knowingly smiled at the woman's husband. "I think she likes what she sees."

He smiled back. "You better start sharpening your pencil," he joked.

She winked. "I use a computer nowadays." Another trick of the trade. In her business, it paid to read her clients' senses of humor. She attributed it to her success.

He laughed. "Oh, yeah, I did hear something about that invention. New fad. I don't think it will catch on."

She laughed. *Yep.* She'd read him right.

They'd been admiring the view for a while when Jaycee's phone sounded. *Piper's ringtone? Odd.* Piper never called her at work without texting first, so she wouldn't disturb Jaycee when she was with a client.

No text.

Jaycee held up her phone. "I need to take this. I'll let you enjoy the view." Besides, it would give them a perfect time to talk without her listening.

She stepped inside the house. "Hi, Piper," she said into the phone.

"Thank god you answered." Piper's voice came out breathless.

Jaycee's heart raced. "What's wrong?"

"It's Mitzy. Officer Turner just stopped in, you know the cop that volunteers at the shelter. Well, he just got back from a call...hold on." Jaycee heard rustling on the other end of the phone and then Piper said, "You can pick up Paxton and Maddie from school?"

Sergio's voice came through the phone. "Yep. Push those newspapers aside."

Jaycee heard more rustling and then a car door slam. She wanted to ask what the hell was going on, but instead she paced the bedroom, waiting for Piper to say something.

An engine roared and then Piper said, "Sorry. Sergio's dropping me off at the hospital."

"Hospital?" Jaycee's pulse quickened. "What's the matter?"

"Officer Turner said a business owner found Mitzy in the alley. Badly beaten." Piper was breathless as she spoke. Jaycee suspected she was fighting back tears.

"Is she going to be okay?" Jaycee paced faster as she talked.

"He didn't know. She was pretty messed up. I haven't contacted Donovan yet. I wanted to assess things first. Donovan is going to be out of his mind."

"Good call. Does Turner know what happened?"

"Not yet. Sounds like it might have been four or five teenagers. Witnesses saw them running from the alley."

"Fuck." Jaycee ran her hand through her hair. "Hate crime?"

"I don't know, but it's possible. Can you come?"

Dumbass. That should have been the first thing she offered. "Of course. I'm showing a house, but I'll cut it short and get there as soon as I can."

"Thank you." The relief was evident in Piper's voice.

"Hang in there. I'll be there soon. I love you."

"I love you, too."

⚜⚜⚜⚜

Piper shoved her hand into her pocket, so the woman behind the counter wouldn't see her clenched fist. Since she wasn't Mitzy's family, she was having trouble cutting through the red tape. Sometimes hospital staff were cooperative once she showed her credentials from DOTS, but other times, they weren't. Unfortunately, in her work at the shelter, she'd been at the hospital with a client more times than she could count.

The woman behind the desk turned up her nose at Piper's credentials. "You've already showed them. I've told you I'm going to have to check with my superiors on this."

Piper resisted saying, *I'm sure you have many superiors.* Instead, she smiled. "That's what you told me twenty minutes ago."

The woman rolled her eyes. *Seriously?* Who

allowed people like that to work in a place where people were in heightened emotional states? "I'm awaiting a callback. You're going to have to be patient." The woman turned away and began typing on her keyboard.

Piper walked away from the desk before she said something that would get her kicked out. She circled the waiting room; pacing was the only way to keep herself calm. Somewhere behind the imposing doors Mitzy lay. In what condition, Piper didn't know.

She just completed her third lap when she spotted Jaycee. Piper rushed to Jaycee, not caring if she made a spectacle.

Jaycee wrapped her arms around Piper. "How is she?"

Piper shrugged. "I don't know. I'm not family, so I'm getting the runaround."

Jaycee stiffened. "We'll see about that."

"No. We have to play by their rules, or we could get tossed." Piper knew Jaycee wouldn't like the answer.

Jaycee stepped back. "This sucks."

"Walk with me. I need to get some of this energy out."

As they were making their fourth lap, Piper grabbed Jaycee's sleeve. "Now's our chance."

"For what?"

"My *friend* isn't at the desk anymore. It looks like a young woman replaced her, so we should try again."

They'd only taken two steps when a tall man strode into the room. His shoulders were squared as he marched across the room.

"I think I know that guy," Jaycee said. "I sold

him his house."

"Maybe he'll loosen things up. He looks like he's on a mission."

"He's driven."

When they approached the desk, the man was speaking to the young woman in a controlled voice, but his anger was evident. "I received a call that my son was brought into the ER. I want to see him. *Now!*"

"Yes, sir," the young woman said and stood. "You said his name is Anthony Clark?"

"Yes."

"Um, I'll go check and be right back." The young woman didn't wait for a response before she bolted from the room.

The man huffed and turned away from the desk. He'd taken one step forward before he registered that Piper and Jaycee were standing in front of him, so he nearly walked into them.

His brow furrowed. "What in the hell..." He abruptly stopped. "Jaycee?"

"Derrick." Jaycee reached out her hand. "I hope everything's okay."

He took Jaycee's hand. "I hope so, too." His eyes softened. "I got the call that my son had been in an accident."

"I'm so sorry," Jaycee said.

"It's maddening that I have to wait around until they figure things out." He let out a heavy exhale. "I hope you're okay."

"I'm good. One of Piper's clients was brought in a while ago." Jaycee took the opportunity to introduce Piper.

As they were exchanging greetings, the young woman returned. "Mr. Clark, if you'd follow me, I can take you to your son."

Mr. Clark turned to Piper. "I hope you get some answers."

"You too," Piper said.

He smiled and then disappeared into the bowels of the hospital.

They remained standing by the desk, absorbed in conversation.

"Are you back again?" The acerbic older woman had returned. When she spoke, her tone was condescending.

Her gaze landed on Jaycee, and the woman's entire demeanor changed. She pointed at Jaycee. "I know you. You're on the side of buses."

Jaycee put on her brightest smile and then looked sheepish. "I am. It's so embarrassing."

"Nonsense," the woman responded. She smiled and pointed again. "And you're wearing your suspenders. I thought that was just for the photo."

Piper watched in astonishment as the surly woman turned into a fan girl right before her eyes. Jaycee masterfully pulled out just the right amount of charm and humility mixed with a twinge of celebrity. Piper tried to stifle her grin as she watched the maestro at work. No wonder she was such a good salesperson.

After a bit of small talk, Jaycee said, "I was hoping that my friend and I could get in to see her client."

"Certainly." The woman beamed. "Let me take you back now."

As soon as the woman turned her back to make her way to the door, Piper mouthed, "Seriously?"

❧❧❧❧❧

Hospitals always made Jaycee uneasy. The antiseptic smells, the rushing medical personnel, and mostly the worried and pained looks on the faces of the visitors. She focused on her breathing and tried to block out her other thoughts.

"Here we are." The woman pointed to a door.

"Thank you so much, Edie," Jaycee said, having checked out the woman's name as soon as they'd begun talking. Something else she'd learned in her trade.

The woman smiled, and her cheeks reddened. "It was my pleasure. Let me just check and see if it's okay for you to go in." She knocked and disappeared inside.

When she returned, she said, "There's already a family member inside."

Jaycee looked to Piper, whose face showed the same surprise that Jaycee felt.

"We normally only let two people in at a time." Edie leaned toward them. "But in this case, I'm sure we can make an exception. I asked the gentleman if it was okay, and he said yes."

"You have been such a great help," Jaycee said. "I so appreciate you."

Edie smiled. "Just doing my job."

Jaycee complimented Edie again before she pushed open the door and motioned for Piper to enter.

They'd only walked in a few feet when Piper abruptly stopped, causing Jaycee to run into the back of her. Derrick Clark stood beside Mitzy's bed. His eyes went from fury to confusion.

He pointed at Jaycee. "You work with my son?"

Jaycee shook her head. "Well, indirectly. I volunteer at DOTS where Piper works."

"I see. I agreed to let you in, so I could meet the people who *worked* with Anthony." He spit out the word worked as if he were saying a foul word.

Jaycee knew that someone like Derrick would be more apt to listen to her than Piper, so she stepped past Piper and walked farther into the room. Piper followed behind.

Jaycee looked down at Mitzy. Her face was so swollen that she was barely recognizable. A large bandage extended from her cheek to her jawline, and blood seeped through the gauze.

Seeing Mitzy like this had Jaycee rattled, but she needed to pull it together so she could talk to Derrick. She tore her attention from Mitzy and met Derrick's gaze. "I can't imagine what it feels like seeing…um…." *Shit.* How did she walk this minefield? "Seeing your child like this." Jaycee put her hand against her heart. "I know how it's affecting me, so I can only imagine how you must feel."

The anger in Derrick's eyes softened slightly. "I haven't seen him in two years. This isn't how I wanted it to be after all this time."

"Understandable."

"Do you know what the hell happened?" Derrick shifted his gaze toward Piper.

"I don't, sir," Piper said.

"Then how did you know he was here?" His eyes narrowed.

"An officer that volunteers at the shelter contacted me."

Derrick turned to Jaycee. "And why are you here?"

"Like I mentioned, I volunteer at the shelter, too, and Piper contacted me." When Jaycee registered a confused look on Derrick's face, she continued. "I've grown quite fond of Mitzy."

Derrick stiffened and crossed his arms. "I suppose you approve of this?" He waved his hand over Mitzy.

Shit. Dumbass. There was no sense fueling the fire. "It's not for me to approve or disapprove. I just want everyone to be able to live as their authentic selves."

Derrick scoffed. "Seriously? And where has that gotten him? Oh, yeah, beaten half to death and laying in a hospital bed."

Jaycee bit her tongue. Now wasn't the time to point out that had Derrick been more accepting, then Mitzy would likely not be in this state. She weighed her words carefully. "Since we don't know what happened yet, it's hard to speculate. Unfortunately, the world isn't an accepting place for people like...um..." Jaycee took Mitzy's hand. She couldn't bring herself to call Mitzy him, but she knew saying *her* would likely set Derrick off. As much as she wanted to take a stance, it would do Mitzy no good at the moment.

Before Derrick could respond, the door flew open, and a tall, elegant woman rushed into the room. Jaycee recognized Lucinda Clark immediately. "Oh, my god," Lucinda said when she saw Mitzy. She pushed past Jaycee and Piper and rushed to Mitzy's bed.

It was as if she didn't notice anyone else in the room as she gently took Mitzy's hand and began speaking to her. Jaycee stared at her feet, feeling uncomfortable. This was too intimate for her to be eavesdropping on.

She helplessly glanced at Piper. Could they back

out of the room slowly without being noticed? Piper shook her head as if reading Jaycee's mind.

Jaycee shoved her hands into her pocket and studied the IV bag. Anything to not look at Mitzy and her mother.

After several minutes, Lucinda finally recognized that she wasn't alone in the room. She glanced at Derrick with a questioning look.

"Lucinda, you remember Jaycee Ward, don't you?"

Recognition dawned on Lucinda's face. "Of course. You sold us our house, or should I say houses? Why are you here?"

Derrick didn't give Jaycee a chance to speak; instead, he filled her in on Piper and Jaycee's role. Jaycee bit back a retort at the unflattering way Derrick was portraying Piper and the shelter. At the hospital while bearing witness to a mother's pain wasn't the time to educate.

When Derrick finished, a cool anger filled Lucinda's eyes. Jaycee braced for the onslaught. Lucinda's steel gaze swept over Jaycee and Piper, and then she abruptly turned her attention back to her husband.

Lucinda raised her hand and pointed across the bed at him. "Put your self-righteous indignation away. You're responsible for this. I'm responsible for this, so stop trying to blame these two women."

Derrick opened his mouth to speak, but Lucinda cut him off. "No, you've done enough talking. It's time you listened for a change. I let your words, your bigotry cloud the way I saw our son...our daughter."

Derrick flinched as Lucinda said *daughter*.

"Get over yourself. This is our baby." Tears streamed freely down her face. "I should have done more than slip her money."

Derrick's jaw clenched. "You've been seeing him?"

"Her," Lucinda corrected. "No, I've been too much of a coward. But at least Derrick Jr. has courage. Anthony has been staying with him sometimes."

Realization dawned. Maybe Mitzy hadn't been turning tricks. She'd been visiting her brother and getting money from her mother. Piper and Jaycee's gazes met, and Jaycee could tell that Piper had come to the same conclusion.

Piper leaned over and whispered, "I think we should give them some privacy."

Jaycee nodded, happy to escape.

They'd nearly made it to the door when Lucinda called, "Stop!"

Jaycee froze but didn't look back.

Piper turned and said, "Pardon me," as she tugged on Jaycee's hand.

Reluctantly, Jaycee turned, as well.

"I don't want you to go," Lucinda said. "I've lost two years of Anth...um...what name does she go by?"

"Mitzy," Piper answered.

"I've missed two years of...Mitzy's life. I'd like to hear a little about it."

"I understand." Piper smiled. "How about we give you and Derrick a little time alone? Jaycee and I will grab a bite to eat in the cafeteria. We'll wait for you there." Piper pulled a card out of her purse and handed it to Lucinda. "If something changes or you need us to come back here, give me a call."

"Thank you." Lucinda wrapped her arms around Piper. "And thank you for looking after my baby."

Jaycee blinked back tears and looked away. Her

gaze met Derrick's. His eyes glistened and were so
filled with pain it nearly took Jaycee's breath away.
She walked around the bed and held out her hand to
him. She was surprised when he didn't take it, and
instead, he pulled her in for a bear hug.

Chapter Forty-one

Donovan flopped onto the picnic bench next to Piper. "Ugh, those two wore me out." He pointed toward Maddie and Paxton, who were enthralled by the woman weaving cornstalks into decorations.

Jaycee smiled. She'd lost track of how many times Paxton and Maddie had dragged Donovan into the corn maze.

Piper shook her head. "Never try to keep up with children. You'll lose every time."

"No doubt." Donovan groaned. "They were trying to talk me into going again."

"How about I give you a break? You and Jaycee have been doing most of the work today." Piper smiled. "It's kinda nice having extra hands with all the energy those two have." She reached across the table and patted Jaycee's hand.

At Piper's touch, warmth spread inside Jaycee. Doing family things with Piper and the kids always made her happy. Each passing day, she grew more and more attached. It still frightened Jaycee at times, but she'd been able to keep her fear at bay.

Since her and Piper's talk over a month ago, things had gotten better. Jaycee had returned to spending more time with Piper and the kids and resumed volunteering two days a week at DOTS. She still saw the Wilsons frequently, but she'd found a balance.

"I can take them." Jaycee started to rise.

"No." Piper shook her head. "As busy as both of you have been, you haven't had a chance to talk to Donovan lately."

Jaycee picked up on Piper's meaning. "I'd like that." Jaycee held up her empty cup toward Donovan. "What do you say we go get ourselves some more cider?"

Donovan beamed. "Absolutely."

It had been nearly a month since Mitzy's hospitalization. While Piper had spoken to Mitzy several times since, Donovan had remained tight-lipped.

"You've got forty-five minutes." Piper pointed at her watch. When Jaycee gave her a puzzled look, Piper said, "Our hayride reservations are for three." Piper rose and made a goofy face. "Wish me luck."

Donovan and Jaycee laughed as they watched her walk away.

"She's terrible with directions," Jaycee said. "Do you think they'll get lost?"

"Those kids are like bloodhounds," Donovan answered. "I don't think we have anything to worry about."

"Okay, let's go find that cider then." Jaycee waved at the kids as they dragged Piper toward the start of the corn maze.

They'd been talking about Donovan's job and the housing market when Jaycee decided to test the water. "How's things going with Mitzy?"

He shrugged. "You know."

Jaycee smiled. "If I knew, I wouldn't be asking."

Donovan laughed. "Good point. I don't know. I guess she's doing good. Her family's trying, and I know she's happy to be back home." A shadow crossed his eyes, but then they brightened. "I know living in a tiny rundown apartment wasn't for her, obviously."

"It has to be a relief that she wasn't lying to you."

"Yeah. I feel like an asshole. She's forgiven me, but I don't know if I can forgive myself."

"You weren't thinking anything the rest of us weren't."

"I still don't understand why she couldn't have told me she was seeing her brother." Donovan snorted. "What if I would have hauled him out of his car and beat the shit out of him?"

"You think that's likely?" Jaycee grinned. "Derrick Jr. is three inches taller than Mitzy."

"I'm scrappy." Donovan chuckled. "I know I would've got my ass kicked, but let me have my delusions."

Jaycee smiled. "You would have put up a good fight."

"Thanks." Donovan took a sip of his cider. "Did you hear they caught the son of a bitches who did it?"

"Piper told me. I hope they rot in jail."

"Last I heard, they'll be charged with a hate crime." Donovan's jaw clenched, and his nostrils flared. "The sick bastards. She wasn't hurting anyone."

"I know." Jaycee's heart went out to Donovan. "Piper said Mitzy's going to start school in January."

"Fashion design." Donovan smiled. "Her dad refused to pay for it two years ago, but things have changed."

"Her parents are doing better with things?"

Donovan shrugged. "Her mom's fine, and her dad's trying. It'll take a while. I went to their house for dinner the other night."

"How'd that go?" Jaycee had already heard it

from Mitzy's perspective, through Piper, but she was interested to hear Donovan's take.

"I felt a little outclassed." He snorted. "Who am I kidding? A lot outclassed. They have a maid and a fucking chef."

"I bet you held your own."

"Nah. I'm sure they were watching for every misstep, and I made plenty."

"What did Mitzy say?"

Donovan blushed. "She said I was a perfect gentleman and was proud how well I did." He glanced at his fingernails. "She says I don't give myself enough credit."

"I'd agree with that." Jaycee smiled at Donovan with affection. While Mitzy had gotten into Piper's heart, it was Donovan who'd stolen hers. "Never sell yourself short."

"I don't come from much," Donovan said.

"It doesn't matter where you came from. It only matters where you go."

"I like that." Donovan gave her a shy smile. "I need to remember it when I'm feeling low."

"You know you can always give me a call. Any time."

Donovan smiled again. "I know Piper'd like me to talk to her about stuff, but she's Mitzy's go-to person. It'd be nice to have you as mine if you're cool with it." Donovan winked. "I know you two tell each other everything. And that's okay. I just don't feel right telling her myself."

Jaycee gave Donovan an encouraging nod, but she didn't speak for fear he'd clam up.

"Mitzy's moods are better, too," Donovan said. "I think it's because she's getting proper estrogen every day like she's supposed to, instead of how it was on the streets." He sighed. "I'm hoping now that I got health insurance and I only need to take care of me that I can get leveled out on the T."

"If you run short, I'd be happy to give you the money."

Donovan held up his hand. "No way. I ain't taking money from you. That's not why I'm telling you these things."

It was obvious she'd hit a nerve with him. "Whoa. I didn't mean to offend you. I just know how messed up it can make someone if they go on and off it."

"I don't want to be no charity case."

"Charity case? What the hell? You're like a little brother to me." Jaycee wasn't sure if her words would make things better or worse, but she decided the truth was the only way to approach it. "You know, I'm an only child. I don't have any family left."

Donovan nodded. "I know."

"And you know why I showed up at the shelter last Thanksgiving."

"Your ex tossed you out of her family." Donovan frowned. "That sucked. But I know you're back hanging with them. That's why I don't see you around much anymore."

Donovan's words hit her like a baseball bat to the gut. Was she going to have this conversation with him? *Yes.* This mattered to her. He mattered to her. "You're upset with that, aren't you?"

He shrugged. "I suppose. Now you're offering me money and calling me family. I don't know what to think."

Ouch. Another gut punch, but he had a point.

"You're right."

"I didn't expect you to say that. I figured you'd make excuses like everyone else does."

She held up her hands. "No excuses. I'm just trying to figure this all out. I was pretty messed up last year. Losing an entire family overnight was tough."

He nodded. "I get that."

Duh. Jaycee had been so blinded by her own pain that she'd never considered how Donovan felt. He'd lost his entire family. "I guess we have something in common, but I'd never really thought of it that way."

"I had." Donovan smiled. "Maybe that's why I feel comfortable with you."

"But I haven't been treating you right lately."

"I've been busy, too. Been working a bunch of OT now that I don't have Mitzy to go home to." He paused. "I keep busy, so I don't have to think about the people I'm losing."

Jaycee suspected she was included in that sentence. "I'm sorry. I need to do better." Jaycee put her hand over her heart. "You're part of my life now. You're my family, too."

Donovan's eyes brightened, but they still held a hint of guardedness. "I still don't want your money. It changes things. But I could sign up for the other."

"Little brother?"

He nodded. "Yeah, I'd like that."

❧❧❧❧❧

The tractor turned down the lane, taking them back toward the farm. The hayride had been a blast. It had been a perfect day, warm for so late in October, but as the sun sank lower in the sky, the nip in the air increased.

Piper shivered. Before she could zip her hoodie, Jaycee moved closer and draped her arm over Piper's shoulders. Jaycee's warmth radiated from her, immediately taking the chill away. They'd planned on getting more apple cider when they returned, but hot chocolate might be in Piper's future.

The kids were finally beginning to wear down, which suited Piper. She wasn't sure what had gone on with Jaycee and Donovan, but both were acting different. Recently, Donovan had been sullen, but now he was practically buoyant. And it was as if Jaycee couldn't keep her hands off Piper. Not in a sexual way, but with every bump of the hayride, Jaycee had put a steadying hand on Piper's back, leg, or arm. It felt nice having Jaycee so attentive again.

Jaycee was always playful with Paxton and Maddie, but during the hayride, she'd been more animated than usual. She had the kids laughing so hard they had tears streaming down their faces. Piper expected that all the laughing had aided in causing their drowsy eyes.

"We still have to pick out our pumpkins," Piper said to Maddie and Paxton. "That is, if you two plan on carving pumpkins this year."

Their eyes immediately lit up. *So much for being tired.*

Jaycee clapped her hands and wiggled in her seat. "I can't wait. I want to carve Santa Claus in my pumpkin." She winked at Donovan.

"I'm going to do a reindeer," Donovan added.

Maddie wrinkled her nose and put her hand on her hip. "You can't do that."

"I can't?" Jaycee feigned surprise. "Donovan,

did you know that?"

He shook his head.

"I know." Jaycee snapped her fingers. "The Easter bunny."

"No!" Maddie said.

Paxton sat beside his sister and grinned. He was too old to fall for Jaycee's game.

"A leprechaun?" Donovan asked.

"No." Maddie scowled.

"Fireworks?" Jaycee said.

Maddie drew her lips together and shook her head. She pointed at Jaycee. "You do a spider." Then she pointed at Donovan. "You do a bat, and Mommy does a witch."

Jaycee glanced at Donovan. "We have our assignments, now we just have to pick a pumpkin."

The hayride had stopped, and Jaycee was helping them off the rack. Maddie squealed with delight as Jaycee tossed her into the air.

Paxton held out his arms. "My turn."

Jaycee glanced at Donovan. "I think I'm gonna need some help with him."

Donovan nodded. Piper held her breath as they tossed him into the air and caught him before he crashed to the ground.

"Awesome." Paxton's grin stretched his cheeks.

"On to the pumpkins," Jaycee said. "We should be able to do it quick. Grab a few and hit the road."

"Oh. No. You. Don't." Piper pointed at Jaycee.

"What?" Jaycee said with concern.

"Choosing pumpkins is not something one does quickly."

"Oh?"

"No. We need to find the ones with the best

faces."

Jaycee shot Donovan a look. "Did you know pumpkins have faces?"

He shook his head. "Not before they become jack-o'-lanterns."

"And that's where you two are uninformed. To have a good jack-o'-lantern, it starts with a good pumpkin face."

Donovan shrugged. "Who knew?"

"I didn't." As they walked, Jaycee draped her arm over Piper's shoulder and pulled her closer. She bent so her mouth was near Piper's ear and said, "I love you so damned much."

Piper's heart filled, and she leaned into Jaycee's warmth.

⁂

"Are you okay?" Piper asked.

Jaycee nodded but didn't speak.

Piper studied Jaycee, who'd been quiet, almost distant, since they'd returned from the pumpkin patch. At first, Piper assumed she was imagining it since the kids were so excited and left little room for Jaycee to say much. Maddie and Paxton had been in bed for nearly an hour, and still something seemed off.

"I should probably head home." Jaycee stood up from the couch and stretched her arms over her head. "I have four showings in the morning."

"Okay." Piper drew her knees against her chest but didn't rise from the couch. Jaycee's distance was making her uncomfortable, and her instincts were to close in on herself.

Jaycee looked down at Piper and ran her hand through her hair. She pointed at Piper's closed posture. "What's going on?"

"Isn't that what I just asked you?" Piper tried to keep the edge out of her voice, but the discomfort inside her made it difficult.

Jaycee sighed and sat but positioned herself on the edge of the sofa. "I caused this, didn't I?"

Piper nodded. "I know something's off with you. It scares me when you shut me out."

"I don't mean to scare you." Jaycee put her hand against her forehead and rubbed her eyes. "I had an amazing time today."

Piper stared. Whatever she'd expected Jaycee to say, this wasn't it. "Um, isn't that a good thing?"

"You'd think." Jaycee gave Piper a half smile. "It's just hard sometimes."

"Hard? It's hard having a good time?"

"No. Just the aftermath."

"There's an aftermath from having fun?" Piper shook her head. "I'm afraid I don't know what that means."

Jaycee's eyes were sad when she met Piper's gaze. "What if something happens? Something bad."

"Why do you think something bad is going to happen?" Piper wanted to reach out to Jaycee, but she held back since she wasn't sure what was going on.

"Sometimes it just does, and I'm terrified that I'll lose another family." Jaycee shook her head but didn't look up. "Sometimes after a really good day with you and the kids, when I drive home, I can barely breathe, and my hands are shaking so hard I worry that I'll drive off the road."

Piper gaped at Jaycee for several beats before she

scooted down the couch and put her hand on Jaycee's knee. "Oh, honey. Why didn't you tell me?"

"I'm telling you now," Jaycee mumbled. "Besides, it's embarrassing. I'm an adult, for fuck's sake."

"Adults get scared, too." Piper squeezed Jaycee's leg. "No shame in that."

Jaycee looked up and met Piper's gaze. "You don't think I'm pathetic?"

"No." Piper smiled. "I think you're sweet and honest."

Jaycee rested her back against the couch and opened her arms. It was all the invitation that Piper needed. She cuddled up against Jaycee and rested her head on Jaycee's shoulder.

"That's better," Jaycee said.

Chapter Forty-two

"O no," Maddie said with a huge grin. Since she'd lost another tooth last week, she was even more adorable. At least Jaycee thought so.

Donovan groaned. "These two are card sharks." He put a blue card on the pile.

Paxton intently studied his cards and then shot a glance at Maddie. He started to play one card but at the last minute thought better of it and threw another. "It's all up to you, Jaycee."

"No pressure." Jaycee laughed. She stared at her cards. When she'd first started playing with the kids, she'd intentionally let them win. Then Piper caught on and told her that Maddie and Paxton could hold their own and needed to win legitimately. Even though Jaycee now played to win, most times, the kids still beat her. She grabbed the yellow five and threw it down, guessing that Maddie held blue.

Maddie triumphantly slammed her yellow card onto the pile.

"Another?" Paxton asked.

Before Jaycee could answer, Ole Freddie ambled toward their table. He had a huge grin on his face. "I see they beat you again," he said to Jaycee.

"Nothing new." Jaycee laughed.

Ole Freddie pointed at Paxton. "Your mom sent me out here to get you. She says it's time to make the pudding."

"Can I help?" Maddie asked.

Paxton looked Maddie over before he said, "Okay. I suppose you gotta learn sometime."

Jaycee stifled a laugh, but Ole Freddie let out a cackle. "Kids," he said as Paxton and Maddie scurried toward the kitchen.

"Hey," Jaycee said. "I hear congratulations are in order."

Ole Freddie beamed. "Piper telling tales again?"

"I heard the same tale," Donovan said. "You got a job working at the VA."

"It's only part time, but if things work out, it could turn into full time." Ole Freddie glanced around the room and leaned in. "I bet she didn't get the chance to tell you. I got my letter today."

"Letter?" Jaycee said.

He gave her a huge smile. "I got approved for transitional housing."

"Yes!" Donovan jumped from the table and wrapped his arms around Ole Freddie.

"You two don't have to make such a fuss over it." Freddie's face was bright red when Donovan released him, but the huge smile had never left his face. "I best get back in there and finish up, so Piper doesn't come hunt me down."

Jaycee wanted to say more, but she suspected that Ole Freddie had had enough attention drawn to himself for one day.

After Ole Freddie had shuffled off, Jaycee said, "How's things going with your job?"

"I started learning how to do electrical work." Donovan beamed. "Do you think I'm too young to have found my calling?"

"Absolutely not."

"It's not just a job to me. I'm building houses. Places for families to live. It might sound stupid, but I try and put extra love into my work." He tapped his chest. "I hope it'll help a family get through the hard times." He shrugged, and his face reddened. "I know, dumb, right?"

"No, not at all." Jaycee clapped him on the shoulder. "I believe houses have energy. I've seen it in my line of work." She shook her head. "There's been houses I've refused to sell."

"Really?" His eyes widened.

"It's only happened twice." Jaycee shook her head. "You'd think it'd be a house where someone died, but neither was. To be honest, I have no idea what might have happened there, but I got this horribly dark feeling whenever I walked in. I couldn't bring myself to sell it to some poor, unsuspecting family."

"Wow. That's cool."

"How's Mitzy?" Jaycee asked.

"She's all right." He glanced down at his fingernails and picked at his cuticle. "Can I tell you something?"

"Anything."

"It's been kinda nice that she's living with her parents." He met Jaycee's gaze. "I don't have to worry about her all the time, and I can focus on myself. Is that selfish?"

"Not at all." Jaycee filled with pride at how much Donovan had matured the past year. At nineteen, he was wise beyond his years. "The better you are with yourself, the better any relationship is going to be."

"I believe that." He smiled. "I'm starting to actually like myself."

His words caught her off guard. At first, it made

her sad, but then she realized he wasn't sad for himself. She needed to show him support not pity. "Well, I like you, too. I've known people in their sixties that haven't figured that out."

"Mitzy and I clung to each other, wanting the other to make us whole." He shook his head. "It didn't work."

"It never does."

"Can I tell you something else?"

"Like I said, anything."

He met her gaze. "I love Mitzy with all my heart and would do anything for her, but I ain't sure we're gonna make it. And I'm okay with that."

Donovan was full of surprises tonight. "Did something happen?"

He shook his head. "No, but we're going in different directions. Things are gonna be different when she starts college. She's got big dreams. Wants to work in the fashion industry in New York."

"And what do you want?" Jaycee suspected their dreams were different.

Donovan got a goofy grin on his face. "I want kids. A family." He chuckled. "Somehow, I don't see Mitzy as a mother."

Jaycee laughed. "You got a point."

"We're still hanging out and all, but there's no guarantees for tomorrow."

Jaycee smiled. "You're telling me this, so Piper and I stop worrying about you, aren't you?"

His eyes danced. "You're pretty smart. I know you guys worry about me, about us, but you don't need to. We ain't gonna fall apart without each other. We both have things we need to do for ourselves first."

Jaycee's heart filled. If someone would have

told her a year ago that she'd be sitting in a homeless shelter, talking to a transgender man who'd become like a little brother to her, she would have laughed them off. But here she was, happier than she'd ever been.

Paxton raced across the room toward them. At first, Jaycee thought something bad had happened until she saw the huge smile on his face. He pulled to a stop at the table and met Jaycee's gaze. "I was wondering…uh…if you'd like to learn how to make pudding, too."

Jaycee's heart filled. Paxton's invitation said more than any words could. Jaycee glanced at Donovan, who sported a huge smile, before she turned back to Paxton. "I'd love to."

※※※※

Jaycee dried the bowl and put it into the cupboard. She and Piper had put the kids to bed earlier and were cleaning up from the ice cream they'd eaten for a snack.

"Hey, I forgot to tell you the good news." Jaycee couldn't believe it had slipped her mind all evening.

"I love good news." Piper smiled.

What was it about Piper's smile that still caused her heart to race? "Stop giving me that look."

"What look?"

"The sexy one."

Piper laughed. "I smiled, for god's sake. I'd hardly call that sexy. Are you trying to get into my pants?"

Jaycee smirked. "Always, but that wasn't my intention when this conversation began."

"Oh, so it's your intention now?" Piper overexaggerated licking her lips and then stuck them out in a duck pout.

"Stop, or you're going to make me forget what I wanted to tell you."

"Fine." Piper squeezed the water out of the sponge she'd been using to wash the dishes. "Should we go sit in the living room? I think we're done."

Jaycee glanced around the kitchen. Everything looked spotless. She reached out her hand to Piper, and Piper took it.

"Why are you grinning?"

"Do you realize that we hold hands even when we walk from room to room?"

Piper glanced down at their interlocked fingers. "Is that weird or pathetic? Or both?"

"It's romantic."

When they arrived in the living room, they sat next to each other on the couch, and Piper burrowed against Jaycee. Piper kept her heat at sixty-five, so Jaycee was happy for the warmth.

"Okay, I'm comfy now," Piper said. "Tell me the good news."

"Actually, I have two pieces of good news."

"Even better."

"Betsy called today. She got the results of her PET scan. No sign of cancer."

"Oh, god. That's great." Piper hugged Jaycee tighter.

"And Tessa and her girlfriend decided to fly to Paris for the holiday."

Piper gazed up at Jaycee. "Why's that good news?"

"Betsy invited us to come to Thanksgiving."

"But we planned to get together with the Wilsons on Saturday," Piper said.

"Yeah, but the whole clan couldn't make it on Saturday, but they'll be there on Thanksgiving Day."

Piper stiffened and moved away from Jaycee. "I can't go."

"Why not? They invited you and the kids. Betsy considers you part of the family." Something was upsetting Piper, but Jaycee struggled to figure out what.

"Are you serious?"

"I know I'm missing something, but I'm afraid I don't know what it is."

"Fine." Piper stood and faced Jaycee. "I have obligations. Commitments."

"Oh. You mean DOTS. I'm sure someone can cover for you."

"It doesn't work that way." Anger danced in Piper's eyes. "Sergio's going to Chicago again this year."

"You said Caleb was staying back because his mom's sick."

"He is, but that doesn't change anything. He still needs my help."

Jaycee's face dropped. "I'm sorry. I wasn't thinking." Jaycee shook her head. "I got overly exuberant and forgot you'd be shorthanded."

Piper put her hand on her hip. "Even if we weren't, it wouldn't make a difference. It still wouldn't be right for me to shirk my responsibility less than a week from Thanksgiving. The people coming for dinner deserve better from me."

Jaycee nodded. "You're right. I'll tell Betsy we can't make it."

Piper held up her hand. "No. You go."

"But I don't want to be away from you."

Piper shook her head. "I'm not going to be responsible for keeping you away from your family."

"But I'll miss you."

"And I'll miss you, but you can stop by later that night."

"Okay." Heaviness set in. Jaycee patted the couch next to her. "Will you come back and join me?"

Piper gave her a weak smile and sat in the seat next to Jaycee.

Chapter Forty-three

Jaycee pulled to the curb outside of the Wilsons' house. The memory of a year ago flooded her thoughts. Sitting here now, she felt the humiliation she'd endured that day. She could still see Tessa's angry face as she sent Jaycee away. How had she allowed herself to sink so low? She glanced at the boxes of macarons sitting on the passenger seat.

Her heart ached. It had for the past two days. *PTSD?* She'd baked the cookies by herself. Why did she have to make such an elaborate dessert? Paxton and Maddie would have loved to help her bake cookies, but macarons were too difficult. Too much could go wrong for her to allow them to assist.

A year later, she'd gotten what she wanted. Her family back. A loud rapping on her window caused her to jump. Her heart raced, and she gazed at the twins, who smiled at her outside the window.

"Jesus, you two scared the crap out of me," Jaycee said after she rolled down the window.

"What are you doing sitting out here?" Josh said.

"Waiting for you to help me carry in the cookies."

Megan's eyes lit up. "Macarons. I'll help."

Jaycee grinned. "But you'll keep your hands out of your cousins' boxes."

Josh laughed. He pointed at his sister. "Remember the year she sneaked into everyone's cookies?"

"She thought she was so clever." Jaycee chuckled.

"She only took two from each box and thought she'd get away with it."

"I would have if I hadn't gotten sick." Megan glowered.

"Hmm, I wonder why you got sick. You ate at least twenty."

"Cut me some slack. I was eight."

Josh and Jaycee laughed.

The heaviness in Jaycee's chest lightened, but it remained. She scooped up the boxes and handed them out the window to the twins.

⚜⚜⚜⚜

Piper dropped the potato peeler for what must have been the fourth time. "Damn it. This peeler is a piece of shit."

Caleb walked over and picked the potato peeler up off the floor. "Do you want to tell me what's got you so riled up, or would you like me to guess?" He went to the sink and rinsed it off before he returned.

She glared at him as he handed her back the peeler. "I don't like subpar equipment."

He crossed his arms in front of him, making a giant X, and then made the sound of a buzzer. "Try again."

"I don't know if I'm mad at myself or Jaycee," she admitted.

"That's better." Caleb smiled. "Honest communication is the only way to solve problems."

"We don't have a problem." Piper frowned. "I mean...nothing lasting. Today will be over soon, and then things go back to normal."

"But you're hurt."

"I shouldn't be." Piper sighed. "The sooner this day is over with, the better I'll feel."

"I'll say it again," Caleb said. "You're hurt, and you need to be honest with Jaycee about it."

"How?" Piper's brow furrowed. "If I told her, she wouldn't have gone, and then I'd feel guilty."

"You wanted her to come to the realization herself."

Caleb was right, but how selfish was it of Piper? "We're not teenagers. We don't have to spend every minute together. She's been doing great since we talked in September, so I need to cut her some slack." The conversation was making Piper uneasy, so she began peeling potatoes.

"This day means something special to you, though."

Piper blinked back tears. What she'd give for a good onion, so she'd have a reason to cry. "I guess."

Caleb snorted. "There's no guessing. It was last Thanksgiving the two of you met."

Piper waved her hand at him. "Need I remind you again? We aren't in high school. We don't have multiple anniversaries. The day we met. The day we went on our first date. The first kiss. The first..." *No.* She'd said too much already.

He chuckled. "Weren't those last three all on the same day?"

Piper's cheeks burned. *Damned Sergio.* He couldn't keep his mouth shut. "I am not having this conversation." She began peeling the potato again.

"Holy hell. You're going to have those done in record time if you keep that up."

Piper looked down at the potato peels that had flown in all directions. "Okay, maybe I'm a little upset, but it's not fair to burden Jaycee with my insecurities."

"Give yourself a break," Caleb said. "You've been dealt a shitty hand. First by your parents, then Emma."

"And I've done plenty of therapy to work through it, so I don't sabotage myself." Piper dropped the potato in the pan and grabbed another one.

"I know you have, dear. Just don't be so hard on yourself." Caleb smiled and nodded at the potato in her hand. "And don't be too hard on them, either."

Piper laughed, happy to release some of her tension.

જીજીજીજી

Jaycee was mobbed when she walked into the Wilsons' house. Most everyone she'd seen since she'd reconnected with the family, but it was the first time being with them all together.

She'd forgotten how loud and chaotic it was at the Wilsons', although nothing compared to DOTS. At the thought, a wave of emotion washed over her. She'd talked to Piper earlier that day, but their conversation had been weird. Subdued. Maybe it was just Jaycee's imagination or her guilt.

No. She didn't have any reason to feel guilty. Piper even told her so. She pushed her thoughts aside.

"Where's Betsy?" Jaycee asked.

"In the kitchen," Chuck said with a frown. "I told her she had no business in there while she's still recuperating."

"She wouldn't have it, would she?"

"Nope."

One of Tessa's brothers shook his head. "She's

supposedly only supervising, but I'm not sure she can keep her hands out of it."

"Maybe I'll go in and see what she's up to," Jaycee said.

"Please." Chuck smiled. "Maybe she'll listen to you."

Jaycee lifted her eyebrow. "Doubtful."

"Tell her you won't read any more of those smutty books to her."

Jaycee groaned. "I still can't believe she's making me reread all of them. There's like twelve in the series."

Tessa's brother laughed. "That'll teach you for leaving out the sexy parts."

⚜ ⚜ ❀ ❀

Piper was still sad that Jaycee wasn't there, but the kitchen had gotten busy. She thought back to last year, when somehow, they'd pulled off getting the meal on the table. Today, there was a full team of volunteers, but everything was running behind schedule. Except for Mrs. Akers, who'd cut up all the pies into uniform-sized slices.

Maybe it was her imagination, but even Paxton and Maddie seemed off today. In fact, Maddie had thrown a tantrum when Piper asked her to put on her dress shoes for the occasion. She'd caused such a ruckus that Piper gave in and let her wear her tennis shoes.

It wasn't the best parenting, but it was rare for Maddie to act that way. Besides, Piper didn't have the energy to argue with her. Paxton was acting the opposite. He was such an independent boy, but he'd been clingy and hadn't wandered far from her all day.

She wondered if it was his way of protecting her. Piper smiled down at him. Likely it was. "Hey, sport," she said. "Would you mind carrying the pie out to the dessert table?"

"You sure you don't need me for anything?" His eyes held a hint of panic.

"I'm good. I really need for you to take care of the pies."

He nodded and shuffled toward the table that held the pies.

"Hey, Paxton," she called. When he turned, she said, "Everything's going to be okay."

His eyes welled. "Why isn't Jaycee here?"

"Oh, buddy." Piper went to him and wrapped him in a hug.

❧❧❧❧❧

Jaycee smiled at Betsy, who stood in the kitchen barking orders. Jaycee greeted Betsy's minions before she turned to Betsy. "Do you have a few minutes that we could talk? Alone."

Tessa's sister called out, "Take her for more than a few minutes."

Jaycee laughed but stopped when Betsy shot her a look.

"Do you all think you can handle things without me?" Betsy asked.

She was met by a chorus of yeses.

"I'm all yours," Betsy said and pulled Jaycee into the dining room that was already set up for the feast that would soon cover the table. "Spill it."

"What?"

"Come on. I've known you long enough to realize when something's bothering you. It's written all over your face."

Jaycee's mind raced. She didn't want to appear ungrateful or make Betsy think she wasn't happy to be there.

Betsy held up her finger and circled it toward Jaycee's face. "I see those wheels turning, and I know you're trying to answer without hurting my feelings."

Uncanny. It was true that Betsy knew her well.

"I...uh...I'm so grateful to be reunited with the family. For you to have invited me. But I, well, I..."

"You don't want to be here," Betsy said.

"It's not that. It's just—"

"You want to be with Piper." Betsy put her hand on her hip.

Jaycee's mouth dropped open. "Yes," she said barely over a whisper. "I should never have accepted the invitation."

"Why did you?"

Tears welled in Jaycee's eyes. "I was afraid to disappoint you—everyone. To lose you. But instead, I've hurt the woman that's my entire world."

"So what are you going to do about it?" Betsy asked.

Jaycee's hand trembled. "I'm going to go into the other room, give everyone a big hug, and leave so I can go to DOTS."

"Atta girl." Betsy smiled.

"You're not angry?"

"Absolutely not." Betsy put her hand on Jaycee's arm and patted it. The warmth from Betsy's hand and the gesture was comforting. "Piper is your partner. Your lover. You need to choose her over me. Over us."

"But—"

"No buts. What happened last year never should have, and I apologize from the bottom of my heart. But the one thing I promise you is it will never happen again. You have a place in this family for the rest of your life."

Jaycee struggled to breathe, and tears welled in her eyes. She was terrified. The realization hit her like a runaway bulldozer.

"Oh, sweetie." Betsy moved closer and grasped Jaycee's hand with both of hers. "I'm so sorry we caused you so much pain."

"You always told me family was forever." Tears rolled freely down Jaycee's cheeks, and she didn't try to stop them. "But then it wasn't true."

"I will regret that for the rest of my life. That I didn't reach out to you. That I allowed myself to believe Tessa."

"It wasn't your fault." Jaycee wanted to erase the pain in Betsy's eyes.

Betsy shook her head. "I had culpability. I'm the matriarch of this family. I should have held it together better."

"No, you shouldn't—"

"Stop," Betsy said, raising her voice. "You need to understand that you don't have to choose one over the other. Kids move out of their parents' house. They fall in love. They start their own family. It doesn't mean they're deserting anyone. It means they're building their own lives. And what they're building adds to the family and makes it bigger. You don't have to lose one to have the other."

Jaycee ran her hand through her hair, messing it up, but she didn't care. "So I've gotta leave the nest."

"Bingo." Betsy smiled.

"But I'm not kicked out of the nest. I left on my own accord."

"Exactly."

"I can come back whenever I want?"

"Yes again."

"And I can have Piper and not lose you."

"Hallelujah." Betsy raised her arms over her head. "But you better get your ass out of this nest and go find her."

"I'm going." Jaycee hugged Betsy.

≈≈≈≈

Piper let out a long breath. The volunteers had just wheeled out the food to put in the service line. *Thank god.* With the new Chefs with a Heart program, DOTS had gotten a lot of publicity, which Piper assumed would bring more people to dinner.

She'd been right, but she hadn't anticipated that this many people would show. Caleb assured her they wouldn't run out of food, but she'd have to hold her breath until everyone was served.

Piper pulled on the garbage bag. It had been so overfilled that she had trouble pulling it out. An arm reached around beside her and easily pulled it from the trash can.

Her heart skipped a beat. *Jaycee?* She turned and gazed into Donovan's eyes.

"Looks like you could use some help," he said.

She smiled. "Thanks." It had been so busy that she'd barely seen him let alone had the chance to talk to him.

"No problem. I'll just take this out to the dumpster." He paused as if he were going to say more, but he turned away.

"Did you have something else on your mind?" Piper asked.

He turned back. "Is Jaycee planning on showing up at all?" His jaw clenched.

"That's the plan. Later tonight, after everyone's gone."

"Kinda sucks that she bailed."

Shit. How was she supposed to answer that? She didn't want to bash Jaycee, but she didn't want to discount Donovan's anger, either. "It's tough for her right now."

Donovan snorted. "Sure, life sucks for her."

By his response, he was more hurt than she'd realized. "Cut her a little slack." Piper wondered if she was saying it for Donovan's benefit or her own. "She's trying to get her footing in two worlds, and she's struggling."

Donovan nodded. "I get that." The tightness in his jaw was gone. "But we're her family, too."

"I'm sure she has us in her thoughts today." Piper was certain of that, but she'd been struggling with her role in Jaycee's life. It had been a long time since Jaycee had asked Piper to move in with her. *Unfair.* She'd turned Jaycee down twice, so what did she expect? For Jaycee to continue to ask and face rejection?

Ugh. She hated feeling so insecure. She'd be done with school in a few weeks. Then it would be time for them to talk. Until then, she couldn't let herself question Jaycee's commitment just because she chose to spend Thanksgiving with the Wilsons.

Donovan was staring at her, probably waiting

for a response. She smiled. She opened her mouth to say something upbeat that wouldn't match the way she felt. Instead, she decided on honesty. "I know. I'm just struggling today…a little emotional." Piper shrugged. "But I love Jaycee, and she loves me."

"I have no doubt about that." Donovan smiled. "Someday, I want someone to look at me the way Jaycee looks at you."

Chapter Forty-four

Piper high-fived Caleb. They'd gotten all the food to the serving tables, and the volunteers were ready to serve the patrons. The line snaked around the tables. There were more people here than last year. The lead volunteer called for quiet, so they could say a prayer of thanks.

When Piper lifted her head after the room said, *amen,* in unison, Caleb said, "I can't believe how packed this place is."

"Is it wrong to say I'll be glad when it's over?"

"Cut yourself some slack. This week has been stressful for you."

Piper placed her clenched fists against her cheeks and pretended to scream. "Ugh. I've always prided myself on handling whatever life throws at me, and instead, I'm throwing this pity party for myself."

Caleb put his arm over Piper's shoulders. "Tomorrow, things will look different, but you and Jaycee need to talk."

"I know." Piper let out a deep breath. "I know. I just wish it could be sooner rather than later."

"What do you say we get in line, and you stop thinking about it for a while?"

Piper held her stomach. "I don't think I could eat anything."

"Just a little." He pointed toward the middle of the line where Paxton and Maddie stood with

Donovan. "You don't want them to have to eat without you, do you?"

"No, it's not fair to them." She wasn't sure she'd be able to eat, but she needed to be there for her kids, so she followed Caleb to the back of the line.

"Jaycee," Maddie screamed and took off running across the dining area. Paxton followed.

Piper's heart pounded as Jaycee slowly walked across the large room. Piper couldn't help but smile when she saw that Jaycee wore one of her stupid stocking caps. Piper resisted the urge to act like the kids and sprint to Jaycee.

When the kids got to Jaycee, she knelt and held her arms open wide. They threw themselves into her arms, and she engulfed them in a hug.

Piper tried to appear nonchalant as she stepped out of line. With each step, she fought against running or at least walking faster.

Jaycee looked up, and their gazes met. She kept her focus locked on Piper, even as she hugged Paxton and Maddie.

There was something in Jaycee's eyes that Piper couldn't read.

Jaycee gave the kids one final squeeze before she stood with Piper's arrival.

"Hi," Jaycee said sheepishly.

"Hi back at you," Piper said.

Piper was stunned when Jaycee tenderly cupped her cheek. They'd never hidden their affection, but normally, Jaycee wasn't this demonstrative in a packed room.

Jaycee gazed deep into Piper's eyes and held it for several beats before she spoke. "I'm so sorry for not being here. I never meant to make you feel unimportant. Second best."

"No. You did nothing wrong." Piper wouldn't let Jaycee take the blame for her own insecurities. "You need other people in your life. You'll sometimes have other commitments."

"True. But today I made a mistake." Jaycee put her hand against her chest. "I broke a commitment to you. And that's something I don't plan on doing again."

"Thank you." Piper swallowed the lump in her throat. "It's not the end of the world."

"It felt like it to me." Jaycee smiled. "I never want to feel as horrible as I have today."

"Me neither."

"So there's only one thing for me to do."

Piper narrowed her eyes, curious at what Jaycee meant.

Without warning, Jaycee dropped to one knee. She held Piper's hand.

Piper stared at Jaycee, speechless.

"Today, I realized I want to spend the rest of my life with you. I don't have a ring, and I don't have a plan. I just know that I don't want another day to pass before I ask you this."

Tears welled in Piper's eyes. This couldn't be what she thought it was. *Or could it?* Her heart raced.

"Piper Marsden, will you marry me?"

A collective gasp went up from the crowd that Piper had all but forgotten as her focus had been fixed on Jaycee. She needed to say something, but her mouth was suddenly dry.

Maddie pulled on Piper's shirt. "Mommy, did you hear what Jaycee just asked?"

"Yes," Piper said.

Jaycee pursed her lips. "Is that a yes to Maddie or to me?"

"Both," Piper practically shouted and grabbed Jaycee by the shoulders. "Yes, I'll marry you."

Jaycee sprang to her feet and pulled Piper to her. Piper's feet left the ground as Jaycee swung her through the air.

"You just made me the happiest woman in the world," Jaycee said into Piper's ear.

Piper held on to Jaycee and laughed. She alternated between laughing and crying as she clung to Jaycee.

❧❧❧❧

Jaycee fell back against the pillow. "Holy shit. I should propose to you every day."

Piper collapsed on top of Jaycee. "Thank god we came back to your house, or everyone on the third floor would have heard that."

"Shit." Jaycee gulped for air. "You don't think the kids heard, do you?"

"Not the way this house is designed." Piper kissed Jaycee's neck. "Relax. You're going to have to get used to having sex with them in the house."

Jaycee's heart filled. Finally, they'd live under the same roof. "Can we revisit the conversation we started earlier? Before you seduced me."

"Seduced?" Piper raised her eyebrow. "I'd hardly call it seduction. I believe all I did was run my finger around your nipple like this." Piper slid from on top of Jaycee and moved her finger toward Jaycee's nipple.

"No." Jaycee laughed and covered her breast with her hand. "I won't be seduced again until we talk about this."

"Fine." Piper pretended to pout. She lay her head on Jaycee's shoulder. "Let's get on with this conversation because I have parts of your body that I still want to explore tonight."

"Stop." Jaycee laughed. "Who knew proposing would make you so horny?"

"Commitment is sexy," Piper said with a smirk.

"Perfect segue."

"Ugh, I walked into that one." Piper groaned. "I'm assuming this is the negotiation you started earlier?"

"Negotiation?" Jaycee smiled. "You're not buying a used car."

Piper laughed.

"I want you here with me. Every day," Jaycee said. "I want to start our life together. Now."

Piper smiled. "I think we already have."

"You know what I mean."

"The next month is going to be so busy," Piper said.

"All the more reason to get here sooner rather than later. I'll be here to help."

"But I'll be finishing up with school. I won't have any time to pack."

"If you'd trust me, I'd be honored to do it."

"I'm embarrassed." Piper looked away. "I know you understand we don't have much. But it's going to be more evident if you pack us."

Jaycee hugged Piper. "It's just stuff. Stuff doesn't mean shit. You've taught me that. In fact, I was thinking that maybe we could build a new house after our wedding. A more modest one."

Piper's eyes lit up. "Seriously?"

Jaycee nodded. "This house is gigantic. Too big for a family of four." Jaycee's breath caught in her throat. *A family of four.*

"Are you okay?" Piper put her hand against Jaycee's cheek.

"Yeah. The family of four thing choked me up."

"Would you be willing to make it a family of five?" Piper asked.

Jaycee's heart raced. "Are you serious? I never asked because I figured since you already had Maddie and Paxton... Oh, my god...that would be so amazing."

Piper laughed. "So is that a yes?"

"That's a hell yes." Jaycee pulled Piper on top of her.

Their lips met, and their kisses grew more intense.

Piper pulled away and said, "You know we can't make a baby this way, don't you?"

Jaycee smirked. "We can try."

"Ah, I like the way you think."

Piper kissed Jaycee's neck.

"Don't think this is going to get you out of picking a moving date." Jaycee moaned as Piper continued to nuzzle her neck. The discussion would have to wait.

Chapter Forty-five

Jaycee sat in front of the fireplace and stared at the gigantic Christmas tree in the corner. She'd turned off the other lights in the room, preferring the glow from the fire and the tree. The burning logs warmed her. It wasn't just that. It was the feeling of love in her once cold and empty house.

The stockings hanging from the mantel confirmed that she had a family. Maddie. Paxton. Piper. Jaycee. And Donovan. Her heart filled. What a difference a year made.

She'd talked Piper into moving before Christmas. True to her word, Jaycee had taken care of the entire move with the help of Donovan and the kids. Piper had been right; they didn't own much. At first, it had broken Jaycee's heart until she realized that Piper was richer than most people she knew.

The fire crackled. Jaycee gazed around the room at the decorations, several of which the kids had made. It certainly wouldn't win a decorating contest, but to Jaycee, it was the best her house had ever looked. In the past, she and Tessa hired professionals when it was their turn to host Christmas. All other years, it went undecorated.

Jaycee glanced at her watch. In less than an hour, they'd be hosting their first Christmas Eve party. The Wilsons. Sergio and Caleb. Mary Ann and Margot. Donovan and Mitzy. Ole Freddie. The house would be as full as Jaycee's heart.

Jaycee adjusted her tie. Maybe it was silly to dress up for a casual party, but she wanted to look nice for Piper. No doubt, a lot of pictures would be taken since this was their first Christmas as a family.

She'd offered to help get the kids ready, but Piper had sent her downstairs to set out the food that didn't need to be refrigerated. It had only taken her ten minutes, so she'd been sitting in front of the fireplace contemplating her life for the last half hour.

"We're ready," Piper said from the doorway.

Jaycee's breath caught. *Stunning.* Piper wore an off-the-shoulder red dress that fell just below her knees. Her calves were perfection in two-inch heels.

"Wow. You look amazing," Jaycee said. "Beautiful."

Piper twirled. "I wanted you to get all your drooling out of the way before I had the kids come down."

Jaycee laughed. "You know me so well." She wrapped Piper in a bear hug. "Seriously, you look amazing."

Piper pulled back and looked Jaycee up and down. "You're looking rather dapper yourself, especially with the reindeer tie and suspenders."

"The kids helped me pick them out."

"I never would have guessed." Piper lifted her face toward Jaycee, and their lips met.

Jaycee was breathless when they separated. "Stop that. We have guests coming soon."

Piper laughed. "Are you ready for the kids' grand entrance?" She leaned over and whispered, "They wanted to look nice for you."

Jaycee smiled and nodded, afraid that words

would fail her.

"Okay, guys, Jaycee's ready to be dazzled."

Maddie walked into the room first. She wore a red dress, too, but hers was long sleeved and had thick white puffs at the end of her sleeves and her neckline. She had on black patent leather shoes with white leotards. She looked adorable.

Jaycee knelt and hugged Maddie. "You are as pretty as your mom."

Maddie giggled. "Thanks."

"And can we have Paxton?" Piper called.

Paxton did his best to strut into the room. Jaycee blinked back tears. He wore a tie and suspenders just like Jaycee, but his had elves on them.

"Dude," Jaycee said, knowing he wouldn't want the mushy stuff when he was trying to be cool. "Those are some nice threads you're wearing."

He beamed.

She opened her arms, and he gave her a bear hug.

When she stood, Piper leaned over. "Apparently, he likes your fashion sense."

Jaycee didn't think her heart could be any fuller.

The doorbell shocked her out of the moment. She glanced at her watch. "What the hell, are guests showing up this early?"

"Paxton, would you get the door?" Piper asked.

He raced off, and Piper busied herself with Maddie's hair.

Paxton came into the room with Donovan in tow.

Piper clapped her hands together. She smiled at Donovan. "Now that we're all here, we can give Jaycee her present."

"Present?" Jaycee's gaze went among the four

standing in a semicircle in front of her. Something was up. "But Christmas isn't until tomorrow."

"We thought we should give you this early." Piper turned to Donovan. "Did you bring it with you?"

Donovan handed Piper a legal-sized envelope. Why did Donovan have it?

Piper smiled. "I didn't want you to accidentally stumble across it, so I asked Donovan to hold it for safekeeping."

Piper stepped forward and put the envelope in Jaycee's hand. The others stood staring at her with big grins on their faces.

Tentatively, Jaycee unhooked the metal tabs and opened the top. She slid the papers out of the envelope. *Cavendish, Stintson, and Clark.* Had Piper had a prenup drawn up?

"Read it," Piper said.

Jaycee began to read, and her eyes widened. *No.* It couldn't be.

"Are you going to say something?" Piper asked. Her eyes were full of concern.

Jaycee met her gaze.

"Oh, honey." Piper took a step forward and wiped her finger across Jaycee's cheek.

Jaycee blinked. She hadn't even known she was crying. "Is this…is this…what I think it is?"

"It is." Piper's smile lit up the entire room.

"Oh. My. Fucking. God." Jaycee practically yelled. "Oh, sorry." She looked down at the children.

Donovan laughed. "Of all the responses I thought she might have, that wasn't one of them."

"And you knew about this?" Jaycee asked.

"Duh. That's Mitzy's dad."

Jaycee glanced at the paper again. *Clark.* Of

course, why hadn't she figured that out?

"How'd you think we got something drawn up so quickly?" Piper asked. "We still have to go to court, but the papers have at least been drawn up."

Jaycee dropped to her knees and motioned the kids forward. Maddie and Paxton went to her. "You're okay with this? With me being your second mom?"

In answer, they both threw themselves into her arms. As Jaycee hugged the kids, she glanced up at Piper, who had tears streaming down her face.

"Damn it," Piper said and swiped at a tear. "Good thing I planned for time to redo my makeup."

After Jaycee hugged the kids for several more minutes, she stood. "I'm speechless," she said to Piper. "I can't believe you pulled this off without me knowing. This is the best present ever. I'd be honored to adopt Paxton and Maddie." The tears that had stopped now flowed freely.

"I know how afraid it made you that you could lose another family." Piper smiled. "Not that I'm planning on going anywhere, but I wanted you to never feel like you could lose your family again. Plus, it protects the kids should something happen to me."

Jaycee stopped trying to wipe away her tears. "Family really is forever."

They all swarmed Jaycee, and *her* family wrapped her in a gigantic hug.

About the Author

Rita Potter has spent most of her life trying to figure out what makes people tick. To that end, she holds a Bachelor's degree in Social Work and an MA in Sociology. Being an eternal optimist, she maintains that the human spirit is remarkably resilient. Her writing reflects this belief.

Rita's stories are electic but typically put her characters in challenging circumstances. She feels that when they reach their happily ever after, they will have earned it. Despite the heavier subject matter, Rita's humorous banter and authentic dialogue reflect her hopeful nature.

In her spare time, she enjoys the outdoors. She is especially drawn to the water, which is ironic since she lives in the middle of a cornfield. Her first love has always been reading. It is this passion that spurred her writing career. She rides a Harley Davidson and has an unnatural obsession with fantasy football. More than anything, she detests small talk but can ramble on for hours given a topic that interests her.

She lives in a small town in Illinois with her wife, Terra, and their cat, Chumley, who actually runs the household.

Rita is a member of American Mensa and the Golden

Crown Literary Society. She is currently a graduate of the GCLS Writing Academy 2021. Sign up for Rita's free newsletter at:

www.ritapotter.com

IF YOU LIKED THIS BOOK...

Reviews help an author get discovered and if you have enjoyed this book, please do the author the honor of posting a review on Goodreads, Amazon, Barnes & Noble or anywhere you purchased the book. Or perhaps share a posting on your social media sites and help us spread the word.

Check out Rita's other books

Broken not Shattered - ISBN - 978-1-952270-22-2

Even when it seems hopeless, there can always be a better tomorrow.

Jill Bishop has one goal in life – to survive. Jill is trapped in an abusive marriage, while raising two young girls. Her husband has isolated her from the world and filled her days with fear. The last thing on her mind is love, but she sure could use a friend.

Alex McCoy is enjoying a comfortable life, with great friends and a prosperous business. She has given up on love, after picking the wrong woman one too many times. Little does she know, a simple act of kindness might change her life forever.

When Alex lends a helping hand to Jill at the local grocery store, they are surprised by their immediate connection and an unlikely friendship develops. As their friendship deepens, so too do their fears.

In order to protect herself and the girls, Jill can't let her husband know about her friendship with Alex, and Alex can't discover what goes on behind closed doors. What would Alex do if she finds out the truth? At the same time, Alex must fight her attraction and be the friend she suspects Jill needs. Besides, Alex knows what every lesbian knows – don't fall for a straight woman, especially one that's married…but will her heart listen?

Upheaval: Book One - As We Know It - ISBN - 978-1-

952270-38-3

It is time for Dillon Mitchell to start living again.

Since the death of her wife three years ago, Dillon had buried herself in her work. When an invitation arrives for Tiffany Daniels' exclusive birthday party, her best friend persuades her to join them for the weekend.

It's not the celebration that draws her but the location. The party is being held at the Whitaker Estate, one of the hottest tickets on the West Coast. The Estate once belonged to an eccentric survivalist, whose family converted it into a trendy destination while preserving some of its original history.

Surrounded by a roomful of successful lesbians, Dillon finds herself drawn to Skylar Lange, the mysterious and elusive bartender. Before the two can finish their first dance, a scream shatters the evening. When the party goers emerge from the underground bunker, they discover something terrible has happened at the Estate.

The group races to try to discover the cause of this upheaval, and whether it's isolated to the Estate. Has the world, as we know it, changed forever?

Survival: Book Two - As We Know It - ISBN - 978-1-952270-47-5

Forty-eight hours after the Upheaval, reality is beginning to set in at the Whitaker Estate. The world, As We Know It, has ended.

Dillon Mitchell and her friends are left to survive, after discovering most of the population, at least in the United States, has mysteriously died.

While they struggle to come to terms with their devastating losses, they are faced with the challenge of creating a new society, which is threatened by the divergent factions that may tear the community apart from the inside.

Even if the group can unite, external forces are gathering that could destroy their fragile existence.

Meanwhile, Dillon's budding relationship with the elusive Skylar Lange faces obstacles, when Skylar's hidden past is revealed.

Thundering Pines – ISBN – 978-1-952270-58-1

Returning to her hometown was the last thing Brianna Goodwin wanted to do. She and her mom had left Flower Hills under a cloud of secrecy and shame when she was ten years old. Her life is different now. She has a high-powered career, a beautiful girlfriend, and a trendy life in Chicago.

Upon her estranged father's death, she reluctantly agrees to attend the reading of his will. It should be simple—settle his estate and return to her life in the city—but nothing has ever been simple when it comes to Donald Goodwin.

Dani Thorton, the down-to-earth manager of

Thundering Pines, is confused when she's asked to attend the reading of the will of her longtime employer. She fears that her simple, although secluded life will be interrupted by the stylish daughter who breezes into town.

When a bombshell is revealed at the meeting, two women seemingly so different are thrust together. Maybe they'll discover they have more in common than they think.

Betrayal: Book Three - As We Know It - ISBN - 978-1-952270-69-7

Betrayal is the exciting conclusion to the As We Know It series.

The survivors at Whitaker Estate are still reeling from the vicious attack on their community, which left three of their friends dead.

When the mysterious newcomer Alaina Renato reveals there is a traitor in their midst, it threatens to tear the community apart. Is there truly a traitor, or is Alaina playing them all?

Dillon Mitchell and the other Commission members realize their group might not survive another attack, especially if there is someone working against them from the inside. Despite the potential risk, they vote to attend a summit that will bring together other survivors from around the country.

When the groups converge on Las Vegas, the festive

atmosphere soon turns somber upon the discovery of an ominous threat. But is the danger coming from within, or is there someone else lurking in the city?

Before it's too late, they must race against time to determine where the betrayal is coming from.

Whitewater Awakening - ISBN - 978-1-952270-74-1

Can two lost people find themselves, and possibly each other, halfway around the world?

After a tragic accident, Quinn Coolidge leaves everything behind, hoping to find solace in a secluded life in the Ozarks. Her solitude is disrupted when her best friend unexpectedly shows up with a proposition she may not be able to resist.

Faced with a series of failed relationships, Aspen Kennedy is left wondering why she can't find true love. With each new partner, she immerses herself in their interests, hoping to find the connection she's been missing. That should make her the perfect girlfriend, shouldn't it?

Come along with Quinn and Aspen as they travel to Africa to take on one of the most grueling whitewater rafting courses in the world. With the amazing Victoria Falls as their backdrop, the pair will have to look deep inside to discover what holds them back. Will the churning waters of the Zambezi River defeat them, or will it lead them to a whitewater awakening?

Out of the Ashes - ISBN - 978-1-952270-84-0

When unusual seismic activity is detected on Mount St. Helens, volcanologist Nova "Cano" Kane, along with a team from the United States Geological Survey, is sent to investigate. The year is 1980, and there hasn't been a large-scale eruption on the mountain in over one hundred years.

Dr. Allison "Allie" Albright is a prominent professor at the University of Washington where the seismic activity is being tracked. As more scientists pour into Seattle, she braces for the possible return of Cano.

Neither Allie nor Cano has fully recovered from their breakup four years earlier. Both live with the pain and regret of how their relationship ended. Maybe it's best to leave it in the past and focus on the job at hand.

They must battle the limits of predictive science, the shortsightedness of bureaucracy, and the bias of the media, while fighting their complicated feelings for each other. As Mount St. Helens continues to churn, so too does their attraction.
Which will erupt first—the volcano or their feelings for each other?

Love or Hate - 978-1-952270-96-3

In a world full of divisiveness, what would it be like to walk in someone else's shoes?

Two worlds collide when Rain Hargrove, a progressive lesbian, and Ivy Nash, a conservative Christian, clash at a political rally. Normally, that would be the end of the story, but it's just the beginning when they're approached by an old woman. Her bizarre chanting about love and hate disrupts their argument, and the two go their separate ways, pushing the incident from their minds.

That is, until, without warning, they find themselves in each other's bodies. Then they're suddenly switched back. This can't be real...can it? Did the old woman have something to do with this? The unpredictable body swaps continue, sometimes with hilarious consequences.

While Rain and Ivy search for a way to stop these unsettling events, they're forced to see the world through each other's eyes. As the unlikely friendship develops, they must face some of their deeply held beliefs and prejudices.

Is it possible to not only accept their differences, but also embrace them? If so, could the bond they've developed lead to something deeper?

Printed in Great Britain
by Amazon